JAMES COX

ROPPONGI

Black Rose Writing | Texas

The author grants the final approval for this literary material.

Second printing

This is a work of fiction. Names, characters, businesses, places, events, and incidents are either the products of the author's imagination or used in a fictitious manner. Any resemblance to actual persons, living or dead, or actual events is purely coincidental.

ISBN: 978-1-68513-102-9
PUBLISHED BY BLACK ROSE WRITING
www.blackrosewriting.com

Printed in the United States of America
Suggested Retail Price (SRP) $22.95

Roppongi is printed in Garamond Premier Pro

*As a planet-friendly publisher, Black Rose Writing does its best to eliminate unnecessary waste to reduce paper usage and energy costs, while never compromising the reading experience. As a result, the final word count vs. page count may not meet common expectations.

For Dad

ROPPONGI

ROPPONGI

1

TOKYO 1992

"Here's to the tilt in your kilt, Adam me boyo!" Dan Bronsan, Quasimodo with a Ph.D. Three hundred and fifty pounds. Fifty-five going on seventy. Boozer, philosopher and Celt today due more to the demographics of the bar than to any ancestry that may have existed within his loins. The old Woody Allen movie *Zelig* comes to mind. The one where Woody literally "becomes" the people he is with. Dan the social chameleon. That was it. Beneath the thatch of graying hair one was immediately struck by the lazy bloodhound-like eye peering this way and that like a lighthouse beam in the crazed control of a lunatic.

A beautiful spring day in Tokyo. The tall, bent figure sitting at the bar next to Dan would not be aware of this. Dan's words just adding to the ambient noise that Adam Welsh hears buzzing around his head. Numbing in a way. A feeling of serenity for this thirty-six year old alcoholic. Fire Controlman First Class Adam Welsh, drinking away the pain here at the Sanno Hotel bar. A year or so to go till retirement. Then what? No matter. Anything but this. Some type of change. Anything but the living hell he was in now. The problem, as Jack Bender was always quick to point out, was that no geographic move would make a difference. Adam Welsh would be there wherever he went.

"Adam, have you even heard one word I've said. Jeez, well here comes another round anyway. Maybe it'll improve your disposition. I worry about you my boy."

A curious feeling of impending doom mixed with euphoria engulfs Adam Welsh as the dark figure approaches. This Angel of Death, gliding towards him, maneuvering through the assemblage of lost dreams and hopelessness, his fellow travelers in despair. Closer, closer, until she is in front of him now. The receptacle is delivered. The daughter of John Barleycorn smiles.

"Here is your drink, Adam San," she says, and floats away.

Adam takes the double Jack Daniels with trembling hand and brings it to his lips, bracing for yet another fall from the wagon. Down the hatch. The brutal bite (He never drank for the taste) and then the warmth. The glow. The filling of the void that only alcoholics know. Mission accomplished. He is normal. The sins of the father repeated. This the way Dad had gone.

Five years ago at Rikers. Middle class white man dying alone on the infirmary floor at Rikers Island prison. Adam remembered seeing him on the stoop years ago puking the scotch; Dewars, no Cutty for him. It was gangster booze and wasn't that how that scumbag Joe Kennedy made all his money during Prohibition?

"Adam, if I ever see you drinking, I'll break your arm," and then puking again.

No way. Adam would never drink that horrible stuff. But a funny thing happened. He did, and it wasn't for the taste. Effect. All effect. He felt normal with the booze, and now this normalcy was taking his soul. He had probably died at thirty. They could bury the body later.

Adam thought about the A.A. meeting. God it had only been last week. This was going to be it. He was done with the booze. Yet after the meeting, he drank again. Life was a shambles. Seventeen years in the Navy. Still a First Class. Two rehabs already. The new Navy. Zero tolerance for booze, drugs, and don't even look at a female the wrong way - or the right way for that matter.

Would I need another visit to the emergency room? Jesus, the last one was bad. A lost weekend of booze and women (more of the former than the latter) capped off by a day at the Tokyo Bowl, or Big Egg (so called for the oval appearance of Japan's version of the Houston Astrodome.)

He drank with Benny Carter. Good game. Kansas State against Nebraska. Adam surprised at the Kansas State's quarterback. Great arm. Never heard of him, though. He remembered thinking the kid must have had a father who was there. Always there for him. Shit, maybe even a real-live TV dad. Laughing a bit to himself.

They had the flask of scotch, but then the shakes came. They always came, but these were different. Coming out of his skin. Thank God Jack had been around.

Jack Bender, thirty years sober, retired Navy ET1. He'd been in Japan forever. His wife Yumiko who somehow loved him even though the bomb at Hiroshima had incinerated her family. Little Yumiko, a mere child at the time, safely away in the hills. Her family wiped from the planet before her tears could even begin to form. All these years later and still the hate and anger could engulf her just like the cloud had engulfed her mother on that beautiful/horrible day.

Jack Bender was a good man though. He had helped a lot of people through the horrors of the booze. Perhaps because Yumiko had lived in her own hell she could more readily understand her husband's.

Jack had taken Adam to the emergency room that night a few weeks ago. Adam ended up spending a week in the hospital detox. Got out and felt great. Good enough to drink a double bourbon in Roppongi the very night he got out. Insanity.

The Sanno Hotel was located in the center of Tokyo. Convenient to the bar and entertainment district of Roppongi. The bar where Dan and Adam were imbibing this Thursday afternoon, a cosmopolitan upholstered sewer that on weekends attracted a mix of State Department employees, Japanese nationals, expats and the usual sailors and marines on liberty. All looking for romance with the liberated New Age women of Tokyo; the modern day geisha who though the country was liberated in 1945, were just now beginning to join in the emancipation, much to the chagrin of the Japanese male.

Dan Bronsan was not always this bulbous mound of flesh that sat with one lazy eye frantically searching for a target. He had been born in New York to a good Catholic family. His mother was so dedicated to the Church that his father said she had in fact been a waitress at the Last Supper. Dan was schooled by Jesuits and could speak on any subject related to the history of the Church. His childhood was uneventful save for a brief stint in seminary when he was twelve, which ended abruptly with the onset of puberty he liked to say. After a tour in the Navy, where he first had the opportunity to visit Japan, he returned to New York and became an engineer. Of course, what Dan had done was take some engineering courses at the undergraduate level. To hear him tell it, especially after a few Beefeaters, Dan Bronsan was a veritable expert on the subject of telecommunications. He wrote a paper from which he was awarded a Ph.D. The degree was not from an institution that one would instantly recognize. His friend and sometime tormentor, Art Chambers used to like to tell him that it was from the same place that the Reverend Al Sharpton had received his degree. This inevitably lead to the usual string of epitaphs and charges of racism from Dan the liberal Democrat launched at the "Ignorant Neo-Nazi," Art.

Despite all this, Dan had worked his way through the complex hierarchy at Svenson to become the Chief of Training at Svenson Telecommunications, Tokyo. It mattered little to Dan that he had landed this position in spite of what he knew or didn't know of electrical engineering. What Dan Bronsan did have was the ability to teach. A gift. He could communicate to his Japanese students in a way that few if any gaijins in the field could match. Of course, the Dan Bronsan that existed outside of the classroom in social settings was very different indeed. The term, "Pompous Ass," seemed to be invoked by both friends and enemies more often than not.

"His Holiness, Peter O'Mara! As I live and breathe."

Adam struck sober by Dan Bronsan's exclamation. The name cutting through the din.

Peter O'Mara, the Irish Ambassador to Japan approaching the space between Dan and he. A shutter going through Adam. The Catholic priest, Father Ribauld, years ago at St. Rose's. Altar boy practice over.

Please stay, Adam. You're my best helper. Eleven, maybe twelve at the time. The feelings of shame, guilt. All rushing back now as Peter O'Mara pulls up a bar stool and lightly touched Adam's leg.

"Adam Welsh, I would like to introduce you to Ambassador Peter O'Mara. Hailing from Belfast, but aye we will not hold that against him. Anyone who pours the Jameson the way this man does has got to have a bit of the Irish Republican in him."

"Now bite your tongue, Danny old pal. There may be some Orangeman spies about. One never knows these days. In any case, I have had the pleasure already of meeting Adam. I can call you Adam, Petty Officer Welsh?"

The knowing look passing right by Dan. In any case the word "subtle" was not in Dan Bronsan's vocabulary. The ambassador and Adam Welsh had in fact met before. A glance at Adam as the ambassador addressed him would have tipped this fact. The revulsion palpable.

"Mr. Ambassador, nice to see you again."

Dan missing everything. The alcohol buzz precluded any chance he may have had of picking up the utter contempt and hate floating in the air that separated Adam from this O'Mara fellow.

"My God, you do get around. The New 'Yawk' thing I guess. Maybe something to it after all. Aye, Peter, if you ever need a room at the Sanno, this is your man. Mr. Sanno, they call him. Got a room on New Year's Eve, a bloody suite no less. He's promised to get my daughter, Kelley, one as well; that is if I'm off me head enough to let her fly over here."

"So you could get me a room, Adam?"

"I think it's time for a head call. You know you only rent it, right, Dan? Please excuse me...Mr. Ambassador."

"Hurry back, Adam. We have a lot to catch up with. I may be joining you shortly. Kidneys don't hold as much as they used to, don't you know?"

Adam about to lose what little food he had in his system as the disgust and shame overcame him. Rushed headlong into the stall. Thank God no poor soul inhabited it. He power-puked off the seat. Most of it found the bottom of the toilet though. A success. Time passed. *Why was the bastard here?* He needed a drink. The puke helping clear some room for more poison. The alcoholic way. Thoughts of his father but only for a second.

The ambassador was behind him.

"Are you all right there my boy?"

Turning now, the ambassador's member out of his pants. O'Mara laughing out loud now. Christ, you could hear him back at the bar, Adam thought. Turning away abruptly. Pissing in the urinal now.

"Jesus my boy. Don't worry; I'm not into that golden shower stuff. Get yourself together and get back to the bar. I'll buy you a few. We need to talk. In private, of course."

Adam Welsh had performed oral sex on Peter O'Mara, Irish emissary to Japan about a year earlier. The fact that the act was staged while Adam was in an alcoholic blackout making it no less devastating. It occurred in the men's room at Paddy Foley's Pub, an Irish bar located in the Roppongi District of Tokyo. Adam was drunk of course. Pictures were taken appearing to show Adam engaged in the act. No picture of the ambassador of course, other than his member. All four inches of it. The Irishman's disease. Still, enough to keep Fire Controlman First Class Adam Welsh in the pocket of Peter O'Mara, ambassador to Japan and I.R.A. liaison to the Aum Cult. Adam for his part did not know why.

"Bill Clinton will be one of the greatest presidents this country has ever had. Christ, you Nazi bastards are already out for blood. The guy will be a great statesman. Read my lips on that one. I mean look at the man's family? That's the true test of character. Have you ever seen more of a loving couple than him and that one, Hillary?"

"Well I'll say one thing for him, he should be given the Navy Cross for banging that one. We know he did; at least once."

The bar in an uproar now. Dan holding court in rabid debate with one of the "Unwashed" as he would have no doubt called this young sailor who was pushing the Republican talking points. Adam had seen it all before. The ambassador missing though.

The Japanese waitress beside Adam now.

"Excuse me. Adam San. The gentleman would like you to join him."

O'Mara at the table just off the dance floor here at the Sanno. This being a Thursday, no DJ on duty. They would be alone.

"Jesus, God help me," Adam murmuring under his breathe.

"Yes, yes, thank you very much. Please bring me a Jack Daniels. A double please."

A glance over to the bar. Dan busy with his new found antagonists. It seemed that the man was not happy unless he was involved in some type of confrontation. O'Mara motioning Adam to come over now. He could not ignore it. Had to go. Staggering now. He'd had more than enough for a buzz. Of course the puke had helped and the sight of the Irishman's flaccid Chipmunk would make anyone sober.

"Sit, sit, old pal. Please take a load off."

Then, under the breath, reeking of stale whiskey, "Me cock is in its house. Not coming out just yet. No worries."

This meant to be O'Mara's way of breaking the ice. Welsh could have killed him. The temporary presence of reason but more likely the absence of a weapon the only thing stopping him.

"Haven't seen you at Paddy's lately. Miss you. Miss our chats. Things going well aboard ship? How is Keiko?"

"Talk of anything, anybody. Leave Keiko out of our conversations. We spoke about this before. She doesn't exist as far as your concerned."

Trembling. Visibly shaken.

"Aye, my boy. Certainly. Here's your drink now. Take a good blast. Things will be fine. Just need to get your head straight. Everything's going to be just fine. Thank you so much, my dear."

Using the leprechaun look for the waitress. Safely out of earshot and then, "Look you fucking piece of Yankee dung, we... you have a problem. I need access to certain areas of your base. I've told you this before. If you would draw a sober breath perhaps you would hear me. At least remember. Bender is your friend. We need him. I need to, shall we say, monitor his movements. For his own good, of course."

"Look, I've told you before, I'm a sailor onboard a godamn ship. Enlisted for Christ sake. I don't even have a security clearance worth a shit anymore. Why me? Why the fuck me?"

The ambassador shifting to Father Confessor now.

"My boy, now, now, please. The booze may be getting to you a bit. Ease off on that Tennessee shit. You need to drink the good stuff. The nectar of the fairies."

Pausing to let the shaken American take this all in and then, "I just want a meeting with your friend, Mr. Bender. We have mutual business associates, that's all. You won't be involved. I promise you."

Adam mind's eye flashing to the picture that O'Mara had shown him. The "BJ pic" as the ambassador gleefully referred to the compromising photo that O'Mara had taken of Adam while he was drugged and drunk. Slipped him a Mickey. Adam had actually found some bizarre humor in the fact that "A Mick" had "slipped him a Mickey."

O'Mara's voice bringing Adam back from his latest excursion.

"All right, all right. Look, give him this. You will see him soon?"

Handing Adam the business size envelope. Adam grasped the parcel. Maybe one sheet of paper in it.

"Ship gets underway tomorrow. I'll see that he gets it. I'm supposed to meet him before we go to sea and anchor. Of course he thinks that I'm at an A.A. meeting now."

"Yes, damn things would be much simpler if you would be going to those meetings on a regular basis."

"Sea and Anchor" referring to Sea and Anchor detail. This evolution took place at least two hours before the ship actually got underway. Preparations had to be made such as manning the lines and starting and testing the weapons and navigation systems. A U.S. Navy warship could not just be backed out of its parking space and set on its way as it were. Adam would be part of the evolution. It was approaching 8 PM or 2000 in military terms. He would have to be back at the ship and conscious in less than eight hours. He knew this yet ordered another one. The alcoholic way.

I'll worry about it tomorrow.

Adam took another belt as he placed the envelope in his pocket.

2

The seventy empty containers sat motionless in the bleak, sanitized fortress. Aum Cult storage facility #1 was located in the entertainment district of Roppongi. An area that consisted of restaurants and clubs all open most of the day and night. A land where all types of desires could be satisfied providing one had some yen. Gas Panic a bar within walking distance of Roppongi Station. Packed this Friday evening with a cosmopolitan crowd. There were American sailors, French computer programmers, Japanese, Chinese, Filipina. The Japanese office ladies or "OL's" eager for a good time. Take away the strain of the long six day, sixty hour work week. Demure and humble to a fault one would scarcely recognize these ladies now as they were transformed into modern geishas. These Bathsheba's of the East on the prowl now with their cigarettes and condoms part of the standard hunting attire.

The music blasting to a crescendo not experienced anywhere except perhaps in the wheel well of a 747 on take-off. The Cult soldiers worked two floors above Gas Panic oblivious both to the din and the irony of the aptly named bar where just above a factory of death would soon be in full operation.

"The Leader will be here tonight."

"That is ridiculous. Too risky."

"I heard it I'm telling you. One of the others mentioned it, thinking no one was listening."

"Move along now you two. There is much to do."

One of the Aum lieutenants barking at the workers. No time to waste. The Event drawing close. History would be forever changed. The Truth of Creation ingrained in everyone's mind that survived. A new world would begin. Shoko Asahara himself would be here at Gas Panic this very night. Arrangements had been made. The catastrophic Event would take place but first a precursor to the apocalypse. A message would be sent soon. A lesson taught through a horrible death. A microscopic foreshadowing of what was to come.

Shoko Asahara, the leader of Aum Shinrikyo, like so many insane zealots before him, had a flare for the dramatic. The Hindu god Siva, presiding over death and destruction. What better deity to worship for Shoko. Destruction after all no different from Creation. A kind of creation in itself in fact. From death springs life. Life to death. Death to life. Aum was doing what nature had intended all along. The sarin gas replacing the aging process that nature usually used in the birth to death cycle. A minor detail. The Science and Technology Agency, with scientists recruited from every major university in Japan, broken up into teams for the Cult. Specializing in chemistry, biology, physics and medicine. Quite similar in fact to what another fanatic had done decades before.

The little boy sat quietly watching, The dark brooding figure sang softly, rocking in the chair. The boy was terrified. Nine years on this planet and terror and guilt his primary feelings. His only feelings. Mother not here. He hadn't seen her for months in fact. Only the boy and the figure. Tall, dark, menacing, in a curious way. Getting up now. Moving towards him as he sang softly. An old Japanese nursery rhyme perhaps? Opening his robe now.

Sweat poured out of The One. The dream/nightmare again. The father dead years ago. Hacked to death as he slept. The protruding enemy inside the robe turned to mincemeat first. The beast butchered and buried by 17 year old Shoko. When the police came, the boy singing a nursery rhyme. Almost unintelligible but yes, a nursery rhyme. Years at the hospital. Shock treatments. Probing. Always probing. They would never know though. He would never tell of the nightmare. It was gone forever. Banished along with the beast they called his father.

Released after four years, quietly slipping back into a society that had decided he was safe now. Staying with his aunt while attending university. A good student. Quiet. Serene, yet something lurking below the surface.

Don't get close to me. Stay away.

No women. No friends at all until he met Atashi. In the park they talked of Siva, God of destruction and creation. Creation out of destruction. This made sense to Shoko. How could it not? He had killed his father and the thing that had tormented him for all of his young life. Shoko had been reborn when he had destroyed his father.

Wasn't this world just like father? Everyone out to torment me. Especially the women. All of them whores.

They had made his body experience unmentionable things. He had wanted to cut it off at times. Like he had done to the beast that lurked in the robe of his father. He would destroy all of them. The women and their American soldiers who paid them and made them cheap and disgusting.

Everything would change. Shoko knew this with the utmost of certainty after that first meeting with Atashi. A new world. One free from tormentors. The whores would be cleansed. The ones that still lived that is. Atashi had told him of the sarin. Goro Atashi, the disgraced lawyer. Brilliant with a beautiful family. Long gone now. His distant and strange behavior too much for his young wife and child. The wife now remarried to an American sailor.

At first progress was slow. A few scientists, fringe types. No focus. The breakthrough happened when Atashi came to them with the news on the gas. Saddam Hussein had used it with great effect during his war against the Kurds. The fact that these were his own people, a minor detail to Aum. Sacrifices had to made. Certain collateral damage a necessity. The twisted, grotesque forms of the dead, women and children seen all over CNN.

A simple gas to manufacture and transport, it was nonetheless, once weaponized, lethal. Lethal to the extent where seventy containers of a relatively small size could wipe out over half the population of Tokyo. An act of horror that would be blamed on America herself. This was the brilliant addition to Aum's plan. Launch the world into a war that would eventually reap total destruction. The Aum Cult waiting to rebuild civilization in their image from the wasteland.

They had left the coffeehouse with a feeling of demonic euphoria that night after realizing that this dream could indeed become reality. No more chants against the American dominators, the rapists of the Japanese women. No. Time now for action. A real statement. Destruction and then the Creation. A new world with Shoko at the helm. The torment would end with the last gasp of the last martyr. Yes there would have to be martyrs. Not enough to merely destroy the evil West. No the Japanese would die as well. After all, they, particularly the women had been soiled forever by the American semen.

• • •

The nondescript Japanese man walks through the cacophony of the Gas Panic bar. Most of the occupants if they noticed him at all would take him for a beer vendor there to replenish a keg or two. No matter. He walks to the back of the bar almost stumbling over a body. American. Drunk of course, fondling the Japanese female. Soon this would end, Shoko Asahara, leader of the Aum Cult, thought as he walked through the back door and up the stairs to the sarin gas factory.

She walked through the archway of cherry blossoms, oblivious. The petals like so many miniature Kabuki players dancing gaily in the light breeze. The figure is small, fragile yet somehow ominous. She stepped on the fallen petals, staring straight ahead. Eyes black. A young man approached and smiled. No response. He flinched at the abyss lurking in those eyes. Still, she is beautiful.

Twilight. A mother pushed her stroller with infant past the figure, and their eyes meet ever so briefly. A touch perhaps of a smile? Gone in an instant as the brooding, broken, beautiful shell continued on. Now at the front of the house, she took out her keys, opened the door and entered.

Keiko Watanabe stood inside the non-descript building on the outskirts of Tokyo. A petite beauty on the downhill side of her twenties. Not showing it though. Beautiful almond eyes, Cheshire cat in black skirt, stooping like an old woman but not pulling off the disguise at all. A beauty for the ages. A tragic beauty that Shakespeare would have cast in some Globe Theater east if he had made it this far. Alas, she would have to be satisfied with playing a real-life cross between Lady Macbeth and Juliet opposite an American Romeo and a Japanese Richard III.

Keiko Watanabe, the lover/victim of Adam Welsh, had attended university in Ebisu and was the product of a wealthy Tokyo family. Her father owned a well-established trucking company, and her mother had never wanted for the finer things in life. It was in fact rumored that Keiko's maternal grandfather had made his fortune through some "creative" weapons contracts with the occupational government of Douglas Macarthur just as the war had ended. An ebullient girl for most of her life, it was just recently that friends had noticed a change. Some would say that a darkness had seemed to fall over this lovely, vulnerable creature. Those who did not know of the botched abortion, of the heart that had not been merely broken but shattered into an infinitesimal amount of jagged pieces, never to be repaired, would not understand. They would find the scene here at this Aum Cult house all the more surreal and ironic gazing upon the image of this small, placid-looking Japanese woman here in this factory of horror.

In a different world, one removed from contradiction, deceit and utter insanity, Keiko would be strolling with her lover in the Harajuku Park. Instead, here at this Aum Shinrikyo staging area, she was a participant in the planning of an attack on humanity so devastating in its potential for slaughter that its successful completion would dwarf both Hiroshima and Nagasaki.

"Keiko San, so good to see you."

It was Daiki meaning "bright one" as his mother had called him. Before this insanity had begun. Years ago when he was loved and he himself was capable of the emotion. Finished now. A pawn of the Aum. No return ticket available. A young, wide-eyed, former university student turned soldier for Aum. Recruited right out of university. Once a promising law student till he came under the spell. Working with the ardor of the possessed now. The Cult would be in the courts again this week. Time was of the essence. Briefs would be needed. Motions filed.

"Is there tea?"

She spoke in that inanimate way she had. Daiki, accustomed to it now. After working with this woman for only a short time, he had come to realize that she was driven in a far different way than the others. The otherworldly way she had about her could be quite disconcerting in fact.

Thoughts of Adam came to her. Just recently he had been visiting inside her head. Unannounced. Thinking back to one of her last meetings with him.

"It's going to be fine, baby. I'm going to get sober. This is it. I feel it. Things will be different this time, baby. Jack is really helping me."

Adam had been visibly shaken. The booze coming out of his pores. She wanted to believe him with every bit of faith she had in her being. She forced herself to. Against all logic. Adam had said these words in one form or another so many times before. The alcoholic's mantra. I'll quit tomorrow. The problem was that quitting was not Adam's problem. Living sober was. There was the rub as Dan Bronsan might have said on more than one occasion. In the end, Keiko forced herself to believe.

So long ago when he had spoken these words. A park bench on a beautiful sunny day under a cherry blossom tree in Hiroo. She had looked at him with a look, which was at once loving yet also one of fear.

Dread.

So strange now to think that she had once been capable of any human feeling at all. She would be an accomplice, albeit unwittingly, in the annihilation of a third of Tokyo in a very short time if all went as planned. Probably a couple on that same park bench would be part of the carnage.

"Keiko Chan?"

Daiki again. Back to her senses now.

"Your tea, Keiko. You were away there for a few moments. Are you okay?"

A slight smile on the lips of Keiko Watanabe now. The thought of anyone ever being "okay" again in this cold world that she now inhabited, devoid of anything or anyone making any sense or semblance of logic. There was no feeling here. Not even a hint of compassion. The suggestion that Daiki would have any empathy for her almost insulting to Keiko now. She took the tea without acknowledging the young lemming. Daiki not bothered by this. At one time he might have been. No time now for personal feelings. There was paperwork to file. He left Keiko to her private Gulag, sitting at the sparse desk which had been her place of toil for the last weeks. No idea or concept of time dwelling inside this tormented woman. She gazed across the barren floor towards the windows, closed despite the spring heat. Rumors of a shipment coming within the next weeks. No need for any prying eyes. The lawyer, Shoko Asahara's right hand man and chief confidante had said as much to the soldiers here during the last Cult meeting. A kind of pep talk. A phrase that Adam had taught her. A slight turn to her lip as this fragment of her lost love flooded through her. Just for an instant though. Gone as quickly as it came. Mercifully.

4

Jack Bender fumbled with the crumbled piece of paper, oblivious to the din of the early afternoon bar crowd. Staring at the words neatly typed on the paper now.

The contents seemingly innocuous to the casual observer, but Jack Bender, Supervisor of the Toxic Waste Facility, Yokosuka Naval Base knew that the people that would be looking though the waste in his classified material-only disposal receptacle would not be doing so in a casual way. Jack had spent enough time around "spook types," as Adam Welsh had referred to them, to know that anything put in a burn bag was subject to investigation before being incinerated. True, the message he held in his hand now from Peter O'Mara was innocent in and of itself. But placed with other parts of an intelligence puzzle by someone with a trained eye, it could be devastating to the crusade of Jack Bender which was nothing less than total retribution for the injustice done to his beloved Yumiko.

"FINGAL O'FLAHERTIE PER USUAL"

The paper spread out on the back booth here at the Roppongi bar. Jack foregoing his normal lunch at the base enlisted club. The ritual of coffee, pecan pie, chicken sandwich on white bread (in that order) would have to be missed today. The other diners at the club would no doubt be thankful for this as they would not be subjected to the inevitable culmination which included a spirited dental flossing right there at Jack Bender's table for all to see. Adam, his usual dining partner still at sea. The paper in front of Jack Bender now the only content from the envelope Adam had given him before he got underway. The message from Peter O'Mara. A code of course. The Irishman with an unabashed affinity for Oscar Wilde. The middle name of the Irish, alcoholic, gay bard agreed upon as the signal for a meeting at Paddy Foley's Irish Pub in Roppongi. The time always 2PM.

"A drink, Jack? How about a nice Jameson? Take the edge off, don't you know?"

The ambassador had arrived discreetly as usual.

Peter O'Mara slithered into the seat across from Bender. The man knew that Jack was a sober alcoholic in recovery. Very aware of it. Still asked if he wanted a drink. A game. Bender never having a problem with this. He knew that O'Mara was in essence a weak, grandiose human being. The hate that he did have for the man spawned from what he had done to Adam Welsh. Adam a surrogate son in many ways. Jack Bender had heard of the pictures. He knew that the blackmail was O'Mara's way of insuring that he could communicate with Bender indirectly by using the unwitting Welsh. Jack understood this but still knew that in a different time, a different world, he would have not hesitated to kill O'Mara, Irish Ambassador to Japan or not.

"No, Mr. Ambassador, just a Diet Coke. As always. I do admire your tenacity though. We have business to discuss?"

"I'll have a Jameson and a Diet Coke for my friend please."

The Irishman never taking his gaze from Bender as he placed the order. The young Japanese waitress appearing on cue. The bar full even at this early hour. Some kind of Rugby Match had just finished. Jack noticing the multicolored shirts worn by the gaijin and Japanese players. Sony and Guinness both well-represented. As if they needed any more advertising, thought Jack. O'Mara noticing the slight smile.

"Something amusing, Mr. Bender?"

"Oh, not really. Just ironic. A bit of irony, yes. Nothing important. One thing though, before we start. You saw Adam Welsh the other night of course. In the future, please contact me directly by cell phone using the usual phrases. There is no need to cause Adam any more pain. Are we understood?"

"Ah, but Jack..."

Jack cut him off with a look and then, "I was reading The Japan Times the other day. Curious story from the AP wire in Bangkok. Poor fellow. Woke up after a night of drinking with his nuts gone. Could you imagine that? Waking up with one's testicles gone. Seems the boy deserved it, if anyone could. Turns out he was a pedophile, and out and out rapist. Specialized in young boys and men. Don't ever call me 'Jack.' Don't go near Adam Welsh again. Ever. Now, the business you called me here for?"

The steady look, one of contempt and something else. Perhaps even more foreboding. The ambassador recovering immediately though. No heart or soul to the man. As if he had been bothered by a flea for just a moment. Back in stride now.

"Yes, Jack, I.... Jesus, God please...."

The table here at Paddy Foley's very intimate. Couples could sit directly across from each other yet still be close enough to hear through the noise of the crowd. Even fondle each other's lower extremities if the relationship had reached that point or the booze had accelerated it. In any case, Jack Bender now had the "Diplomatic Pouch" as it were of Peter O'Mara, Irish Ambassador to Japan, securely encased in his clenched fist. He began to twist. O'Mara turned a curious tint of pale gray. A moment or two before unconsciousness, Bender released his testicles.

"Please bring Mr. O'Mara a glass of ice water and of course another whiskey. He appears to be working too hard lately. Out of breathe a bit. Yes, Peter, you need to get some exercise."

Jack Bender never breaking eye contact with O'Mara even as the waitress once again appeared out of nowhere. No doubt responding to the man's cries of pain. She nodded with a quick bowing movement and rushed off for the drinks. O'Mara gasped for air, slowly regaining the composure or as much of it as a man whose balls were just placed in a vice can regain within any period of time. The thought that the scum would not be touching any young men for a while gave Jack a nice feeling of serenity.

"Ja... Mr. Bender, for the love of God, was that really necessary?"

Not waiting for a response. In any case, the consummate politician in Peter O'Mara holding full sway now. He would kill Bender for what he had just done. Would have killed him for a lot less, but alas, there was business to take care of. Sweet retribution later.

"To the point, yes. We have a mutual acquaintance, you and I. The One, I believe he is called these days. I would very much like to know what you are doing for this man. You may be, how do you say in America, "In a bit over your head?"

Jack Bender's relationship with ambassador Peter O'Mara had been promulgated on their mutual interest in the head of the Aum Shinrikyo, Shoko Asahara. Bender, in his position as Head of the Toxic Waste Facility at Ship Repair Facility, Yokosuka, Japan, had first met the ambassador at the Navy Day Ball ceremony a couple of years ago when it had been held at the Sanno Hotel ballroom. The Navy Day Ball an annual ceremony celebrating the birthday of the United States Navy. It was an affair that included a dance and was steeped in tradition. Adam and Keiko had been there as well. Of course it was also a perfect excuse for one to get shit-faced to borrow the parlance of Commander Steve Blasingame, who hosted the party in his role as the present senior officer. In any case Jack's first sight of the ambassador was in the men's room of the Sanno. He stepped over his power-puking torso as he made his way to the urinal. Jack had even thought of taking the man to an A.A. meeting, but any thoughts of rehabilitation for this man were dashed the night that Adam Welsh had come to Jack in a fit of utter despair and related the story of the black-out with O'Mara and the ensuing compromising pictures. Adam had let it be known during a drunken rant with O'Mara that Jack Bender had many highly placed Japanese friends and hinted that Asahara might be one of them. Of course Adam had hit the bullseye so to speak without even knowing it. His idle boast actually turned out to be true. Using Adam and the pictures, the Irishman had been trying to get a meeting with Asahara through Jack ever since. Finally, after several rejections, Jack had agreed to a meeting. Jack despised O'Mara, but he felt he would be useful for the time being. A way to get him closer to Asahara and Jack's ultimate goal-the destruction of the besotted West that had destroyed his Yumiko's family so many years ago. O'Mara of course not knowing of Jack's intentions either. Both men operating in the blind. All this considered, the particulars of the call to meet here at Paddy Foley's a mystery to Jack.

Until now.

"Why would you want to know that, Mr. Ambassador, even supposing it was true. You may want to lay off the whiskey a bit. I know that I could become quite delusional when I wrestled with the demon rum. Even believed in leprechauns."

Jack hitting a nerve here. Adam had mentioned that the ambassador was called the "Little Leprechaun" with emphasis on "Little" behind his back. Jack continued.

"Look, Mr. Ambassador, we are both very busy men. I deal with many Japanese people of all classes. My job as well as the fact that I have lived in Japan for a long time now makes this a necessity. This person called The One that you speak of, I have no recollection of having met. So if there is nothing else, I must be going."

O'Mara nodded slightly and passed the glossies across the table. Time encoded digital pictures. Very good quality. Bender in front of the Gas Panic bar. Another interior shot. Bender and Asahara himself. Trying not to betray any emotion.

How did he get these?

Jack's mind racing now. No one knew he was meeting Asahara. Only Adam. Of course. Adam had given everything away. At least the little that Jack had let him know. Adam not aware that Jack Bender was involved with Shoko Asahara. Unfortunately, when Adam was in a drunken stupor he just assumed Jack knew all Japanese of note. O'Mara, a drunk but alas no dummy. He had evidently put it all together, thought Jack. Realizing now that there was more to it than Adam's explanation that Asahara was an old family friend of Bender's wife, Yumiko. *God damn, that boy needs to get sober!*

"Mr. Bender, I have certain acquaintances, shall we say, that are very interested in Mr. Asahara and his group, cult, whatever you want to call it. I need to meet with The One as soon as possible. We could be mutually beneficial, symbiotic I believe they would call it in the animal world. In any case, let me put it a bit more direct. If you do not arrange a meeting, your

NIS, is that what they call it, Naval Investigative Service will be delivered these self-same pictures you see in front of you. The originals of course. Yes, it is a rather unfair world. Do not go for my jewels again. You are only alive right now because I need you, Mr. Bender. I want the time and place of the meeting by tomorrow morning. Have another Diet Coke. Make it a double. It's on me."

The Irishman got up, not waiting for Bender's answer. Immediately joined by three men who seemed to come out of the woodwork. Bodyguards possibly. Or something else. Jack watched him slither out of the bar. No one even noticing him. Just another afternoon patron.

Jack Bender stared into space momentarily and smiled at the waitress as she walked over with his drink. Without further ado, took out his cell phone which had been entangled in some old dental floss in the bottom of his worn Navy issue jacket and dialed a number which could only be answered by Shoko Asahara himself. One thing at a time. One step at a time. He would kill Peter O'Mara but not just yet.

Of course Jack Bender had heard the rumors of Peter O'Mara's involvement with the Provisional I.R.A. Hadn't really paid much attention to them. Until now. These days, any Irish politician had some sympathy for the Irish Republican Army. Jack thinking that the Irish scum or the Provs, as the Provisional wing of the Irish Republican Army was called, must have the world's best public relations firm. Only rivaling whoever Yasar Arafat, that other renowned scumbag, had.

Bender's musings interrupted by the Japanese voice on the other end of the cell. The usual code words spoken and a meeting arranged. The Gas Panic bar. Tomorrow. 1PM. As good a time as any to find out what the Irish vermin was up to before he killed him. Of course, Bender might not even have to. Asahara may well rid himself of the cancer that had plagued Adam Welsh and was, at least now, a minor annoyance to Jack Bender. Funny how things worked out if one worked a good A.A. program, thought Jack with a smile to himself. Lunch hour over. Time to get back to work.

But first, a floss.

5

"Stand by for heavy rolls as the ship comes about."

Another turn, godamn it. Like it's not rough enough out here.

Fire Controlman First Class Adam Welsh aboard the USS McClusky (FFG-41) somewhere off the coast of Japan. Been out there for two days. Exercises. That's all the Navy did these days was exercise. Pull out for a week. Come in for a week. Good in a way for an alky though. Chance to dry out. Adam would surely have been thrown out long ago if he'd been in the Air "Farce." Shore Duty in all the choices places. Nine to five job. Might as well be a civilian. Yea, he would never have made it. The Navy was perfect. Couldn't drink at sea. Well you could but what was the point? Adam was a bar drinker. He needed the camaraderie. The crowd. If he drank out here it would be like dropping acid in a mental asylum. The bar scene in that old Star Wars movie came to mind. The one where Luke Skywalker goes to the bar with all of the aliens. *Yea, it would be just like that, come to think of it.*

The first day at sea had been hell. The usual shakes. Coming out of his body. Thank God he had made it through. Thanks to Rose and Starsky at the front desk of the Sanno. Threw him in the shower and poured him into the cab to the train station. Jack had been waiting at the brow of the ship. His look of disgust had abated somewhat when Adam had handed him the envelope from the ambassador. He just nodded, told Adam to "Keep coming back" and left rather hurriedly. Unlike Jack, Adam thought now. Weird.

Of course the Chief had been a pain in the ass. The Mormon bastard, Chief Petty Officer Bonner. Bucking for officer and on Adam's case all the time. Finally, after the ship was underway, he was able to lock himself in his space and sleep off the drunk from the night before.

Hoisting a few with Art at the Sanno bar. Trying to erase the memory of the latest meeting with the human refuse, O'Mara. One too many Jack Daniels. He just needed to get his remaining time in and he'd have the retirement and the pension. Stay here in Japan. Teach English. No going back to the States. Nothing there for him. The suffocating mother and the brother who wouldn't talk to him unless he got sober. Well he had no intentions of that. Not now anyway. He was doing all right playing the game. If only the Mormon piece of shit chief would get off his back.

Lying in his rack. No Watch until tomorrow morning. About 2200 now. Taps. Lights out. Finally alone. He hated dealing with the people he worked with. The younger guys were the worst. The looks of disgust were seldom hidden these days. They knew he was a useless drunk. Things had been different a few years back. Respected. Off the sauce. Doing his job in Navy Intelligence. Yea, a contradiction of terms. A great life though. He knew his job and was respected.

Different now. All over. Lost his security clearance. The Operations Officer at Edzell Base, a comms intercept site in Scotland might as well have put a knife in his heart when he came in to tell him. Escorted out of the building. One drink too many. Felt like scum. A nothing. All the things Dad had said years ago had come true. His life over. Felt like someone had died. Like when his father had died in fact. He hadn't thought about the old man for a while. Hadn't dealt with it. Come to terms with it. Funny the things you thought of in your rack floating around in the middle of the dark, endless sea. The harpies all came out to play.

"You're a zero! You hear that! Nothing. Not my son!"

Years ago but just like yesterday. Davey Welsh standing at the bottom of the stairs. Drunk again. Adam's mother crying in the other room. Adam not knowing what to think. Trembling. He loved his father.

Why was he angry?

Must be Adam's fault. It had to be. He was a zero. Everything was his fault. His father and mother fighting, unhappy. All his fault. Ten years old. The cause of everything that was wrong in a family that lent new meaning to the word "dysfunctional."

Denial became the operative word in the life of Adam Welsh. Inherited from a mother whose life contained more secrets than the National Archives. Dad in and out of the bars. Getting sober for a while but never staying that way. Always back to the solace of the bottle. Funny how Adam could never understand it then, but it seemed clear as the nose on his face now. Booze was the answer. Life too much and God knows his father had his demons.

Adam just a kid then. Getting off the bus from school. Walking towards the house. There at the door, Davey Welsh. The look of a dead man. Face as white as a ghost. A few drinks leading to a few more the day before. Walking into a supermarket with a loaded .38. At least that's what it said in the police report. Davey went into the blackout after the third drink. Picked up by the Nassau County cops while swerving aimlessly on the Southern State Parkway. Beaten to a pulp. Body still alive but spirit absent. No more castles for Davey Welsh.

The next time Adam would see that death pallor was at the Rikers Island morgue. Davey Welsh on the slab for identification purposes. Adam thinking he was ready but then the curtain coming down, and there was his father. Naked and in some ways surreal. Like a department store mannequin but this man on the table was not a mannequin. Could this be the human being that sat at Adam's bedside and told him that life would be wonderful? Davey about thirty-four then and Adam, seven and already troubled by nameless fears.

Back on the ship now. God he hated to space out like that. Go back to those days. If he only had a Jack Daniels, he would deal with it. Deal with it by not dealing with it.

Beautiful Keiko. Here she was now. Floating around in his head as he sailed through the Sea of Japan. No escaping her. He would never forget the look on her face as she left for the abortion clinic. Alone. The tears had dried by then. She had wanted the baby. He didn't. Responsibility was not in Adam Welsh's vocabulary. He hadn't even paid for it. Couldn't. After all, he was a good Catholic. Dealt with it like he had dealt with everything else. Did nothing.

Poor little, beautiful Keiko. Adam hadn't seen her since that day. The doctor had been a drug-addicted butcher who partook of the same drugs he gave his patient. Keiko, the beautiful Japanese girl who only wanted two things in life, the love of Adam Welsh and to bear his children, would now never be able to have a child of her own.

Adam prayed for sleep to come. He knew it wouldn't though. Not without the booze. He was trapped here with all of his demons. Keiko holding court over them all, *Why did you do this to me, Adam?* At once her face in pain but then turning a ghastly hue of yellow. Contorting now, her mouth trying in vain to form words that would never come out. Only a guttural, tormented scream. One that encompassed all the pain in the world. At least it seemed that way to Adam as he tossed and turned along with the ship. Two more days. Then back to Tokyo. He would find Keiko. He had to. Time to banish the demons forever.

6

The ambassador had left an hour ago. Or maybe two? No matter. Adam was in the zone. Thirty-six, gaunt. Ichabod Crane with a Navy ID card. The booze had taken its toll. "Nothing ages like whiskey," Jack Bender had stated on more than one occasion. Still there was some semblance of the fresh-faced kid he had once been. Brilliant blue-eyes that got brighter with a shot of Jack Daniels or a woman's touch. The warmth had enveloped him. In this dark cavern called the Sanno Hotel bar with its smells of old whiskey and lost dreams he passed into and around any memory he wanted to visit. No shakes now. He appeared normal to the occasional visitor to his space here at the darkest corner of the bar.

Dan was here of course. Going on now about Rose and Art and how Art was an old fool...you know, nothing like one.

"Damn, Art, I'm your friend. Don't you understand that? She's no good for you. No good. Find yourself a young Japanese harlot."

"Fuck off, Dan. Stop with the harlot shit. Just because that thing between your legs hasn't been inside a pussy since you were..."

A laugh from the assembled cast of characters. All drunks. All with potential. The dreaded "P" word. Rose in the ladies room now. Out of ear shot.

Rose Carney, thirty-nine-ish but built like the proverbial brick fertilizer house. Platonic consort for Art Chambers. A painkiller with breasts. Art had spent all those years in Vietnam. He had seen everything or at least it seemed that way. Left a bit of himself there. His friends were on that Wall. He went once, touched the names. It somehow-what was the word-validated them. They were once alive. They had dreamt the dreams. Fell in love. Had their hearts broken. All dead now. Art would never go back to that Wall. It was okay. Enough to know that Billy and Walt were there. They had lived, and all those who filed past would know that they had.

No, Art didn't fit back there anymore. He was sixty-five, strong as a bull. first gaijin stick fighting master in Japan, hopelessly in love with Rose. She was back from the ladies and was sitting next to him now but might as well have been on another planet. In another dimension. She turned to Adam.

"So Mr. Sanno has got himself a room again! How do you do it, Adam? All those guys on waiting lists, and you just saunter up here and get one. Amazing."

"Oh, Adam is amazing, yes he is."

It was Dan interjecting as always. On his tenth gin and tonic. Beefeaters, always Beefeaters. Adam just nodding now. A wry grin. The "Luke" smile from that old Paul Newman movie maybe. "Hey, you just have to treat people right. It's a New Yawk thing, right, Dan?"

"Yes, Adam, we know how you are, and then we know how you are. Just make sure you make it to the bloody ship. Christ, ease off on that stuff. It's almost eleven for the love of God. You will never make your retirement at this fucking rate."

"Double Jack and one for Dan, Yoko San."

Dan shaking his head in disgust but taking the free drink nonetheless.

"Art, are we going to watch *It's a Wonderful Life* this year?"

Art, smiling kind of weakly now, lips pursed, looking at Rose. Rose getting closer to Adam, touching him every now and then.

"That's 'Lieutenant' to you."

Joking now. He loved Adam. Like his son.

"Christ, it's not even close to Christmas. Yes, I would love to watch it though. You could ask Keiko to join us."

As soon as the words left, were out there, irretrievable, Art knew the enormity of his gaffe. The look on Adam's face, stark confirmation that he had hurt his friend.

"Well, old son...." Trying to regroup now... "You two haven't seen each other in a while. Well, of course...what's that they say about the heart growing fonder. Yes, we'll all watch it together. A good time for all. Yes. That is an order."

A partial success. The faint smile on Adam's lips. Better than nothing, thought Art. Another story as far as Rose was concerned.

"Oh, Art don't bring poor Adam down. Maybe it's better this way."

A quick glance at Adam. Rose reaching. Digging. Nothing.

Finally, "How about another drink, gentlemen? About time the lady buys. Women's Lib and all that."

A muted cheer. Keiko momentarily placed on the back burner. Salutations all around. The self-inflicted pain inherent with the pursuit of unrequited love alive and well for one Rose Carney.

• • • • •

The air is alive. Columns and columns of clouds, like so many dark sentinels, watching and waiting. Crowds move to and fro below. Everyone with a story, a life. The human desire for survival is uncanny. What must these sentinels think as they look down at this humanity; this mass of intelligence going hither and yon, bustling, driving on and on? To what purpose? To whose plan?

Art Chambers struggles to breathe. His last breath? Gasping now in his one-bedroom apartment here in Hiroo. Stick-fighting had been a bit harder today. He had been struggling. The price for the cognac last night more than likely. He'd wanted to leave, but as always Adam had bought him one.

"One more, Art."

"It's okay. You're retired now. Enjoy."

"Here's to the tilt in your kilt."

Dan, the pain in the ass. *Jesus come up with another one! Original, maybe.* His jokes as tired as his hand on a good Saturday night.

Funny how much the human mind could spit out and take in as it is expiring. How would it happen? Like a light switch being turned off by some celestial janitor locking up for the night?

He woke. Birds singing. Sunlight. A dream, only a dream. This time. Too many lately. Good to be alive.

Time for some tea. The warmth of the bag reminding Art of a newborn baby. Alive. How strange. He would see Rose today. Tell her how he felt. Hell, she knew already. Tell her anyway. Ask her to move in.

•   •   •   •   •

Sunday, mid-morning in Tokyo. Art Chambers at the subway. Right on time. The Tokyo trains are never late. Well, if they are it's due to another drunk salary man or cheated-upon housewife hurling themselves onto the tracks. The wreckage, human and machine, is cleaned up and the grieving family billed for the expense. All very efficient.

Art never would understand the Japanese completely. He had lived here most of his adult life, learned the language, married a Japanese girl. Hell, he was about to be named the number one (Ichiban) practitioner of Kendo for his age group in the entire country. A gaijin no less. Still, he'd never be accepted completely. Fine with him though. Art loved Japan. The people, the culture, the peace. God, the peace!

Growing up in Los Angeles was not a good time. Stabbings and then the gangs. Mexicans, blacks, whites. They were all insane, out of control. L.A. today was a City of Fear. Anger permeated everything. Thoughts of the 110 from Pasadena to the 10 freeway and on to Santa Monica. Sitting in the traffic. He had taken the sales job right after retirement.

Lily, his wife, gone now, had desperately wanted to live in the States, the land of the free. But Art had dreaded getting up in the morning. Getting in the car, speeding off to his on-ramp, only to sit in the parking lot called 110 South with all the other zombies. No way to live. Out there with the Low-Riders and their nuclear-powered stereos. Art would look over and envision disemboweling the ignorant driver. He could deal with stupidity but never with ignorance. Capital punishment for the ignorant. It would be a better world indeed.

Everyone angry, frustrated, unhappy. After a year, Art couldn't take it anymore. When he started carrying his service revolver with him every day, he knew that it would not work. This quest for the American dream here in a place that looked nothing like the America he had grown up with. Christ, English had become the second language!

No, Art had no regrets. Rose was another matter though.

The subway stopped at Ebisu station. Art Chambers walked out of the car and turned towards the stairs. No escalators for this aging warrior. Climbing now, passing scores of Japanese school children, his bald head and goatee gleamed in the morning sunlight.

Rose Carney lived in Ebisu in a one-bedroom apartment near the train station. The apartment was almost plush by Tokyo standards. Anyone tall enough to purchase an E-ticket at Tokyo Disneyland would of course have to bow slightly as they entered and made their way from room to room. Nevertheless, the apartment was a bargain at 100,000 yen a month.

Reaching the subway exit, Art trudged up the crowded street towards Rose's apartment. The Tokyo Tower loomed in the distance like some Behemoth's discarded erector set. What were they thinking when this monstrosity was built, he mused.

He was wearing the good suit today. Shoes shined. Art Chambers was a civilian who had never really left the military, spit shine and rigid all the way. The green and white flowered tie had been a gift from Rose. Expensive silk purchased at the Ginza when she still had the big job with Coca Cola. The first foreign female at the corporate level of Coca Cola Japan. She had spearheaded the Diet Coke introduction into Asia. That seemed so long ago now. Let go for various reasons all of which lamely tried to cover the truth. Japan was still a racist and sexist country when it came to competition in the business world. Business was indeed war here but fought without weapons if one was a female gaigin.

She taught conversational English now, in turn caring for Art and longing for Adam Welsh.

Art walking briskly now. The anticipation of being with Rose. God she was a beauty. Couple of Japanese teenagers approaching. One wearing a T-shirt proclaiming "Fuck You." It might as well have said "Have a Nice Day." The kid had no idea as to the meaning. In this land of contradiction, it was cool to wear anything with English on it.

Art smiled and shook his head. *What would this kid's life expectancy be in Compton?* What a difference of cultures. Like being on another planet. Winding down the narrow street he reached the apartment and rang the bell. Within moments a female voice with a sexy, husky tone answered, "Hi, Art, I'll be right there."

The door opened and Rose stood before him. She was wearing jeans and a T-shirt that said "New York Mets Baseball Club." A gift from Adam. Art winced but recovered quickly.

"I've been cleaning the place up. You know, the spring-cleaning thing. Tea?"

"Love one, thanks. The place looks fine."

"You look great, Art."

Rose looking at him now, her face pink from the house cleaning. Ravishing though thirty-nine. Still a beauty. Like a fine wine. His loins ached. Been awhile since that feeling, he thought. No Viagra necessary with Rose around.

"Have a seat while I make the tea, Art. Sumo's coming on in about 10 minutes."

Akebono would be wrestling in the title match against Takanohana. Both Yokozuna (Grand Champion). Art had helped train Akebono in his early years. An American kid right out of Hawaii. Samoan mother and father, 650 pounds if he was an ounce, 6'7" tall. The heart of a small boy though. Great kid. Art had once eaten with Akebono and his stable mates. Rather he had watched them eat as they had polished off the entire Saturday night Mongolian barbecue at the Sanno Hotel restaurant. Akebono had washed his down with at least twenty bottles of Budweiser.

Now that he thought of it, Keiko was there that night. Her and Adam. Better times. They held hands and kissed like a couple of school kids. Art still had the picture somewhere of Keiko sitting on Akebono's lap or, more accurately, his massive tree trunk of a leg. She looked like a little girl engulfed by this man-child. A good night until Adam started drinking again. Keiko wanted him to stop, but he would have none of it. They had their usual argument and then retired to the room to make-up. The next morning saw a different Keiko though. At brunch she was distant, a different person all together. Art tried to cheer her up but to no avail. She spoke little and did not even look at Adam. Art had not seen her since.

Rose brought the tea.

"What time did you get back home Thursday night? I heard you and Adam really tied one on."

"About one, maybe two," Art answered. "You left early."

"I had some things to do. Working on the resume, you know. Art, I've got to find some godamn work soon! My savings are going fast and the fucking yen is kicking my ass!"

Rose angry. *What else was in her voice? Desperation? Maybe. Over the job or something else? Someone else? Adam?* Adam Welsh would always be there. The gorilla in the living room. Unspoken. Art knew it. Rose knew it. Tension in the air now. Palpable.

"Damn it, woman! You'll get something soon."

Art in his officer/father mode now. Rose comfortable with this part of him. No aging Lothario now. Daddy Art, a good man.

"I talked to Dan last night. Svenson is looking very good. He thinks he might be able to get you set up with an interview."

I don't want to make coffee and suck the occasional Japanese cock!"

"Jesus, Rose! It's a Swedish company!"

"We're in Japan, godamn it!"

Time to end this. Art knew she was right. As an American woman in Tokyo, no matter how fluent or intelligent, she would never be fully accepted. Smile, go to late-night bars, always be available, The trophy gaijin girl for some frustrated, rich, married salaryman. Art wanted to take her in his arms right now but knew better. In any case, the tirade was not over.

"What the fuck does Dan know anyway? Self-centered, fat bastard. He just wants to pump up his ego and get in my pants!"

"He means well on this one, Rose. Dan does have a few decent bones."

"Yeah, the one between his legs, right?"

"I'm not even going to go there, young lady."

Damn, the fatherly mode again. Art hated it when he went there. Sixty-five/thirty-nine, that's not really a big gap, he thought. Yea, it was. He knew it. She knew it. Hell, Rose was in her sexual prime. Sure, he was in good shape for his age but...that wouldn't do. Adam was on her mind. Art knew it. The tension was Adam. Not the job. Not Art. It would always be Adam.

"Let's watch the godamn sumo! Akebono is coming on soon. Sit down...please."

7

"Just eat the spaghetti, Dan San!"

The Japanese director irate now. Dan Bronsan had been at the commercial shoot for two hours and had already gone through about four bowls of spaghetti. A good way of adding to ones income for an ex-pat in Tokyo, Dan had been making commercials for Japanese television now for about five years. He knew all the ins and outs including the fine art of getting a free meal or two along with his daily wage by purposely screwing up take after take.

"Well if the cameraman knew what the hell he was doing, maybe. What was this guy's last job, special effects for the *Godzilla* movies?"

Gaijin asshole! The director had worked with Dan before. The only reason he kept hiring him was that he had the exact look that they wanted, a fat, obnoxious, pseudo-intellectual; in short, the Ugly American.

"Please, just look at the camera, and as you take a bite of the spaghetti, smile and say your line."

"Look, I've done this before. The other directors didn't seem to have this problem."

"Yes, they were all fired. It happens when you triple the budget!"

"Barbarians."

"Okay, here we go. Action."

Dan picked up a forkful of spaghetti and shoved it in his mouth like it was the last bit of food he would ever have. Visions of feeding time at the Tokyo Zoo came to mind. Looking into the camera, a large piece hanging from his nose, he said, "Toto Pasta, oshi!!"

The director surrendered with an audible sigh.

"Cut. Okay, let's stop for today."

Dan needed a drink. As the prop manager tried to pick up his plate, Dan almost gobbled up the poor man's hand as he devoured the rest of the pasta.

Back in the Sanno Hotel, Dan ordered his usual double Beefeaters and sat down at the empty bar. It was 4 PM on a Tuesday. Probably no sailors in today. Adam was at sea for the week. Art might come in, though.

How did I end up here?

The usual thought as he gulped the drink. Dan gulped or devoured everything. No delicacy to the man. Making love was reminiscent of bull elephants engaged in a struggle for the female. Not that this happened much lately. No, the lovemaking had decreased in direct proportion to the weight increase. He was up to about three hundred now and his cholesterol was very high. The doctor had told him just the other day that the bad cholesterol was getting much higher in fact. This brought a small smile to Dan's face. *So there were good and bad cholesterol. Well, what exactly determined this? Was the "bad" cholesterol a product of a poor upbringing? Did it come from the wrong side of the tracks?*

Funny. He had to remember those lines. Rose had told him that his jokes were getting old. Well, he would show that tart. Just because she was the only gaijin piece of ass that came into the Sanno with a pulse, she thought that she was Sophia fucking Loren!

God she was doing a number on Art. He liked Art. Sure, he got on his nerves, and they had huge spats over politics. Art the right wing Nazi, Dan the compassionate liberal Democrat, Old School, not this punk Clinton. The democrats of FDR and Harry Truman. Jack Kennedy, even. God, Kennedy looked like a saintly statesman compared to Slick Willy. Of course, Dan would never admit to Art as much. In public conversation, Clinton would make a great president.

Deeper in thought now. The Beefeaters taking effect. *Was it one, two?*

How many? Shit, like it mattered. He was fifty-five. A very old fifty-five. Sure the booze was no good but he had given up the fags. Fags as they called cancer sticks in London. Days of London past. Dan thinking about his younger days now. Dangerous territory. *What was it that Adam used to say: One foot in the past and the other in the future and you're just pissing on today. Oh well. So be it. What was it. Twenty years ago?* Dan, just out of the Navy. Working for a "Boiler Maker" operation near Soho. Selling charity. My God. How had he done it? All day on the phones calling total strangers.

"I'm Dan Smith, and we'd like to thank you for your contribution to the London Orphan Children's Foundation last year. Can we count on you again? The kids will love you. They all had a great time last year."

"Fuck you. Yank bastard,"the normal response. If he even got that far. Normally they just hung up. Another Beefeater. Feeling the glow now. Needed to cut down. Oh, what would it matter? He had never really been in great shape since his high school days. Why start now. He didn't smoke anymore and could hold his own with most of the decrepit ex-pat specimens around his age.

Thoughts of Father Terry. A Jesuit of course. Way too liberal for the Holy See. A talk with Father Terry years ago came to mind. Dan, maybe 16 at the time. A senior at St Pius in Brooklyn. They were talking about where Dan would attend college, and Dan just blurts it out. No reason. "Father, is there really a heaven? I mean is there something after this? Do we really go someplace else?"

He had regretted saying it as soon as it came out. Couldn't believe he had said it. He had though. It was out there.

Father Terry. Was that a look of doubt? Surprise? To this day, Dan wasn't sure.

"Dan, my son, why do you ask a question like that?"

He hadn't answered though. Just asked a question himself and then, "How about those colleges? Notre Dame looks good." Mindless small talk but no answer.

Back now at the bar. The glow. He belonged here. Wished he could stay here forever but reality lurked just outside the door. The world. Sure he didn't have any savings. Never would. The medical bills for Kelley just too much. The job at Svenson paying them thank God. She had just graduated from Cornell though. A miracle considering she had been given next to zero chance of living into her twenties just a few years ago. She'd be coming out to visit him next month. First time in Japan. First time out of New York. Feelings of elation mixed with fear. Fear for his little girl and fear for himself.

"Buy that old fart a drink too! Where's the sumo? Put the sumo on, godamn it! Is this Japan or not? Jesus Christmas!"

"How the hell are you, Dan? You're thinking too much."

Benny Carter. Retired Air Force. Viet Nam Vet. A black man and product of South Central L.A. Another survivor. Dan admired him and resented him all in the same breath.

"The hell with that shit. It's fixed. Just like that wrestling in the states now. Everybody knows it, I mean if you have a brain in your head!"

The arrogant Dan now. Coming out. Always did with the increase in Beefeaters.

"Now, Dan, who shit in your Wheaties today?"

Benny had had a few already himself. Must have been over having a liquid lunch at the restaurant. The afternoon crowd would pour in soon. Dan didn't like crowds. Only ones he felt comfortable with these days were Art and Adam and sometimes Benny. He even wished Rose were here. He could use the smell of a woman.

And where the hell was Keiko these days? He missed her. *What had Adam done to her? What had they done to each other?* Adam drinking more lately. Starting to get into trouble with the Navy. Not long to go till retirement. Made the ship the other day by the skin of his teeth. If the staff at the Sanno hadn't almost broken down the door and thrown him in the shower he never would have made it. Rose had helped as well. Everyone had known that she had spent the night with Adam. Everyone of course but poor Art. In any case, Missing Movement, the Navy's term for not being on one's ship when it goes out to sea, not something the Captain of the McClusky would have appreciated at all. With Adam's history, it would have been most certainly the last straw. Kicked out with over eighteen years with no pension to show for it. He'd have been in a cardboard box in no time, probably joining the growing legions of the destitute at Ebisu and Shinagawa Stations.

The rising number of homeless something that a society that was all about "saving face" finding increasingly harder to deal with. Oh, well, if he blew it, so be it. See how he would do in the real world. Dan a little pissed off at Adam for always bringing up the fact that Dan had only done two years in the Navy. Shit, it had been in Nam though. Not in some Boy Scout fight in the Persian Gulf. Hell, that was like playing a big video game.

"Should have come over to lunch."

Benny standing next to him now, 6'2". Chrome dome. Still in good shape though. Needed to get off the cigarettes. Wouldn't listen. Just told Dan to lose weight. Pissed him off. He could be ignorant at times. God, the whole world could be.

Dan deciding not to mention the commercial. It was good work, and he didn't want any competition. Part time work for gaijins wasn't as good as it used to be. Besides, Benny was doing fine with his English school. As many of the expats had done, Benny Carter had become an English teacher upon leaving the military. Teaching English for a Japanese company really a form of indentured servitude. Benny had played his cards right though. Made some contacts. Saved his money. Now he owned his own school. Helped out Art by throwing him some translation work. Good man. A survivor. They all were, thought Dan, with a sudden flush of camaraderie.

"I had Mongolian before I came over. Great spread down the street. Hard to hold down the Mongolian though!"

"Jesus, the same joke again."

Benny took another gulp of the Courvoisier.

"I saw Keiko today."

Dan taken aback. Keiko had not been in the Sanno since last New Year's. No one had seen her, in fact. There were rumors. Weird friends. Nothing solid though. Adam never mentioned her, and one didn't mention her in front of Adam.

"How is she?"

"How is she?" The voice loud and guttural now. The cigarettes and alcohol maybe doing some damage.

"Couldn't tell ya, Dan. She breezed past me. It was eerie, like she was another person. Just stared straight ahead. I could tell she recognized me. At least something inside her recognized me. She was dressed in black, all black. No make-up. That was weird. She never saw the light of day without make-up when she was with Adam. 'Hey baby,' I said. Couldn't even finish. Just flew past me. Jumped in a cab and she was gone. It was her though. I loved that little girl. God, what happened to her, Dan?"

"Adam was an asshole. You know how he could be."

"Yea, but they always got back together. Dan, this was another person I saw today. I got goosebumps. I can't get that look out of my mind. Hopeless. No feeling. Like the devil was inside her."

8

It was late. He should start the trip back to his small apartment, Art thought as he looked at Rose with a longing that could not be quenched. The sumo had been uneventful. Takanahano had beaten Akebono again. A leg thrust that brought the man-child crashing to the Dai. Art would always believe that the Japanese would never let a gaijin succeed completely at sumo. After all, it wasn't just a sport. It was a national institution. A religion for God's sake.

The drama outside the television had been predictable as well. Rose had been distant. After the initial tirade over her job status, she seemed to withdraw, to leave the scene. Other things on her mind. Not Art. Adam, of course. He'd be back in a few days. Ready for the booze again. Dried out for a week. Rough and ready to go. A bizarre triangle. Rose, Art and Adam. Of course Keiko the tragic missing part of the equation.

"Well, Rose, I'm off. Got to say a few things first though. I'd hate myself if I didn't."

"Yes, Art."

A look perhaps of disappointment. Did she want him to just leave? No matter, he would say his piece.

"I love you, girl. Damn, I said it. Feel like a damn fool. But, that's it. It's out there."

The unspoken now spoken. Lines drawn.

"Art, shut up."

She cut him off with a kiss to the cheek. Held him. The loins again aching. Was she grinding against him? Couldn't tell. She moved away before there was time.

"Art, you will always have a special place in my heart."

He was finished. He knew it and swallowed hard.

"You are the older brother I never had."

The coup de grace. She had killed him.

"I need you to be there for me, Art. Please be there for me. I can't be what you want me to be but..."

Art sensed the dread "F" word coming, tried to think of something before it came but too late.

"I want you to be my friend."

It hit him like a .50 caliber round at close range. Devastated but not entirely surprised.

"I'll always be there for you, baby," all he could say as he grabbed his hat and turned to leave.

"I think I'll stop at the Sanno on my way back. Talk to you tomorrow."

"Adam will be back in a few days. We'll all get together this weekend, maybe."

A lift to her voice now. Eagerness mixed with elation.

"That would be fine."

He opened the door and was gone.

Rose sat on the bed for what seemed like a lifetime after Art had left. Adam would be back on Friday. He had come to her the night before he left. Heavy drinking with Art and Dan at the Sanno. He cried. It was Keiko again. It would always be Keiko of course. As only a woman could know, Rose realized in her weary heart that Adam was deeply, tragically in love with Keiko. A dangerous foreboding love but all-consuming nonetheless.

Human beings were a tragic and foolish lot, she thought. What did Jagger say? "You can't always get what you want." So true. She would never get Adam. Not the way she wanted at least. Thirty-nine, her biological clock winding down. There would be no white picket fence with babies. Too little time. Too many mistakes had been made. No chance for a "Do over." Maybe in the next life but not now. Adam was unattainable and she could never love Art the way he wanted, deserved to be loved.

She looked at the pills. Sitting there, the bottle seemed to nod in agreement. A come hither look, perhaps. She was tired. The wine she snuck during the sumo had hit her. Head spinning just a bit now. It was really the only way she could get through a meeting with Art these days. He didn't seem to notice her trips to the small kitchen for a quick nip. Maybe he didn't want to notice.

Yes, Adam would return on Friday, but what of it? Keiko would always be between them. No real chance for her and Adam. No real chance for a life for Rose Carney. Her mind racing now. She grabbed the pills. Not thinking. Brought the bottle to her mouth and then...threw them to the floor. Screaming.

Not this way. Never this way. Not the way Mother had gone so many years before.

Rose Carney would carry on.

As long as we are breathing, honey.

Dad's words coming back now to save her.

As long as we can take a breath, we're in the game, Rose, hon. At least for another day.

Finally exhaustion overcame her.. No bad dreams on this night. At least for another day. She slept.

9

Art stood on the subway for the short trip to Hiroo station. He would stop at the Sanno for one. Hell, maybe two. The train was crowded as usual. Salarymen and housewives with children. The salarymen returning, many of them from weekend trysts with their mistresses. A reward for taking care of the family over the years. The Japanese culture. What a paradox, Art thought. It never ceased to amaze him. A society which on the one hand could worship honor and the ability to tell the truth but on the other hand could look the other way while one cheated on one's wife.

It was all about saving face, Art realized after years of living and working here. It was not so much about telling the truth but rather about not getting caught when one told a lie. Never get caught. Never lose face. The salaryman could spend time with his nubile twenty-something mistress as long as the wife did not know of it. As long as he did not flaunt the relationship. All about saving face.

The way of business as well. Art had seen many young Western executives with dreams of striking it rich in Tokyo, feeling that they only had to be truthful with their Japanese counterparts to succeed. Be upfront and they would have no problems. The Japanese are an honest people. A breath of fresh air compared to the decadent land in the West where the likes of Donald Trump, Bill Gates and Warren Buffet held court, the conventional wisdom.

Of course, these young dandies invariably went home with their tails between their legs because they failed to understand what Art knew. With the Japanese, business is war. Any bit of lying and deceit was okay in order to achieve the end result – Victory. The deal was the thing, and the Japanese would do anything to win. As long as they were not caught in the lie. This was the difference. This was the true meaning of honor in Japan, "Do not get caught." To be caught in a lie, not the actual lying, was the ultimate disgrace.

Art smiled as he thought of this. What a world. Oh well, none of his business anyway. He was surprised at himself actually. How he didn't seem to be as devastated as he thought he should be over Rose. Maybe he had known all along that there was no real chance for him. Not the way he wanted it anyway. Just needed some closure. Closure is what he had got. So be it.

Actually, Rose and he were so much alike in this respect. No chance for poor Rose either. Adam loved Keiko, and Rose loved Adam. The eternal triangle. Art loved them both. That's why he could survive. Adam the son he never had and Rose, well, not a daughter. She would never be that to him. He cared though. Always would. Loved her. Would protect her to his death.

10

"You will not kill him, Mr. Ambassador. The One thinks of Mr. Bender as a very valuable commodity. The test of his trustworthiness seems to have paid off. Our sources have no indication that he has reported your little meeting to his supervisors. In any case, The One believes that we can all benefit in the end from mutual cooperation."

Peter O'Mara began to object, but the look from Goro Atashi, lawyer and right hand man to Shoko Asahara, said that it would be fruitless. The ambassador made a mental note of when and where he would eventually pay Bender the retribution he deserved for not only the current swelling in his crotch but also his overall disrespect. He never did like the wiry little bastard. Who could trust a man who doesn't drink, he mused.

The meeting that Jack Bender had arranged in progress now. It included Shoko Asahara, Goro Atashi, and Peter O'Mara, Irish Ambassador to Japan and informal liaison between the Cult and the Irish Republican Army. Jack himself not present. Atashi had told Bender that it would be in his best interests and the security interests of the Cult if he were not there. In any case, he had assured him the ambassador would be dealt with. Atashi addressing the Irishman now. Asahara rarely speaking at these meetings.

"Mr. Bender will be very useful to us and to you, Mr. Ambassador. A red herring, I believe the Americans call it. A way of diverting attention from the real plan to another, shall we say, lesser plan."

O'Mara taken by surprise by this. Uncomfortable. Off-balance now. Unknown territory for the ambassador.

"Forgive me, Atashi San, but how do I know that you are not playing Bender and myself against each other for your own gain?"

A thin smile from the Japanese. A knowing, perhaps conspiratorial one.

"You do not know, Mr. Ambassador. That is the beauty of the plan. The genius of The One. *Fail-Safe* - to borrow a term from one of my favorite American films. Yes, Mr. Ambassador, it is better this way. Now to the real business at hand. The plans for the Tokyo water purification system. You have an update for us? The One is very anxious to hear your input on this issue.

O'Mara a drunk but still fairly lucid. Enough to realize that Bender was a pawn. No immediate gratification from this since, of course, he himself might be one as well. The plans to contaminate the Tokyo water supply with ricin obviously unknown to Bender. The man being used. Yes, a pawn. The Cult expert in using people. People in various stages of misery. In Bender's case, it was his demons that came forth anytime the anniversary of Hiroshima was marked. O'Mara knew that the man's wife had been there. Another bit of information provided by Adam Welsh by way of a fifth or so of Jack Daniels. God, he wished the boy would get off that toxic stuff. Graduate to the choice of the immortals, Joyce and Company, Irish Whiskey.

"Yes, you will give us some news now, Mr. Ambassador. Please. Entertain us. It has been a very uneventful day. The One is not happy. Please make me happy."

The hot, rancid breath of Shoko Asahara, leader of the Aum Cult, touching Peter O'Mara's face. Inches away now. Hands out of view but busy below the table. Leaning over in excited anticipation. Like a little boy, thought O'Mara.

"So nice to see you, Asahara San."

Atashi flinching ever so slightly at the pedestrian salutation used by the Irishman. No matter. The ignorance of the Westerners would be tolerated for the good of the end. The final solution as it were. In any case, Asahara did not seem fazed. Staring into space. Waiting for the answer to his original inquiry. Despite his bizarre façade, the man had the uncanny ability to stay "on message," thought Atashi.

"Yes, the business at hand. Two of the most efficient elements of the Provisional Irish Republican Army are in place as we speak. Final preparations should be finished by week's end. The logistics are the only piece of the puzzle to be completed."

Atashi nodding approvingly. The One stopping his self-gratification suddenly. Looking directly into O'Mara's eyes.

"Please, Mr. Ambassador. Tell us the plan once again. It makes my heart sing the way you present it. Please."

The man disconcerting. O'Mara feeling violated. The irony lost on him. It happened every time he was near Asahara. It bothered the Irishman. Not used to being intimidated. Smooth as ice. Not now though. Not here with the Madman. He struggled to bring himself together. He needed to find the coolness. The consequences unthinkable if he failed.

"Of course Omnipotent One. While our French and Middle Eastern friends are concentrating on the sarin agenda, we along with our brothers in Al Qaeda will be doing things to the Tokyo water supply that were unimaginable even a few short months ago. If all goes as planned, millions will perish within a week after our experts have released the ricin into the reservoir system. I believe Atashi San has recruited a scientist to coordinate the project with my I.R.A. associates. I must say, Asahara San, your subway diversion is a stroke of genius."

"Ahhhh yes. Yes. My, my. So sorry, gentleman. Please excuse me. I must wash up. You do understand. Thank you so much for the briefing, Mr. Ambassador. It has done much to bring excitement back into my day. I bid you adieu, gentleman."

Having finished his masturbation, Shoko Asahara made his exit. The ambassador could only stare after him. No words applicable to this situation. He merely looked at Atashi for perhaps an answer. None forthcoming. As if nothing had happened, Atashi addressed O'Mara.

"Yes, well done. Very well thought out. We have great confidence in you, Mr. Ambassador. One more thing. For security reasons it has been decided that no communication between your organization and Aum will take place until after our diversionary tactic is carried out."

"The sarin..."

"Yes, please, no further discussion on this point," Atashi interrupted. "I'm sure you understand."

The Ambassador rising to leave now. Atashi with one last instruction.

"We have completed the indoctrination of the courier who will handle the ricin. He will be arriving in Ireland before the night falls. Please be sure that your people treat him well. Although his wife and child are being tended to with the utmost respect by The One himself at one of our country estates, he will no doubt be suffering some anxiety. Perhaps a couple of pints of your Guinness will balance him a bit. Not too many though. Not all of us have the capacity for alcohol and some of life's other vices that you have, my dear ambassador."

Atashi did have a way of keeping one unnerved, thought O'Mara, deciding not to make too much out of this last remark. Responding in a business-like manner instead. In the end it was only business, thought O'Mara. A tool he used to let himself sleep at night. This along with the booze and the young men and boys.

"Yes, Atashi San. All is in place. My associates in Dublin will take care of the courier. No worries."

11

"Well, of course if it wasn't for the turncoat, Michael Collins, we wouldn't be sitting here crying in our Guinness."

"Aye, but we've had some great bards though."

A pub. Any pub in Ireland. It could have been any establishment where men drink and seek the validation of false dreams. The Stags Head this day. The two figures sitting at the corner table, "three sheets to the wind" yet lucid. The mark of the practiced drunk. Tolerance built up over the years. Shamus Burlie and Rafferty Grogan. Salts of the Earth, every mother's son and career Irish Republican Army. Trained killers each in their own way, Burlie the Bomb –Maker and Grogan the Water Treatment Specialist.

Shamus continuing his tirade against the traitor, Michael Collins of the early Irish Republican Army and Sinn Fein who signed over Northern Ireland to the British in the early 1900s. Many think he was duped into the signing, but the men imbibing here today would have none of it. Michael Collins would always be a traitor and a British lackey.

"Aye, to be sure, the sainted Eamon De Valera, a much too trusting lad to be dealing with the English scum and the likes of Lloyd George. It cost us our country and years more of bloody struggle. We will win in the end though. Aye, you can be sure of it."

The reference to the partitioning of Ireland brought about by the perceived double-crossing tactics of one Michael Collins. Sent to England to bring back a proposed treaty to Ireland for debate in the Irish Parliament, Collins, for reasons still not quite clear, signed the treaty himself. The treaty gave the south of Ireland independence but kept the north a part of the United Kingdom. Thousands had died since then, and the mention of the name of Michael Collins in the south of Ireland could still be guaranteed to start a pub uprising. For his part, De Valera, the patriot and first Prime Minister of the free Ireland never forgave Collins.

Grogan taking a liberal swallow of the Guinness before draining the dram of whiskey. Guinness used as chaser here, unlike the "Colonies" where it was consumed on its own more often than not.

The Stags Head located here in Dublin away from the normal tourist haunts. If one took the daily ferry from Liverpool and debarked at the East Docks, the curious traveler would more than likely walk right past the place. The nondescript location one of the reasons that this pub was the central meeting place for the Provisional Irish Republican Army.

"The business at hand now, my friend."

Shamus, the captain moving effortlessly to operational mode. No time to waste. The schedule not to be altered.

The four other men in the pub involved in their own conversation. In any case, all the regulars here struck deaf and dumb whenever they happened to be interrogated by the local police who, though they made regular sweeps through the pub, never came away with any information other than the price of a drink or perhaps a good horse in the Galway Races. Mutterings of connections between the Provs and the budding Al Qaeda network in Saudi Arabia. NSA picking up higher traffic levels than usual in their intercepts in Europe, the Middle East and curiously, Asia. Specifically Japan. Something in the works.

Shamus Burlie and Rafferty Grogan had been involved with the IRA since they were both teenagers. Shamus brought in after his father was shot right in their living room during Gaelic football viewing one Saturday afternoon. His mother and brother in the kitchen but Shamus there to see it all as the Orangemen broke the door down and put a pistol in his beloved Dad's mouth before sending him to oblivion. The hate fueling his dedication to the struggle early on but now things considerably different. The IRA just another part of global terrorism. Shamus knew this though he would never verbalize it. Not even after a fifth of Jameson. No, the murder of his father was enough for him. No matter that the IRA was now motivated more by money and politics than by any kind of idealism. Those days were gone forever. The sainted Eamon De Valera would never recognize the current bastardized version of what he had helped to create so many years ago. These the thoughts of Shamus Burlie as he prepared to brief his comrade on his role in the upcoming Event in Asia.

"The Jap will be landing at Shannon within the hour. He'll take a taxi here. The transfer will be made over a few pints. The coppers won't know what the hell to make of it. He'll be here under the cover of the Dublin Scientific Symposium on Water Purification. Aye, the irony of it all. Joyce himself would have been proud."

"Can we trust the boy bugger though? That is my question."

"Aye, the bastard gives me the shivers every time we even talk of him."

Grogan's reference to Peter O'Mara, not lost on Burlie. Part of the game. In order to play it, one had to get dirty. This scum, O'Mara, part of the price paid to avenge Burlie's father's death. He could rationalize anything at this point. A bit worried about Grogan though. Still a bit of humanity in the man. Something long since gone from Shamus Burlie.

"A necessary evil my friend. You may want to keep your voice down a wee bit. No worries here, but still one never knows."

A quick sweep of the surroundings by the Bomb-Maker. No problems here. The normal three or four regulars minding their own business. Lost in the bottom of the glass. One could never be too careful though, thought Shamus. The Italian in a few weeks back now coming to mind. In two nights in a row. Kept to himself. Watched the football on the telly. Of course he had been Interpol. When would they learn, thought Shamus as he drained his glass. The poor bastard never knew what hit him. One of the regulars luring him out back with some bullshit information. One shot to the base of his skull. In the back. Favorite method of the Chinese. Body sent down to the local meat packing plant. The coppers may well be having some Italian food with their tea Shamus had thought. A slight grin on his face as he thought about it. Work to be done now though.

12

Dan and Benny were at the Sanno Bar when Art arrived. Yoko was behind the bar. The crowd was light. Three or four people besides the regulars. Sumo had ended a couple hours before. Tomorrow was Monday. Most of the sailors and marines were heading back to Yokosuka on the last red train, a weekend of ecstasy with a local Japanese girl at an end.

Yoko was about thirty, Art would have guessed. He remembered that she had been a good friend to Keiko when Adam and Keiko were still together. She had always spoken with Keiko when she came in, especially after Adam had poured down a few Jack Daniels and dug in with Art and Dan and Benny and whatever inebriated soul was around to solve the problems of the world.

Yoko felt sorry for Keiko. She had felt that way from the start. She saw Keiko as a tragically flawed soul even when things were at their best between her and Adam. There were rumors of an American boyfriend in Yoko's past, but she never spoke of him. He'd returned to the States in any case. Now she just tended bar here at the Sanno and took care of her ailing mother. A good kid, Art thought as he walked to the bar. Unusual, thought Art. Benny normally left after the sumo ended. Some sailor or jarhead must have plied him with a few Courvoisier. Benny the affable, gregarious drunk. Everybody's friend. Dying of cancer. It was in his throat now. Art knew his doctor at the Naval Hospital. Six months at the most. Benny had refused to have the surgery that might save his life. The trade-off just too much. Surgery would have meant the loss of his voice.

"I might have known I'd see you two characters here. Art, how are you my son?" Dan Bronsan into his "Father Dan" persona now. Still a little of the catholic school education in him. His religion fueled by the gin rather than any higher power now though.

"White wine, Art San?" Yoko had glided over.

"Yea, you twisted my arm, lovely lady. Just one and then I'm on my way down the road."

Art stared at the television set. Not really listening to the banter between Dan and Benny. Something about that crazy Aum Cult was on the news. The Aum or something. They'd just shown some file footage. He couldn't hear anything. A picture of the leader flashed on the screen. Art trying to remember his name but couldn't think of it.

The Aum Cult had been making some noise lately. Demonstrations that were mostly peaceful, though. Most Japanese didn't really pay any attention. Art Chambers, Lt., USN, (Retired) knew better. He still had some friends on active duty at Yokosuka Naval Base. Intel types. Spooks. The ones who said, "I'd have to kill you if I told you," in response to any question about their job. Mostly boring stuff but interesting on occasion. One of Art's old shipmates, a crypto type, had hinted that some threats had been made by Aum against U. S. Navy interests. Threats that were being taken seriously. A few years earlier, one of the group had gotten a hold of some sarin. It was in powdered form and raw. Nowhere near weapons grade as it was called behind closed doors at the Pentagon. This guy had actually climbed halfway up the Tokyo Tower and dumped a whole bag of the stuff on an unsuspecting lunchtime crowd. Thankfully the only damage done was some ruined suits and skirts. The wacko was eventually taken into custody. The public never really told that it was sarin, a chemical agent that if refined could have killed everyone walking below the Tokyo Tower that summer's day. Art knew this though, and so he gestured for Dan to keep his voice down while he watched the rest of the report. Art, with over 20 years in the Navy, knew that many threats were just bullshit but, in any case, still had to be taken seriously. "Remember Pearl Harbor" and all that.

Here was this Aum clown now. Very sedate looking. Shoko Asahara his name. Art remembered it from the informal briefing he had received. A distant look. Like he was on drugs or hypnotized. More likely the former, thought Art. In the same picture with Ghaddafi. Not a good thing. Art made a mental note to ask his buddy about this the next time he visited the base. Maybe he'd ask Adam to do some snooping also. Adam the ex-Cryptologic Technician washed up now due to the sauce. Funny how the Navy had pulled his clearance and then made him a missile tech. In charge of operating multi-million dollar shipboard weapons systems. Art smiled as he swallowed the drink and put it back on the bar unfinished. "Permission to go ashore, Ma'am," he bellowed as he snapped a salute Yoko's way in his customary ritual of leaving for the night. Yoko laughed and Art left amid a smattering of drunken salutations from Benny and Dan.

13

It is evening. An ordinary storage room wreaking of Suntory Whiskey. Located above the Gas Panic bar. What better place to hide a book but in a library, Keiko had thought when she first came here. An idiom Adam had taught her. Seemed like light-years ago. She forced herself to block the visual and succeeded. Becoming adept at this sort of thing of late. The One himself present. Holding forth to his minions. Keiko Watanabe was here at least physically. She stared at Shoko Asahara with a look reminiscent of a long ago day in Jonestown just before the Kool-Aid was to be served. Asahara stands alone in the front of the room. A silk robe with nothing under it. The protrusion at the groin area a testament to this. Asahara obviously excited. Keiko taking note of the erection with no sense of revulsion. It did not matter what her feelings were these days. Just biding time till the end.

The Test would take place soon, The One explained to them. Keiko here along with Asahara's confidante, Goro Atashi. The One rarely without him at these gatherings of the faithful. Scientists who had been recruited from the Ministry of Technology in attendance. All hanging on the Madman's every word. Asahara speaking softly, forcing the others to listen. A practiced technique although The One did not have to rely on it. His was indeed a captive audience, spiritually, physically and emotionally. He owned them.

Everything was in place, Asahara continued in the drone-like mantra. Everyone knew their role. The deadly capsules had been acquired, and there would be complete surprise. The American knowing something was in the air, and oh yes, something indeed would be in the air. Not where they guessed though. A soft target as they called it these days. Like when the IRA blows up post offices or schools. Soft targets. Not heavily fortified but enabling one to kill the enemy none the less. Of course there would be "collateral damage" as the women, children and other innocent civilians were referred to these days by The One. A suicide mission. The member who delivered the deadly sarin gas would have to die as well. This bit of information not conveyed to his enraptured audience this night however. No reason to spoil the moment. In any case, all the Cult members were expected to die at a moment's notice for the cause. Indeed part of the recruiting process involved the candidates very desire to be released from an existence he or she found unbearable for various reasons. A small price to pay for a quick and deadly thrust leveled at the evil West. The perpetrator would be guaranteed immortality. A hero almost as exalted as The One himself.

The meeting adjourned. Keiko aware that the drone had stopped although she had not really heard it. Aware that the noise had ceased. Asahara was in front of her now. The room empty but for her and The One. A faint sense of alarm began to overcome her but then ended. Behind her a voice. Familiar and foreboding all at once.

"Keiko San, so nice to see you again. You are looking well, my lass. Yes, you always were a beauty. That drunken sot of a boyfriend...Adam? Was that his name?" The name of the man who had once been her salvation. The love of her life momentarily bringing her back to life. She turned around and without looking, kicked Peter O'Mara, Irish Ambassador to Tokyo directly in the balls. He went down like the sack of spoiled potatoes that she knew he was. The tormentor of her Adam. All coming back. Too late. Asahara on her now. A pin prick in her arm. Vaguely aware of the angry screams from the Irishman. Asahara whispering over the din.

"Let go, my Cherry Blossom."

The rancid smell of the Irishman here. On her as well. Pushes her gently to the floor. He enters her and then, mercifully-only darkness.

14

"Moored. Shift colors."

Back in port. Yokosuka. Thank God. Fire Controlman First Class Welsh rushed to his rack to change. He had the weekend off. No duty. As long as the Mormon Bastard, the hypocritical SOB, did not come up with a reason for him to stay, Adam would be free. Free to drink and fuck. The two things that killed the pain.

He was dressed and ready to leave. The shower could be taken at the Sanno. The Sanno Hotel in Tokyo. The refuge where Adam Welsh could drink and talk to the expats and be a civilian, at least in his own mind. A brief respite from the torture he endured as a First Class Petty Officer in the United States Navy. A mere enlisted man who was smarter than most on the boat. He lived a lie on the McClusky and would live a lie at the Sanno, but this deceit was easier to take by far. Art, Rose, Benny, all of his confidantes would be there. The warmth of the Jack Daniels would envelope him, and he would be released from the agony of reality. The price he would have to pay on Monday inevitable but denied at least for now.

It had not always been this way. Waiting for Liberty Call, Adam began to space out, to daydream. One of the ways to fight the pain. This was not quite as effective as the booze but a good substitute nonetheless.

Thoughts of Massapequa Park, New York. Small town in the suburbs. Dad, a war hero. A marine on Guadalcanal during WWII, the Big One. None of this police action shit like these long-haired, drug-addicted Vietnam vets were in. Davey Welsh never missed a chance to get on the young Nam vets at the V.A. in Northport. Adam with him. Another pre-operation checkup. Davey still paying the price for the lost lung and still smoking two packs of Kool Menthols a day. Dad saw no problem though. The one lung was growing and was just as good as two, he reasoned.

Adam Welsh could see his father as clear as day now. Davey Welsh holding court at the kitchen table. Adam and his brother and sister leaning on every word. Their father talking about how he lost the lung now.

The yellow bastard Jap sniper. In the back. Bullet holes through his chest. The bazooka buried in the mud. Sullivan, the poor bastard, his loader, running terrified. Not remembering much. Lt. Lando running across the open field like John Wayne spraying the BAR rounds. The Jap sniper cut in half. Hanging out of the tree. Davey Welsh saying, "And I woke up from a coma and there was Kate Smith singing 'God Bless America' on the pier! Gave me Last Rites five times but here I am! Takes a lot more than some Jap bastard to kill your old man. Not a TV dad though. Never will be."

Adam finding out that it was all a lie only later. "Friendly Fire" the cause. Dad more Don Knotts than John Wayne. What was the depth of the pain that his father endured that he had to make up such a story?

Adam thinking about poor Lucy Welsh. His sister sitting right next to their father as he smoked and smoked. Lucy, maybe seven. How she didn't have the cancer from the secondhand smoke was a miracle, he mused. Shit, it was first hand when it comes billowing down directly into your little mouth and nostrils. Lucy survived though. Mentally and physically. Good job in Los Angeles now. Married with a normal life. *What was normal?* Adam never really wanted normal. Drama at the Welsh house. Everyday something new. Dad always planning. Things were always going to be better.

"Dad's not like those losers." The losers being the neighbors who took the train to work every day and provided for their family.

"Liberty call. Liberty call."

Adam back to reality. How ironic life in this world could be. The old man's life destroyed in a war against the Japanese and here was the son, defending Japan. Leaving the boat now. No sign of his Chief, AKA, "Mormon Asshole."

The run to the train station. Boarding. The large beer for the ride. Bliss. Temporary but bliss in any case. The red train. Just in time. Always. Not as fast as the green but would do. Less crowded. The beer, Asahi safely encased in the paper bag. For an instant, Adam saw his reflection in the train window. A sense of revulsion came but then mercifully went. A quick blast and then the glow. He could always count on the booze until he couldn't.

Sitting on the train, hurtling towards Shinagawa Station. No subway from there. He'd pay the taxi. Adam needed to get to his habitat. The place he flourished. Sometimes he wondered what the staff at the Sanno Hotel really thought of him. This tall, thin gaijin who shook violently at times but shrugged it off.

"Too much coffee," Adam would explain, and they would laugh with him albeit uncomfortably. Just paranoia. You know what they say, "Just because you're paranoid, doesn't mean someone is not out to get you."

Cute little Japanese girl on the train. Across from Adam. Maybe five years old sitting with her mother. Adam loved to play little games with the children he came across. He loved Japanese children. Especially little girls. A faint twinge now. It was something about what Keiko had said when she was pregnant. "It's going to be a girl, Adam. We're going to have a beautiful little daughter." *What had he said to her?* Mercifully, the answer not forthcoming, at least for now.

The little girl looked over. The large Godzilla-like gaijin too much for her to ignore. Adam gave her his best playful dinosaur look. She went into hysterics. Adam looking away just as quickly before the mother could see the source of her little daughter's glee. One of life's few real pleasures for Adam these days. It helped pass the time as well. Very important in a life that had become nothing more than a series of brief respites between drunks.

15

The train stopped at Shinagawa Station, on time as usual. Adam Welsh finished off the large bottle of Asahi and searched for a garbage receptacle. There was one at the exit ramp to the taxis outside. He rushed towards the exit and immediately crashed into the Japanese man scurrying across the platform. A box of Coca Colas scattered as the man fell to the ground. He gave Adam a quick look. *What was it? Fear, hatred?* Maybe both. Picked up the Cokes almost as if they were pieces of China and continued towards the subway.

"Ignorant Jap bastard." A little of his father in Adam. Resentment and anger. Blaming the Japanese people for his lot in life. In the taxi now.

"Sanno Hotel."

Thank God, the driver spoke English. Adam, three years in the country and still only a smattering of Japanese. Mostly bawdy phrases learned on barstools from inebriated young Japanese women.

"What color is your panty?" a favorite. The driver sped off to the Sanno and escape for Adam Welsh. The pain would soon go away.

Naoyuki Enomoto brushed off his pants and tried to slow his breathing as he picked up the Coke cans and entered the subway. Ebisu station would soon be here. As the train hurtled towards Ebisu, Naoyuki thought of the American. He would be dead in the near future when the Event was complete. Tonight though just a test. A taste of things to come. The crowd at Ebisu would be heavy.

Rose Carney put on her make-up. Adam would be back tonight. A few drinks. Talk. Adam, Rose, Art and even Dan. God she was so happy, even Dan would be bearable tonight. She would tell Adam that she loved him and later in the room, make him forget Keiko. At least for the night. Rose Carney rushed out the door towards the train station. Ebisu Station. Leaving the apartment she would never see again. She ran towards the station. Had to see Adam. Everything would be okay. The Japanese man passing her. The Coke can slipped into her purse. So light Rose not noticing. No beverage in this can. A small hole. Not visible to the naked eye. Something had started to seep out, unnoticed. Rose entered the elevator. No stairs. Amazing how a minor decision in one's day to day life can alter everything. No one in the elevator. Doors closed. She reached for the 2nd floor button but...something ...a smell. Her chest very tight now. Alarmed. Eyes teary. Burning. Rose fell to the floor. Terrified. *My God, what is happening*? Opened her mouth to scream. Nothing. Like a nightmare when she was a little girl. But then she would wake up as her scream finally came out. Her father holding her in his arms. *It's going to be okay, Rose, hon. Just a little nightmare.* How she loved her father. Not here now though. No scream coming out. Elevator door shut. No air! God she needed air. The can of Coke rolling on the floor. Rose threw up. Her entire intestine attempted to leave her body. Her bowels released. *Not this way. My Jesus, not this way.* Half-conscious now. *I love you, Adam. I always will love you.* Art's smiling, fatherly look. They were waiting for her just about a mile away. She was lying in a heap on a elevator floor in Ebisu. Lying in her own puke and shit. Her breathing stopped. Adams face. Blackness. The abyss.

16

Keiko Watanabe knew that something would be happening that evening. She had heard little at the earlier meeting, but it was still enough to indicate that Aum would take a major action this evening. A statement. The One believed that Aum would be taken seriously only by striking a blow directly to the solar plexus of the American debauchers. The heart thrust would follow soon enough.

Adam had been trying to contact her now for over a month. Since he was a member of the military arm of the evil American empire, tabs had been kept on him. His every move scrutinized. Keiko's old girlfriends had been seen with him in Roppongi, and in his drunken rants, he had on more than one occasion screamed her name. Keiko had of course left her old apartment long ago. The one in Meguro where Adam and she had stayed. Had she actually made love to him there? So distant. So far away. In any case, Keiko had ceased to think of herself as a woman. Even a human being. She was now a soldier to be utilized by the forces of Aum. As such she would serve her purpose and then be discarded. All for the cause. This had been understood from the beginning. Deep inside Keiko's inner being where a bit of humanity still flickered weakly, she wished, yearned in fact for this end to come. Her soul had died when the fetus that would have been her daughter was ripped from her body. The occasional violation by Asahara now just an inconvenience to her. No feeling anymore anyway. The presence of the Irish scum almost bringing her to some type of feeling. The heroin took care of that though. All just a fog now. At one time she would have killed O'Mara with her own hands. Now though she was satisfied to merely exist devoid of any feeling. "Comfortably numb" as one of Adam's favorite bands had sung, what seemed like eons ago.

Shoko had come into her life shortly after the abortion. Adam had run as was his bent. A good man but the alcohol and his father had taken his spirit. While Adam was at sea, Keiko had been recruited by Aum. After the breakdown she had been visited by an old girlfriend who had come under the spell of the True Creation. One look at the shell of this woman who was incapable of love for anyone or anything assured the Cult that Keiko could be an invaluable soldier.

They had taken her out of the hospital under cover of darkness, and since that night, for all intent and purpose, she was more machine than human.

The police sirens in the distance brought Keiko back. The deed had been done. She knew. Somewhere in Tokyo this night, the first blow had been struck. A sense of relief filled little, broken Keiko as she now knew that her pain would be at an end soon. The hint of a tear came and went. There was work to be done.

17

Adam Welsh was met by scores of armed military police as he entered the Sanno Hotel. The hotel was in fact a U.S. Department of Defense installation despite its five-star appearance and was now at a high state of military readiness. The bar packed with gaijins all mesmerized by the figures on the television screen –"Ebisu Station"- in bold letters at the bottom of the picture. Bernard Shaw saying something about deadly gas and an American woman. No identity released as yet. Pending notification of relatives.

Art visibly shaken. No greeting for Adam. Only, "God, have you seen Rose!? Jesus, I should have brought her here myself!"

"What about Rose?" Adam not putting things together yet.

"She's not here, god damnit! She was supposed to be on her way from Ebisu, for god's sake, man! Jesus, have a drink. Useless."

Dan pulling Adam to the side now. Not his usual self. Not the normal Dan. Benny either for that matter. Everyone different. Bad vibes in the air. Like the morning in San Diego when the news of his father came. The smell of death permeating everything.

Dan saying, "Rose was supposed to be here two hours ago. It looks like there's been a gas attack of some kind at Ebisu Station. Gaijin female dead according to the news. Late thirties."

Adam dazed, now staring at the screen with the others. Deer lost in the eerie glow of the cathode rays emitting news of death.

"Just got the goddamn answering machine."

Art not holding up well. The calls to Rose's apartment had been answered by a disembodied voice. Beautiful, lost Rose. Would that be the last he would ever hear from her?

"I'm not at home. Please leave a message and I'll call you back. Have a great day!"

Will you Rose? Can you call me ever again?

"Lt. Chambers. Phone call for you, sir. You can take it in the lobby."

Art gone in an instant. Fleeing the bar.

"She's probably just stuck at the station. Jesus, between the Jap Swat teams and the American Military, it's a miracle you got here, swabbie."

Benny, hopeful. Heart of gold. Trying to reassure Adam and the rest. For all his attributes, a lousy liar.

"Double Jack. One for Benny. Dan, Gin?"

"You twisted my arm. Double. Here's to the tilt in your kilt."

Dan, merely mouthing his trademark salutation now. Real trouble brewing. A bad feeling all around. Death. The rest grateful though for the attempt at, what was it, normalcy? Status quo. Anything to beat back the growing tide of impending doom that felt like it could wash over all of them at any second.

18

Keiko Watanabe left her small shanty of a domicile and hailed a taxi for the trip to Aum Headquarters number 2 as preordained. The taxi dropped the small dark figure, and for some reason the driver, a student of American literature at the University, was reminded of "Laura" the tragic figure of *The Glass Menagerie*.

Keiko had not spoken throughout the entire trip except of course to instruct him where to take her. Arriving in this seedy area of Shinjuku, the driver thought it unusual for her to get out here. Somehow out of place but then after a quick glance maybe not an unusual destination, this place of seedy bars and discarded souls. She paid her fare and walked into the strip club.

Days later, Kenji Abe, taxi driver and student, would find a picture of a happy couple — he American, she Japanese — while cleaning out the back of his cab. The newspaper would portray this picture prominently for many days and weeks afterward. The glowing faces of Keiko Watanabe and Adam Welsh in a time when everything seemed possible.

19

Adam entered the lobby in time to see his best friend in the world dying on the floor. Art Chambers had taken the call from the base. His contact at Operations was well-informed. The dead American woman was Rose Carney.

A cry had emitted from somewhere deep in the bowels of Art Chambers psyche, and the massive stroke had followed. Brain waves stopping but not before a Polaroid like image of Rose smiling, probably manufactured by one last synapse connection, had flashed before Art.

Keiko watching the small television above the Pussy Cat Bar. Music throbbing from below. Keiko oblivious. The CNN reporter talking of the dead American woman. Showing the face of Rose Carney. Keiko bursting into tears. Her entire body shaking. Convulsing now. Falling off the chair and rocking in the fetal position. An inhuman shriek emitting from her small body. Coming from the depths of hell itself.

"Oh my God, what have I done. Not Rose. Please, God, don't let it be Rose."

Tears cascading down her face. A small flood on the floor beneath her. Her kidneys emptying. Pent up rage, anger, sorrow. Everything leaving Keiko Watanabe at once now.

Why Rose?

Out of thousands of gaijins, why Rose Carney? Of course only later would Keiko find out that Shoko had picked Rose specifically. Had known that Rose Carney and Keiko Watanabe had been like sisters at one time. What seemed like centuries ago now but alas not long ago. Keiko the pretty Japanese girl who had been schooled in all things American thanks to numerous visits to LA and New York as a young girl and various trysts with American men. Never falling in love. Just the sex. The feeling of power. Until Adam of course. Adam had changed everything.

The Sanno Hotel banquet room appeared in Keiko's mind's eye as she slowly lost consciousness. There was Rose and Adam and Art and John Bannister, the sports medicine guy. The man who had advised sumo wrestlers like Akebono, Konishiki, as well as numerous American baseball players looking for one last hurrah in the Japanese baseball leagues. John a little on the wacko side as Adam would say. Good guy but one of those conspiracy theory nuts whose list of UFO sightings and government condoned massacres of Venusians increased in direct proportion to the number of champagne glasses piled in front of him.

The Sunday brunch at The Sanno. *God, we were happy then.* Keiko and Adam in love more than any human beings deserved to be. Adam and Art and John and sometimes Dan and Benny would join them, although the group soon lost patience with Dan's arrogant presence. Eventually he would leave in a huff, being sure to include everyone in his blistering diatribe of inventory taking and personal insults.

Keiko and Adam fresh from a morning of blissful lovemaking. She could die at these moments and make a heaven out of these memories alone. *Was I really that alive then? Yes. More than alive. Everything was Adam. My universe.*

So long ago now as Keiko lie crumpled on the floor of this tawdry strip club.

Shoko entered the room.

No words. None necessary. He knew. Walking over to the broken angel, he administered the needle in a quick sterile fashion. Keiko not having a chance to reject it. Not that she had any intention of doing so. The heroin doing its job now. The vacant look returning. Any life, emotion, feeling, a thing of the past. The old Keiko gone again.

Naoyuki had done well. The American cunt had been banished. More to be done now. He would be here soon. Asahara would talk with him. Explain why he would have to die. To die for the cause. What an honor. Shoko pensive now thinking of the next move. Naoyuki a good soldier but must be removed now. Too much chance of being captured and then all would be for naught. All the plans drawn up over the last few years. Actually longer than that. Shoko had started planning probably from the first time that his father had molested him. A way of cleansing. A purging of all that had poisoned his young body and soul. Now the final purge was at hand.

20

Adam Welsh in the waiting room at Tokyo Hiroo Hospital. Thoughts of Christmas past. A meeting with the man who would become like a surrogate father to him.

"You're looking pretty good for an old fart. Damn good. A drink for this guy, please, Yoko."

"Lieutenant to you."

The brash façade cut through in an instant by the kind look in Adam's eyes. There was love there. The potential for a father-son kind that was in a way indestructible. Something Adam had never had with his own father. Davey Welsh never there for him. From the first night that Adam had met Art Chambers, the bond had begun to form. The old salt officer and the troubled enlisted man.

It's a Wonderful Life playing to an all but empty bar except for the strong "Burl Ives" shape of Art Chambers. Christmas Eve and he was alone. Rose probably entwined with another young marine for the night. She would call him the next day in tears of course, but now he would hurt in solitude. Dying inside as Jimmy Stewart kissed Donna Reed in a world which had ended a long time ago. A world that as Art thought about it over the martini, probably never existed.

"God, that Jimmy Stewart was a national treasure, you know. Donna Reed too. A real woman. Jesus, these American chicks these days. Don't need us anymore. Women's Lib screwed up everything."

Adam Welsh speaking to anyone who would listen. Art chuckling out loud.

"Huh! Well now you know why I've been over here for almost thirty-five years!"

"Damn! God Bless you, sir."

"This is one of my favorite movies of all time. Capra was a genius, and of course Stewart and Donna Reed are classic."

Adam moving over to the seat next to Art now. Two lost souls on Christmas Eve in the middle of Tokyo. Talking about this and that. Adam remorseful, about to go into another crying jag. Talking about his old man. Art having none of it.

"Look, you're a young guy. Your old man is dead. He did the best he could."

"The bastard," voice breaking now. The tears starting as they always did.

"I never had a chance, Art. The booze and the drama. Shit, now I'm in it. Hard whiskey. Just like him. Said I would never be like him, but here I am. No turning back. Ah, fuck it. Give me another, Yoko."

"No more, Yoko. Beer only for this swabby. Pulling rank now. Sorry. You'll thank me."

They talked. Surrogate father and son. Adam thought he saw a tear in Art's eye at the end of *It's a Wonderful Life*. Friends forever. The bond created.

21

Adam waited outside the emergency room. Not much hope. A massive stroke. The Japanese doctor not wanting to relay the worst, but Adam knew. Could see it in his eyes. In one horrible night, what was left of Adam's world was being torn asunder. Rose dead. Art probably gone. Keiko nowhere to be found. Dan Bronsan sitting alone at the Sanno. Benny had gone home. The cancer and trauma of the nights events sending him to an early departure. Staring at the screen now. CNN reporting that no suspects had been found as yet. The American and Japanese authorities working closely. Lifting the drink to his lips slowly and then gulping it down. If Art was here he would have told him to get a funnel. No need for a glass. He missed him already. He seemed already dead when they wheeled him out. The loss of Rose too much for the old warrior. In a better place now. "God be with you my friend," and then an Irish toast in Gaelic.

Dan's thoughts turning to his daughter, Kelley. She would be coming over from the States next week. He had a bad feeling. Should he ask her to postpone the trip? He knew the answer already. His daughter like her mother even more so since she had been diagnosed with MS. A bad hand for his little princess. She'd overcome it though. Twenty-three now and as normal as any girl her age. Same emotions, likes, dislikes. Probably even more well-adjusted in fact.

At the Hospital, only a few blocks from the Sanno Hotel, the emergency room lights glaring. Adam trying to find out about Art. He hadn't been able to get any information since he arrived. His Japanese not that good. No chance to learn it. All the girls wanting to learn English. Adam accommodating. Wishing he had been more interested in their minds now than the patch between the legs. *Trembling mound of Venus*, an old porno he had read as a kid. Probably written by some out of work English teacher. He had heard they use to do that in the seventies. All these soft-core pornos being written by high school English teachers. Made you wonder. Wouldn't want to be a parent. Dan in fact was the one who had told him about it. His daughter Kelley's teacher had been doing it. They found out at the school one day when one of the parents heard him bragging about it at the bar, "My throbbing member between her trembling mound of Venus..." Actually maybe he had stolen it from Henry Miller. Anyway, the poor English teacher was history once Dan found out about it.

Different times then of course. These days the same guy would probably be promoted to principal. Definitely in New York or California, Adam thought. He remembered how Dan and Art would argue about the respective education systems. Art lambasting Dan about the level of education in New York City. How the public school system was a joke there. Dan with the usual retort about Catholic schools and the sainted Jesuits, "Put the Jesuits in charge and everyone would speak English in 'LALA' Land," he would say.

The reality now. The lights coming into focus. Emergency room. Hiroo Hospital. Art somewhere in the other room. Going fast. *How was he?* "Doctor! I need to see a godamn doctor." No one stopping. Bustling around like cross-eyed ants. The red ones that Adam used to destroy with firecrackers when he was a kid. This their revenge now.

The ants. All the goddamn ants that he had killed as a kid. Jesus he was losing it. Screaming now. *My God where are you, Art. Please Jesus, don't die. Don't die, Dad. Jesus, don't die.* Sobbing now. Out of control. The ant in the white jacket turning and staring.

"Please, sir. Sit down. Here. Nurse, get some water for this man."

"Dr. Tsurahara," the tag read.

Adam calmed down. "Doctor, my friend is here. His name is Art Chambers. They just brought him in less than an hour ago. I think he had a heart attack or something."

"Please God, let it be "Something."

Adam faded out again. His father was in the bathroom with the .38. Mom screaming, "Please, Davey, don't do it." Joyce Welsh. Standing at the door. Davey inside with the gun. Probably pointing it at his head. Drunk on his ass. Adam, eight years old, trembling on the stairs. *Must be my fault. Has to be my fault. What can I do? Nothing.* The helpless feeling. Leg shaking up and down. Thumb in the mouth now. Waiting for the gun to go off. Waiting.

"I'm going to do it!"

Silence. Sobbing. Sobbing from the depths of Davey Welsh's soul. Door opening. Joyce's arms around him.

"Everything is going to be all right kids. Go to bed. Nothing wrong here. Tomorrow's Sunday. I'll make a big breakfast for us all. Dad's just a little upset. You know he works so hard."

Adam had gone back up to his room. Leaving part of himself on those stairs. The part he lost waiting for the sound of the recoil of the .38. The sound that never came. Back in bed now. Scared. Empty. Guilt-ridden.

The next morning, Mom smiling. What planet was she on? Dad whistling "My boys." Arms around Adam and Sammy.

Sammy his brother, two years younger. Adam hadn't thought about him much. Left home. Got into crack cocaine. Dead now. Overdose. His girlfriend killed herself. Blocked out of Adam's mind. A little of Mom in him. A lot. "Denial is not just a river in Egypt." He'd heard that at one of the meetings. Bullshit now. All bullshit.

22

Shoko Asahara laughed. A strange laugh. Not amused. Not in any way joyful. Satan would laugh this way, thought Atashi. CNN blaring the news of the American woman's death. Shoko beside himself. A cleansing had taken place of sorts, thought his loyal comrade in arms, Atashi. What better first victim than a woman and an American for that matter. Of course nothing left to chance. Rose was as good as dead three weeks ago. Keiko's best friend from her earlier life. Her life amongst the gaijins.

Everything had been methodically planned to the last detail. Keiko followed and then Rose Carney's apartment staked out. No accidents in the world of Aum. Every action taken had a distinct purpose. Naoyuki's body found under a train at Shinagawa Station. An apparent suicide. No sign yet of the sarin in his system. Only later would this information unfold.

Naoyuki a hero of the cause albeit a very hesitant one. The thought of his wife and family being tortured and killed enough prodding for him to inhale the Sarin.

"At this time we go to Tokyo and the American Embassy where the American Ambassador is making a statement on tonight's grisly events."

Shoko sensing a bit of irony in the one pundit's reference to Hiroshima. Of course the Americans had dropped a second bomb days after the first. The attack tonight at Ebisu Station had indeed been Aum's response to Hiroshima, and the more devastating apocalypse in the next few days would

77

probably be viewed by historians as Nagasaki. Of course history is written by the victors. Smiling. Content now. Atashi could see it, even sense the relief that had come over Shoko's body after the successes of the night.

"Make certain everything is in order for our final victory, Atashi San."

Shoko touching himself under his robes now as he watched the news cast. Atashi bowing and leaving seemingly on cue.

23

"I'm all right, bern." Dan using the Gaelic form. Not really Irish. More French but the *Zelig* thing kicking in now. Needed to be something, anything other than himself. Kelley was on the phone and frantic.

"I called as soon as I saw it on the news. It's horrible, Dad. What is the world coming too? I thought Japan was such a safe, non-violent place?"

"It is, honey. Don't worry it's, but..."How can he say it...She saw it coming.

"Oh, Dad, please I've bought my ticket. I've had my heart set on this trip. I have to go! Please don't cancel on me. This is the biggest thing that's happened to me."

Dan knowing it was true. Beautiful Kelley. The diagnosis of multiple sclerosis years ago only strengthening her dream to be the best that she could be. Her body and her soul still able to take flight and sing with the angels. He couldn't/wouldn't take that from her.

"Of course you can still come visit. I just thought that maybe you could come next summer instead."

"Jesus, Dad."

The Lord's name in vain. The apple not far from the tree.. Dan wanting to bellow something about it but stopping. Mellowing know. He loved his only child. Probably the only thing Dan did love or have any real feelings of the human kind towards. His own fear had removed him from the world.

From the company of his fellows. Never could be a worker among workers. Probably the reason he always spoke in literary phrases so much. A defense mechanism against intimacy someone had told him.

Actually now that he thought of it, Adam had told him that. Something from one of the boozer meetings Adam attended between drunks. Can't be much of a program if Adam just kept drinking anyway. Of course Dan had it under control. Still had his job, 800,000 yen a month, thank you. God bless the child who got his own. Bravado. A good mask for fear.

"I've already booked the flight, Dad, and you have no idea how hard it is to book these things if you're disabled. As soon as I get elected to Congress, I'm going to make sure that the American's Disabilities Act gets changed to something worth a crap. Not something the Republicans wave around so they can prove that they're in touch with the masses.

Ah, that's my little girl.

Dan the old-time Liberal now. Kelley, definitely her father's daughter. Part of her anyway. There was hope. He knew that the argument was over before it started. Dan no match for the love of his life.

"I'll pick you up at Narita. Make sure you confirm the day before."

"Yes Dad."

Kelley the mature twenty-three year old now. Putting up with her father's condescending attitudes. "My brain is in excellent working order, thank you very much."

Point, Set, Match.

"I'll see you on Friday. I love you very much."

"Love you too, Dad," and then the click.

He hadn't told her about Art. Art had been like an uncle to Kelley. She would not take it well. Maybe it was better that she was coming. Tell her in person. Console her. Dan Bronsan gulped the last of the gin and headed for Hiroo Hospital to be with the last friends he had in the world.

24

A Japanese hospital is, in a very real sense, a microcosm of the society itself. When one first enters the emergency room, the Westerner is struck by the seeming apathy that permeates the entire waiting area. Old, sick people, with every injury imaginable, all waiting on stretchers with no help at all from the various nurses and doctors scurrying in an out of various rooms like ants through a colony. The injured and infirm are ministered to by friends and family who do the best they can until a white suited ant converges on the scene to take the patient away, almost like a small morsel of bread being taken back down the hole for the queen to feast on at leisure. Of course the patients do for the most part emerge back out of the lair of the queen to lead productive lives, and the system is quite efficient capitalizing on Japanese society's insistence on taking care of one's own family as much as possible with the government or any other institutions for that matter having little or no intervention. Of course when one is dying, this all changes but grudgingly at best.

Perhaps the West could learn from this self-reliance, thought Dan Bronsan as he entered the ant colony searching for Adam and his dying friend, Art.

"No news yet. One of them came out earlier and just said something about him being stabilized. Haven't seen anybody in about an hour," Adam said as he sat down next to him.

"Here, take some of this, Adam me boy. A bit of the hair of the dog that bit ya. Of course normally I would frown on anything that even remotely smells of alcohol going into that screaming liver of yours, but this is definitely an exceptional day. A dark day for us all."

It was good to have Dan here, thought Adam. A steadying influence. Adam grabbed the flask and took a drink. Jack Daniels. Perfect. The anesthetic of choice in a world filled suddenly with interminable pain.

"Rose didn't suffer, did she, Dan?"

The voice pleading in tone. Dan not expecting this.

No talk of Rose. Just Art. Enough to think about Art. Everything happening too god damn fast.

"Sure, Adam. The gas put her to sleep. Never felt anything," Dan lied.

Her death had been horrible. Acutely aware of everything that was happening to her no doubt. Art had talked to a Swedish friend of his at Svenson who knew of these things. Sarin was a derivative of mustard gas only much more lethal and unmerciful. One lost control of all bodily functions in a very short time, but one was also cognizant till the bitter end.

Doctor Tsarahara approached them both now. He didn't look good. The news would be devastating. Dan clutching Adam's shoulder.

"Mr. Welsh, your father..."

"He's not my father."

"A very good friend," volunteered Dan.

"Yes, I'm afraid he has suffered a catastrophic stroke. He is on life-support."

"Jesus, God!"

"Adam. Here take a blast."

The doctor ignoring this.

"I understand he has no living relatives?"

"We're as close to family as he's got, after tonight anyway."

Adam bracing himself after the whiskey. "What do you need from us?"

"I'm afraid we must get your consent to take him off life support. There is no brain activity whatsoever."

Adam rocketed back to a similar, horrible time. Rikers Island Hospital. His mother, telling him to rub his father's hands.

"Rub his hands, Adam. He'll recognize you. The doctor says it will help."

Joyce Welsh the Denial Queen of all time now. Adam staring into the dead eyes of his father, Davey. No life there. In a coma. They'd found him on the floor of Rikers Island. Been there over an hour. Massive cardiac arrest they had said.

Why an hour? Adam knew his father had had enemies. It came with the territory of an obnoxious arrogant drunk. One didn't attract a lot of bright and shiny people. Adam back there now. Rubbing his father's hands. Cold. Dead. His mother hysterical, saying the Rosary.

"Pray for him, Adam. It's all going to be all right. Pray to Jesus, Mary and Joseph. Pray for Daddy."

So he did. He knelt down next to his father in a prison hospital in New York City. Knelt and prayed with all his heart. The doctor taking him aside later.

"Your mother needs to make a decision about taking him off the respirator."

"There is no hope, Doctor?"

"None, I'm afraid."

It wouldn't matter of course. Mom would never pull the plug. The whole Catholic thing. She would never do it.

"Go home and rest. We need to know by tomorrow."

That night Adam Welsh had gone to an Alcoholics Anonymous meeting in the city. Not really wanting to stay sober. Asking his father's old A.A. buddies to pray with him. Coming home, his mother had met him at the door. Tears of joy.

"The hospital called a few minutes ago. Dad went on his own. Thank Jesus."

"Yea, thank Jesus."

Adam returned to the ship in San Diego. A DUI four weeks later. Never looked back. The booze the only answer.

Now here again. Another time. Another place. A nightmare revisited. So Adam asked the question again. The one he already knew the answer to but had to ask.

"There is no hope," the reply from the doctor.

"Can we see him?"

"Of course."

The feeling of impending doom now. Not New York City anymore. Tokyo. Hiroo Hospital. The ashen-faced figure devoid of any sign of life. The machines hooked up more as an acknowledgement of technology than for any practical utilization. One look and Adam saw that his friend was gone. Dan and Adam now kneeling next to the hospital bed. Dan spoke first.

"Here's to the tilt in your kilt, my friend. We went around a few times. You might have even been almost right some of the time. I'll miss you, Art."

Adam just staring now. Finally, "The next one is going to be a wonderful life. I'm sure you're holding hands with Donna Reed and talking to Jimmy Stewart now. Old Frank Capra there to. Thank him for that movie, will you, Art? I mean that's what brought us together. Both of us alone on Christmas Eve watching *It's a Wonderful Life*. Did I ever tell you that that was the best Christmas Eve I ever spent?"

Adam breaking up now. Dan putting an arm around him. Dan and Adam standing now. Saluting their lost friend.

"Permission to go ashore granted."

25

"My name is Jack Bender, and I'm an alcoholic."

"Hi Jack."

The small room adjacent to the Yokosuka Naval Base Chapel was on this night the site of a meeting of Alcoholics Anonymous. Jack Bender, retired U. S. Navy Electrician's Mate and recovering alcoholic was leading the meeting. Since there were no real leaders in A.A. meetings, this chore was more an act of facilitation than one of authority. One just basically guided the group through the meeting by asking members to "share" and make sure the meeting ended on time. Jack was good at this job. He took it very seriously. A.A. had after all saved his life. Saved his family as well. Sure things were not going as smooth as he would have liked with Yumiko, but that would change soon.

The group consisted of 12 people tonight. A good turnout. Normally the demographics consisted of young and old, all American. Over the last month or so a quiet Japanese man had been escorted to the meeting by Jack himself. This being a U.S. military base, all foreign nationals had to be signed in and escorted by an American I.D. card holder. Jack of course was retired and employed by the base, so he was more than qualified to sign a guest onboard. He called himself "Peanut," the Japanese A.A. members an extension of the culture that valued "saving face" above all else. It was still considered a disgrace in Japan to have a member of one's family who was an alcoholic, regardless of whether that member was courageously trying to get help. In most of the West, men of good will realized and accepted alcoholism as a disease. Not so in Japan. Thus the curious, giant of a man would announce himself only as "My name is Peanut. I am an alcoholic," and leave it at that. Jack was the only one he conversed with, and even these exchanges were brief and generally out of earshot.

"If there are no burning desires, we'll close the meeting with the Lord's Prayer. Bill, would you like to lead us?"

"Our Father who art in heaven..."

Jack chatting in his low key almost otherworldly manner now to the stragglers. Meeting having ended a half hour ago. Clean-up done. Now only Jack and Peanut.

Jack Bender was fluent in Japanese. Decades in Japan. Drinking heavily in the early days. Horrible things done to his Yumiko. Beloved Yumiko. What his country had done to her family and then he himself years later. She still loved him though. He would set everything right. Last night had been a beginning. He would do more. Do all he could to wipe away the guilt and shame that he carried. Finally dry the tears of his anguished wife forever.

Waking up in a cold sweat, Yumiko feeling the heat of the bomb on that horrible day so many years ago. Just like it was yesterday. Watching, away in the hills with her uncle. Packed away by her parents before the plane came. The small plane. The Enola Gay. A curious name. The name of the pilot's mother in fact.

The American Satan must suffer what Yumiko and her family and her friends had suffered. Jack there with her every night. Working long hours at the ship repair facility. The pension not enough to survive in Japan with the increasing strength of the yen. As supervisor of the waste facility, he was responsible for the storage and disposal of all toxic waste on Yokosuka Naval Base. Thank god for A.A. Couldn't have held a job for five minutes when he was on the booze. Couldn't function. Hurting everyone around him.

"You always hurt the ones you love." Corny but God it was never truer than with alkies. Came home many a night and beat Yumiko senseless. One night she was waiting though. The knife hidden under the mattress on her side of the bed. Too many beatings. Too much hate already for the

Americans. Now Jack epitomized everything American on that day at Hiroshima. He might as well have been behind the controls of the Enola Gay. Might as well have dropped the bomb. Jack lunging at her.

"Come here, you Jap cunt. Come here, you bitch."

Slurring, stumbling. Collapsing on the bed. Yumiko over him now with the knife. At his throat. His eyes opening right before the penetration.

"Oh my dear God, baby, please don't!"

He had snapped and was changed forever. Perhaps the last brain cell had disintegrated in the booze or the shock of being so close to the "Final Curtain." Jack Bender never the same. A spiritual awakening of some kind. Yumiko over the edge as well. Changed forever. Dropping the knife and hugging him. Letting all her pain pour out. Jack puking and then staring into space. Not Jack anymore. Of course Jack Bender had ceased to exist awhile back. Sometime shortly after his first heavy drinking sprees. The soul gone. Something had replaced it though. Something else inhabiting the body of Jack Bender. Something evil.

Yumiko not noticing. She had gone somewhere else as well. It was calm and safe there. Jack though was in a turbulent area. Unfinished business. Getting sober only the beginning. A quest had begun that night. The nervous breakdown after coming out of an alcoholic blackout had precipitated what was to become the last piece of the puzzle for the Aum Cult.

Jack Bender stayed sober a day at a time. He helped a lot of sailors as well as Japanese. Being a retired enlisted man made him a natural to help young sailors with drug and alcohol problems.

Along the way he had met Adam Welsh. Took him to meetings for a while. Adam not making it though. Tough odds. Family history there. In the genes. Adam knowing Jack was always there for him though. Yes, and Adam would reciprocate thought Jack. When the time was right. One day at a time.

26

HONCHO I- YOKOSUKA, JAPAN 1965

The young sailor fell to the ground hard. Nausea had set in. Blood. Tasted it in his mouth. He started to get up but thought better of it. Jack Bender, Seaman, United States Navy, power puked all over the shoes.

Whose shoes were they?

The vague thought amongst the spinning and outrage in his gut. Head pounding. Eyes blurred. The cute Japanese girl. Yumiko, of course. Memory returned. Yumiko Abe. Talked to her most of the night. Drank him under the table. First woman on earth to do that. Reason enough to fall in love. Another rough duty day for Seaman Bender. Everyone on his ass. A worthless drunk. That was Jack. No mean feat to achieve the moniker of drunk on a ship full of red-eyed swabbies. The drunk he was though. All coming at the age of twenty-five. This exalted status. An old twenty-five thought Jack now here in Honcho I, the name for the bar and entertainment district just outside the Yokosuka Naval Base gates.

A connection with Yumiko though. Something there. Between them. Alive. The pain, that was it. The common denominator. The great equalizer. The bridge between the oceans. Yea, they shared the pain, mused Jack. The third sake had brought Hiroshima into view. The Bomb. The terrible days.

Yumiko Abe had talked of that day. All coming back to Jack now as he took her hand to right himself.

"Jack San, you ruined new shoes. My new shoes!"

"I'll buy you another pair. As many as you want, my beauty."

Staggering down the narrow streets towards the Love Hotel. Japan way ahead of the West, in matters concerning sex. Love hotels specifically set up for young lovers and cheaters of all ages. Very practical. Most Japanese houses were built with walls as thin as paper. No privacy. One reason for the Love Hotel – fucking. No allusions. If you took a girl to one of these dens of iniquity you were going to have sex. She knew it. You knew it. Nothing dirty about it at all. The neurosis of the West not existing here. No one slithering in and out. Perfectly acceptable. Sex as normal as breathing here in the Land of the Rising Sun.

As they had entered the hotel, Jack saw a giant replica of the Statue of Liberty adorning the very top. Jack never did understand why all of these hotels had decorations of this type. If one saw the Statue of Liberty or the Washington Monument (actually that one made sense, thought Jack) it was a dead giveaway that you were not entering a Motel 6 but rather one of the numerous Love hotels throughout Japan. Yumiko had picked the room by pressing a button affixed to a picture. The faceless woman behind the counter, her hands the only visible part of her anatomy due to the partition blocking any other view. This another feature which was uniquely Japanese. Complete anonymity between the customer and the proprietor. The key passed through the slot, money exchanged and then straight into the elevator.

The embrace was immediate and cataclysmic. A hunger. One born more out of fear and anger than anything else. Yumiko engulfed the man who represented the destruction of her family and her way of life while rejoicing in the excitement of a new beginning. A new life. Jack looked up from the void. The blackness that he had wandered in for what seemed an interminable time now being wiped out by the passionate, all-consuming kisses of this wanton siren. Jack beside himself now, grappling with her breasts, falling back on the bed. Mounting her now as if his entire existence depended on this moment. Lips, loins interchangeable in this dance of passion. On and on now. Jack in a veritable delirium. Yumiko crying out her testament of love for this man whose soul had almost passed into the night but for the intercession of the beauty now passing out in ecstasy beside him.

27

YOKOSUKA NAVAL BASE, 1992

Walking back towards his office at the Ship Repair Facility, Yokosuka Naval Base, Jack Bender pondered his life to this point. Peanut beside him, trance-like. Waiting for direction it seemed. Jack, content to stay within himself for a while longer. A kind of escape for the man who had not drank in a very long time. There would be time for stress very soon in any case. Jack Bender, retired United States Navy walked with Peanut, a man who would not be given a second glance by the passerby on the street. "Peanut" known as Haruki Okamoto within the circles of Aum Cult. A valuable soldier, he had killed the daughter of a former Aum lawyer who had been guilty of testifying against the Cult. Killed her while she slept. A lesson. The lawyer saving them the trouble by killing himself soon thereafter. The wife and mother now in an insane asylum. The grief too much. The human mind dealing with grief by switching on the automatic shut-down valve that we all have. The pain threshold only so high and then the valve opened and all pain gone along with one's very sanity. Some would say a fair trade.

A chance meeting by a roving security patrol. A more alert marine on duty at the gate and the events of the next week may have been averted. This was not to be. Jack Bender entered the empty office with one of the most notorious terrorists in the world with the ease of the unlocking of a door.

Here in the Supervisor of Toxic Waste's Office at Yokosuka Naval Base, a different Jack Bender. In no way reminiscent of the man who just an hour earlier had spoken of "One Day at a Time," "Easy Does It," and "God Grant Me the Serenity." No this was the Jack Bender born of years of guilt. A result of his alcohol consumed torture of the tragic Yumiko. Reparations had to be made now. Amends due.

"Soon we will move the gas out of the caves. I have a scheduled hazardous material pick-up just outside of Yokohama. We'll make the switch then," he barked to Okamoto.

"There will be no suspicion?"

"I've worked here 15 years now. Half of the Japanese base workers respect me, and the others think I'm crazy and leave me alone," Jack pausing but no laugh forthcoming from the caved in forehead that was Haruki Okamoto.

Jack continued, "Adam Welsh will be with me. He doesn't have any idea what's going on. He's been assigned to me on a Temporary Duty Status since he has complained of depression. He'll be just the diversion we need."

"The lover of Keiko."

"Yes, but I wouldn't bring that up when we're there tomorrow, even though he doesn't speak any Japanese and we can converse freely. The transfer will be made as planned."

They studied the map Jack had kept hidden in his lunch box. Stored underneath the dental floss that he would bring out from time to time at the base restaurant. Right in front of God and everyone, Jack Bender would floss his teeth. This after a lunch of apple pie and ice cream, fishcakes and a burrito. All in that sequence. Eccentric would be a word used for Jack if one were feeling thoughtful and kind. "Horse's ass" would be the term most often that came to Adam Welsh's disgusted mind as he looked upon the absurd visage of Jack Bender pulling morsels of burrito, ice cream and fish from his nonetheless stained teeth on those occasions that they dined together.

An hour, perhaps two passed. Now about midnight. Time to leave the base. Take Okamoto to the taxi. No chancing the trains just yet. Next week, of course, no problem. But taxis for now. No public viewing. No one able to say, "Yes I saw him. The man in the newspaper." The man who undoubtedly would be found under the wheels of a train somewhere after the Event. His usefulness passed.

28

Jack Bender dropped the terrorist at the taxi stand and without a word began the walk to his humble abode. Twenty years in the Navy and ten more with Ship Repair Facility and Jack Bender was living in an apartment the size of a room at the local YMCA in Schenectady, New York. This apartment he shared with his soulmate in torture, Yumiko. Walking towards the hovel, Jack thought back to that night in 1965. The night of the metamorphosis for him and his beloved Yumiko.

Something else had happened though. The sense of impending doom had hovered over them almost from the beginning. Even after Jack had stopped drinking for good, the anxiety and fear would always creep under their door like the Casper character of the cartoons that Jack watched in his youth in Bakersfield, California. Funny he should think of that now. Hadn't thought of Casper in years. Crazy what a guy can think of on a clear night with Armageddon approaching.

The apartment in Yokosuka was small even by Japanese standards. One entered to a tableau of two figures speaking quietly. Jack Bender and Yumiko Abe, husband and wife, but Yumiko, despite her deep love for her husband, unable to bring herself to take his American name. Too much. Enough for Jack that this Asian beauty had chosen to stay with him for all these years now. Through the drinking, the beatings, the insanity. Sitting here at the table few words needed. Two human beings who had shared so much over the years did not need to rely on verbal communication. Periods of silence were not awkward in any way. They were welcome in fact. Language such an imperfect, flawed device anyway, Jack thought. One always reading things into what had been said.

What did she really mean by that?

A simple look would suffice now. A gesture. Body language the order of the day. Most days they could reach each other's minds in Japanese and English. The talk tonight did not touch on the events at the train station. They both knew that Jack had been an integral part of the Event. The eradication of the American woman a deposit on the past due note from Hiroshima. A note that Jack Bender prayed would be paid in full in less than a week.

Yumiko Abe ate her rice and Kobe beef tentatively. The Kobe an unspoken gesture of celebration from Jack. In her senior years now, she was a small woman. Average size for her generation but still dwarfed by the modern day Japanese woman. Diet of course as well as the inbreeding with the West being the difference. Yumiko rationalizing her union with Jack by refusing to bring even half an American into the world. The Japanese women of the day disgusted her. Yellow Cabs, she called them whenever the subject came up. The inference of course being that these girls were "ridden" by American men with the ease of riding a local taxi. Too much coddling. More and more like their Western sisters. Trying to be like a man. Women should be a woman. Number one job was to please the man. Man of course always sure to show respect.

Yumiko had given Jack a good life. The sex had been in Jack's words, "Out of this world." Her own vengeance though could be other-worldly as well. Jack had witnessed it first-hand the night of his last drunk when she had pressed the naked blade against his throat.

Yumiko had been a young woman when she met Jack on that summer night on Honcho I so many years ago. Leaving Hiroshima after the War, her uncle getting work at the American Naval Base at Yokosuka. Yumiko drinking at an early age but able to function. Always in control. A tolerance of sorts. Breezing through a series of American sailors and marines in rapid succession. "Kicking 'em to the curb" as one of her broken-hearted quarry had blurted out to his sympathetic shipmates.

Jack was somehow different. She hadn't planned to fall in love with him. Hadn't planned to fall in love with anyone in fact. In the end, she had and a gaijin no less. An American, the enemy. Her enemy. The remitter of all of her suffering. His vulnerability was what had sealed her fate. The broken soul badly in need of repair.

Since that night in the Honcho, Jack and Yumiko had barely been apart. A slight of build man, Jack nonetheless had the intensity of a pit bull when he set his mind on something. Once he put down the booze, all the energy that had hitherto been focused on the hard work of leading the life of a functioning drunk had been re-directed to whatever the mind of Jack Bender determined to be the good. Alcoholics Anonymous, more specifically Alcoholics Anonymous in the Tokyo, Japan area became an all-consuming vocation for Jack. He had started the first Japanese-English A.A. groups in the area and was known throughout the offices of the Navy brass at Yokosuka Naval Base as the man to send a sailor to who was having problems with the "Demon Alcohol," as Jack called it.

Yumiko did not always support these efforts of her husband. At first, being young and still uncomfortable in the circles that Jack traveled, which included many Americans, she felt resentful. Just another phase of his, she thought. He'll tire of it soon enough. It wasn't until she realized that the days of sobriety were turning into weeks, then months and finally years did she accept that Jack's work with other alcoholics would indeed be a significant part of their life.

In point of fact, acceptance had been imbedded into the psyche of Yumiko Abe from the first flash of the Bomb, and she had used it as a drowning victim clings to a raft.

The headaches came for Yumiko about five years into her almost perfect union with Jack Bender.

"Where are you, Nami? I can't see you."

Screaming. Cold sweat. Jack in his low-key, unassuming voice now.

"Honey, wake up. It's the nightmare again. Only a dream."

"She's gone! I can't find her! Jack, what happened!"

The flash again and then the heat.

"My head. It hurts so much. Hold me. Please, Jack, Make it go away. So painful. Where is Nami? Where is my sister? Where did she go?"

Jack holding her tight now. The human being in his arms; his wife. His very life. The reason for his existence. His Savior.

Nami Abe had been incinerated at Ground Zero on the day of the Bomb. The clean-cut boys from the Midwest United States. The land of corn and Oz. The apple of their mothers' eyes turned in an instant to the Furies that day. The deliverers of death parcels that were still being received by generations of innocent Japanese. Little Yumiko had made her way out of the city with her uncle. For reasons Yumiko still did not know, her older sister, Nami, had not. In the recurring nightmare, Yumiko would see her sister briefly. Nami, two years older. A look of confusion. Fear. Trying to call out to Yumiko. The white flash and then, nothing. The dream at least once a week now and always the intense pounding in her head afterwards. Jack doing his best to console and comfort but to no avail. An impossible task in any case. Doctors, both Japanese and American all saying the same thing. The headaches a result of some catastrophic blow to the nervous system. Yumiko not forthcoming. Jack knowing the source. It could be found years ago in the bomb-well of a B-17 with the incredulous name Enola Gay. The tumor in the brain of Yumiko Abe would be discovered a year later. Not malignant. Aggressive drug treatments wiping it out but taking part of Jack Bender's wife as well. The spark that had attracted Jack in the beginning now but a flicker. Yumiko becoming more and more distant. Withdrawn. The love-making, while continuing becoming less and less emphatic. What was once a toil of bliss now a workmanlike chore for Yumiko. A wifely duty.

Jack more and more involved with helping other alcoholics. Promoted to Toxic Waste Facility Supervisor at the Naval base. Doing a bang up job. People talking. What a change. The drunk nobody could count on a ghost of the past. Of course the eccentric with the dental floss during lunch still alive and well. The good outweighing the bad. An amicable trade-off. Meanwhile, Yumiko, his soul-mate for the ages, falling into the void. Communication with friends non-existent. The meetings helped. The program the saving constant. Not enough though. A.A. had kept Jack

Bender alive and saved his marriage with his beloved Yumiko but still the recurring nightmare. The horror that he and his wife would always face. The need for retribution would always be there. Thus the alignment with Asahara and now the Irish scum. Unpleasant. Jack hated them both, but in the end, they were a necessity. An evil one but albeit a necessity. Once this was all over, he and Yumiko could live again. Did Jack Bender really believe this? Not important. It would be so though. Then he would gladly face his judgment. Always a price.

29

The state of the art modern day chariot navigated through the security checkpoint at John F. Kennedy Airport with the ease one would expect from a vehicle being piloted by a Formula One driver. Alas, the driver today was a twenty-three year old woman, and the mode of transport was airport cart not a super charged race car.

Kelley Bronsan took her carry-on bag from the conveyor belt and moved to the departure area. The plane to Tokyo would be boarding soon. Her heart was racing. Thoughts of Dad and Japan. A different culture. Another planet, her father had told her when they talked last week.

Dan not wanting his little girl to make the trip. Not now anyway. Too much happening. The murder of Rose Carney at the Ebisu Subway just a few days ago. Tightened security all around although the Japanese government, no doubt with prodding from the Ministry of Tourism, had assured all prospective visitors that travelers to the Land of the Rising Sun would have nothing to fear. The suspected terrorists had all been found. Dead unfortunately and no way to interrogate them, but dead nonetheless.

Three of them discovered under various trains throughout the city. Rumors of death by sarin gas played down by the police. The events of the last few weeks just an aberration. Things would be back to normal in no time. In the dark nooks and crannies of Roppongi, the perpetrators smiled with a sense of glee. All going according to plan, the day of reckoning coming very soon.

Kelley Bronsan did not think of herself as crippled in any way, and God help anyone who even suggested it. First exhibiting the tremors of MS when she was fifteen, she had become even more determined to do everything a normal young woman could do. Here in the departure area she thought of her life thus far. No shrinking violet by any means. Jesus, if only Dad knew. Better the inequities of her past and present for that matter kept a secret. The fact that she had MS did not keep Kelley from a full life. Brown eyes that could flicker come hither in an instant. Men were caught off guard more often than not. Expecting to deal with a shy, insecure woman because of the MS, they (the ones that didn't run away) were pleasantly surprised to find an intelligent self-assured woman.

"Excuse me, miss. Is this seat taken?"

"The one I'm in is, but you can have the other one. By the way, it's 'Ms.'"

The grimace on the poor guy's face told Kelley in an instant that the quick, acerbic mouth that she had inherited from her father had once again worked a bit too well. The poor bastard was beside himself with embarrassment.

"Jesus. I mean, damn...No I didn't mean your..."

"Hey, lighten up. I know. It's just the New Yorker in me you know. Please, sit down. I'm Kelley Bronsan."

"Joe, Joe Dickwell. Nice to meet you, Kelley."

Kelley, trying not to lose it completely. Dickwell. Bending over in the chair. Head between her legs. Shaking violently.

"God, are you all right?"

Lifting her head now, a face full of tears. Scarlet red. Laughing out of control. Joe totally mortified now. Getting himself together.

"Do you always make new acquaintances feel so at ease?"

Very good. He has some balls. A little bit too much the gentleman, but straight when it counted.

"Look, Joe, I'm sorry. I can call you Joe right or would you prefer..."

"Joe is fine."

"So where are you going, Joe?"

"Tokyo. I teach English at a small school there."

Another conversational English teacher, thought Kelley. Japan needs gaijin English teachers like America needs more lawyers.

"Oh, that sounds interesting."

The socially acceptable comment now. Kelley working very hard at being civil. The guy seemed okay. She had that tendency to sabotage a relationship before it even started. A "defense mechanism," one of her teachers at Cornell had called it. The apple not falling far from the tree. The old man exactly the same in this respect.

"Yes, I love the country. I never thought I would though. It's like another planet over there. I mean you can visit Europe and it's great, you know, the culture and everything, but after a while, you realize that it's just America with an accent. I don't think Japan will ever be like that. I mean sure, they have McDonalds and Kentucky Fried Chicken, but that culture will never break down completely."

"I've never been there"

"Oh, visiting friends?"

"My father works for Svenson in Tokyo."

"Oh yea, the cell phone makers."

"Don't tell him that. He'd give you the long bit about Svenson being the Cisco of the East. Leader in all things dealing with telecommunications. But, yes, they do make a decent cell phone."

"Forgive me for asking, but why does your hand shake? You seem to have a slight tremor."

Kelley, caught completely off guard by this. At a loss for words for one of the few times in her life. About to answer but,

"Okay, hey that was probably crude. The reason I asked though is I had a bad experience. I know this probably sounds selfish, but I just don't want to repeat it."

"I have MS. Other than the tremor, some fatigue and depression, I am a normal young woman. Everything works. Now, the bad experience?"

Joe had no choice. This new found acquaintance was a force of nature and he liked that. He liked it a lot.

"Last year I'm in this bar in upstate New York. Yuppie type crowd you know."

Kelley took him for a yuppie. Not a bad butt though and slim. No fat. The complexion showing a little age. Nice blue eyes though. She was a sucker for the eyes. Pegged Joe for about thirty-eight. Older man. A plus also. No bullshit.

"Friday night. Real crowded. By myself as usual."

A hint of self-pity. One step back for Joe, she mused. Still in the game though.

"So I belly up to the bar, and there's this beautiful black girl sitting there. By herself from what I could see, anyway; I had had a few glasses of Chivas."

Dad would like his taste.

"I start the basic small talk."

"Kind of like what you're doing now?"

"Ah...Yea."

"Go on."

"She says her name is Rita, and she's waiting for some girl friends for dinner. By the time they show up I'm in love."

"You mean lust."

"A little of each."

"She asks me to join them for dinner, and I of course accept but excuse myself to the restroom first. When I come out, everyone is already seated. We talk for a while, and I am enamored. I can't believe I'm telling you all this."

"Go ahead. I have that therapeutic effect on people. If I were a man I'd probably have ended up hearing confessions much to the delight of my sainted father."

"Okay, well I end up asking her if she'd like to go to a movie after dinner since she had subtly hinted that she would be available after her friends went home. I'm ecstatic. Then we get ready to leave and..."

"She was crippled."

"My god, yes. How did you, I mean oh I guess you ..."

"Happened to me more than once. It's why I stopped going to the 'meat markets.' I mean I can deal with it, but it seems that most men, present company included, can't it seems."

"It's not that I can't. I mean I saw your tremor. It's not that. It's just that with Rita I was afraid to bring the subject up the whole night. We walked to the movie. I had left my car at home since I was drinking, and it was painfully obvious that she had cerebral palsy or some type of palsy. You know, whatever that is when people walk in that herky jerky motion. I felt sure that she would say something, but she didn't, so I didn't. God it was awkward."

"For you or for her?"

"Touché. I know now that I should have said something. Hindsight, twenty- twenty and all that. We're sitting in the movie and, I don't know...I think it was a love story, and right in the middle she starts crying. It suddenly dawned on me then that this was probably Rita's first date in a long time. I mean here she was, this beautiful girl, late twenty's and all of the pain..."He stopped.

My God what was he doing. What did he do?

The hint of moisture at the corner of Kelley's eye. The beautiful face all knotted up. Contorted. Fighting something. Winning. A smile.

"Hey, don't worry. Go ahead."

"I'm sorry."

"Don't be. It's okay. I'm okay. Never pity a cripple, Joe. Or at least don't let on that you are. Lesson number one. I understand now why you asked me about the tremor. Get it out there right away. Everything out in the open. Oh, and I am capable of having sex."

"Will all First Class passengers please begin boarding..."

Kelley extending her hand, "I hope to see you in Tokyo, Joe. Maybe we'll bump into each other on the flight."

"Well, I'm in economy, but you never know. A pleasure making your acquaintance, Ms. Bronsan."

"You're all right, Joe."

Joe walking away now.

Kelley following her new acquaintance with her eyes as she made her way onto the plane and First Class while poor Joe headed for the land of the unwashed, Economy. Kelley again thinking the way her father would. Getting back to the matter at hand. She was excited. Excited about the idea of finally seeing her daddy. God, she missed him. One wouldn't know to listen to her talk about him to mere acquaintances but Kelley Bronsan was indeed Daddy's Girl in all respects. Her mother, a different story entirely. Ever since the divorce, Cathy Bronsan had worked overtime to destroy the love that Kelley had for her father. Of course it had worked at times. Only briefly though. To Cathy Bronsan's eternal frustration, no matter what truths, half-truths and outright lies that she poured into her daughter's head to poison the bond that she had with her father, his "Little Angel" would always come back to him. Dan seemed to send a letter at just the critical moment. Or call. Always managed to catch Kelley on the verge of tears after one of her mother's orchestrated smear campaigns against her father. Dan always saying exactly the right thing. The Irish Bard indeed. Some truth to that after all. At least with his daughter.

The excitement building now as the Captain made his pre-takeoff announcements. Looking forward to seeing Dad. Love-hate still the order of the day when it came to this relationship. Still it had been three years. A long time. Of course, Mom everyday trying to pull Kelley farther and farther away from her Old Man.

"If he loved you dear he wouldn't be living in that God forsaken place. Drinking and whoring."

"Mother, shut up please. I know he hurt you, but he's my father and I'm going to see him."

Mother immediately going into silent mode. Not even saying good-bye. She could be hurtful, but in some ways Kelley understood her bitterness. Forgave her the inequities that she set upon her, Kelley, her only child. Looking forward to talking to Dad. Get things out there. Really communicate. Hard to cut through someone's real feelings over thousands of miles of telephone cable. Life short anyway. The terrorist thing or whatever it was bringing that to mind. That poor woman. Rose her name. Couldn't remember her last name. Friend of Dad's and Art's. Funny, Dad avoiding the subject when she mentioned Art. Art Chambers like an Uncle to Kelley. Oh well. Probably in some political argument again. She knew the love her father had for Art but God, when they got into politics! She'd be the peacekeeper in any case when she arrived. Take them both out to dinner. After a while she'd have Dad toasting Art. The "Here's to the tilt in your kilt" toast being proclaimed with more frequency than the spellchecker in a George W. Bush speech.

The movie on now. *Black Rain* – a Michael Douglas flick set in Tokyo. Very good actually. The stewardesses...God forbid; the flight attendants announcing to their captive ambivalent audience that the original new release movies had not arrived in time for the flight. Kelley amused with the idea of the Japanese Ministry of Tourism finding out that a movie about the Japanese Yakusa or Mafia had been shown in the First Class section of a flight that contained first time visitors to Japan. The land of non-violence.

Four hours into the flight Joe arrived beside her seat.

"Okay, I know this must seem ridiculous, but I was wondering if you could help me drink my mimosa? Bizarre drink. Half orange juice and half champagne."

"Joe, you are weird."

Kelley unable to conceal her delight. Happy to see her new found friend.

"Excuse me ,sir, but I'll have to ask you to leave the First Class area."

The Northwest flight attendant extolling the code of the airline – *"Always on time, fuck customer service, and last but certainly not least, if you are not booked in First Class, you, my Gentlelady or Gentleman, are not shit!"*

He's with me. He's taking care of me. Can't you see that I have MS."

Just loud enough for most everyone in the cabin to hear.

"Yes, ma'am. Of course. I didn't realize."

"Of course you didn't. Two mimosas, please."

"Of course. Right away."

30

Standing outside Hiroo Hospital. Dan, Benny and Adam. No talk. The gruff banter of drunks not present here. Stunned silence. A living memorial to a friend who had just left. Gone forever. In the blink of an eye. Life. *What the hell was life anyway?* Dan Bronsan bouncing this thought around inside the archive of personal history called his brain.

"What the fuck, shipmates! Sorry Benny. No insult intended. I always did consider you a shipmate though. Air Force but not 'Air Farce.' You did your time in that horror called Nam. You too, Dan. I never did tell you guys that, but I really respect you for it. Respected that man...," voice quivering a bit...Getting it back. "God I need a drink. Okay I mean that man in there."

"We know, Adam. We know how you feel...felt about Art. We all feel the same. But you know, Jesus...Without Rose he was dead anyway."

"Bullshit, he had us."

Dan now, the obnoxious drunk taking a peak out to test the waters. Quickly subdued.

"Damn, aye, maybe you're right. Yea."

Arrogance subdued for now. Another day perhaps but not this night. Art Chambers was gone. A good man had departed the scene. There would be a void.

"You know I was just thinking, how the hell am I going to drink at the Sanno and look at Art's chair? Empty. I mean we should put some kind of memorial there. A plaque or something."

"Come on, Adam. Mary and Joseph. Memorialize Art in our hearts not in the bottom of a glass."

"Godamn it, Dan. Don't get fuckin holier than. Not now."

"Look, maybe you need a bit of the holier in thou in you, Adam my boy."

Benny stepping in between quickly. Adam and Dan had never come to blows, but this just might be the night. Benny, the calming influence now. Dying himself but no one would know. Art the only one and he was gone. The rest with a hint but really too busy thinking of themselves. Benny joking now.

"I'll take both you squids down if you get into it here. I have a damn reputation to keep up. Damn Japanese already think we expats are just a bunch of good for nothing drunks anyway. Don't need to give them any more ammunition," said Benny.

Dan grunting something. Adam pulling back. Fight not really in either of them right now.

"Here's a taxi. Let's go home. Adam, you need to get back to the base tomorrow anyway."

"I'll just walk to the station. God knows I need the exercise."

Dan leaving now. A handshake for Adam and Benny. In death Art had kept his friends together. At least for now.

"Let's get together at the Sanno tomorrow, Benny speaking to Dan as he passed into the night. You too, Adam. We need to take care of the funeral arrangements."

"I'll be there."

Adam's voice different now. A resigned resonance to it.

"See you there at 1800."

Dan passing into the night completely now.

"C'mon, Adam. Let's get you back to the base and me back to my wife. I could use some TLC tonight. Come on, old son. Let's get you back. She knows you love her, Adam."

The younger man taken aback by this last. How had Benny known that Keiko was on his mind? "Old son" the term that Art would use. Did Benny really say that? Probably just tired. Stressed. The older figure turning towards the light before Adam could speak.

31

"Keiko San, I love you."

The figure in the distance. More like an apparition. Tall with a glowing effervescence surrounding it. Another figure next to it now. Older perhaps. Wiser. Keiko not knowing how she knew this. Everything around her unreal. Dreamlike.

"Art San?"

Screaming, she wakes from the trance. Something next to her touching her. Hair of some kind. The eyes glowing and then...purring. Chibi, the cat with her now. Consoling in a way no human being could ever be for Keiko Watanabe. Struggling now to remember the events of the past few hours, days, months? No concept of time. The sting of the needle still there in her arm. The tracks. Vague remembrance of Shoko coming towards her saying something. *What had it been?* Keiko angry. In a rage. Full of remorse. Something about Rose. Yes, Rose. They...No she had killed Rose. Might as well have taken a gun to her head and pulled the trigger. Keiko a pawn of Aum but nonetheless deep in her heart aware that something terrible would happen. Happen it did. Rose gone. Everything coming back into focus now. Boiling the green tea. It always helped. What a simple remedy for all of life's ills, green tea. The beverage of serenity. Wasn't that what Jack Bender had called it? My God that was a long time ago. Probably only a couple of years but an eternity now. So many changes. The world ...Her world destroyed.

Not reborn. Just brought back to some animate yet deathlike state. Zombie the word. She had heard Adam use it once when they were at the Sanno champagne brunch. Keiko not feeling well. Too much to drink the night before. Not speaking just staring into space.

"Jesus, Keiko, you look like a zombie. Snap out of it. Are you okay?"

He had held her, and of course she was okay. Okay then. Now a different story entirely. A true zombie in every sense of the word. The undead. That was Keiko. Neither dead nor alive. The green tea enveloping her now. It did impart some feeling of serenity. Probably some type of herbal remedy. The simpler things the best. Something had happened to Keiko last night. Before the heroin delivered by Shoko had sent her into unconsciousness, Keiko had felt almost alive. The news of Rose. The horrible news of Rose. Her death at the station. The realization that she was gone forever. Keiko a part of it. Unwittingly, but indeed part of it. When this news had hit her, it had entered her entire being. Flooded through her every pore. The reanimation had occurred. Keiko Watanabe had risen from the dead. Awakened by feelings for another human being. After all the cosmic trash was cut through, digested and finally regurgitated she knew that what we had was only each other. If there was a God we certainly weren't meant to understand him/her/it. It would be like the ant understanding the human, something Adam had said. The final answers were there in our fellow human beings' eyes. A smile. A touch.

How are you today?

I'm here for you always, Rose had said. Meant it.

Strange how the whole concept of the Aum Cult – Creation from destruction, actually was true in the case of Keiko Watanabe. Through the destruction of Rose Carney, the soul of Keiko Watanabe lived again. With another sip of green tea, a look at Chibi, a thought of Rose, a decision made.

Keiko Watanabe would live.

32

"The caves were built in the late thirties. Don't believe any of the bullshit you might hear about the Japanese not knowing that they would be going to war with America. It was a foregone conclusion. Economics. America was stopping the oil flow. The Japanese had to have the oil."

The flatbed truck rumbling forward with its human cargo of hopelessness, despair, rage and raw unabated hatred. Jack Bender, Adam Welsh and the man called Peanut. Bender regaling this captive audience with his knowledge of World War II history here in Yokosuka. Rumbling along in the flatbed truck headed to Ikego just a few miles from the base.

Adam not really listening. Staring straight ahead. Peanut with two years of English grammar but feigning ignorance. On and on down the road to Ikego. Relentless. Adam taken off the ship yesterday. Reassigned. The despair too much. Art Chambers gone. Jack Bender requesting a body to help with a routine supply run to Ikego. Adam's chief gladly turning over Adam. Adam shuffling off the boat. Not really here. Not really anyplace. The soul gone. The body there but the soul gone. Benny Carter noticing it when he left him at the hospital. After they had said goodbye to Art. Him and Dan. Dan and Adam almost getting into it. Benny the peacemaker. The empty suit that was Adam Welsh accompanying his friend Jack Bender and the terrorist known as Peanut. Empty suit a term used by Davey Welsh many times. A reference to someone that didn't have any substance to them.

Of course with Davey this more often than not referred to intestinal fortitude. The intestinal fortitude that Davey himself lacked but covered up with the bravado spawned by large intakes of booze over long periods of time. Strange that Adam should think of his father now. All these years ago. Down the Yokosuka Road. Route 1. Short trip. A few miles. Still, a bit of friction in the atmosphere. A bizarre trio. Peanut staring out the passenger side window. Adam between him and Jack. Jack speaking. Forced.

"No rain today. Thank God. Good day maybe. Yes, a good day."

The reality of Rose and Art both gone. A fuzzy reality but in Adam's alcohol drenched brain a crystal clear one nonetheless. Art and Rose. Two living breathing human beings. Walking and talking. Just last week he'd seen them. Touched them. The smell of Art's pipe. The knowing look. Rose's perfume. Her girlish manner when Adam looked directly into her eyes. A teenager again. Adam returning to the ship last night. The Asshole Mormon chief on duty. Different. Receptive. Sensing Adam's pain. Adam ignoring the empathy. *Shit, the self-centered, hypocritical bastard just wanted me off the ship. One less headache.*

Adam long ago losing the respect of his shipmates. Sleeping off the countless hangovers in the armory. Locking himself in. Against regulations of course. Ship going to general quarters- battle stations drill. Serious stuff. Adam passed out in the space. Ship failed the drill. Mormon Asshole getting chewed out by the skipper big time. Mormon Asshole beside himself with rage. Couldn't prove Adam was passed out drunk. Couldn't burn him. God, he wanted to. Adam Welsh, piece of human refuse keeping Chief Mormon Asshole from his Ensign bars. It would only be a matter of time though. Mormon Asshole would be ready when that time came. Adam Welsh would never retire in Mormon Asshole's Navy. Not on his watch. No way. Good excuse to get Welsh off the boat. Ship Repair Facility requesting someone. A body. Adam Welsh was indeed a body. No soul requested so not a problem. The body would be delivered. Temporary duty under Jack Bender, supervisor of all hazardous waste disposal for Yokosuka Naval Base. Mormon Asshole thinking he was a strange bird. No matter. Welsh would be his problem for a while. The McClusky would conduct exercises for ten days in Yokosuka Bay.

Adam Welsh would not be missed.

Entering Ikego now. Ikego basically an annex of Yokosuka Naval Base. Jack giving Adam the history lesson that seemed centuries old. Jack the all-knowing one when it came to Japanese history. A veritable encyclopedia of Japanese history. World War II era. Jack the soft spoken gaijin turning into something akin to a Samurai when it came to World War II as seen from the Japanese view. Animated not a word normally used when describing Jack Bender but applicable indeed when the subject of World War II in the Pacific was brought up. Troubling to Adam. Something desperately attempting to come to the surface. Escape from the bowels of Jack Bender's psyche. Lurking just behind the wild blue-grey eyes.

"The Imperial Navy started digging these caves in the Thirties. War was a foregone conclusion. U.S. blocking the oil. No choice. Cut Japan off. Unreasonable. Roosevelt the pompous ass. Everyone better off if the polio had killed him early. A better world."

Stopping abruptly. Struggling for an instant and then back to low key subdued Jack. Uncanny. Scary. Adam's look bringing him back.

"Sorry, shipmate. Didn't mean to get carried away."

Adam relieved to move on. Change the subject. Still it was all very unsettling. Jack Bender a mystery. A riddle. Unfortunately, for Adam, the subject did not change at all.

"Stored the torpedoes in these caves. Best damn torpedoes built for that time. Germans didn't even come close."

Jack sensing and cutting off Adam's impending question.

"The Germans? Shit! Just a bunch of barbaric bastards. Huns actually. Great uniforms. Sure. You can dress 'em up but you can't take 'em out. Always reverting back to Huns. Germans given more credit than they were due in that war. Japanese a noble people. Honorable."

Adam smiling inside. Knowing what Art would have thought of all this. Knowing what his response would have been. One mentioned at his extreme peril the "honorable" Japanese around Art Chambers.

Through the gates now. No sentry. No security whatsoever. Not in this area. Strange. Jack Bender rolling the flatbed past two or three Stone-Age like excavations. Seventy years old. God the stories they could tell. The horror.

Peanut still staring. Motionless. Adam imagining the Japanese soldiers buzzing in and out of these fortresses. High spirits. Victory at hand back in '39 or '40, or whenever they were here. The Emperor and God on their side. The Rising Sun getting higher every day. The Koreans, Filipinos, Chinese not sharing in this glorious empire. Butchered daily. Anger, resentment to this day. Never would end. Shouldn't end, thought Adam.

"Everybody out."

In front of cave number 134. Not much different from the others. Two very large wrought iron bars going across a steel door which almost looked new. Adam thinking this strange for a moment, then drifting away again into the release of his dreams. Switching everything off. Able to respond to the simplest command and carry out the most basic of tasks. Jack of course knowing this. Knowing the pain and loss. Relating to it. Adam the perfect specimen for this job.

The door opening now. Jack releasing two padlocks. Darkness. The flashlight providing sudden illumination. Adam entering just in time to see the giant spider two inches from his nose. A start but in his naturally medicated state not the response a normal human being would have. Jack knocking the creature away. Peanut with no emotion. A walking Buddha from Hell itself.

The fifty-five gallon drum sat in the farthest most corner. "Hazmat" painted on its side, along with "Property of U. S. Navy" and a skull and crossbones.

No one would go off into the night with this. Jack pausing as the irony hit him. There was indeed hazardous material in this receptacle. Not the disposable kind. If the drum would have been perforated at this moment, thousands of living, breathing human beings in the surrounding areas would die in a horrible fashion.

The drum would be transported directly into Roppongi soon. It would take place on a Saturday in Roppongi, the Sodom of Tokyo. A Saturday night full of gaijin revelers. Partying at Gas Panic, Hard Rock Café, Motown and scores of assorted passion pits where the young gaijin sailor with but a drink and a smile and perhaps a room at the Sanno Hotel could entwine himself in the willing arms of a young Japanese girl fulfilling her fantasy of wild, uninhibited sex with a young American sailor or marine. This moral erosion of an entire generation at the hands of the evil gaijin eating away at the heart of hearts of Jack Bender, Retired ET1, U.S Navy now the avenging angel of an entire race; the fallout in the figurative sense of Hiroshima itself. Jack Bender and Peanut would drive right down Roppongi Road. Into the very heart. Stop directly in front of the Almond Café, "Almondo" to the Japanese girls who rendezvoused with their new American boyfriends there. Impossible to miss. The drum with its lethal cargo would be opened and rolled into the street. Jack and Peanut would be wearing NBC or Nuclear, Biological and Chemical protective suits that Jack had procured from the Yokosuka Base under the guise of conducting a training exercise. Thousands would perish. Yumiko, beautiful, suffering Yumiko redeemed at last. The sins of the Enola Gay paid for in full with interest. Jack not bothering to inform Asahara of the slight change in plan. The emergence of the ambassador as well as the failing health of his beloved Yumiko changing everything, at least in the mind of Jack Bender.

"Just need to clean this area up a bit gentleman."

Peanut moving before Jack had finished. Towards the drum. Checking it from top to bottom. Adam finding this strange. Just a drum of Hazmat. Peanut handling it like it was a priceless giant vase.

"What's in there, Jack. Let me take a look."

Adam not really caring, going through the motions. One step further towards the back of the cave. Heading for the drum.

"Baca gaijin... !"and then something else.

Adam of course familiar with "Baca Gaijin" – "American bastard," but not the rest. Adam retorting, almost unconsciously. Shaken though. Strange look on Peanut's face.

"Hey, asshole, who the fuck you think you're talking to?"

Davey Welsh, his father rearing his ugly head within his son. Adam and Peanut toe to toe now. Peanut grabbing for something. His back pocket. The box-cutter coming out. Still out of view to Adam. Jack in an instant around Peanut. A bear-hug and then, "Samisen, my friend." Under his breath. "Come on now. Chill as they say in South Central these days."

An usual joke for Jack. Adam coming back into reality. *Why was Jack holding Peanut?* Something behind him and then gone. Out of sight. Peanut turning abruptly. Back towards the cave entrance. Motioning to Jack.

"I will kill him," muttered under his sordid breath.

Jack pushing him out the door.

"Let's go, Adam."

Back in the truck now. This trip just a partial run-through of the real thing which would take place very soon.. The canister checked out for any sign of damage. Peanut passing on the information to Jack in Japanese on the way back. Adam motionless. Enraged, yet confused. Unawares how close he had come to joining Rose and Art.

33

Huffing and puffing. Only a few more steps to the arrival area. The bulbous gaijin rolling through the microscopic Japanese like a boulder through a group of field mice. Relentless. Dan Bronsan made his way to the Northwest arrival area. A quick glance with the rolling eye to the flight status board indicated that Kelley would be in his arms very soon. Flt 1 from New York was on time. Well at least they were punctual. Still didn't make up for the nightmarish service. Dan recounting briefly the experiences he had had with the barbaric stewardesses aboard Northwest Airlines. Better than PLA – Philippine Air Lines or "Plane Always Late" as Dan loved to call the Philippine national airline after a few gins at the Sanno. Used it almost as much as the "Tilt of your kilt." Oh well. The others just jealous. A great line could and should be used over and over. Jesus, look at Shakespeare. Of course Dan not comparing himself to the Bard but the point had to be made. No drinking today. His little angel would be arriving. It had been a long time. God he could use one though. Maybe later. Back at the Sanno with Adam and Benny and Art...No, Art wouldn't be there. God, how could it be that Art and yes, Rose were gone? Forever. He had prayed for them at Mass this morning. The irony of Dan Bronsan. Praying for his friends every day at Mass yet not missing a chance for character assassination at the slightest provocation – real or imagined.

An open seat. Dan spying it. Locking in with the good eye. The crazed one warding off any insane Japanese that would have the audacity to attempt to seat him or herself at what Dan had now targeted like an aegis missile. Homing device locked. Warhead engaged. Dan Bronsan's enormous ass mating with the poor Japanese-made airline waiting room seat that screamed with a loud creak as the gathered bemused Japanese travelers looked on in horror, albeit discreetly. No gawking here.

The plane would be landing in fifteen minutes. With customs and the other necessities, he would be talking to the love of his life in the flesh in about an hour's time. Added security these days at Narita Airport of course. Very subtle but there no less. Dan had noticed the numerous dogs roaming about the baggage areas as well as the gaijin FBI and Secret Service who gave themselves away with their uniform like suits. The attack at the train station just a few days before. Poor Rose. Very much on the minds of the Japanese. The news not releasing the cause of death- sarin gas. Still Dan had heard some American Intel types talking about it on the base. Hard to keep a secret like that. Reports that the gas had been smuggled in somehow from the Middle East. No one sure how.

A long couple of days. Dan drifting in and out of consciousness. Sleep a welcome lover at this juncture. Soon the few Japanese nearby scattering in comic terror as the thunderous otherworldly sounds emanated from the 350 pound Goliath's nostrils. Snoring like no one in this part of the world had ever heard. Little Japanese children gathering around the behemoth. Innocent to any danger. Sensing there was none. Giggling. Young mothers leading them away. Trying to keep their own giggles from becoming uncontrollable laughter.

The beautiful young girl with the trembling hand approaching without warning. The young mothers whispering frantically to the young children. "Don't look."

Kelley Bronsan in front of her father now. Breaking into laughter herself. Out of control. Dan awakening with a lurch. A blur at first. Then the realization. His daughter. The only real reason he had for living. Leaping forward now. Almost knocking her off her feet.

"Kelley, It's you. My god I have missed you. You look beautiful. A woman."

"I certainly hope so, Dad."

Kelley trying to be the self-assured cocky young daughter from New York City. Succeeding for about thirty seconds.

The tears came.

"Dad, I missed you so much!"

Collapsing in his bear-like arms. Falling out of the chair. Her father supporting her. No fear. Embracing now like a father and his baby daughter. The tears coming for both of them. Dan's tears a culmination of the events of the last few days and the sight of the love of his life. Holding each other for what seemed an eternity. Finally, Kelley breaking the hold. Slowly moving back into the chair.

"What a horrible flight. Those stewardesses. Dad, where do they get them. All "waitresses at the Last Supper."

Dan smiling at this. His line. She had remembered it. What was that about "the highest form of flattery?" A mental note to look that up and use it the next time the unwashed at the Sanno ridiculed his platitudes.

"And the movie. My god, they showed *Black Rain*. You know the one about the Japanese mafia?"

"Yakuza."

"Yea, that's right."

"The Japanese actor who played the young Yakuza was great though. I wish I knew what else he was in. I'll have to research it."

Dan not ready to lower her spirits just yet. The actor had died right after the completion of the movie. In fact he was dying of cancer as the movie was being made. Courageous guy. National day of mourning when he died. Many Japanese heartbroken. A tragedy. So young and full of promise.

Like Kelley.

"Well, maybe when you get back, young lady. We have a lot to catch up on while you're here."

"I can't wait, Dad. I want to see everything!"

Kelley, living life to the fullest. Dan feeling the pall that had been lowered over him the last few days being lifted away by the sheer spirit of this courageous young woman.

Dan pushing her baggage cart towards the airport exit now. The rented car outside. No train. Insanity with the baggage. Dan not enthused about the drive but it would be a straight shot to the Sanno. He had managed to book a room for Kelley there with Adam's help. The new Sanno Hotel a Department of Defense facility and so only for the use of Department of Defense personnel and their families and guests. Adam Welsh tipped the front desk every chance he got and was loved by most of the staff. Despite all of his demons, Adam Welsh had a heart, and the Asian staff at the Sanno saw and felt it.

Something Dan could never understand. Dan still looking at Adam as a common drunk. Obnoxious. Takes one to know one, the late Art had said. Dan thinking about this now. Adam had procured the room. Under his name. Kelley would be signed in as his guest and for all intents and purposes it would be her room. This was the kind of thing that Adam did on occasion that made Dan forget about all the other self-centered bullshit. Almost even made him forgive him for what he had done to Keiko. Almost but not quite. Take a lot more to right those wrongs. Probably in the next life. He would pray for him at Mass this weekend though. Light an extra candle for dear Keiko wherever she was.

"Joe, get over here."

Joe Dickwell had witnessed the reunion of the father and daughter from a distance. No desire to intrude.

"Jesus, you're unsociable."

Kelley, exalting in her ability to make Joe uncomfortable. Another one of the inherited sins of the father. No chance for maudlin reminiscing. Not with Kelley Bronsan about. Live life to its fullest. Today is all we have. Her sermon on the flight.

"Meet my old man. Don't worry, he's had his shots."

The grimace from Dan noticeable even from a distance. Joe filing this. Unless you were his daughter, Dan Bronsan would be laughed at only at one's extreme peril.

"An honor to meet you, Mr. Bronsan. Your daughter has spoken very well of you."

Dan the gruff handshake. Kelley interrupting before the salutations could be completed.

"Ask him what his last name is, Dad."

"Jeez, Kelley."

Departing from the intended "Jesus" as he remembered Kelley's description of her sainted father. Never diss the Catholic Church, and never take the Lord's name in vain.

"I actually have an Old English name, sir."

Kelley breaking up again out of view from her father. Joe seeing her.

Turning red.

"English, aye. Spent some time there in my day. I've got a bit of the bard in me, don't you know." *Zelig* coming out again. The old Woody Allen movie. Dan the chameleon. Becoming whoever he was around. The ultimate people-pleaser.

"Well what is it, my boy?"

"Dickwell, sir."

Kelley thought she would pee in her pants.

"Yes, sir. From the Old English."

Dan, still oblivious.

"I believe that 'Dickel' is actually the common variation of the name. You've heard of the whiskey George Dickel?"

"Yes, sir."

Joe, breathing easier. Dan either entirely ignorant to what was going on or purposely casting a blind eye to his daughter's impetuousness.

"In any case, a good English name. A pleasure to meet you, son."

Kelley with mixed emotions that the storm she had created had been weathered. She liked Joe very much and didn't want to hurt him, but there was a big part of her that wanted to push him away. Her survival instinct she supposed.

"Here on business or pleasure, Joe?"

"Actually a little of both, sir."

"Call me Dan."

"Sure, Dan. I'll be teaching English in the Ebisu area for Berlitz. It's a one-year contract with an option to extend. I'm really excited about it."

"Another English teacher. Just what we need." Under his breath but heard by Kelley.

"Excuse me?"

"No, yes you should have a great experience."

"Where are you staying?"

"Actually, Berlitz has put me up in an apartment in Ebisu. I think this is my shuttle right now."

Looking at Kelley. A look of encouragement. Seeing something there but not really able to nail it.

"I'll be at the Sanno in Hiroo. Give me a call if you get sick of explaining idioms to cute little Japanese girls."

"I'll call."

"Nice guy."

"Yea, he's all right."

As they drove towards Hiroo, Dan thinking that despite all of his daughter's wonderful traits, she would never win any Academy Awards for acting.

Joe Dickwell had definitely lit the flame.

34

"That Jap bastard!"

Adam Welsh sitting at the Sanno Hotel bar. Thoughts of the altercation in the cave come and go. Third Jack Daniels of the night. The daughter of John Barleycorn delivering them as fast as he could drink them. A Thursday night. Unusual even for Adam Welsh.

If Adam had his way, he would never see the States again. At least not California. Maybe New York. A few visits to Mom every year. That would be it though. Settle here in Tokyo or the Philippines. Wherever he could work. Always wanted to write. Needed to get off the booze though. Time to go back to the meetings. First another drink.

The last few days a blur, yet so final. Rose, Art both gone. Adam staring over at Art's old seat. Countless conversations over the last few years. Art the father Adam never really had. Davey Welsh never really present. "Present," a word the therapist would use. Adam almost chuckling over this now. True enough though. Davey Welsh, the "Don Quixote of Long Island." Tilting at windmills with John Barleycorn, his Sancho Panza.

"Adam. Things are going to change. Getting out of this dump. Moving to..." (fill in the blank here – the destination changing every week.) The main thing was to move. The geographic as the therapists would point out. Problem was, wherever Davey went, there was Davey. Change needed to be made from within, and the poor bastard was too godamn scared to go inside.

Joyce, the loving, loyal wife staying till the end. Mixed feelings here from Adam. The shrinks would probably say that he blamed his blessed mother. Mom at church daily. Front row. Lighting the candles. Five decades on the Rosary.

"Another Jack Daniels, Adam San?"

Daughter of John Barleycorn this day disguised as a modern day geisha. Chiyo, the barmaid smiling at him now. Cute girl. He had asked her out numerous times after the obligatory nine or ten shots. She'd actually accepted once. A night of Roppongi bar-hopping ensuing with poor Chiyo ending up praying to the porcelain god at a restroom in McDonalds. The price one paid for attempting to match drinks with an alcoholic with the tolerance level unique to the last stages of the disease. Somehow she had gotten home in a taxi. No help from Adam who was busy chatting up an oversized belt buckle that belonged to a female member of the Medellin Cartel. The buckle coming perilously close to his face in response to a rather obnoxious and lewd retort. One of Adam's failings with the ladies. Small talk more often than not tending to go from "What's your name?" to "Let's fuck" in a nanosecond. Amazing how it worked with the Japanese girls. Not so with this weathered Latina veteran of the sex wars who, if Adam had only known the backstory, so to speak, would make most of Adam's one-night stands look like Newport debutantes. The five African-American semi-professional basketball players present were more than happy to come to "Eva Peron's" defense, one with a glancing blow to Adam's balls. The rest accelerating his departure from the Motown bar with a few shoves down a flight of stairs and out the door and into the street. Adam having none of this. A stable person would have flagged down the first taxi and returned to the hotel to sleep it off. Adam, accused of many things but stable not one of them. Getting up. Dusting off and heading directly to the Roppongi Police Station. Adam's disheveled, bloody, drunken entrance into the station being met with the same reception as perhaps another atom bomb drop. *Let the gaijins kill each other for all they cared.* Adam adamant. Finally the decidedly unenthusiastic police suiting up in riot gear and following Adam back to the Motown. The tall gaijin Ichabod Crane on acid, leading the munchkin-like police to do battle with Eva Peron and her mercenary "Watusis." Eva and the Watusis still there when Adam and his entourage arrived.

"God-damn, he brought the Five-0," emanating from the would-be "Nutcracker." The crowd jeering. Screaming at Adam.

"His fault! He started it!"

The crescendo deafening.

Adam beside himself with rage. Incredulous. The eternal victim mode snapped on in Adam.

Back to the station. Riot gear clad munchkins, Ichabod, Eva and the enraged Watusis in tow. Eva muttering something in Spanish alluding to Adam's future as a eunuch.

"Why did you have to go and get Five-0!?"

The Nutcracker and then, "Man you shouldn't drink!"

Adam never forgetting this one.

Dropping the charges. No doubt influenced by Eva's castration comments and numerous death threats from the Watusis. Ignoring the recommendation of the munchkins to return to his hotel. Staggering down the road a few hours later.

"There he is!"

The Watusis on him in an instant. Lucky for Adam, better with a jump shot than a roundhouse. A few scuffs and bruises. Pride suffering the worst. He called Keiko. Keiko whom he had stood up coming to his rescue nonetheless. Listening to his pathetic commentary.

Soon after she had disappeared.

35

The office of the United States Naval Investigative Service was located in the basement of the Hardy Army barracks in Hiroo, Japan, a section of Tokyo. It would perhaps seem strange to the layman for the Navy to be cohabitating with the Army, but this was the age of the new military. The Army, Navy, Air Force and Marines not so much fighting forces as such but slickly advertised conglomerates competing with Fortune 500 companies for the services of the youth of America. The military looked at by many as a vehicle for further training and college funds. A bridge to the eventual "real job."

Lt. Joe Dickwell, USNR, flashed a bemused smile as these thoughts ran through his head as he approached the check-in desk or rather the quarter deck to put it more accurately. Even ashore the Navy still the Navy. Thank God that had not changed yet, he thought.

"Yes, sir, may I help you?"

"Lt Dickwell, here to see Commander Blasingame."

A slight pause and the Navy enlisted woman on duty had won the internal battle that pretty much everyone that had ever been introduced to Joe Dickwell had to fight. The burst of laughter repressed.

Good for her.

"Please follow me, sir."

"Joe, great to see ya! How was the flight? You didn't get stuck with an old Air Force pilot did ya? Those wingnuts bore me to tears! Can always tell the Navy Comair pilots though. Landing just like a carrier trap. Love it. Gets the juices flowing. Might as well turn the Muzak on when the wingnuts bring it in. Shit though, I guess we need 'em."

Commander Steve Blasingame got up from behind the large oaken desk in the Naval Investigative Services C.O.'s office and shook Joe's hand firmly. It was a wonder he was even able to rise at all from the chair given the seemingly endless array of battle ribbons he carried on his broad chest. Diminutive in stature but not to be underestimated. Joe knew that many a taller man had made that mistake and paid a painful price. The nickname "Bulldog Blasingame," an appropriate moniker.

"Great flight, sir. Thank you for asking. You're looking fit if I may say so. Shore duty seems to appeal to you."

"You may suck my..."

Trailing off. The female Third Class Petty Officer within earshot. Admirals had been forced into early retirement for less. The new Navy-Post Tailhook version.

"Belay that. Whatever. Yea, I love it here, Joe. Believe that and I'll tell you that Clinton is a great Commander in Chief."

"Yes, sir, underway the only way."

"Aye. Let's cut to the chase, Joe. What did they brief you on in Washington before you left? The office is secure. No worries."

"Well, sir, I was told that the subway attack that killed the American woman was orchestrated by a Japanese terrorist organization."

"Do you know anybody here in Tokyo, Joe?"

Thinking about Kelley now. The "teaching job" cover story. *What if I run into her?*

"No one, sir."

"How about on the plane over? Meet anybody? Small talk. You know, eleven or twelve hours. God, I'd have to talk to somebody."

"Actually there was a girl, sir. We spoke a good part of the trip."

"What's she doing here? Business? Pleasure?"

"Pleasure, sir. Her father's an ex-pat. Works for Svenson Telecommunications, Japan. She's staying at the Sanno Hotel, I believe."

"Jesus, that's about a stone's throw from here."

"I told her I was here to teach English in Ebisu."

Blasingame paused for moment. Satisfied.

"Okay. This is the deal, Joe. The consensus among the spook types is that the death of the American woman was just a taste. A precursor. We have reason to believe that a shipment of sarin gas is right here in Tokyo."

"How? From where?"

"Possibly a mole inside one of the American bases. More than likely, Yokosuka. We've got some real good leads now, but time is against us. N.S.A. and Japanese Intelligence seem to think that the next strike will be very soon. Possibly a few days from now. Aum knows that the gas can't be hidden for an extended period. Joe, you're here because you know what that shit can do. What it has done."

The horrible image suddenly appearing from some deep recess in Joe's brain. Grotesquely disfigured human beings. Picasso's *Guernica* in all its horror. Not on a canvass now. There in the Kurd village. Saddam testing the horrible gas on his own people. An entire village wiped out by the sarin. The children the worst. Miniature hellions in death. CNN not covering this. The American government zipping it up like it was Area 51. The widespread panic that would have ensued had anyone known just exactly what this horrible agent could do. An entire village of Kurds. Over five thousand human beings annihilated by little more than a cupful of the sarin pellets.

"We believe the stuff is being staged somewhere on or near Yokosuka Naval Base. Our investigation is focused on a 'Jack Bender,' retired Navy, ET1 type. Here's his file."

Jack, looking up at Joe from the inside page of the Naval Investigative Service report. Unassuming. Docile even. Like someone's favorite uncle. Something behind those eyes though. Joe thinking of old pictures of Ted Bundy for some reason. Not the physical resemblance of course. Bundy much younger. That thing behind the eyes though. Something lurking there. Waiting to pounce.

"Why don't we just pick him up?"

Joe, wanting to pull the words right back into his mouth but too late. Jet lag must be still with him. Had to be. Of course they couldn't take Jack Bender down. That would be suicide. As soon as they brought him in, the Cult would let loose the sarin that they had and promptly wipe out God knows how many innocents before anyone could do anything about it. Cult members dying themselves. A glorious death. The way they'd want it. No, had to wait. Let him lead them to it somehow.

"Need you to get inside, Joe. Meet this guy Bender. Not much time. The English Teacher thing could actually work out."

"How do I get close to our Mr. Bender?"

Commander Blasingame couldn't suppress the almost devilish grin that came over him.

"When was the last time you got so drunk that you thought you were going to shake out of your damn skin the next morning, Joe?"

"Been a long time, sir. Don't know if I have ever actually got to that point."

"Well, Joe, time to start. When you leave this office, you will commence the bender of all benders. No pun intended."

"Don't think I follow, sir."

"You will, Joe. You will. Tomorrow night, you'll be attending your first meeting of Alcoholics Anonymous on Yokosuka Base."

Joe Dickwell woke up with the mother of all headaches. The events of the night before slowly coming into view now. Like some yet unrecognizable creature stampeding towards Joe. Captured in the rear view mirror of his alcohol soaked psyche. The meeting with Commander Blasingame. Yes, coming back now. The creature taking more of a distinct form albeit not a less menacing one. Talk of the Aum Cult. Shoko Asahara. The American woman's death on the subway. The gas that was located somewhere in

Tokyo. Jack Bender – The mole. The necessity to infiltrate the Aum through Bender. Finally, the decision to use Bender's Alcoholics Anonymous meetings to gain access to the Aum. Joe Dickwell, a tee-totaler by nature, would have to feign a booze problem. Blasingame had not wanted to rely on Dickwell's acting ability. He needed Joe to actually get drunk and possibly be seen by Adam's friends in a Tokyo bar. Maybe even by Adam himself. (Adam of course would tell Jack.) Adam dry now but that changed by the moment, Blasingame knew.

A bulge next to Joe. Flesh of some kind. The smell of orange juice and sake. A concoction that should be administered to serial killers and child molesters, thought Joe as he tried without success to stop his bed from spinning by using his trembling foot as a brake. He saw the torso beside him and promptly vomited the entire contents of his intestinal tract onto it.

Upon further review, the mass of flesh was in fact a rather large Japanese woman. The marine escorts that Blasingame had been assigned to watch Joe from afar had apparently not done their job of keeping him out of danger. *Jar-head assholes.*

Aside from a short grunt, she seemed non-plussed and simply rolled over and continued her erratic snoring.

Joe had ended up in Shinjuku, a bar district in Tokyo full of booze, Yakusa and loose women. Joe had met "Orca" after his tenth or eleventh sake and orange juice. (The number of drinks Blasingame had suggested.) From the looks of his surroundings, cracked walls, putrid smells and stale alcohol, Joe was in the abode of the whale-woman.

Leave immediately.

The sudden urge. All-consuming now. Joe had to get out of there. Another overpowering need to puke, his esophagus retracting rapidly. Nothing. Joe had heard some heavy hitter friends speak of the dry heaves. This must be what he was experiencing now. He tried to think of a time that he had felt worse. The incident remotely similar to his current state involved his testicles being impaled by the handle bars of his sting ray bicycle with its banana seat so many years ago.

With all the self-will he could muster, he pulled himself off the bed and lurched for the door. Please God be open, his thought as he approached the bright red knob. With feelings that he was sure Jonah could empathize with, upon final regurgitation from his whale-prison, Joe exited the apartment and headed for the train station with the fervor that only those who have seen the light and returned can muster.

Joe Dickwell was going to an A.A. meeting.

36

"Glad you could make it, Adam. I really am happy to see you here."

"Yea, Jack, maybe the billionth time is the charm."

The A.A. meeting would be starting in about an hour. Adam Welsh here early to help Jack Bender, his curious savior, with the coffee and general set-up. This an important part of the whole sobriety process. Commitments, the old-timers called them. Art's death a couple of days ago putting Adam at a crossroads of sorts. He could continue drinking to escape the pain and eventually die or go insane, or he could kill himself.

There was a third option as well. A "jumping off" place would be the term used in the rooms to describe this pivotal point that Adam Welsh had arrived at in his heretofore turbulent existence. He really didn't want to drink anymore. The booze was, after all, no longer the friend it had been. At one time it had been his best friend. The friend had turned though. The "rapacious creditor," taking and taking without giving back. The agony of staying sober, a major problem as well. Therein lies the rub. Adam didn't want to drink but at the same time did not know if he could do what he knew from years in and out of the rooms of Alcoholics Anonymous would take an act of monumental willingness on his part. To drink was to die though. Even absent the minor detail of the physical demise of the body, it would still be a living death of the soul for Adam if he continued to consume the demon alcohol. The death of Art Chambers had been a major catalyst to start the journey to Jack Bender's meeting here at Yokosuka Naval Base. Perhaps, though, even more of a factor was Adam's new awareness of his overwhelming love for Keiko Watanabe and his intense desire to right the wrongs that he had administered to her over the years.

The weird bastard, Peanut, was sitting by himself as usual. There in the corner, never speaking to anyone save an occasional few words to Jack, always, curiously out of earshot. Jack claiming it as normal behavior.

"He's a newcomer. Give him time. He's still shaky, plus, he's Japanese."

The reference not lost on Adam. To drink oneself into a stupor in Japan was a disgrace. To ask for help, even more of a reason for family, friends, hell, the entire society, to disown the drunken sot. Still Adam had run into a few Japanese at the meetings, and they didn't resemble this whack-job in any way. In fact, a few of the Japanese even questioned Peanut's sincerity in respect to his very alcoholism, under their breath of course.

The altercation in the cave at Ikego the other day. Ominous now for some reason. It didn't seem like much at the time to Adam, but afterwards, on the way back, Adam noticed something very different in Jack's look. His very demeanor out of kilter. A sense of fear seemed to run through him. Jack Bender knew the Tokyo traffic better than most Japanese, yet his driving was unusually erratic all of the way back. A couple of near accidents in fact. Adam sensed later that just maybe Jack had seen something different in that cave. Something that Adam had missed. A feeling not unlike someone walking on his grave. A brief chill. Putting it down to the booze, finally. Shit, he only had a couple of days dry. It was a wonder he wasn't having nightly visitations from the Tooth Fairy let alone these ominous feelings. Feelings of impending doom. Yes, that's what they were. All alkies in early sobriety experienced them. Kind of a senseless paranoia. Of course, you know what they say? – "Just because you are paranoid, doesn't mean everyone is not out to get you."

Jack saw the small smile on Adam's face and felt a sudden love for the young man he cared for like a son.

37

Kelley Bronsan fell in love with Japan instantly. Only here a day and a bond had developed. The sights, the sounds, the smells; yes, the smells. Mostly the smells in fact. She had been at the fish market near Shinagawa this morning and had been mesmerized immediately. It wasn't just the seemingly endless activity. It was the aroma. The beautiful almost diabolical aroma of the newly killed fish mixed with the scent of the damp sidewalks fresh with the morning dew. She had dreamt how it would be here many times as she tried to envision her experience. Of course as is almost always the case, it was nothing like she had expected. It was so much more. So all encompassing. She cursed the fact that she did not have the writing skills of her father. That part of the Irish gene had bypassed her generation. She would have loved to be able to put her experience into words. Instead she settled with internalizing the sights and sounds of this remarkable land which was indeed another planet, just as her father had told her. Joe Dickwell had reiterated this during their magical meeting which now seemed to have taken place ages ago in anther galaxy.

Adam Welsh had delivered as promised. "Mr. Sanno" had booked Kelley into a beautiful suite. One of the two that had handicapped access in the hotel. The room had all the comforts of home and even included a bidet. Kelley smiled as she remembered her father's awkwardness as he briskly pointed it out. Kelley, of course without mercy,

"And what is this for, Dad?"

Dan saved by the Japanese maid who whispered what Kelley already knew into her by now scarlet ear.

The news of Art's death had hurt Kelley deeply. As was her wont, she gave away only her initial shocked and distressed feelings before retreating into herself and placing the "I'm fine" sign on the now neutral façade of her outward being. This disturbed her father, but he never made an issue out of it, partly because it had been handed down by way of DNA and perhaps more importantly, it was a defense mechanism which Dan believed his daughter needed.

38

"Excuse me, is this the alcohol meeting?"

Jack Bender looked at the frazzled, unkempt figure in front of him, smiled and extended his hand. "That's right, my friend, and I believe you are in the right place. My names Jack, and you?"

"Joe, Joe Dickwell. Nice to meet you, Jack."

After consulting with Blasingame, they had decided against having Joe use a fake name. The logic being that this operation would not take up much time, and if and when Jack Bender decided to investigate Joe, it would be too late.

"How about some coffee. Rough out there, ha?"

Joe not getting the full meaning of this last allusion of Jack's. Thinking he meant the weather at first but then catching the glances from the rest in the room, realizing Jack had meant a state of being rather than a place.

He nodded and sipped on the coffee.

Joe had planned on getting to the meeting as close to starting time as possible so as not to draw too much attention to himself. He had never actually attended an Alcoholics Anonymous meeting before, but he had an old uncle he remembered had attended, and nonetheless, he had been thoroughly briefed by Commander Blasingame and his staff.

"Get there as close to the beginning of the meeting as possible. Find Bender and introduce yourself. Once the meeting starts, you'll just have to raise your

hand and say your name when they ask for any newcomers or visitors. Don't say a lot. Just tell them that your drinking has gotten a bit out of control, and you think you might have a problem. You're an English teacher at the Berlitz school in Roppongi. That's all they need to know. After the meeting, you won't even have to approach Bender. He'll come to you. He loves helping newcomers. Try to get him to take you out for coffee. Feel him out. You know the drill. Find out as much as you can without raising any suspicions. NSA needs to know the basics – where, when, how, and they need to know fast. We're talking not more than 48 hours. We have to know where they're keeping the sarin and where and when they plan to use it."

Joe pondered the briefing with Blasingame just a few days ago. Time was indeed running out. CNN had been sniffing around as had the Washington Post. The fact that sarin had actually been used by terrorists in a major metropolitan city would not be able to be kept under wraps much longer. Mass hysteria would no doubt ensue once the populace of what had once been a city practically devoid of violent crime found out that a chemical agent had been used to kill a human being right in its midst. This of course part of the Aum Cult's plan. The hysteria causing the needed confusion right before the strike to the jugular.

There was one other American in the room besides Joe and Jack. Joe watched Adam as he fidgeted and shook visibly. Felt bad for the guy. Definitely an alky but something more. A darkness to him. Couldn't put his finger to it. The rest, Japanese all stereotypically bent over and humbled.

All except for one. The guy in the corner. Away from everyone. Strange, thought Joe. All the Japanese sitting together and this guy, who called himself Peanut when they asked for newcomers, he was sitting by himself. Uncomfortable but with a look that said "don't come close." Don't even think about it. A dangerous bastard. Joe getting this not from any empathy for alcoholics but from years of schooling and experience in tracking assholes just like this guy. He filed him away in the back of his brain for further development later.

• • • • •

"So how did you like the meeting? Feeling any better?"

"Did I look that bad?"

Joe, a bit cocky with him, thought Jack. Sensed it right away. A shadow moving across Jack's otherwise empathetic exterior. In an instant, gone. The sun breaking through the clouds again.

"No, you look fine, Joe, just fine. Thanks for helping with the clean-up. It's much appreciated."

Jack turned towards Adam now, "Adam, Let me introduce you to a new friend; Joe Dickwell, Adam Welsh."

The quick handshake. Adam self-conscious. Joe reminded of the Tasmanian Devil as Adam's hand shook violently in his.

"Nice to meet you, Adam. Active duty?"

"Yea, three hundred eighty-one days and a wake-up till retirement from the New Navy, but who's counting."

The sarcasm mixed with bitterness unmistakable to Joe.

"What brings you here?" Adam adding quickly.

"Teaching English for Berlitz. Did a few years in the 'Canoe Club' myself. Wish I would have stayed."

Jack fought off a smile. If he'd had a thousand yen for every vet who had said he should have stayed in, well, he'd be a quite a rich man now. Definitely wouldn't need this GS12 job and the meager Navy retirement. No time to think those thoughts though. He was in the right place. Everything happened for a reason. Yumiko wouldn't be avenged if Jack wasn't right where he was. Head of the Toxic Waste Facility at the largest American Naval base in the Pacific. No, Jack Bender was right where he wanted to be. Needed to be. No regrets.

Back to the present now. The scene in front of him. Adam Welsh, hopeless alcoholic speaking with Joe Dickwell, impostor. Jack Bender had been around the rooms of A.A. a long time, and one thing that Joe Dickwell definitely wasn't was an alky. Who was he, and why was he here? Jack needed to know, and he needed to know immediately. Nothing would stand in the way of his beloved Yumiko's retribution.

"Joe, any plans tonight? We usually get together, myself, Adam and have coffee. There's a nice place in a quiet part of the Honcho." "Honcho" a term used for a section of the entertainment district in Yokosuka.

"Damn, didn't know there was a quiet part of the Honcho." Laughing a bit. A tad too self-conscious for Jack. Adam noticing that Jack didn't treat this guy like the rest of the newcomers, as anyone with less than thirty days was called. Adam noting that Jack's behavior a bit out of the ordinary in any case. His sponsor not one to ask someone out for coffee. Jack always told Adam and all that would listen that the most important thing that a newcomer to sobriety needed was willingness. The willingness to do whatever it took to stay sober. The fellowship of the program was one of the things that insured sobriety. In the words of Jack Bender, "If you want what we have then you will do what we do." Jack had not waited for Joe to ask about coffee. He had made it easy for him.

"I'd be honored."

Again the inappropriate attitude. Newcomers were not honored. They were terrified, restless, irritable and discontent. Aside from being a bit under the weather from a recent drunk, Joe Dickwell did not exhibit any of the symptoms of a "real" alcoholic in Adam Welsh's eyes.

"Fine. Let me just escort Peanut out the front gate, and we'll be on our way."

•　•　•　•　•

They sat in the back of the VFW Hall in Honcho One, just about a mile from the main gate. Walking distance. The Hall a quiet watering hole for expats and young sailors and marines who usually only paid one visit to the place. Visiting more as a sign of respect or more often than not by mistake. Nothing much here for a twenty-something who ached for the harbor of a young and willing Japanese girl. No, just some burned out expats talking about the "Big One, WWTWO." The only Japanese females here were well past their prime. If AARP had a geisha division, this would be it. A crack that Dan Bronsan had made on more than one occasion, thought Adam as he sat drinking coffee with Jack Bender and the new guy.

"So, Joe, what makes you think that you're an alcoholic? Sorry, I don't mean to assume. You are an alcoholic?"

Caught a bit off-guard by the immediacy of the question. Dickwell briefed on what to say by Blasingame, but still...something about this Bender. He felt uncomfortable. For the first time in a long time, Joe Dickwell not completely at ease with his wits. He was flying on instruments. Alone.

"Well yeah, Jack. I mean I drink too damn much."

"Not really about how much you drink, Joe."

Adam joining the inquest now.

"More about how it affects you. I mean I drink my share, but there are some normies out there who probably drink more than me on occasion. The difference is that they don't have that feeling of incomprehensible demoralization that the Big Book talks about. You do have a Big Book, don't you Joe?"

"Oh yeah, most definitely. Read it yesterday, in fact....Not the whole thing of course."

Joe uncharacteristically screwing up. He just came off a binge. At least that's what he had told Jack. How the hell could he read the damn book in his condition?

If Jack caught this misplay he didn't let on.

"Well, Joe, you're in the right place. I'll do anything I can to help you stay sober as will Adam."

"I'm grateful. I really do appreciate your help. Both of you."

Jack smiled. Adam nodded. Neither bought it. Jack excused himself.

"Got to make a head call, gentlemen. Coffee like the beer in a way. You only rent it."

A laugh from Joe. Adam had heard it more than once. Preoccupied. Somewhere else. They both watched as Jack headed to the front of the hall, disappearing around the corner.

"Great guy, that Jack. He really does seem to care."

"Oh yeah. The best."

Adam snapping out of his momentary lapse of consciousness. Coming back to the present reality. Joe realizing he hadn't fooled anyone. Jack would be gone for a few moments at the most. Needed to go with his gut. Not a lot of time left.

"Petty Office Welsh."

"Hey no need to go military on me."

"Petty Officer Welsh, look at me. I don't have a lot of time."

Dickwell staring directly at him now. A complete transformation. No Berlitz teacher here. Regular Navy.

"I'm Lt. Joe Dickwell, Naval Intelligence Service or NIS as you may have heard us called."

"Jesus, you're a Narc."

Dickwell not taken aback by the remark. Most Navy personnel, particularly enlisted, had a very negative view of NIS. The only time you really heard of them is when they infiltrated a ship's crew with a thirty year old agent that looked twenty playing a Boatswain Mate and busted some poor bastard for smoking dope or dealing it.

"Look, I'm going to forget you said that, and I'm going to call you Adam. Frankly, I don't give a shit what you call me. I need answers from you, and I need your trust. A lot of lives are depending on it."

Joe glancing quickly towards the front of the Hall. Bender would be returning any second.

"Okay, copied and understood. Go ahead...sir."

"We have reason to believe that your friend, Rose Carney...."

"How did you know..."

"Please...let me finish. Rose Carney was murdered as part of a preliminary strike by the Aum Cult. We have further intelligence that indicates that Jack Bender has aided and abetted Aum."

"No fucking way, Lieutenant! Goddamn where the hell did you guys get that shit. Should have known, fuckin NIS!"

"Keiko Watanabe is involved as well."

Adam, beside himself. Unable to speak. Finally finding the words and...

"Sorry, gentlemen, you know when you get old like me the plumbing is just not the same. Just when I think I'm done...well you'll know in your time. Why the terrified look, Adam? You look like you've seen a ghost."

Dickwell was finished. Bender knew. He didn't miss a thing. Of course now Welsh knew as well.

"Well, Jack..."

Dickwell starting to speak but Adam cutting him off.

"Jack, Mr. Dickwell here is a fraud."

Adam looking directly at Joe now. Dickwell thinking he had misread him badly. Then..."No he isn't an alcoholic. He's a REAL alcoholic."

A pause for effect and then Jack and Adam both laughing at the little joke. Adam had not turned on him at all. He was going along, for now. The term, Real Alcoholic something used by the old-timers to discern the high-bottom drunks from the low-bottom ones.

"Yea, Jack, he's definitely one of us. Just keeping a low-profile. What a story though. He'll be a great circuit speaker one day."

The small talk continued a bit longer. When Joe Dickwell got up to leave, he shook hands with Jack and Adam. The palmed business card that Dickwell discretely placed in Adam's hand not missed by the trained eye of Jack Bender. He had never believed him in any case. The exchange of the business card the nail in Joe Dickwell's coffin as far as Jack Bender was concerned as he headed home to his beloved Yumiko. Changes would have to be made. Immediately.

39

The first indication to Jack Bender that something was wrong was the door. More accurately, the position of the door. Ajar. He had always kept the door to the apartment locked as had Yumiko, even when they were at home. Jack had been adamant about this.

"Please, always keep the door locked, baby."

Baby. Funny, he still called her that after all these years.

The sight Jack Bender dreaded the most met him as he forced the door. There behind it, Yumiko Abe lay motionless. She had tried to leave and had apparently collapsed where she now lay. Here was the geisha doll of Jack Bender's universe. Thankfully, his military training was still with him. He quickly leaned over and delicately held her head as he checked for pulse and breathing. Both were there, Thank Jesus, he thought, heart pounding, sweat starting to appear on his brow. He called Yokosuka emergency and in what felt like forever, although only about five minutes, the ambulance arrived.

She was in ICU now as Jack paced in the waiting room. All the years together, *What was the line from that song-* "The hopes and fears of all the years..."came flooding through his very being. From his brain, his subconscious, all the way down to his gut. Exploding there like one of those giant "Daisy Cutter" bombs he had heard about. The shrapnel here though was not laced with bolts or nails but substances much more lethal – broken promises, indiscretions, drunken rages.

The doctor was speaking to him now.

"Mr. Bender, your wife is stable now. I'll have to ask your permission to operate, however."

"Operate? Why? The tumor wasn't/isn't malignant. They told me. Jesus, did they lie? Was there a mistake?"

Jack in a dream-like state now. Not really speaking to the doctor. The doctor, a young, fresh-faced Lieutenant - *Was he from Oz too? The Cornfields, the son of one of the Furies of long ago. The Messenger of Death here to finish what the Enola Gay started in another day, on another planet?*

The doctor spoke now. Appearing as an apparition to Jack rather to any flesh and blood human being.

"No, sir. All the information you were given concerning the tumor was correct. There has been a complication, however. An aneurysm. The aneurysm was probably caused as a result of the unexpected growth of the tumor. Regardless of how it got there, it is imperative that we reduce its size."

"No other options? There is no other way to do this, doctor?"

Jack knew the answer already. He suddenly knew that his feelings now must have been eerily similar to those that Adam had experienced when he had asked the same unnecessary question the night his dear friend Art had died. Jack recalling the ashen, broken look on Adam's face as he spoke of his friend's loss. What would Adam think of him now if he knew that Jack was the mole for Aum. Had indeed played a pivotal role in the demise of his friend? When Jack had "aided and abetted," to borrow the police phrase from the Bakersfield of his youth, in Rose's death, hadn't he basically killed Art as well?

"I'm afraid not, Mr. Bender. Mrs. Bender's..."

"It's not 'Mrs. Bender,' it's 'Abe.'" Jack cut him off, regretting it almost immediately. Deep down he had yearned for his beloved Yumiko to take his name. It broke his heart to hear a stranger refer to her in the way he had always wished, especially in the time and place and the dreadful circumstances of the moment.

"Yes, sir, your wife's only chance of survival is this operation. She will most certainly die without it, I'm afraid."

"And if she has the operation?"

Again the interminable wait before the inevitable response.

"She has about a thirty percent chance, Mr. Bender. I'm truly sorry. We will do the very best we can. I can assure you of that much. I wish I could give you better news, but it is my duty..."

"Yes, yes, of course. Please operate, doctor."

40

"I am a guest of Mr. Carter. Could you please contact him. I believe he is in the bar."

The marine looked at the small, fragile Japanese woman. It was 2000 or 8pm in civilian time, and she was wearing sun-glasses. A bit too anxious as well. Probably should contact the Captain, but hell he was going off duty in just a few minutes.

"Okay, Miss Watanabe, just one moment while I call the bar."

Benny Carter was at the front gate of the Sanno Hotel in five minutes. He shook his head as he passed the recently constructed cement barricades and the detachment of U.S. Marine guards that had just last week been transferred here from the marine barracks at Yokosuka Naval Base. God, how times had changed. Benny, the Vietnam vet who along with dear, departed Art Chambers, had fought a conflict where at least one knew who the enemy was. Now, well, different times. He did know that two of the dearest people in his world were dead, however. Somebody would pay. Benny Carter. U.S. Air Force Master Sergeant, Retired was as certain of this as he was of the fact that the cancer, currently residing in his lymph nodes would eventually kill him.

"Is that my long, lost daughter out there? Could it be? My God, it is. My beautiful Keiko. How's my little girl? My cherry blossom!"

Keiko had wandered over to the new construction site where the newly installed cement blocks stood. Preoccupied momentarily. Walking back now toward the gate as Benny's voice brought her out of her trance.

The sight of Benny, her big teddy bear, suddenly bringing Keiko back to the beautiful, innocent times. Not ready for this. Welling up now. Shaking. Holding Benny now. Sobbing uncontrollably.

"Hey, hey now, my baby girl! Please, I can't bear to see you cry."

"Oh, Benny San, I miss you so. Everyone, everyone all gone. My life, gone."

Benny, signing her in now, walking her past the bemused Lance Corporal Henson.

Keiko overwhelmed with a kind of sensory overload almost immediately as she entered the lobby of the Sanno Hotel. The furniture reeking with the smell of new leather. As a girl, on her first day of school, the smell of her new book bag. The best that money could buy. Leaving the lobby, walking towards the lounge. The sounds of bells now. A "ding, ding, ding" sound. Art Chambers had told her and Adam one long ago afternoon that a lot of angels were getting their wings that day. Adam had laughed and shook his head in a knowing way.

"Yea, that's it. Art. Angels getting their wings," and then, seeing the quizzical look on Keiko's face, laughing louder and holding her close.

"It's okay, baby. I'm sorry. You never did see *It's a Wonderful Life*, did you? We'll change that soon."

That night they had watched the movie and saw Clarence the Angel gleefully explain to an incredulous Jimmy Stewart how another angel was getting his wings as the bell on the cash register at Martini's sounded.

Of course, the bells that Keiko was hearing now were emanating from the slot machine room which was conveniently located adjacent to the Sanno Hotel Bar and Lounge.

"Aye, Art, there may be a few angels getting their wings, but there are a few poor souls in there losing their shirts as well," Dan Bronsan had retorted that day.

"There's a booth in the back there, Keiko San. Do you want something to drink?"

Looking at the lounge now. Memories flooding back. She almost lost her balance. This return to a place that had represented so much hope so much love along with a good amount of pain. She steadied herself on Benny's shoulder.

"You okay, baby? Here, sit down. I'll get us a drink."

"Just juice for me, Benny San. I'm okay, really."

"It's so good to see you, little daughter."

Keiko smiling weakly now. Benny just looking at her. Both caught up in one of those awkward pauses that occur probably millions of times a day throughout the world. *Why don't we just say what we really feel*, Benny thinking now. *Shit, so much easier.* Thinking of Art and Rose. He loved them so much. Never told them though. *Hell, they probably knew.*

Benny Carter, a black man in the U.S. military when men of color were still treated in a less than manner. Art, always treating Benny like a man though. Sure they would argue. Art, the "Right Wing Nazi" as Dan liked to refer to him and Benny the "Bleeding Heart Liberal." Still they cut through it somehow. 'Nam, the common denominator of course but Benny still believing deep down that Art Chambers would have been the same decent guy, war or no godamn war.

"How long has it been? It seems like forever. There were rumors that you were in the hospital."

"Oh, Benny San, I...I don't really know. So much has happened. Changed. Have you..."

Shaking visibly now. Voice cracking.

"...I mean, I'm sorry..."

"Adam? Yes, I've seen him. Are you okay, baby? How about a small cognac?"

Smiling, she nodded. Benny already on his way to the bar to order.

Alone now. *What am I doing here? Is this the right thing to do? The right way to do it even?* Too late in any case. The die cast . Keiko Watanabe formerly a member of the Aum Cult terrorist organization now banished. Here now in a United States military facility. Despite the lax security at the gate, she had no doubt that she had been recorded by the ever present security camera. It would only be a matter of time. Benny her only chance now.

"Here you go, daughter. Drink this. Medicinal purposes don't you know."

Benny smiling. The raspy voice a bit rougher than she remembered. He had lost weight as well. Benny not looking healthy at all. She took the drink.

Courvoisier. Memories flooding in now. Benny's favorite drink. She eyed it tentatively for a brief moment as if she dreaded yet at the same time desired the release. A Pandora's Box of emotions of sorts. Finally, she gulped it and gagged.

"Hey, hey, baby doll. Scoshi, slowly. I can't have my favorite daughter getting sick now."

The warmth coming as she finally swallowed. She was better now. She would be able to do what was needed.

"Adam is fine. He's off the sauce. Been hanging around the base a lot lately. They took him off the ship. Probably for the best."

"He is working on the base now?"

"Yea, works with the civilians now. Retired guy named Bender is his boss. So how are you, Keiko? Really. Where have you been? What have you been doing? God, I missed you, Keiko Chan."

"I had to leave, Benny. Adam...well you probably know about it. I just couldn't..."

Her voice breaking now. Benny the consoling father-figure.

"Hey, It's okay, baby. Take another shot of courage there. You don't have to tell me everything at once. Drink your Courvoisier. Relax. Everything is going to okay."

"But I do, Benny San. I do. I need to...I have to tell you everything. Everything and everyone that I care about in the world depends on it. I just don't know how to start."

Benny holding her hand now. The fatherly mode. Keiko reminded of a bald Nelson Mandela. The soft Benny Carter emerging. The part of him only those closest were allowed to see.

"Why the sunglasses, baby. You were wearing them when you came in and it was dark outside. Not a star in the sky even. Pretty dark in here right now too. You know they keep it this way so that the old drunks like me can turn into Billy Dee Williams after a few snorts."

"Who is Billy Dee Williams?"

"Don't worry about that, girl." *Jeez, I'm getting old.*

"Unless you're trying to be the Japanese Stevie Wonder, those sunglasses don't make sense to me. You always did have the most beautiful brown eyes. If I were only younger. Jeez what a ..."

Stopping now. No need to go into a tirade concerning Adam. Not now.

A brief smile just at the corner of her mouth now. Benny didn't miss it though.

"Anyway, honey, you couldn't pull it off. Much too pretty and Stevie is getting up in years now. He's a might darker shade of yellow too. "You are the sunshine of my life..."

Benny singing to her in that raspy voice.

"You brought a lot of sunshine to all of us when you were here. Tell your father everything. It's okay."

Maki, just starting her shift at the bar. Tray in hand, she was standing over Benny and the weeping Keiko now. Benny with a dismissive gesture of his head, ever so slight but caught by Maki.

"Everything is daijoubu here. Bring us another round will you, pretty lady? Courvoisier, two of them. A couple of glasses of water too. I can die now. Here I am with the two most beautiful girls in all of Tokyo."

Maki smiling as she left.

"I'll bring it right away, Benny San."

Keiko crying softly now. Finishing her drink. She would be okay. She had to be.

Leaning back in the booth, she missed the entrance of the head of security for the Sanno Hotel. The man accompanying him a tall stooped shouldered individual but with an otherwise unmistakable military demeanor about him. Joe Dickwell, Lieutenant, Naval Investigative Service gave the room a quick studied sweep before turning towards the bar with his companion.

The words she needed suddenly came to Keiko.

"Benny, I need to tell you some things. Please listen to everything that I have to say before you ask any questions. I'm sure you will have many. I know that a lot of what I am about to say will be very hard for you, but please know that I never wanted to hurt anyone."

Benny gesturing as if to cut her off. Keiko having none of it.

"Please Benny, you must listen to me."

No music playing. Only a few people in the lounge. Joe Dickwell heard the loud female voice with the Japanese accent. He turned ever so slightly, just enough to note the source.

"Okay, baby, I'm here. I'm listening."

When Keiko finished, an hour had passed. There were pauses, a few tears, consolation from Benny, but she got it all out. Told him everything. How she had left the doctor's office in a daze following the horribly botched abortion. The initial meeting with Shoko Asahara. How he had mesmerized her from the very moment she looked at him. His eyes seemed to look deep into the abyss of her very soul. He had dared to venture into the dark pits and recesses and had brought out all of the horrid bile and emotional excrement that she herself would never look at let alone even attempt to remove. In a sense, he knew Keiko already. At least her pain. In fact, he seemed to thrive on pain. His own, hers, the world's. He had talked of rebirth from destruction. A theory that Keiko was as ripe for as any being could be.

The meeting had taken place in a room above the Gas Panic bar in Roppongi. Keiko had run into one of her old girlfriends at a local upholstered sewer. She had been drinking heavily for days.

"He has all the answers, Keiko. He will help you. I know. It's a new religion. A spiritual revolution."

Of course, Chiyo had not mentioned or probably even known that the decimation of half the population of Tokyo was an integral part of the Spiritual Awakening sought after by the Aum Cult, the name its founder and leader, Asahara, had given to his menagerie of lost souls and broken angels, all of whom would die for the cause with the eagerness of one who had been given an escape route from a life of interminable pain.

Shoko Asahara had the gift. The ability to see inside any human being and bring up all the refuse that most never examine in twenty lifetimes, let alone one. The lost and anguished, his specialty. The refuse boiling over within them. A look, a touch, a few well-chosen words and the process began. The expurgation of all of the pain. Once finished, one indeed felt cleansed but with a kind of void. The kind that one would feel when one's humanity had been taken as well. A trade off curiously not mentioned. No worries though. The shell was now devoid of the malignant abscess as well. What the lemmings did not realize at once but would learn later, when it was too late, was that their benefactor would return this abscess of pain and utter human suffering magnified to the nth degree when and where it served his purpose to do so. The ultimate insurance policy for Asahara. The pain of the lemming gladly remitted ten-fold.

"You look troubled, my dear."

"I..."

"Please, don't say anything. Not yet."

She had noticed the eyes at first. Black, seemingly empty, yet, something there. Almost imperceptible. Drawing one in. The black orbs like magnets for all of the pain in the universe. Closer and closer, she felt herself being carried into them till, finally, a latch in some deep, dark confine buried away in her soul shut. Not a loud noise. Just a click. Shut nonetheless. The world ending with a whimper, not a bang. The poet was right.

Keiko had not mentioned the heroin use to Benny. It would complicate matters. He would insist that she enter a hospital to kick the addiction. Keiko would have none of it. There was no time in any case. Her life meaningless when measured against the loss of humanity that would most certainly take place in a very short time if she did not act.

Shoko Asahara himself had injected Keiko with heroin during that first meeting. It was like leading a lamb to slaughter. Keiko, in her already trance-like state under the spell of Asahara, offering no resistance at all.

"It is a kind of an initiation, little one. A test to show that you trust the Cult above all else. A necessity to prepare you for the arduous days ahead. Be strong," he had whispered as the needle pricked her skin. Immediately enveloped in an exquisite warmth she had never experienced and would never attain again. Although, true to the form of an addict, she would continue to try. The difference between an addict and an alcoholic very simple. One always became addicted to narcotics upon the first administration while ten different people could drink a few glasses of whiskey and only two or three would end up drinking alcoholically.

The injections given at staggered times. Different locations after the first. Keiko never knowing when or where they would come. This another technique used by The One to maintain complete control over his troubled minions.

As the days went by, Keiko Watanabe became privy to certain aspects of the Aum Cult's plan of Rebirth from Destruction. It became her understanding that Aum had acquired a lethal chemical, a gas of some kind. Rumors were that it had come from the regime of Saddam Hussein in Iraq. Keiko was not a stupid woman by any means, but in her drug-induced, spellbound state she was incapable of concluding the obvious. Rather than use the sarin gas that Asahara had in his possession as a bargaining chip to somehow force the West into ceasing the export of the decadent military men sent over to soil the young Japanese women, the Aum Cult would in fact unleash the deadly sarin on the population of Tokyo itself. There would be no warning or room for negotiation as Asahara had led all but his inner circle to believe. It was only after Rose Carney was killed by Aum that Keiko was awakened to the horrible truth and made the decision to bring down Asahara and the Cult itself.

Benny needed another drink. He motioned to the bar.

"Another Courvoisier, please."

The animated, larger than life Benny not present now. A seriousness of the deadly variety falling over Benny Carter's dark visage.

"Did anyone follow you here, Keiko?"

"I don't think so. No one would be expecting me to come here."

Of course, Asahara had seen the change in Keiko. Her breakdown on hearing of the death of Rose Carney an indication that she could no longer be trusted, let alone depended on. As Keiko sat here in this booth at the Sanno Hotel lounge, a confessional booth of sorts, she had no way of knowing that plans for her eminent demise were being drawn up only a few short miles away in the rooms above the Gas Panic bar.

"Look, honey, you're not safe."

Benny back to the fatherly mode if only briefly.

"I'll get you a room here tonight. You'll be safe here."

Keiko started to protest, but Benny's look indicated that negotiations would not be forthcoming on this issue.

"Wait here, baby, while I get the room."

Benny gone in an instant, never noticing the brief glance from Joe Dickwell. A studied look. Just long enough to file away essential information of a descriptive nature. This done, his eyes moving towards the small Japanese woman seated alone now in the booth a few feet away. The woman known to both Japanese and American intelligence as possibly the last hope of averting a holocaust of the chemical variety the likes of which the world had never experienced.

·   ·   ·   ·   ·   ·

"Dusty, how about a real drink?"

Bill Dwyer, retired Army Colonel. White-haired pixie, about 5'6" tall but strong as a bull, at least before years of living off the good graces of a filthy, rich Japanese wife took their inevitable toll.

Dwyer had been a hero in the Korean War. As a young Second Lieutenant, he had damn near saved his entire platoon after he and his men were caught at Chosin thanks to the brilliant planning of an egotistical demagogue by the name of Douglas MacArthur.

These days though life for William Dwyer, USA (Ret) consisted of a daily regimen of nickel slots and pitchers of beer sprinkled with war stories for any poor bastard who happened to be sitting within earshot.

"Thanks, but no thanks, Bill. Still on duty and all that."

Dusty Rhodes knew that this response would always work with Bill Dwyer. The laugh and conspiratorial nod followed with Dwyer turning his attention, limited as it was these days, back to the bar television.

"Subject has exited the lounge. Make sure you give him a room if he asks for one. It'll make our job a lot easier if 'Geisha 1' stays here voluntarily."

"Affirmative. He's at the front desk now."

The "hands-free" hook-up very discreet indeed. Just two businessmen talking to themselves. Nothing out of the ordinary here in Tokyo, or for that matter, any major city in the world these days.

Keiko Watanabe had been followed. Art Chambers, in one of the last heroic acts in a life resplendent with them, had managed to figure out the connection between his beloved Rose and Keiko. His old friends in Naval Intelligence had made sure he was given a daily brief, albeit unofficially, on all they had on the Aum Cult. To be sure, Art's initial reaction was one of outrage when he was told by the Naval Investigative Service that Rose was being followed by Asahara's soldiers. N.I.S. and Japanese Intel was in turn able to keep tabs on Aum. Tragically, they were not cognizant of the fact that Rose was actually a target herself until it was too late. In a sense, Rose Carney's death had served a purpose in that it exposed the fact that the Cult had sarin gas but, even more importantly, had developed a weapons grade variety of the lethal nerve agent. The night that Rose died, Art was to have let her know everything when they met at the Sanno. It was not to be, and Art Chambers died with the knowledge that he may have been at least partly responsible for his love's demise.

"Yes, Mr. Carter. No problem at all, sir. We have a suite available. Would that be all right?"

"Yea, great. I'm not sure how long I'll be staying...ahh...okay, reserve it for two days."

"Very good, sir."

Walking past the guy talking to himself. Benny Carter could spot a surveillance team a mile away. He'd noticed the first two as soon as they entered the bar. Keiko undoubtedly the mark. Benny approaching Keiko, the two agents no longer at the bar.

"Well, cherry blossom, one of us is living a good life, and I know it's not me, so...."

"Mr. Carter? Benny Carter, is that your name?"

The large, heavy frame of Dusty Rhodes directly behind Benny. Joe Dickwell a few feet to his left. Benny and Keiko cornered in the booth.

"Master Sergeant Benny Carter, United States Air Force, Retired to you, Mr....

"Rhodes, Dusty Rhodes, FBI Special Agent-in-Charge but in a previous life, 1st Marine Division, Khe San, Vietnam 1965 - 1968, Gunnery Sergeant...but you can call me Dusty. Life goes on with or without us, Master Sergeant."

A pause sensing the tension boiling over now and then, "This is Lieutenant Joe Dickwell of the Naval Investigative Service. May we join you? We'd just like to ask a few questions. Miss..." The nod towards Keiko, ashen faced now in the dark recess of the booth.

Benny smiling at Dickwell. Rhodes could be dealt with later. The rage at his earlier introduction temporarily put on the backburner. Not forgotten by any means.

"No problem. As long as you don't call me sir. As I said, I was enlisted. Tough break, Dickwell."

"Excuse me?"

"Kind of a double-whammy. Born with that last name and then becoming a Zero."

The derogatory term enlisted men used for officers not seeming to bother Dickwell.

"I'm proud of my rank, Master Sergeant, as I'm sure you are of yours. As for my name, well, let's just say I've kind of gotten used to it. Helped me learn how to fight as a kid too, if you get my drift."

Benny with the big smile now. This Dickwell maybe not such a bad guy. Some balls anyway.

"Yea, I had a few fights growing up myself. Course they weren't about my name, more about my "colorful" personality if you get my drift."

The tension easing. Rhodes sensing it. Glancing at Keiko as he sat down next to her. Dickwell moving in beside Carter.

"And how are you today, Miss...?"

"Look, you guys know exactly who she is already. This place is crawling with spooks. Let's cut to the godamn chase. She told me everything."

Keiko exploding, "Benny, no!"

Cutting her off, "This is for Art...and Rose, baby, We have to do this. It's the only way. There's not much time." And then to Joe and Dusty, "I got her a suite here as I'm sure you gentlemen already know. Maids probably bugging it right now. What do you say we all go up there?"

41

41

"The traitor is in Hiroo. The American hotel."

The small figure, shaking visibly in the dimly lit room. The heavy bass *thunpita, thumpita* from below. The music from the Gas Panic bar providing a surreal contrast. The group of sociopaths and general societal rejects in their samurai-like attire reminiscent of a scene from a Kurosawa movie. One floor below, the Thursday night crowd picking up. Americans, Japanese, assorted Iranians. Many of the Middle Easterners drawn to Roppongi by a burgeoning illicit phone card industry. All young and following the decadent siren song of the offspring of African slaves turned entrepreneurial millionaires in the West. Their toxic music being injected into first the Americas and now the unsuspecting East.

These the thoughts of the large, brooding bear known as The One to his followers. He stared through the hapless figure before him.

"You have failed, my son. Not only your brothers and sisters but yourself as well. You do understand this, do you not?"

"Master, I...we thought she was asleep. The drugs. She could not have awoke so soon. I only took my eyes off her...a minute, maybe two, or three..."

"Enough. You have failed, and you will die like the dog that you are."

The young man engulfed in pure terror now. With the Cult only a few months. A college student who had lost direction. Drugs, drinking, a perfect tool for the Cult. The other two sentries were already dead. The young man very much aware of this. The slight, almost imperceptive nod given by Asahara. The two soldiers out of the shadows, pulling the young man to his knees. The glint of the sword caught out of the corner of his eye. Thoughts of his mother and father. His first day of school. How odd. The blade taking his head from his body. The torso shaking violently. Asahara almost overcome with excitement. Touching himself. The others not daring to move. The body finally still. Asahara from out of nowhere. The head now in his hands. Raising it to his face. Kissing the dead lips now, tongue probing deep inside the still hot mouth. The dead, sweet mouth. A soldier vomits and runs from the room. Asahara releasing his lips and raising the hot cylinder in the air. The candlelit room lighting the maniacal otherworldly vestige that is the face of Shoko Asahara.

"Throw this garbage away. Atashi San, come, there is work to be done. The time of the rebirth is fast approaching."

"The car is downstairs in the alley, Master. The others are at the compound awaiting your arrival."

Atashi not betraying any outward signs of the horror that he had just witnessed. In the years that he had been with Asahara as his closest advisor, he had been present at many such examples of what most would call pure, unadulterated insanity. Atashi, however, preferred to think of these episodes as acceptable trade-offs when dealing with the evil genius of The One.

In the SUV now. A black Ford Bronco. The driver staring straight ahead as Asahara and his loyal henchman spoke in the back. The bullet-proof partition separating them from the driver who would, in any case, be executed upon reaching the Compound. No loose ends in the world of the divine leader of the Aum Cult.

"In two days' time, the world will be changed forever. A new world, my friend."

Atashi finding it somewhat disconcerting that Asahara had not bothered to wash the blood off his hands and face. When he spoke, it was in the low, almost humble tones that the Japanese people came to expect from sumo wrestlers. The difference though with Asahara was the unpredictable tirades that could transport him from a mild-mannered cerebral man to an enraged animal. No warning. Then, so swift as to be almost indiscernible, the polite, soft-spoken sumo wrestler would reappear. Atashi transfixed on the specks of blood mixed with bits of flesh that were curiously suspended from Asahara's lip.

"The Arabs will be there? All of them, I trust?"

"Yes, and the science and technology people as well, Master."

"Very well. And the cunt?"

"A martyr is in place. She will die within the hour."

In the world of Shoko Asahara, Keiko Watanabe was now a source of unrelenting outrage. The fact that she was a woman and had betrayed The One just added to his fury. She would die indeed. Asahara's only regret that he could not be there to personally carry out the execution. Impossible now though. He should have eliminated her earlier. The death of the Rose Carney harlot had ended the usefulness of Keiko. *Had he had a moment of weakness?*

Atashi's words brought him back to the task at hand.

. . . . .

Aum Cult compound number three was located about fifteen miles outside of Tokyo center. Tokyo, a city very much like Los Angeles in that it is basically spread out. It's prefectures would be called counties in California. Mass transit very much a part of the scene in Tokyo. Unlike Los Angeles though, the train and subway system spread throughout the metropolitan area probably the most clean and efficient in the world. The band of evil geniuses that were meeting in this idyllic country setting among the beautiful trees and singing larks, fully intended to change how the world viewed this system, forever.

As the SUV came to a halt in front of the country estate of Ren Hideo, former Chair of the Biological Sciences department at Tokyo University,

Atashi could have sworn the larks ceased in mid-song. Just his imagination, he thought. A casualty of a long day.

Hideo himself now exiting the house on the dead run. Arriving at the Bronco door just as Asahara himself came out.

"An honor, Master."

Bowing so low as to almost lick the multicolored pebbles that adorned the path to the front door of the house. This splintered genius once one of the most respected scientists in all of Japan. He had been approached by The One himself after a bitter divorce and the onset of heavy drinking. A few meetings, the proper drugs administered (everyone had their drug in the world of Shoko Asahara) and now devoid of a soul yet still intact, the intelligence necessary to accomplish the transformation of raw sarin to weapons grade form.

"I trust that you had a pleasant journey."

A slight stutter now that came and went. The drugs, the shattered life all possible causes. No matter, he would be redeemed. The wife who had helped destroy Ren Hideo would see once and for all the tragic error she had made when she left him. The university as well. Mistaking his genius for insanity. No one understanding him. Leaving the university finally, in disgrace. He needed to drink. The pills, valium, a haven as well. The constant firestorm raging in his mind needed to be quenched. Asahara his savior. Now all would be made right again. In just a few days. The wife would be part of the purification process. Part of the quenching.

"It was a fine journey, my son. Very pleasant, indeed."

The use of "son" not wasted on Atashi. The horrifying slaughter of the errant sentry still imprinted in his mind's eye. *Would Hideo suffer the same fate when his usefulness had expired?* No matter, Hideo's life, like the lives of the rest of the lemmings, had for all intents and purposes ended before their recruitment into the Cult. After all, thought Atashi, with a slight smile, the Cult was not a place for functional, shiny, happy people. Disposable people though. One and all.

"The others are awaiting your arrival, Master. They are in the upper room. All security measures have, of course, been tended to."

Asahara and Atashi followed their feeble host through the front rooms of the house. As they went past the Pollock and the Picasso, Atashi thought of the curious pairing, but then glanced at the owner and shrugged off the thought.

42

The lumbering mass of contorted flesh that was Dan Bronsan passed through the front doors of the Sanno Hotel in the same way that a supertanker might navigate its way through a lock of the Panama Canal. The palsied eye atop the superstructure reminding one of the erratic rotation of the navigation radar on one of those behemoths of the seas.

A tough day at the office for Dan. The Japanese engineers asking even stupider questions than usual, he thought. The trade-off for making the big bucks as Adam Welsh had said on a few occasions. Yes, thought Dan, life full of trade-offs.

"The Black Moses come to save the pagan infidels from themselves."

Dan spotting Benny Carter in the lobby. Eager to try out his latest witty salutation. No use just saying hello when one had a plethora of Shakespearean lines to throw out to the peasants, reasoned Dan.

"Oh, Dan, yea, how are you?"

Strange. No comeback, let alone any perceptible reaction from Benny Carter, one of the few people Dan rated as almost an equal in the art of intellectual banter. Too formal. Something wrong. The lobby for that matter, very different in some way. Too many suits.

"Benny, you old dog. Got some young lovely upstairs, aye? Well, before you go up, you'll have to meet Kelley, my daughter. She's here you know. Just got in yesterday."

The darting glance from Benny. First to Dan then to the dark-suited figure at the elevator about twenty feet away. Dan's look too late as the doors opened and Joe Dickwell disappeared.

"Look, Dan, got to go. I'm sorry. Give my best to Kelley. We'll all get together soon, old buddy."

"Old Buddy," Something definitely wrong with this picture.

"But Ben..."

Too late. Benny almost sprinting to the elevator. Doors sliding open and then closed. He was gone.

"Jesus wept."

Dan muttering to himself. The cute girl at the desk catching his sedentary eye. A new girl. Her bright badge indicating her name and her trainee status.

"Satsu, how are you today? My you are a beauty ... you must have a bit of the Emerald Isle in you, my darling, with those green eyes of yours."

Giggles emanating from the new girl. One of the things Dan loved about this country. The same line in Los Angeles or New York almost guaranteed to provoke a sneer or a dismissive, condescending ,"Can I help you, sir."

The allusion to the Irish not lost on the girl. One of the things one would not know without having experienced the Japanese culture here in Tokyo as Dan had. The close relationship between the Irish and the Japanese. Dan, the eternal historian, had attended numerous well-catered affairs sponsored by the Japanese-Irish Friendship Society. Between numerous bites of corned beef washed down by ample supplies of Guinness, Dan had learned that this unlikely alliance was forged largely as a result of World War II. Japan and Ireland both fought against the allies. This the common denominator in a friendship that was still going strong after all these years. Dan had hoisted many a pint with Peter O'Mara in fact, the Irish Ambassador to Japan at Paddy Foleys, the Irish pub in the center of Roppongi that was the rival of any drinking establishment in Dublin itself. The ambassador a decent enough guy though Dan wondered about his sexual preference at times. Adam Welsh having no doubts. Dan never did understand Adam's disdain for the man. Adam would drink with just about anyone, but when the ambassador arrived on the scene, Adam would go the other way. Dan would not have been so upset about it however except for the fact that it always seemed to be Adam's round on these occasions. Dan had since learned never to bring up the ambassador with Adam. On more than a few occasions he actually felt that Adam was going to take a swing at him.

"My friend, the old black gentleman that was just here..."

"The koku-jin."

Dan grimacing as this lovely lady unwittingly used the racist word which, when loosely translated from the Japanese, meant "chocolate man." She of course not meaning anything by it. Too innocent, her only sin, one of ignorance.

"My dear, yes, but 'koku-jin' is bad word."

"Oh, I am so sorry, I..."

Dan cutting her off with a knowing smile and a gesture to his lips.

"No problem, my dear. You didn't know. It's okay. Do you know what room he reserved?"

Timing. If Dan Bronsan had posed this question a mere ten minutes later when the shift changed, he may never have received an answer. Satsu being an employee in training always erred on the side of the hotel guest. The night manager, Starsky, a nickname bestowed by an inebriated sailor years before after the young man continually mispronounced his given name of Starkeo as Starsky, in any case had been fully briefed on the VIP guest staying in Suite 4012. The presence of the guest was not to be acknowledged, nor was she to have any visitors. Strict orders from Dusty Rhodes.

"It is 4012, sir. Would you like me to call her room, sir?"

Dan thinking quickly now, "No that won't be necessary, thanks. My daughter, Kelley, is here. She's actually registered as a guest of Adam Welsh. Could you call her room, please? It's Suite 3421, I believe. And call me Dan, please."

"Of course, si...I mean Dan San," the blush coming as naturally as a Tokyo sunrise.

"Hi, Dad, come on up."

The lilt in his daughter's voice. God, he hadn't remembered hearing that since her carefree pre-teen, pre-MS days. Maybe this trip was a good idea after all thought Dan Bronsan as Haruki Okamoto, also known as

Peanut, entered the elevator with him. One of the most notorious terrorists alive now dressed in a waiter's garb. The number 4 lit up on the panel. A grunt from the Japanese.

"Floor?"

"Three, please."

43

"The entire floor is closed off. Anybody asks, it's closed for renovation. Make sure everyone gets the word, Captain. No need to cause any panic. A simple renovation. Do you copy?"

"Roger that, Mr. Rhodes. Copied and understood."

Joe Dickwell, Dusty Rhodes, Benny here in the suite. Rhodes hanging up after relaying orders to the marine officer in charge of the security detachment. Keiko just finishing her story. Dumping everything she knew. Helpful, Dickwell thought but still no idea of where the actual sarin was and more importantly where and when it would be used. The target. Godamn it could be anything. Anyone. Anyplace.

"Keiko, you were never told or never heard anything that could give us an idea as to where the sarin gas is being stored. Where it's being refined to weapons grade?"

"Weapons grade?"

"I'm sorry. It's a term used to describe the process whereby the raw chemical is transformed into a product that can actually be lethal in nature. The raw product itself is almost harmless. Hell, a few years ago the Cult dumped a sack of it off the Tokyo Tower. No damage except for some litter and ruined wardrobes."

"I'm very sorry, Mr. Dickwell..."

"Please, call me Joe."

"Yes, Joe, sorry. I mean I worked at their storage facility in Ebisu but there were only empty canisters there at the time."

Dickwell nodded. The Ebisu facility had been used for the refinement of the small amount of sarin that had killed Rose Carney. It was actually owned by Keiko's father and had once contained furnished offices for his trucking company. Her father had passed away though, and Keiko's brothers proved to be as incompetent in business affairs as they were in the rest of their lives. The trucking business had been sold off. All but this building which had been kept under Keiko's stewardship. Dickwell knew by way of the intel that he was privy to, that the refinement of the sarin had been carried out completely unbeknownst to Keiko. The facility had also housed the legal team of the Aum Cult. A front more than anything else. A red herring of sorts. Keiko in her medicated state believing that she was simply part of an administrative effort. God help her when she discovers what she was really being used for, thought Dickwell. The Cult not very interested in operating within the legal system created by the decadent West. The Japanese police had in fact raided it shortly after the train station attack on the strength of an anonymous tip. Nothing there. Barren as a witches womb, to coin one of Commander Blasingame's phrases. Since then, all leads had ended in the same way. Nothing. Any time Navy Intelligence or the Japanese police were set to pick up someone in the Cult, that person or persons invariably ended up unable to provide any information due to the fact that the poor soul or souls had been knifed, poisoned or shot to death. Sometimes all three. Asahara it seemed, thought Dickwell, always one step ahead. Until now of course. The defection of Keiko had changed the game. Keiko Watanabe now the best, hell the only chance Dickwell and his cohorts had in averting the horrible impending slaughter. Burning daylight though, another Blasingame aphorism. Time definitely on the side of the bad guys.

44

The elevator lurching ever so slightly then grudgingly beginning its ascent. The two human beings within staring straight ahead, each with very different agendas this Thursday afternoon. Dan Bronsan wondering whether or not to speak to the rather odd looking Japanese man next to him. A quick glance and he thought better of it. Too much information to dissect and digest as it was without engaging in mindless pleasantries with this whack job. Dan already instantly categorizing the man. Normally an unfair exercise but in this case the assessment more accurate than he knew.

Dan pondering the events of the last few minutes. *What was Benny hiding? Why the unsociable behavior in the lobby that was so unlike the Benny Carter that Dan knew?* Fixated on the elevator wall. Dan thinking it would be a great idea to post copies of the Stars and Stripes, the military sponsored English language newspaper, along with a copy of one of the local Japanese rags. Something to concentrate on, particularly valuable in times such as these when one was stuck in a four by eight space alongside a creature the likes of Dan's elevator companion. Jesus the guy looked like Genghis bloody Khan in a waiter's uniform, thought Dan. The scowl. The Fu Man Chu. *Were hotel kitchen staff allowed to have that much facial hair?* Dan making a mental note to check on that. The bulge around the man's waist curious as well. Could be anything of course. Dan knew that a lot of the staff chose not to store their valuables in the room provided by the hotel. The extra girth on

"Khan" probably one of the waist-wallet contraptions Dan had seen many of the young tourists sporting these days. Kelley had one in fact.

While Dan mulled all of this, the man whose sole purpose left in life was the extermination of Keiko Watanabe stared at the row of elevator floor numbers directly above his head. First 2, then 3, and finally the doors sliding open.

"I'm sorry, gentlemen. Your IDs please."

The young marine guard firmly planted in front of the elevator door. One hand holding the elevator open as his body effectively blocked any exit.

"Aye, Corporal, what's all this?" Dan exclaimed as he passed his ID to the sentry. The terrorist/waiter a stone rendering of a samurai in the back of the elevator.

"Thank you, Mr. Bronsan. Just a routine security drill," he lied.

"We have to check the ID of everyone in the hotel."

Dan knew this marine. He'd seen him a few times at the Club on Yokosuka Base dancing the night away with various Japanese lovelies. Good kid. Name of Sullivan.

"Aye, Sully, understand. God, I don't miss that part of my days in the Nav. All the drills. The Old Navy, of course. I was in Nam, you know."

Sully flashing a brief forced smile. He'd been in this territory before with Mr. Bronsan. Better end the conversation quickly, he mused, or endure an entire watch listening to Dan Bronsan's ever changing personal history of the Vietnam war.

"Yes, sir, well come right out now and have a fine day. Everything seems to be in order."

Dan, not needing to be told twice but not able to resist a parting "Have a fine Navy day" shot to the young marine as he stepped out of the elevator and turned the corner towards Kelley's room.

The marine grimacing slightly at the reference to the Navy. The fact that the Marine Corps was a division of the U.S. Navy a sore spot for all marines. Regaining his composure quickly though. Addressing the Monster in the corner.

"Sir? Your ID please?"

"Of course, Corporal. I am sorry. You see, it seems that I have gotten on the wrong elevator. I wanted to go down rather than up. I am due back in the kitchen."

All of this spoken as Peanut took two almost imperceptible steps towards the marine.

Striking distance attained.

"I will go back down now," the weak smile now as Peanut attempts to close the door. The marine's arm thrusting forward in a reaction born of constant training. The Monster's wrist grabbed and held firmly.

"Sir. I will have to ask you to step outside the elevator and provide me with your identification papers immediately."

A brief pause. The tension palpable.

The autopsy report on Corporal Timothy Sullivan, USMC, would indicate that the young man had succumbed due to catastrophic trauma and extensive blood loss caused by his almost complete disembowelment with an everyday, household, razor-sharp box cutter. Pollen would never be mentioned in the coroner's report although, if the truth be told, the presence of pollen more than anything else was what precipitated the marine's untimely and tragic demise.

A fly on the wall, had he the cognitive and verbal skills of an average human being, would have been able to report that at the precise moment Corporal Sullivan's entire attention should have been focused on the terrorist called Peanut, a microscopic bit of dust that had a one in one billion chance of entering Timothy Sullivan's nostril at this critical moment, did just that. The resultant spasm of the man's sneeze was all that the Monster in the elevator, a trained killer, needed. As the marine's hand involuntarily released his arm, the killer removed the box cutter from the wrap around tourist waistband and in one continuous motion drove the household tool into the marine's lower abdomen, slicing open the man's large intestine in the process. An otherworldly gurgling sound emitted from somewhere deep inside the now critically wounded young man. The trained butcher pulled the blade straight down traversing from the navel to the now dead Corporal Timothy Sullivan's pelvis.

Time of the essence now. The terrorist dragged the butchered marine into the elevator and hit the Emergency Stop button. This action buying time but not much. Ten maybe fifteen minutes at the most was all the time he had. Of course the terrorist knew that he would never leave this place alive. No matter, the mission the most important thing. Destroy the cunt and he would die in the process. No worries. The Aussie expression commonly referring to a feeling of serenity curiously coming to mind. Yes, "No worries." Years of training, all in preparation for this final task. The removal of Keiko Watanabe the last obstacle in the Cult's global purification plan.

Chance an interesting concept. It had worked once in the Monster's favor but now, momentarily disoriented perhaps by the adrenaline needed to kill another human being, he forgot that he was on the 3rd Floor, not the 4th which is where a young desk trainee at the Sanno and sister of a Cult lawyer had said that Keiko Watanabe was being held under guard.

. . . . .

Dan Bronsan never could get used to the layout of these Japanese hotels. Sure this one was owned by the Department of Defense, but the Sanno Hotel still retained the feel and structure of a modern Japanese hotel. The numbering system particularly bothered Dan. In fact most of the suites did not even have the numbers displayed. Just a series of rooms with the names of American states emblazoned on their doors. He had just passed the New York suite in fact.

Thoughts floating back to his recent elevator companion. *Jesus, he was a weird one!* Dan thinking that maybe he should report the guy. No bother though. The marine looked like he would take care of any problems, Dan thought as he walked around the maze called Japanese hotel architecture, in search of Kelley's room.

Turning the corner. Strange the feelings of anxiety he had. No particular reason. Still, they were there though. A foreboding kind of feeling until; there it was. The door to Kelley's room, the New Jersey suite. Right there in front of Dan. His hand now pressing the buzzer and then... the footsteps.

Imperceptible at first. Building to a crescendo. Someone behind him. Turning slowly. Not daring yet needing to look until finally, there in the hallway, not more than twenty steps away, the figure from hell, Genghis Khan. Blood spattered over the waiters uniform. Something glistening in his hands.

"Dad!"

Kelley had opened the door just as the Monster began his death charge. No thoughts from Dan Bronsan. No logical plan. The difference between life and death all in the details of what he would do in the next few seconds. He knocked his daughter to the floor as he fell into the room. His three hundred plus mass of flesh and bone lying inert for a split second looking up at the door. The opened door. With the dexterity that could only have been provided by a power much greater than himself, Dan Bronsan raised himself off the floor and slammed the door shut. Thank God, he thought as he heard the locking mechanism automatically engage.

Silence for a brief moment and then the heavy animal-like breathing.

The Monster was behind the door.

45

"Look, look, Honaka! Up on big building!"

Little Honaka Aki loved to play in the Hiroo Park. In her six years on the planet, playing with her friends here was the happiest time of her life, almost as happy as the dinner hour when her father, Hiroshi, returned home from work at the Tokyo Metropolitan Department of Water. Daddy always brought his little princess a gift. Something every night. It wasn't the gift so much as the anticipation and the fact that Honoka knew that her father loved her more than anything in the world. Well, maybe not more than Mommy, but that was all right. She loved her Daddy and her Mommy with all the love that is contained in the heart of a little girl that is truly cared for.

Honoka, not seeing Daddy as much lately. Mommy telling her that he had to work late but not saying why. Honoka had heard talk about the "Bad People" who were in Tokyo now. She had heard this from her friend, Minato who played video games constantly and scared her with centipedes and generally was not to be trusted.

"Honoka, quick look. Bugs crawling up the side of the big house. Come see."

Honoka broke away from her mediation efforts involving a squabble between Barbie and Ken and looked up in the sky.

The "bugs" were indeed crawling up the side of the big house.

The marine repelling team had begun its journey up the façade of the New Sanno Hotel.

46

"Jack, I don't know what to say...Ah..."

"It's fine, Adam. Fine. Everything is just fine."

Sitting here in the waiting room. Adam and Jack. Yumiko still in surgery. No concept of time for either of them. It could have been an hour. Could have been a day.

Adam had seen Jack's face go rigid as the doctor had relayed the hopelessness of Yumiko's situation. There was a tinge of emotion, violence perhaps, in his eyes but only for a moment. It went out as if extinguished by some unseen force.

Adam thought of the Halon Fire Extinguishing System aboard ship. It was designed to put out engine room fires. Extremely effective but there was one trade-off. Fire is a living thing, and Halon removed what fire and human beings relied on to live – oxygen. Adam had heard of an incident aboard a sister ship of the McClusky's where three sailors became trapped in the engine room after the Halon System had been activated. They died of suffocation. The ship though was saved.

So here, now, his friend Jack sat across from him. Staring through vacant eyes. Something, not unlike Halon had been released behind those cold orbs extinguishing, perhaps forever, the soul of Jack Bender.

47

Adam and Jack back at the ship repair facility office now. Some poor bastard had decided to re-enlist. Another life thrown away and for what, Adam thinking. Three hots and a cot. That was about it. It wouldn't be long now till retirement. Enough waste for one life, he thought.

Rope-yarn an old Navy term for an unscheduled day off, had been declared. Everyone else had left a few hours earlier. Adam and his friend the only ones here now. Jack muddling about, pretending to be busy. The tension between them palpable.

"So will your buddy be at the meeting tonight?"

Adam breaking the silence with the reference to the man called Peanut whom Jack had been escorting to meetings up until the last few days.

"Jack?"

No answer. Jack Bender staring out the window towards the hills of Ikego and the bunkers.

Adam approaching his friend. Jack was shaking now. Something in his hands. A picture of Yumiko. Something pressed inside the picture. A cherry blossom from so many years ago. The tears came.

Adam Welsh hugged his friend. Jack alternately convulsing in a human pastel of tremors and tears only to become somewhat lucid while uttering the likes of, 'She was... a good woman,' Adam. A beautiful girl, you know.

It seems like yesterday. Kind of my higher power, that woman. Oh, I'll be all right now."

Adam feeling a sense of awkwardness at first. Self-centered to the extreme. A common denominator among alcoholics. A common killer as well. What Adam was doing now, despite the fact that Jack Bender was the only real friend he had in the world, went completely against the grain. The irony was that Jack was once again saving the life of his friend by revealing his own vulnerability to another human being. For helping his friend, being there for him, was indeed helping Adam get out of the prison that was his self. A prison that most alcoholics create, adding bits of mortar and brick with every drink until finally the walls surrounding them close in and there is only darkness.

"I'll be okay now, Adam. God bless you. I mean that from the bottom of my heart. When you are lying in bed tonight, entertaining the visitations of your various demons, know that you helped another human being today. The demons will not stay long."

Adam taken aback by the sudden change in his friend's entire demeanor. An emotional wreck a moment ago, at present a coherent, rational human being. Adam had seen this before. The time at the Ikego caves still fresh in his mind. Another day, unbeknownst to him, that Jack had saved his life. That day of course the peril had been to his corporeal being while today his friend, through his outpouring of grief, his vulnerability, had indeed helped save something more valuable - his very soul.

Back to his earlier question now.

"Peanut, have you seen him lately, Jack? You know, the weird guy you use to take to meetings?"

"Destruction, then rebirth, then..."

Adam not quite hearing the mumblings of his friend. Bits and pieces. Unintelligible. Now suddenly, more animate.

"Dying a good thing, right, Adam? A chance to cleanse. Yes, a cleansing."

Trailing off again. His face otherworldly now. Someone else there. Something else. Evil. Adam realizing now that this was the Jack Bender he had seen at the cave. A kind of lucid insanity, if that were possible.

"Sit, Jack. Sit right here at the Lieutenant's desk. You always wanted to be an officer, right? I'll get us some coffee. Real Navy coffee. Made it myself about eight hours ago. Should be just about ready."

The feeble attempt at humor lost on Jack. His eyes seeing something but not anything here in this room. What Jack Bender was seeing was more horrible than anything Adam could ever imagine.

48

"Jesus Christ, there's some asshole outside my room! He's got a knife or something. Send somebody up here now, you stupid bitch!"

Dan Bronsan, for the only time in his life (which he thought could end at any second) not unhappy with his daughter's lack of any pretense of social etiquette. Thankful for it, in fact. Miraculously the door had latched, keeping Genghis Kahn from entering and no doubt massacring them both.

To her credit, the "bitch" manning the desk, who only just recently had relieved the trainee/Aum spy, now in custody, immediately got on the radio.

"Problem on the third floor, Mr. Rhodes. One marine down. Suspect still at large. Converging on him now. Appears to be Japanese, dressed as a waiter. Weapon, razor-like, possibly a box-cutter."

"Keep me informed. Secure the entire complex. No one in or out. Who is the marine?"

A pause. Rhodes knew the worst had occurred.

"We have lost radio contact with Corporal Timothy Sullivan. A team has been dispatched to the elevator, his last known location."

A slight crack in the young marine's voice. Overcome quickly though. *Semper Fi.*

"I'm sorry."

"Aye, Lieutenant; I want the bastard alive if at all possible, but don't risk another man's life. If he doesn't surrender, liquidate his ass."

"Yes, sir."

Joe, Benny and Keiko all sensing the bad news. Rhodes' ashen face spoke volumes as he hung up the phone.

"They know you are here, Ms. Watanabe. They've sent someone to get you."

Averting Keiko's eyes. The deep black eyes. A quick glance and then away. Joe Dickwell knew that Rhodes blamed Keiko for whatever had caused his hands to tremble ever so slightly.

"It seems we have an intruder here, ladies and gentleman. We have reason to believe that he is after Ms. Watanabe. We also believe a marine may have been...assaulted."

Dusty's hands trembling a bit more now. Sullivan a good kid. The best. Nothing PC about him. Marine Corps all the way. Dusty had met Sullivan's parents when they'd visited last year. Proud of their "Little Tim." Now Rhodes likely would be writing them a letter telling them their only son, their world, was gone.

Dickwell, taking all of this in. Intent on Dusty. He had to bring him back into focus. Everything depended on it. There would be thousands more Tim Sullivan's if he didn't.

"Any idea who it could be, Dusty?"

Joe Dickwell knowing full well it was Aum. A soldier. No doubt sent to snuff Keiko before she gave away anything of importance. *What else did she know, anyway?*

A cackle came through on the radio. "Mr. Rhodes. One Marine is confirmed deceased...." and then, "It's a bloody mess. I'm sorry, sir."

Dusty seeming to gain a bit of composure. Years of training. Intent on the task at hand now.

Looking directly into the coal-like orbs now. No backing down.

"Ms. Watanabe, a United States Marine is dead. The Japanese assailant possibly posing as a waiter. The suspect evidently spoke English very well, much like yourself in fact."

A slight pause. A glance at Benny that said, *Don't say a godamn word. A marine is dead.* Benny sits back down.

"The suspect knew the logistics of the area and the building very well. A witness has said that they saw a Japanese national in restaurant worker garb not long ago. Any ideas on who he could be, Ms. Watanabe? He is still here. His own life is of no importance. He wants you at any cost. Of course, I'm sure you know this."

"Jesus H. Christ, stops this bullshit now."

Benny had had enough. Protecting his little daughter. Rhodes starting to move towards him. Fists balling up.

"You'll be safe here, Keiko."

Dickwell looking at Rhodes and Carter. Subtlety moving in between as he spoke to Keiko. Focus. No time for this now. Had to have focus. The god damn world at stake.

"What's the status, Dusty? Have they got the suspect cornered?"

Dickwell moving Dusty back to the matter at hand now. Turning away from Benny. Benny sitting down again. Lowering his head.

"He apparently tried to break into a guest room on the third floor."

Benny with a moment of clarity.

"God damn it, Dan and Kelley are in that room. Jesus I just saw him!"

Dusty not completely understanding.

"What is it?"

"He must have gone up to Kelley's room right behind me. This S.O.B. just missed us. Dan was probably in the f"in elevator with him. The bastard probably got confused."

• • •

The Sanno Hotel ballroom normally used for champagne brunch and wedding receptions was now the Command Center where all information needed for the pursuit and capture of the Aum Cult terrorist, dead or alive, would take place.

"Yes, sir, the entire perimeter of the hotel is secure. Nobody in or out."

"Very good, Captain."

Rhodes turning back towards the curious group in the suite. Benny Carter, retired Air Force Master Sergeant, Vietnam veteran, resident barfly and now, self-appointed father-protector of Keiko Watanabe.

Keiko, a walking, talking character right out of a Kafka piece. Beaten, broken yet here. Perhaps for redemption. Her own and that of scores of others.

Joe Dickwell, an ambiguous character, thought Dusty. Career military. Navy Investigative Service.

"Okay, for now we all sit right here. As I speak there are four teams closing in on the suite where the scum...the suspect is believed to be. We are in direct contact with the occupants of the suite. The suspect apparently has not made any attempt to enter the room by force."

Rhodes' avoidance of any eye contact with Keiko not lost on anyone in the room. Not the least of which, Keiko herself.

How many more innocent lives lost because of me?

When she had first gathered up whatever was left of her humanity to come here, to escape from Asahara and his amateur sentries, to tell all that she knew of Aum, a feeling of release of almost elation had engulfed her. Emotions; she was able to cry again, these had started to return. Maybe she could be a human being again.

Now, sitting in this room, sensing the hate, *yes, it was hate,* from the very soul of Dusty Rhodes, she felt the Harpies carrying her back to the darkness. She deserved the darkness of course, Keiko thought now. The life of drinking, partying, sex, sex and more sex, all to fill the void of course. The void that could only be filled by the true unconditional love of another human being. Never understanding this. Something she definitely had in common with Adam, she thought. *Where had Adam come from?* She thought she had obliterated all memory, yet, here he was again, taking up space, rent-free in her head.

Keiko Watanabe knew that there was only one course of action. Death would bring a cleansing to her. On this point, Shoko Asahara was indeed correct.

"Mr. Rhodes, if I may?"

"Yes, certainly, Ms. Watanabe."

The contempt resonating from his lips like the outstretched talon of a falcon inches from his prey.

Her body now taking on the aura of the resolute martyr. Dickwell couldn't take his eyes from her. *Was this what St Agnes looked like before she was burnt at the stake?*

"I know this man. He will not be taken alive. I alone must go to him. If I do not, others will surely die."

49

The hot, rancid, Navy coffee flowed down Adam Welsh's throat like old bathwater mixed with a heavy dose of caffeine. He had shared the death watch with his friend for what seemed like days but was in reality less than 12 hours

"Elixir of the Gods, my friend," he said as he clicked his mug labeled CTT1(SW) Welsh with Jack's. The mug, a remnant of happier days when he still had the Top Secret clearance. Respected. "Officer material," his old mentor, Lt. George Schue, had said on many occasion. Schue, a George Hamilton look-alike all the way from the slicked back black hair, olive skin, chiseled features to the pencil-thin moustache. One of the people in life that never ceased to be a cause of amazement, along with a twinge of envy to Adam. It seemed to Adam that Schue went through life as effortlessly as a winged dove arcing across the face of the sun on a hot summer's day. What was constant drama for Adam was an effortless journey for Lt. Schue. What further perplexed Adam was that the man actually seemed to expect life to be that way. Success, the attainment of all things desired, a virtual given.

Schue had seen something in Adam. Potential. The dreaded "P" word. What he didn't see was Davey and Joyce Welsh. Destitution and Denial. Schue and Welsh were the same yet very different. Schue had never sat on the top stair leading to his bedroom, jerking his leg in an almost spasmodic rhythm waiting for the .38 that his father had pressed against his temple in the bathroom, to go off. This is where the fork had occurred, one might argue, along the otherwise fairly similar road of dreaded potential that Schue and Adam Welsh had both traveled early on.

In any case, things had changed. After Adam lost his Top Secret clearance for drinking and causing a disturbance at the base enlisted club, Schue looked at him in a different light altogether. Adam would think later that he was now perceived as a pariah to his one-time surrogate older brother, but the truth be told, Schue just felt uncomfortable in the presence of failure. Particularly failure from a person whom he had thought of so highly. The ignorance, lack of understanding probably, did validate and confirm Adam's pariah perception, but it wasn't quite as simple as he thought. Schue was afraid of failure. Terrified of it and stayed away from it as a jonesing junky would flee from the needle. What had once been the manner of the fawning, proud, older brother, now turned to something not unlike revulsion. Schue now assuming the officer-mode with Adam relegated to his enlisted-puke status.

"Good coffee, Adam."

Back now, Jack sitting across the desk. The pictures of Lt. Parker's family, the officer in charge of the Toxic Waste Facility peering back at Adam. Little boy and little girl. Adoring wife. Everything but the white picket fence which in any case Adam felt was just outside the frame of the pictures. Adam had missed it all.

" Navy coffee. Put hair on your teeth, if I do say so myself."

An old joke that was always good for a knowing laugh. Jack's of the somewhat self-conscious variety though. Something there. Lurking behind the facade. Back to the day at the caves again. Adam wanting to speak but waiting. Let Jack be the first. The Inner Voice telling him so. The right thing to do.

"You're going to make it, Adam. I just know it. I just wish you'd take a bit of a more direct route to sobriety rather than the somewhat circuitous one you seem to prefer."

"Jesus, Jack, you think I like doing it this way?!"

Stopping to think. On the defensive now. Maybe he had wanted the booze all along. Still did but not the consequences though. Therein was the rub. Living sober with no booze to get him through the uncomfortability. Life on life's terms.

Jack smiling. Pushing Adam's buttons.

"Adam, you are doing great. I want you to make it. You're one of the good guys. So many don't get this. Try as they might."

"Jack, when you visit Yumiko, I'd like to go along if you don't mind."

Mutterings again. *Save yourself?* Inaudible.

"Oh, no Adam. Routine operation. They'll just go in, remove the poison and sew her back up. Routine. No need for you to come along. Go to the meeting. That's your priority now."

Adam about to interrupt his friend but thought better of it. He had been with Jack earlier when the doctor told them both that there was no hope for Yumiko Abe. Only a matter of time. Adam had helped his friend out of the waiting room with the promise that they would return with some of Yumiko's belongings. Now, Bender obviously in complete denial. Adam knew about denial. He decided to let his friend live in it for a short time longer.

Jack taking a long sip from the borrowed coffee cup that said "Number 1 Dad." A hint of trembling in his hand. Adam never remembering seeing his friend's hand shake.

50

The terrorist stood motionless in front of the suite. A passerby unfortunate enough to come upon the Monster might have mistaken him for a misplaced statue from Madame Tussauds. Perhaps from the Jack the Ripper tableau. The real human blood splattered all over this massive statue would give the lie to this assumption. The knife no wax replica at all. Recently removed from the innards of a once vital human being.

The matted hair atop the head began to shake slightly at first. Soon the entire mass of the fiend shook violently while beginning to laugh. A low guttural sound at first, building though, till finally a demonic-like crescendo of cackles came screaming from the evil within. Laughing maniacally, nose only a half an inch from the door.

Dan heard it first. Then Kelley. She began to scream in surprise and then recognition of the abomination inches away. Dan trying to console her.

"It's okay, my Celtic cutie. It's going to be all right."

Holding her now. Rocking his daughter gently in his arms. Possibly due to the stress of a near death experience, a hint of a smile began to take shape. Dan still rocking her gently. He hadn't called her "Celtic cutie" in years. The last time she could remember was when she was five years old and under an oddly similar set of circumstances.

Lying awake in her room she had been waiting for another kind of monster to go away. Although then, unlike now, the phantasm was of the make-believe variety. Actually, a very diplomatic monster. Believe in me for just awhile with the understanding that I will be gone with the coming of sleep or, in a more severe case, the light of the new day.

That time, years ago, the monster was not playing fair. The diplomacy of Yasser Arafat on a bad day. Simply not playing by the rules. As little Kelley came upon the border between consciousness and sleep where the monster would soon be left behind to be replaced by more user-friendly imaginings like, say the tooth fairy, she heard the moaning.

The moaning then the breathing. Heavy and rapid. The little girl of five getting out of bed slowly, tip-toeing to the door. Reaching it, the sounds became louder. Only inches away. Not knowing whether to open the door or just wait for it to stop.

What if IT came in?

A little prayer to Jesus, the one that Daddy had taught her.

Keep me safe from all things evil, My Lord and Savior, Jesus. Amen.

The five-year-old imp bringing forth the courage of Achilles as she slowly opened the door. The hinge creaking now. She prayed softly for it to quiet. Halfway open now. A shadow or...a figure of some kind? Huge in fact and then...a snore. The loudest, little Kelley had ever heard. A cry not of anguish but of glee. It was Daddy. Sleeping off the effects of Guinness Night at Lucky Baldwin's Olde English Pub.

Now, years later and thousands of miles away, Kelley remembered faintly the relief followed by the sadness. Daddy had been drunk again, and as the years went by, the drinking sprees had continued and with them her parents' marriage slowly crumbled until finally vanishing into the dust of resentment, hurt and love lost never to be regained.

"Kelley, call the desk again. Find out what the hell they're doing."

Before she could reach the phone, the Monster spoke.

"Keiko San, I am here. It is time."

A crashing, resounding thud against the door. Dan perplexed at first but then everything became clear. Not so for his daughter.

"Who the hell is Keiko?"

Kelley screaming again.

"Move away from the door, baby," and then, into the phone, "Hello, Command and Control or whatever the hell this is…"

"Yes, sir."

"Look, the whack job thinks that Keiko Watanabe is in our room. Any reason that he would be interested in her?"

Another thud, louder. Dan making a note to light a few candles at Mass if he ever got the opportunity in gratitude for the fact that this was an American style hotel and not your standard, papier-mâché of the Japanese variety. He and Kelley would surely be history by now if the latter was the case.

"Hold please, sir."

"Hold my Irish balls!"

Oh, Jesus, thought Dan. Kelley smiling though. Good sign. A tension breaker. No problem, Dan thinking. *He wants Keiko. He thinks she's in here.*

"Dad, I don't understand."

"Okay, baby, listen. Adam Welsh reserved this room for us. You remember me talking about him on a few occasions, I'm sure. Nice guy. A drunk. The fatal flaw. Anyway, his girlfriend was, is Keiko Watanabe. For some ungodly reason this assclown from hell wants Keiko and thinks she's in here

"It still doesn't make sense. Why?"

"Keiko San!"

The ranting of the Monster now. Unmistakable. Shaking the room like a boombox reverberating from the car of a recent graduate of the Los Angeles Unified School District. Dan, with a brief smile thinking of his friend Art.

God, how Art hated what Los Angele had become. The ignorance the most.

"Mr. Bronsan, we are working on the situation. We…"

"Dan, Benny Carter here. Stay away from the goddamn door. Help is on its way."

"Benny…"

The explosion knocked the phone from his hand. Smoke all around.

"Kelley, are you alright! Kelley! Jesus, where are you!?"

Silence. Almost serene now.

The plastique hidden in the innocuous tourist bag belonging to the terrorist had worked well. The Monster was amongst them. Here in the room, through the smoke. The silhouette began to shake, then the guttural laugh. The sound of pure evil.

"Daddy, I'm okay. Where are you?"

"Keiko, my darling. At last we shall be cleansed together."

Dan seeing his worst nightmare unfold. Through the smoke he caught a brief glimpse of the Monster. He was standing directly over Kelley. The shiny object in his hand like a beacon through the fog. Not a friendly one however. The knife only inches from his precious daughter's neck.

Then the rains came.

. . . . . .

"Sir, the sprinkler system in the New Jersey suite has been activated."

"Any idea why?"

"Sir, Team One is in the western grid and reports an explosion with heavy smoke throughout the passageway."

"Any communication with the occupants, the civilians in the room?"

"We are trying to raise them now. Stand by please, sir."

Kelley Bronsan would reflect later how inexplicably the image of the Wicked Witch of the East from the *Wizard of Oz* had entered her thoughts. As a young girl she had watched the classic a million times. The constant being her terror no matter how many times she saw the witch. That god damn bitch scared the hell out of her. Apple lying very close to the tree on this point. Dad had mentioned the feelings of trepidation that came over him even as an adult every time he saw that friggin Margaret Hamilton, the actress who played the witch. Her Mom would bring up a great story about it every chance she got to Dan's eternal consternation.

One night before Kelley was born or when she was just a baby, probably in the sixties, Cathy Bronsan could never quite pinpoint the exact date, Dan and his friends were imbibing at a local bar in Asia someplace. This was when he was serving during the Viet Nam War. Anyway they're watching Super Bowl commercials that Cathy had sent from the states. One drawback for the ex-pat or serviceman overseas was that although one could see American television courtesy of Armed Forces Radio and Television System or A-FARTS as it was lovingly referred to, one could not view the American commercials. Sometimes they were even better than the game.

"Anyway," Cathy went on, "while watching one of these Super Bowl commercials, who comes on but Margaret Hamilton riding her trademark bicycle down the lane but this time a can of Maxwell House in the basket instead of Toto. No matter to poor Dan. He actually froze in mid gulp and then put his whiskey back down on the bar. "(An anomaly never seen before or since, Cathy loved to point out.) "The man looked like he had seen a ghost, which indeed, truth be told, he had. His shipmates that day at the bar actually thought he was going to have a stroke."

"Jesus, Dan you okay," Snuffy Perry, a boiler tech who died a year later in the fire aboard the USS Forestall, had asked.

Nothing.

There was Margaret Hamilton, the Wicked Witch of the East, sitting at a kitchen table content as can be drinking a cup of Maxwell House coffee and exclaiming for all to hear, "Mmmm Mmmm good!"

This was too much for poor Dan.

Snuffy recounted that Dan uttered the words "My Jesus God Almighty!" and ordered a double and drinks all around. He shot the double in one gulp. Not a word was ever mentioned in his presence about the incident ever again. Except of course by the long suffering Cathy Bronsan. Kelley heard it probably almost as many times as she had actually seen *The Wizard of Oz*.

An updated somewhat surreal version of Oz now playing in the New Jersey suite. Peanut the Witch to Kelley's Dorothy. Dan the Cowardly Lion watching helplessly as the cold steel descended towards his daughter.

"Ahhhhhhh!"

The sprinkler system projecting water directly into the eyes of the witch. Was he/she melting? The knife falling to the ground. The Monster dropping it as his hand reflexively went to his eyes. Wiping the water and the smoke away with one quick motion. His prey now clearly visible for the first time followed by the realization that this was not Keiko staring up in terror at him from the floor. At this moment the Monster was vulnerable. A window of opportunity for Dan or Kelley, maybe a few seconds. It came and then it went. The Witch/Monster pouncing on Dorothy as she reached for the knife. No Toto in sight. The Lion too far away.

The Monster beat Kelley to the knife by probably a nanosecond. Simultaneously grabbing the knife while wrapping a bear-like arm around her. Standing up now, Kelley in his arms. The knife at her jugular.

"No. Jesus, God in Heaven! Please. No!"

"Be still, gaijin pig. This one is of no consequence to me. Tell the American bastards to bring Keiko to me now or this cunt will die."

Anger enveloping Dan Bronsan. The fear gone. This scum would die. If it took the rest of his days. He would die. Of this Dan was certain.

Fighting to compose himself now though. Everything, his daughter's life at the balance. Winning.

"Yes, yes, anything you want. Who is Keiko?"

Not a good liar. In any case he knew that Keiko was somewhere in the hotel.

Roaring now.

"Bring me Keiko San!"

The tip of the knife glistening against Kelley's pink skin. She stared straight ahead. A look of utter resignation.

51

"That's crazy talk girl. You're not going anywhere. Tell her, Joe. Rhodes, Jesus, someone talk sense into this girl."

Logic, or sense for that matter, were not on the table here in the Missouri suite. The latest communications from Team One at the scene were that the Aum soldier had entered the civilian's room and had taken both hostage. His demands were very simple. Kelley Bronsan for Keiko Watanabe.

Team One had only been seconds from taking the terrorist out when the explosion had occurred. Now the four marines who would have liked nothing better than to have drawn and quartered the murderer of Corporal Timothy Sullivan, U.S.M.C were ordered to remain on station and await further orders.

A fly on the wall in the Missouri Suite may have taken the occupants for mourners at a wake. Keiko, head in her hands, leaning forward slightly, no visible expression. Benny Carter with a pleading, anguished look. Dusty, rigid in his chair, almost at attention, all eyes on him, waiting on the words he had already decided; the inevitable.

Keiko would have to go to the Aum soldier.

Dusty broke the silence.

"Ms. Watanabe…"

"Keiko, please."

"Yes, Keiko, what do you think you could accomplish by confronting this murderer? Even if I were to let you go, which I'm most certainly not going to do. Aside from the obvious guilt factor inherent in having your blood on my hands, there is the problem that you are worth much more to us alive than dead."

Benny, with a glare of utter hate. A jaguar waiting to pounce. Not moving though.

Yet.

Keiko without emotion. Businesslike. The dead Keiko back.

"I have told you everything. There is nothing left to tell. I am of no further use to you as to the plans of Aum. They do not suffer traitors lightly. In any case I am as good as dead now."

"Keiko, no! God no! How can you talk like that, little daughter?"

"Sir, the intruder is giving us an hour."

Rhodes in communication with Command and Control I in the hotel Ballroom.

"Okay, Ms. Watanabe, you have my complete, undivided attention. I let you go to this...soldier. What do you plan to do?"

All eyes on Keiko now. This small, fragile creature. The geisha doll relegated to hell now.

"Bring me to him. I know how to talk to him. You must believe me."

"What about you, baby? You can't do this. Please, little daughter, it's suicide."

Keiko put her small hand on the bald headed black man's now slightly trembling shoulder. He was close to tears.

"I have to do this, Benny San. It is the only way. No more innocents... like Rose."

Trailing off now. You could hear a pin drop.

"Lieutenant, send the auxiliary team up here ASAP."

"On their way, Sir."

Turning back to the assembled cast now. A look of communal, stunned acceptance. A feeling of finality hanging in the air. Keiko would go to the Monster.

52

"Jack, let me go with you. Nothing better to do, you know. No life since I stopped drinking and all that."

The humor lost on Jack Bender. Adam Welsh watched as his now desperate friend scrambled about looking for the car keys that were in his hand. Incoherent. The unnatural, albeit relaxed mood of earlier gone now.

"Ah, what, Adam? No, no...it's okay. Oh, Jesus, the damn keys. Here they are. Senior moment there I guess."

A weak laugh. Adam trying to move the muscles that would have formed a smile on his lips. Might as well have tried to bench press 220 with his tongue. In any case, Jack oblivious.

"Yea, just a routine thing. Probably need me to fill out some paper work. These Japanese hospitals very big on the paperwork. More than the damn Navy hospitals, if that's possible."

Jack had answered the earlier phone call from the hospital. Adam had seen the look on his friend's face as he listened to the disembodied voice on the other end of the phone line. The only paperwork that his dear friend would be filling out would be of the death certificate variety.

"I insist old buddy. Not a problem."

He gently maneuvered his friend out of the office and down the stairs to the car, Jack uttering feeble objections while clenching one of Yumiko's kimonos in his hands. He finally slumped into the front passenger seat, letting the younger man drive. A light drizzle was beginning to fall. June in Japan, the rainy season still a few months off. This weather not unusual though. It would be like this on and off throughout the early summer. The typhoons wouldn't come till later though. A flash crossing Adam's mind. Strapped into his "rack" the loving term used to describe the compartment that he slept in while aboard ship. He was riding out twenty-five foot swells as the ship navigated in between three super typhoons. All of this accompanied by a stubborn hang-over. These lasting longer and longer in direct proportion to Adam's aging process. Not a kid anymore.

Thank God he was off that boat.

Adam turned the ignition on, the radio chiming in simultaneously with the rumble of the 84 Toyota.

"....within a five block radius of the New Sanno Hotel, closed until further notice. No word from any authorities, Japanese or American as to why as yet. We can only assume an exercise. Stay tuned to Armed Forces Radio for further developments. Now back to the Charlie Tuna Show here on AFRTS."

"Jack, Yumiko is in the Hiroo Hospital, right?"

Adam knew of course. A feeble attempt at small talk.

"Yes. Yes...turn the radio back on...please."

Some kind of jingle. No doubt a high-tech AFRTS public service spot. God, Adam missed the stateside commercials. He would be happy with "Mr. Whipple and the Charmin" right now. Anything, but here it was again. The trials and tribulations of the poor Air Force guy forced to have a roommate on base.

"Damn."

Jack muttering; something wrong. Sure, probably upset about the time it would take to reach Hiroo Hospital. Located just a couple of blocks from the Sanno. Adam had gone there after being beaten by the "Watusi" what seemed like eons ago. Just last year though. So much had happened since.

"Jack, don't worry. I'm sure they will be allowing traffic into the hospital. We'll get you there, my friend. Remember that Au...."

"Godamn it, Adam, shut the fuck up. Just drive!"

Someone else in the car now. Jack Bender was having a breakdown of some sort. There was no doubt in Adam's mind. They would find a way to get to Hiroo Hospital. Adam would make sure his friend did not leave once they got there though. He would insist on it.

Mutterings under the older man's breath. Inaudible until...

"Adam, I'm sorry. Please get me to the hospital. Get me to my wife. I need to see my wife before..."

The tears coming now. Good tears, Adam thought. Maybe tears of cleansing. He held his friend for what seemed like an eternity. No words spoken. Finally the embrace was broken without a word and Adam began the drive.

"You know how they're always doing exercises over at the Sanno, Jack. I remember one year they closed it for the whole weekend. Godamn was I pissed. Had a suite reserved, plenty of money...the drunk sailor was going to prove the stereotype."

He winced as he recounted this seemingly minor detail. He was going out with Keiko at the time, but the cheating was at its zenith. The only reason he stayed with her was because the Sanno was closed and one night of partying in Roppongi had depleted his funds. She knew this of course but took him in anyway. Denial.

No response from his friend. Jack sitting rigid in the passenger seat. Eyes glued to the road ahead. Hadn't said a word since his breakdown at the base just before they left.

"Yea, always doing exercises," Adam continued. "Especially now with all of this gas stuff and everything. Yea, just a drill. I'm sure of it."

Jack, even in his current state, not believing a word. Of course he knew better. Jack Bender knew what was happening at the Sanno Hotel. Not exactly what was taking place, but he could piece together puzzles with the best of them. Jack had not seen or heard from Peanut in over a week. That could only mean that Aum was utilizing him in some sort of manner of which he was specifically trained. Peanut was a killer. Pure and simple. There was no drill at the Sanno Hotel. Of this Jack Bender was as certain as the belief that his beloved Yumiko was already dead.

53

"There is a problem, Divine One."

Shoko Asahara stood motionless in the dimly-lit room. His back to the unfortunate messenger who had been given the task of informing his leader that the mission at the Sanno Hotel had not gone quite as planned.

Taka was his name. About nineteen years old. A zealot brought in like many of the others from university. His parents had once had high hopes for the boy whose nickname was taken from his adoration of the sumo champion, Takonahana. His story not unusual The pressure of university to make grades soon lead to drugs, alcohol and finally dismissal in disgrace and then perhaps, inevitably to Aum.

"Leave at once. No one is to enter here."

"It is done, Divine One."

Taka leaving immediately. Relieved to be free from the darkness that was Shoko Asahara.

A minor complication thought the brooding figure, sitting alone now in the antechamber. He would deal with the traitor. Of this he had no doubt. She would be cleansed. Time now to concentrate on the more immediate matters at hand.

"The Master wishes to be left alone."

"Yes, of course. You gave him the news?"

A nod. It had been done. Taka shaking. Glad to be alive.

. . . .

The curious group that had been summoned by Aum all gathered around the 17th century, Louis IV marble table in the library. Each and every one protected by diplomatic immunity. The Iraqi Chief of Staff here for the ambassador. Iraq the supplier of the sarin. The other terrorists seated in statesman-like attire all representing various havens of terror throughout the Middle East, Africa and Europe. Most providing financial and logistical support with the lone representative from Europe, Minister Lemieux, a tall man with a moustache and an accent right out of a Godard film, handling the air transport of the deadly sarin on its travels through Europe enroute eventually to where it rested now – A non-descript World War II era cave outside of Yokosuka Naval Base in Japan. Sitting quietly awaiting the whim of a Madman.

Lemieux had been staring intently at the gold leaf adorning the base of his long deceased compatriot's prize possession, musing on the bizarre twists that history had taken for this exquisite symbol of a truly civilized world, now sitting here in the decadent outpost of a psychopath. His back was to the huge wrought iron door when it swung open as if hit by a Kansas tornado, missing his head by a matter of centimeters.

The One loved to make an entrance, Atashi thought as the door crashed into the wall, fully open now. Shoko Asahara stood before them naked and aroused. The pulsating head of his engorged penis stood, it's one-eye quizzically pondering the aghast figure of Lemieux as he lay prostrate on the palatial floor.

"Gentlemen, don't get up. Please, excuse my tardiness. A few minor matters to attend to. Anyway, you have my undivided attention. Please take your seat, Minister Lemieux."

Lemieux rising slowly, grabbing the leg of the chair. Taking his seat now. The rest of the assemblage remarkably nonplussed considering the specter that now seated itself at the head of the table. Louis IV no doubt in some far off dimension spinning with the G-force of a Saturn V rocket plummeting towards earth.

"Master, your robe."

"Ah, yes, my robe. An appendage almost. Necessary, I suppose."

Rising now, donning the black silk wrap-around.

"Now to the matters at hand, my friends. I can call you my friends? I feel a certain camaraderie, if you will. All we have been through together. Your many sacrifices."

Looking directly into the eyes of Lemieux. The Frenchman's brother had died months earlier during an experiment to develop weapons grade sarin. It had gone horribly wrong. The brother taking weeks to die. Suffering until his final torturous gasp of breath.

Asahara turning back to the assembled state sponsored murderers.

"There is a problem, gentleman. I'm sure that you have seen the news on the unfortunate development at the New Sanno Hotel in Hiroo. Some unfinished business is, alas, still unfinished. A minor hindrance to our all but certain victory."

Lemieux, a slight quiver to his lip, trying to keep eye contact with the Madman, finally looking away.

"In any event, all plans will be expedited. In two days' time, the world as we know it will cease to exist."

"Does Baghdad have the capability..."

"You question me?!"

Lemieux melting back into the French chair. One could have mistaken him for a bowl of Jell-O at this juncture. Asahara screaming so hard that his robe opened exposing himself again to the gathered despots. A mood of unsettledness descending on the room.

"Everything is already in place no thanks to your government, my French friend. The genie is in the bottle ready to be released. It is here, gentlemen. The genie will wreak the wrath of the Almighty very soon, while the American Satan is distracted by the once pure daughters of the empire, now soiled vermin. Yes, the cleansing will begin very shortly. Eternal cleansing and then rebirth. Mr. Atashi will now brief you on the details."

Lemieux fixating on the Madman's love for the idiom. A trait shared by many a Japanese school girl. They loved their idioms. Yes, indeed. This foray into grammatical preferences more than likely his mind's way of providing a release from the overwhelming absurdity of the current situation the Frenchman found himself in. Play the part, though. Play the part. My time will come, he thought. The redemption of his brother.

Asahara with one last soul searing glance at Lemieux, leaving as Atashi stepped to the front of the room.

"Gentlemen, whatever happens at the Sanno Hotel will have absolutely no bearing on our plan, I can assure you. It may actually turn out to be a welcome diversion."

The screen emerged. Originating seemingly from one of the gothic lions perched above them. A hologram of sorts to the unaided eye. Illuminated now to reveal Yokosuka Naval Base, Ikego Caves and Tokyo proper with the entertainment district of Roppongi highlighted.

"As The One so beautifully stated, the genie is in the bottle – Ikego Cave number 134 located here. We would like to thank our Iraqi and Syrian friends who in concert with certain French port authorities made it possible for the genie to make safe passage from Baghdad to the bottle here at Ikego."

Scanning the door quickly, satisfied Asahara would not be coming back, Lemieux spoke.

"What now? The American and Japanese know that there is at least some sarin here in the country. The little debacle at the train station assured them of that knowledge at least."

"A good point my friend. Necessary. Another diversion. The sarin used at the station can be traced to an American biological and germ warfare center just outside of Richmond, Virginia. Before American intelligence finds out where the weapons grade sarin is coming from, it will be too late."

Atashi saw the look of doubt on the French minister's face.

"You have concerns, Minister Lemieux?"

A look at the door and then, "Let's just say I have a feeling that we have not been fully briefed."

"In time, my dear Minister, in time."

54

Yumiko Chan! We are here. Look Yumiko.

The light became brighter and brighter. First, a distant speck, now the brightest most glorious thing Yumiko Bender nee Abe had ever seen. It was the voice of her sister, Kiki. It couldn't be, but it was. Little Kiki, long ago incinerated at Hiroshima. Her and Mother. Barely time to think of Mother and now, coming out of the pure white light, more figures. Her father now. Her dear, sainted father and alongside him, some men. Men in uniform. American men. She knew from somewhere deep inside who they were. The crew of the Enola Gay. The boys from Oz.

"Maam, welcome. I'm Lieutenant..."

"I know who are." No need to tell her. The Voice had made it clear. She felt the pain emitting from the young pilot of the Enola Gay. She reached out to embrace him. To embrace them all. Peace came. Serenity. Unbelievable joy. Her father now. *Father, I love you so.* There were no words to describe her feelings. Moving closer to him, taking his hand and...stopping.

Jack, where are you Jack? I don't want to leave you.

Something from deep inside her. The Inner Voice telling Yumiko that Jack would be "daijoubu" – okay. All was as it was supposed to be. It was time to go and so, Yumiko Bender, the name felt so natural now as she heard herself say it, turned and looked into the forever young bright eyes of the American pilot and knew that she would be okay.

She was home.

55

It was dusk when he pulled the Toyota into the visitors parking space at Hiroo Hospital. The beginning of the end of a long day. Adam turned to say something to Jack, but he was already out of the car and heading for the hospital entrance doors. Nothing really to say anyway, thought Adam. He turned off the old car's engine and followed his friend in.

"I need my wife now. Where is she?"

Adam thinking maybe they should have stayed at the hospital and not left earlier. Jack seemed so exhausted though. It seemed like a good idea at the time for him to get some rest. Hindsight twenty-twenty of course, he thought.

Jack, at the visitors desk, visibly shaken even from Adam's vantage point ten or fifteen feet behind him. From the corner of his eye, a tall lanky figure. An air of authority. Yumiko's attending physician. Adam recognized him from an earlier visit. Right on cue. Maybe there was a God.

"Mr. Bender, please follow me."

Adam falling in behind the doctor, and Jack touching his friend's shoulder.

"Jack, it's going to be okay." Knowing of course that it was not and would never be okay for his friend. Jack Bender taking on the countenance of someone who had just been hit right between the eyes with something cold and hard. Life. Moving now not unlike one of the zombies Adam remembered from a long ago movie he had seen as a kid. Part of a Saturday afternoon double-feature show at the Bar Harbor Shopping Center. Mom would give him a dollar-fifty, the price of admission along with enough left for a popcorn and soda, so Adam would be out of the house when Davey Welsh was having a particularly tough time with his demons.

Carnival of Lost Souls. That was the name of the movie. Funny how certain things, names, places never left you. The main character doomed from the very beginning. Already dead in fact. A lost soul. Not knowing it but a sense of dread and impending doom inhabiting the character from the opening credits, Adam remembered. Watching his friend now.

Jack shuffling along behind the doctor. The Lost Soul.

"Adam, wait for me in the cafeteria. Get us some coffee. Please."

The look from Jack said there would be no discussion. He needed to see his wife alone. For the last time.

"Sure thing, Jack. It won't be as good as Navy coffee but I'll try to make it close. Give my best to...."

The look from the doctor said it all. Yumiko was gone. Jack knew it all along. From the time they left the base. He would see the love of his life one last time. Alone.

Adam started for the cafeteria elevator when he was hit with what later he would remember as a "God Shot," A.A. parlance for a sudden spiritual intervention. For no apparent reason he stopped in his tracks, turned and walked towards his friend Jack. Jack Bender, his savior. The conquering Angel in Adam Welsh's life. He called after him.

"Jack, one minute."

Bender stopped. His back still to Adam but shaking. When he turned, the tears had begun to fall. The face red. Adam took his friend in his arms and held him.

"From the bottom of my heart, Jack, thank you for saving, no, giving me my life. I love you, my friend. My dear, dear friend."

Jack crying softly now. Released the embrace and looked up at Adam.

"No words necessary. I understand. I will go to my Yumiko now."

And then Jack Bender turned to Adam and said the word that would haunt the younger man in the days and weeks to come.

"Goodbye."

56

The silence was stifling. Benny thought he would suffocate in it. They all knew that Keiko was right. They needed to act quickly. If they stormed the room, Dan and his daughter would surely die. No, the only thing left to do was to send in Keiko Watanabe.

Dusty broke the silence.

"Ms. Watanabe...Keiko."

His tone softening now. Joe picked up on it right away. *Good for you, Dusty.*

"A marine escort will walk you down to the room. At the end of the hall, the terrorist's vision zone, you will be on your own. We need you to demand his complete attention for at least one minute once you get inside the room."

"He will have my undivided attention."

Something disconcerting in the tone.

"Yes...well as long as you don't put yourself in any unnecessary jeopardy."

"Jesus H. Christ! Undue jeopardy? She's going to be in the same room with the S.O.B. that just gutted..."

The glare stopped him.

"Jesus, Dusty. Damn, I'm sorry. I know the kid was special to you."

"They're all special. Now, let's move on, shall we?"

. . . . .

The New Jersey suite looking like Newark on a bad day. The smoke still hanging in the air reminding one of a typical smog-filled day in the city.

"Are you all right, Dad?"

"Fine. Don't worry about your old man. I've had worse days, but truth be told I wouldn't be about to name one off the top of my head."

Kelley smiling now. Dad, of course, was terrified. More for her than anything else. If they ever got out of this she silently vowed she would spend more time with him. Maybe even move over here for a while. Take some courses at the University of Maryland Extension on the base. Then there was Joe. She wondered what he was doing at this moment. Out of nowhere. Christ why the hell was she thinking of Joe Dickwell at this of all times? She might die. As good a reason as any came the answer from some unseen inner voice. She smiled.

The phone rang.

"Pick it up, gaijin baca!"

The slur not lost on Dan.

"Yes, this is Bronsan."

"Mr. Bronsan, we are sending Ms. Watanabe down there. She will be arriving in ten minutes time. Please..."

"Are you crazy man! She'll be..."

"The Monster's look stopped him. Dan realizing now that there had to be a method to this madness. Rhodes was no fool. A good man.

"Yes, fine. Okay."

"Mr. Bronsan, this is Lieutenant Farrow at the Command Center. These orders come directly from Mr. Rhodes. Please pass this information on to the ...intruder."

"What are they saying? Give me the phone, now."

Peanut grabbing the receiver which resembled a toy in his massive paw. Nodding now as he listened to the disembodied voice at the other end of the line. Smiling. Satisfied.

"Ten minutes. No more."

Looking at Kelley.

"I will kill then both if there are any, how do you say...mix-ups."

Dan grimacing. Re-filing the mental note that he would send this bastard straight to hell if he ever got out of this. Why did he let his pride and joy, his very life, come to Japan? He would never forgive himself if...

"Stand in front of the doorway. Make yourself visible to anyone coming down the hallway. I am not worried that you roam too far. The crippled bitch will die if you do."

Grinning as he said this. A demonic contortion to the already horrible visage.

"You fat tub of rotten pig lard! Call me a cripple again..."

"Kelley, Jesus, Mary and Joseph!"

Peanut temporarily confused by the pig lard reference. Not really knowing whether to feel insulted or not. Finally, lowering himself onto the couch, a loveseat actually. The only piece of furniture that would accommodate the Monster. Pulling Kelley down next to him, knife poised at her breast. Staring at the clock on the wall. Five more minutes and Keiko would be his.

57

"This is a kind of miniaturized intercom, Ms. Watanabe. We need to monitor everything that is going on while you are in there. It will be hidden here inside this pouch on your belt. Completely discreet. Do not open this belt for any reason."

Keiko nodding. She wasn't really listening though. In any case, none of this mattered. The ending would be the same. Neither she nor Peanut would leave this place alive.

"Sir, we're ready."

"Very well."

Dusty hanging up the phone. Benny head in hand. Keiko, resolute.

"Ms. Watanabe, Lt. Dickwell will escort you to the suite."

"Joe, Godspeed."

"But I thought the Marine guard would be..."

"You will be in the best of hands with the Lieutenant. The marines will be otherwise occupied. Please go. Now."

"Take care, baby. LT, you let anything happen to my baby, it's your ass."

"Message copied and understood, Master Sergeant Carter."

"Shall we, Ms. Watanabe?"

"Good luck, Joe."

"Remember, Keiko, we need him occupied for at least one minute."

"I understand..., Dusty."

The slight smile. Almost imperceptible but not eluding Dusty. Acknowledged in kind. Dickwell led Keiko out of the room and into the hallway.

"I'll accompany you to just inside his field of vision which will probably be right after we exit the elevator and turn towards the suite. Knock once on the door...well of course there is no door anymore...just wait for his instructions. Keep him as far away from the hostages as possible."

"I understand. You obviously want to create a diversion. He is crazy but is by no means a fool."

They entered the elevator and headed down in silence.

"She is on her way."

Dan hanging up the phone and relaying the message with clenched teeth.

"Go back to the doorway. Signal to me when you see her."

Kelley starting to move towards her father. The knife pressed closer to her throat in an instant.

"The girl stays here with me."

"You know I wouldn't have minded this as much if you had taken a shower this week, you fat pig."

Dan grimacing as he headed for the doorway. Admiring and admonishing at the same time.

"Kelley..."

"I'm fine, Dad. Tons of fun here doesn't get it anyway. He was taking Terrorist 101 the day they taught idioms at his English school."

A grunt the only response from Genghis Khan.

"They're here."

Dan spotting Keiko and the American. He'd seen him someplace before. Couldn't place him though for the moment. Not of any importance now. He needed to think as fast as he had ever thought in his entire life. The life of his daughter depended on it.

Keiko smiling thinly as she approached.

Dan praying softly, "God save the little flower. God save us all."

"When she gets to the door, stop her. Wait for my command. Remember where the knife is."

"Hello, Dan San," under her breathe.

The idea that Peanut should know of her relationship with Dan Bronsan could of course be lethal for all of them. The sight of Keiko bringing back a flood of memories for Dan. Better days to be sure. Of course no time to dwell. He leaned forward to give her a hug. She merely bowed and lost her balance. A practiced move. Dan caught her, and as he did, she passed the box cutter that she had picked up from the construction site earlier to Dan's shirt pocket. An unplanned decision that she made while Benny had been talking to the marine guard. The box cutter forgotten by a worker from the cement barricades construction. An impulsive act. One of those gifts from the universe, she reckoned.

"What is this! Bring the cunt to me! Move away from the doorway...Now!"

Dan, taken aback at first by the orchestrated fall, regained his composure quickly. This was all for Kelley. He had to remain calm. Everything depended on it. The cold steel of the box cutter resting against his body now.

"Okamoto San."

Haruki Okamoto aka Peanut and various other handles momentarily caught off-guard by the use of his real name. The name that intelligence and police authorities throughout the world knew him by.

"So nice to see you, Keiko San. It has been a long time...too long. When was the last time? The night in the countryside. At the safe house...mmm yes, a memorable night. A feisty one you were. Is that the word? The English slang is still difficult for me."

Keiko had tried to block out the night the Monster had raped her and almost killed her in the process. With every ounce of courage she could muster, she kept herself from crying out, from showing any sign of weakness. That would mean sure death for Dan and his daughter. She would bide her time.

"I am here now. Let the others go. You have me. Do what you will. Let the others go."

"Of course, of course, I am a man of my word."

Laughing almost to himself now. Caught up in a joke that only he knew. The bag came out from the front pouch hidden under the Monster's shirt in one sweep of his bear-like arm.

"For the love of God!"

Dan staring at the now clearly visible contents of the bag.

White powder.

The Monster raising himself to his full massive stature. Pulling Kelley up with him. The powder poised at her face along with the knife.

He cut the bag.

· · · · · ·

Sir, we have emergency signal from Geisha I."

"Alert Marine One to ready for intrusion. Marine Two will stand-by."

"My God, Dusty."

Benny, overcome with fear now. Fear for them all. Keiko had sent the signal that indicated their lives were in immediate danger.

"Launch Marine One Now!"

Seeing the powder on his daughter's face was too much for Dan Bronsan. He lurched forward despite the pleas of Keiko. The box cutter missing its target and falling to the ground. The Monster laughing as he sent his own knife towards Dan Bronsan's now unprotected jugular.

The explosion threw Keiko into the room and on top of Peanut. The four Marines were inside in an instant. Before they could open fire, an otherworldly scream of pain and horror came from the Monster. One of the Marines would later describe the scene as similar to something he had seen back home at the farm. Keiko was busily ripping the Monster's throat open from ear to ear with the box cutter that had fallen to the ground during the explosion. It was not an easy job, but she did it with the proficiency of a surgeon, ignoring his animal-like screams. As the smoke cleared, Peanut lay there, spinal cord exposed and eyes wide open. No one home though. Dead. Keiko spit on his body almost as an afterthought and collapsed.

Dan stumbled towards his daughter. Her face showing the signs of apparent shock.

"Please stop, sir. No one move."

Captain Arnold of Marine One barking the order.

"Command Center we have a possible nuclear, biological, chemical situation here. I repeat, we have a possible NBC situation. Request NBC unit on scene immediately."

"Copied and understood. Secure area and await Nuclear Biological Chemical unit. Marine Two, do not enter. I repeat. Do not enter. Return to base."

•   •   •   •   •

When the body of the Monster dressed as a Sanno Hotel kitchen worker was inspected by the NBC team with numerous knife wounds and covered with a white powder, it became clear that the sarin threat Haruki Okamoto had used to terrorize his hostages was indeed a farce. The powder turned out to be nothing but cake mix. But of course damage was done. Kelley Bronsan had suffered a sprained ankle during the chaos in the New Jersey suite but had also lost something else. Something much more precious. A part of her soul. It would take some time and possibly the intervention of one Joe Dickwell to get it back.

58

"Look, Benny, I need to speak with you. Now. Not later. It's about the nut job at the Sanno yesterday. I know him. Knew him."

"What in the name of all that's good in Motown are you talking about my brother? You sure that this sobriety thing hasn't dried out that brain of yours too?"

"God damn it, Benny. I'm serious about this. I can't talk now. I think my friend Jack is involved in all of this as well. He's disappeared. I left to get a coffee while he was visiting his wife at Hiroo Hospital, and when I returned, he had left. Vanished. Nobody in the hospital seems to have seen him leave. His wife is dead. I don't know what he is capable of now. Look, I know this sounds bizarre. We need to talk. Please. Where can I meet you? Not at the bar. Anyplace but the bar."

"Okay, okay...aaah...yeah...okay, look, remember that baseball field at the park near the Hiroo Station?"

"Oh yeah, remember it well. When?"

"Meet me at the stands in an hour."

"I'll be there. Thanks, my friend."

In the last twenty four hours, things had started to take shape in the mind of Adam Welsh that were quite terrifying. A connection had begun to form which was too logical in its very insanity to ignore. His connection with Peter O'Mara. The incident at the cave with Peanut . The overall weird behavior of Jack. His vanishing after the death of Yumiko. He hadn't believed any of what Joe Dickwell had told him back then, but now...well, now was another story. All of this starting to make sense in a bizarre way to Adam. He needed to find Jack. Needed to save him from himself. Benny would help somehow. Needed to talk to Benny. Before it was too late for them all.

59

Jack Bender stared into the void. It was quiet here. Peaceful. The cave entrance was open. The pitch black abyss at once tranquil and foreboding. The light breeze along with the soft tapping sound of a nearby woodpecker accentuated the feeling. Jack was always surprised at the presence of a woodpecker in Japan. As it turned out, there were in fact six varieties of woodpeckers in Japan. Something Yumiko had informed him of not so long ago. Memories of Yumiko wafted through the air. One of their first dates. Sitting in a park near Chinatown in Yokohama. Throwing coins into a ceremonial water basin.

"Say a prayer for luck, Jack. Close your eyes. Keep the wish a secret."

"I can't tell even you, my love? The most beautiful and the sexiest girl in all of Japan."

"Jack, we are at a holy place," she admonished.

Jack knew the warm glow that flushed her face was not from anger though. It was one of complete happiness and fulfillment. Yumiko loved the fact that Jack found her desirable.

He missed his wife. A void, yes. Bigger and more all-consuming than the Indian Ocean on a moonless night.

Memories of a West Pac from long ago.

He fumbled for the switch, found it. The bright light, like the time on the ship in the middle of the Indian Ocean. Creeping along the deck, grasping the safety lines. The only thing separating him from a watery grave. Middle of the night in the I.O. If he fell overboard, no one would notice till morning. Then it would be too late. To drown alone at sea would be the worst possible way to go, thought Jack. Just enough time to think of one's life. Nothing but open space. The knowledge that death was imminent but still an eternity to think. Jack would finally make it to the door, pull the dogs open and then the light from within would pierce the darkness like Neptune's sword.

Just like now. Standing inside Ikego Cave 134. Looking towards the rear of the cave now. The innocuous looking fifty-five gallon drum marked Toxic Waste beckoning to him like an evil sibling craving attention.

60

"So what's the deal, Adam? Cut the bullshit. Not enough time for bullshit. Real world now my brother. Yes, indeed. Real world."

"He's my friend, Jesus."

"Fuck that noise! Art wasn't your friend? Rose?"

"Goddamn you, Benny."

"Okay, okay...this is not productive, gentlemen."

Dusty Rhodes. A voice of authority and reason. Here in the Hardy Barracks now. Headquarters for Japanese and U.S. Naval Intelligence. Commander Blasingame's office. Blasingame, Dusty, Benny Carter and Adam Welsh. Adam seated in the middle of them all. All a result, in his confused mind, of a double cross by Benny.

"Christ, Benny! What happened to friendship? Should have known, god damn Air Farce asshole would sell me out."

"Sit."

Blasingame all Navy now. No bullshit indeed. Grabbing Adam's arm before he could get to Benny.

"We're all friends here. Master Sergeant Carter did you a favor Petty Officer Welsh. The only reason you are not locked up in the brig as a co-conspirator is because Mr. Carter has vouched for you."

Benny staring directly into Adam's eyes. There was truth being spoken here, and Adam knew it.

"He has stated that you had nothing to do with the planned attack."

"Planned attack? Jesus."

"Petty Officer Welsh, please just answer our questions. Time is in short supply."

Benny had been at the baseball field in Hiroo of course. Just like he said he would be. Adam knew something was wrong the minute he opened his mouth. Not the same Benny. The appearance of the two FBI agents adding validity to Adam's paranoia.

"For your own good, my brother," as he bowed his bronze head.

"Federal Bureau of Investigation. Petty Officer Welsh, you will come with us."

Adam had been enraged, but deep down he had known that to resist would not only be foolhardy but also cataclysmic. For him and for many more. He had accompanied them without a word.

"We need to know the whereabouts of Jack Bender. We had him under surveillance up until he entered Hiroo Hospital earlier. Somehow we lost him."

The agents in the back of the room lowering their heads in response to Blasingame's quick glance.

"Since you are his friend and, as far as we can tell, are the last person to have seem him, your assistance is vital. Not only to the people in this room but to the very security of the United States of America, Japan and more than likely the world. Do you now understand the need for the utmost expedience in the resolution of this matter?"

Commander Steve Blasingame all business now. Adam looking at him with contempt but also the knowledge that he spoke the truth. Still not understanding the big picture though. Bits and pieces all he had. Parts of the puzzle. Parts that the assembled personages needed. Now.

61

Dan Bronsan was not made for Japanese hospitals, nor their health care systems. Sitting upright in his bed here at the Hiroo Hospital just a few blocks from the Sanno Hotel, he resembled a walrus perched on a buoy. This was the thought that passed through the mind of Joe Dickwell as he entered his room.

"Mr. Bronsan, glad to see that you're up. How's your back?"

"Call me Dan. As for the back, they say I need to lose some weight. Can you believe that?"

"No, I can't. Hmmm...well anyway..."

A slight grimace from Dan. Gone though as fast as it had come. Despite being an inept people pleaser, Dickwell was a good man. Probably helped save his life.

"How's my..."

"Kelley is just fine, Dan. She's just a few rooms away. Quite a personality that daughter of yours. The nurses can't get enough of her. Lights up the room. Really a ..."

Dickwell cutting himself off. Realizing from Dan's look that he was showing a bit more feeling towards Kelley than was probably acceptable at this time anyway.

"Aye. I'd like to see her..."

"Daddy!"

Kelley rolling through the doorway on cue. Almost running over Joe as she drove her wheelchair from the hallway all the way to her father's bed.

"I love you so much. I'm so glad we made it. Are you all right, Dad?"

Dan lowering his massive head to meet hers. Kissing her on the cheek and almost carrying her out of the wheelchair with a hug that a panda would envy.

"I'm fine, my little angel. No worries."

"Well, I'll let you two talk. I need to…"

"Joe, don't go just yet. Some English teacher. Why didn't you tell me you were a Naval officer?"

"Now, Kelley, the Lieutenant was under orders. For your own protection."

Dan bailing him out. Joe thankful. Kelley beaming at him now. Joe becoming weak in the knees.

Damn, I'm not a teenager. Jeez, what's happening here?

"Yes, well, thank you Mr. …ah yes, Dan. I am sorry that I had to mislead you, Kelley. Please understand."

Kelley moving towards Joe now. Looking up at him with those brown eyes. Close enough so only Joe could hear.

"Oh I understand. I just hope that everything else about you is on the level."

A slight grin now. Coy. Alluring.

"Oh yes, Kelley. Everything else is genuine. Yes, indeed."

"Well, I'll let you two be together."

"Please call me. Soon."

Kelley placing her cell phone number in his hand. Locking gazes and then turning back to her beloved father. Dan addressing Joe as he made his exit.

"Keiko… how is she?"

A note of concern in his voice, impossible to hide.

"She's okay, all things considered. She has been through quite an ordeal the last few months. She's in protective custody right now of course."

"Can I see her?"

Joe pausing before giving him the only answer he could. The only true response.

"Yes, of course, Dan. When the nightmare is over."

62

Asahara sat motionless. Atashi had given him the news of Peanut's demise. Having done so, the lawyer waited.

"What would you advise, my friend?"

The very question along with the demeanor of The One catching Atashi off guard. Part of the genius of Asahara of course.

"I'm sure The One will formulate a brilliant…"

"Enough! Do not play with me. Now is not the time for games. Our next move must be a decisive one."

"The caves then."

Atashi surprised at the words emitting from his mouth.

"The American is out of control. His wife has just died. He must be neutralized. In any case, his purpose has expired."

Atashi's ruthless, merciless tone surprising and disgusting himself all at once. He had to continue though. His very existence would be determined by the next few words he conveyed to Shoko Asahara.

"Our sources indicate that Japanese and American joint intelligence know of him and are closing in as we speak. Since the death of his wife, he has failed to make his prescribed check-in times."

Asahara grinning approvingly.

"Yes, my friend, the American must be eliminated. Can he use the sarin? Is it weapons grade? Is that the term? I have no use for these technical issues.

The cleansing. That is what the goal is. Never lose sight. No, the goal, the dream and the..."

"Yes, of course, the dream."

The lawyer taking the calculated risk. Cutting off The One. He had to though. He had witnessed these ramblings before. Soon they would get more confused and disoriented and then someone would die. Horribly.

"We do not know at what stage it is at. Unfortunately, Okamoto San was killed with all the technical data in his brain."

"Yes, of course. Poor Okamoto. And the traitor ? She still lives?"

"We believe so. The Americans have her under heavy guard. She knows nothing. Nothing of value."

"I will determine that. Please make the American disappear. An accident of course. We need to move swiftly. Do we have anyone in place at the Yokosuka base? Use them. I must sleep now. Go."

Goro Atashi bowed and left. No need to press his luck. The sarin was another story. Not quite what it seemed. No need for Asahara to know this however. It would only complicate things.

63

"He was, he is a good man. Jesus. I can't believe all this. It's bullshit."

"Petty Officer Welsh, I know you have a reputation as a... How should I put it? An independent thinker. One who follows the sound of his own drum, perhaps. Those are of course admirable qualities...in a civilian. But godamn it, Welsh! You are in the United States Navy, and you will remember that. Do I make myself clear?"

"Crystal, sir."

Adam looking directly at Commander Blasingame. Mild attempt to hide the contempt. Not knowing whether to laugh or to cry. He still had to play the game. He could appreciate that. One thing Adam Welsh knew how to do was play the game. Three hundred and whatever days and a wake up. Then the pension and the Philippines. Maybe Thailand. Anywhere. Escape into the arms of an LBFM or Little Brown Fucking Machine as the Filipino bar girls were called. Adam hated that expression. Always preferred to look at them as human beings. Women. Girls. Would introduce himself. Have a conversation. Establish an emotional tie. Something. No wham, bam, thank you ma'am and two hundred pesos for Adam. Maybe that was sicker. The emotional ties. Like it was a normal relationship. No matter. It was an escape. Role playing that Freud would no doubt have had a field day with. Of course old Sig had never been to Subic or Angeles City for that matter.

Adult Disneyland. In any case, the lie he had lived for almost twenty years would be over.

"Adam...Petty Officer Welsh, we know that this is difficult for you. Jack Bender was your friend."

"He is my friend, sir."

"Yes, of course. I stand corrected. He is your friend. By all accounts he was...is a good man. The prolonged illness and death of his wife seems to have been too much for him. Not to be cold but this however is really of no concern to us right now, Adam. What is at stake here is much bigger than friendship. However misplaced."

The glare from Adam impossible to miss. Controlling himself. For now.

In the two hours or so that they had been here, Adam had felt the old obsession come back. Hadn't felt it in a while but here it was. Old John Barleycorn, like a thief in the night. Always waiting. The patience of Job. Remembering Jack's comment at a meeting long ago.

He's out there doing push-ups, Adam, waiting. Ready to come right back into our lives. Once an alcoholic, always an alcoholic, my friend. One day at a time. Constant vigilance.

Hardy Barracks was not really a barracks in the common interpretation of the word. More like an office building and low cost military hotel for soldiers stationed or passing through the Tokyo area. Built right after WW II to house the transitional government team. MacArthur himself had been in the very office where Commander Steve Blasingame and Petty Office First Class Adam Welsh now sat. The circumstances not entirely foreign to each other. MacArthur presiding over a pivotal time in the century. A time where a misstep could have adversely changed the future of civilization. A rebirth was indeed taking place then. Now the figures present presiding over a kind of imminent destruction, albeit preceding a rebirth if the Aum Shinrikyo and the fanatic Shoko Asahara would indeed have their way.

"We need you to find Mr. Bender and gain his trust. Actually, use the existing confidence you have with him."

"Excuse me, Commander, but why not just take him now? I mean is he really any kind of threat?"

"That is a need-to-know issue Petty Officer Welsh. You do know about need-to-know access, or I should say, you did know about need-to-know access."

Blasingame hitting home. Adam hated the bastard. The feeling reciprocated in kind by Commander Blasingame. To him Welsh symbolized all that was wrong with the Navy. A guy who had risen to his level of mediocrity not unlike something he had read in an old tome on management called *The Peter Principle*. What was different about Welsh though was that he was a drunk. One of the hopeless variety. Blasingame had seen this first hand. His father for one. Destroyed his mother and his family while also running a destroyer aground during sea trials after the Korean conflict. Captain David Blasingame had been relieved of command and summarily found guilty at a court martial. Booze wreaked from his every pore after the ship had run aground. He was taken off the ship whimpering like a wounded dog. A disgrace. Blasingame had vowed never to be like his father. He had also made a vow to himself that he kept sealed deep in the darkest corner of his soul that he would avenge the outrage that he believed was committed by the Navy and the United States of America against his father. A tee-totaler. He never took a drink. Never would. A weakness. All this disease bullshit was just that. To Steve Blasingame, Adam Welsh was a younger version of his father. All he had to know was his history of alcohol abuse. Nothing else. Case closed.

For his part, Blasingame epitomized everything Adam Welsh hated about the Navy. Phony, back-stabbing, bastard. He made his mind up then and there that he would help his friend Jack. He'd figure out something. Go along with the assholes for now.

"I'll do whatever I can, sir."

A knock on the door and Joe Dickwell entered.

Blasingame nodding towards him and then to Welsh.

"Very well. Joe, brief Petty Officer Welsh on the situation and give him his orders. I will be visiting Ms. Watanabe."

"Keiko! Is she involved in this? Keiko Watanabe? Where is she?"

Adam returning to complete clarity. Cognizant of all.

"Ah, yes, Adam. You know Keiko. That's right."

A quick look towards Blasingame. No use in Dickwell saying anything. The Commander knew he had screwed up royally.

Adam knew nothing of the events that had occurred at the Sanno. Only the cover story. *Kitchen Worker Goes Berserk*, the Japanese tabloids catching up with their Western counterparts in the area of shock news. Rupert Murdoch would be proud. In a bit of blind luck, the tabloid had managed to find a photo of the man Adam knew as Peanut. Otherwise, he wouldn't be in this room right now. However, he did not know of Keiko's involvement.

"Lieutenant, I need to leave right away. Please brief Petty Officer Welsh. A strictly 'need-to-know' basis of course."

"Yes, sir."

Dickwell told Welsh everything. Taking a chance but he needed his confidence. Adam Welsh the common thread between Keiko Watanabe and Jack Bender. Their only access. No time for official need-to-know bullshit. Too much at stake.

Adam sat for a while. Stunned of course. What had he done? What had he done to poor little Keiko. His angel. Now an angel of death. There could never be any amends large enough. All-consuming was her pain. It had to be. How was she even alive? And then it came to him. Hate. Living on hate. The man called Peanut had been the first to realize this.

"Look, Adam. I'm going to call you Adam unless you have a problem with it."

"Not a problem at all...Joe."

Dickwell winced but then saw the look from Welsh that indicated this last was more out of a sense of camaraderie than any disrespect. They were alike in a way. More than Dickwell knew.

"Adam, we believe this Aum Cult is in possession of a significant amount of sarin. We don't know whether it is weapons grade as yet or at least I'm not at liberty to tell you that. I'm actually telling you a helluva of a lot more than I am authorized."

A deep breath and he continued. No turning back now.

"We know that the sarin is in the country. We know that Jack Bender is involved somehow. A mole."

"Hell No!"

Even as he heard himself defend his friend, Adam knew in his heart of hearts that this news about Jack, damning as it was, could be true. To many unexplained incidents like the secret meetings with O'Mara, the association with Peanut and, finally, Jack's mental breakdown as Yumiko was dying.

"Look, Adam, I know this is hard for you. We have a file on Bender going back a number of years. Ever since his wife started to get sick. He began to act a bit strange at work. We sighted him at a few of those rallies put on by anti-American Japanese organizations. You know the ones that want to return to Japan as it was right before Pearl Harbor. Still believing that Hiroshima and Nagasaki were unnecessary. We ceased high level monitoring of Bender recently. Chalked him up as just another nut job. That of course was a mistake. When we started it up again, we lost him."

Adam ignoring the insult to Jack and moving on.

"Still tough to sell nuking Nagasaki, sir. A bit of an overkill I think. I mean it wasn't like we had the Internet where we could inform the people there that, hey we just vaporized one of your cities and your next will follow if you don't lay down your arms. Thought we could have waited a couple of weeks."

"And lost at least a quarter of a million men in a ground invasion. The research was done Petty Officer Welsh. President Truman did the right thing. The buck did stop with him. Thank God. The loss of life was of course horrible. When one looks for blame though, the Japanese people have come to terms. For the most part they know that the militant factions of their government at the time were responsible. Of course they still don't teach Pearl Harbor in their history books."

"I see... I wasn't there....sorry. Please continue."

"As you may or may not know, I make a very bad drunk."

"Don't know of any good ones, sir."

"Yes. Of course the original plan was to somehow infiltrate, get inside Bender and his accomplices by using the Alcoholics Anonymous meetings."

"He knew right away. I could tell by the way he talked to you. It was all bullshit."

" Why didn't you..."

"Narc on you? Well, for one I didn't know the big picture, and of course Jack knew right away so I just went along and bided my time. I was curious more than anything. Also I didn't believe that you were regular Navy at the time. I just figured I'd keep an eye on you. Kind of thought you were just another sick bastard taking refuge in A.A. Not everyone in the rooms is a real alcoholic."

"I see. Yes. Be that as it may, the incident at the Sanno changed everything. With this Peanut character dead, the Cult is sure to expedite whatever plans they have. We think there will be some kind of strike using the sarin within forty-eight hours."

Dickwell thought he discerned a slight flinch from Adam. Regrouping now though. Staring directly into his eyes.

"Are you familiar with the caves at Ikego?"

64

Jack Bender's body was not as sturdy as it used to be, he realized as he labored to position the hand dolly under the fifty-five gallon drum. More than a one-man job this. Couldn't chance Adam though. No. Adam would not be involved. This was for Yumiko. Jack had to do it himself. His last promise to her. He alone would do it. He rolled the drum out of the cave gingerly. The large spiders that resembled bats scampering away. Jack remembered with a smile how Adam hated the spiders.

"Godamn prehistoric," he had referred to them on the occasions that he had helped clean out the caves here.

Jack oblivious to all that now. He felt a sense of giddiness. Like he use to feel right before he took a drink. An alcoholic is different than a normal drinker in many ways. One of those differences is exhibited when the alcoholic is thinking about the drink. A feeling of euphoria, light headedness occurs. A phenomena unique to the alcoholic. Jack used to think everybody had it. All those years sober and here was this feeling again. Not about drinking now. No. About getting even. About dealing with a resentment. The justifiable one that Jack Bender would never let go. No, they would have to pay. Tonight would be the cashing of the promissory note that he had pledged his beloved Yumiko. Vowed to her as he shook in anguish at her bedside the night that her brain had exploded. The promissory note of retribution for what the boys of the Enola Gay from the cornfields of Oz had wrought.

Jack Bender had ceased to exist completely now. An impostor born of hate was rolling the fifty-five gallon drum onto the flatbed truck. Tying down the drum now.

Covering it with the tarpaulin marked United States Navy Property, Jack Bender returned to the cab of the truck. The hand on his shoulder. A slight touch but there it was.

"Hello, Bender San. You seem to be in a bit of a hurry. May I be of any service?"

Jack turning now, the .45 moving ever so slightly in his front pocket. Takashi Ishii stood before him. Grinning. A six inch blade curiously gripped in one hand, the other reaching out to Jack Bender. To shake? Glinting in unison with his rotting teeth which now reflected the summer sun rays creating a quite nauseating effect. Jack thought of flossing him now. Just grabbing the man by the head, ripping his jaw open and then flossing his teeth. Flossing until the blood rolled out of his mouth and onto the ground, finally coagulating at the base of the cave where the fire ants could feast. At this moment Jack Bender could not understand why Ishii, his subordinate at the Toxic Waste Facility and now, would be Aum Cult assassin, here on a mission directed by Shoko Asahara himself, never flossed. Horrible teeth.

The men were standing inches away from each other. Jack unable to keep his eyes off Ishii's mouth. The Japanese man, for his part disconcerted. Expecting Bender to be surprised, alarmed, at least a hint of fear. There was none of this. Only the curious stare of a man who had traveled to the other side of reason, never to return.

"Ishii San, please excuse me, but I have business to attend to."

Jack nodding slightly towards the door of the truck. Ishii ignoring him, eyes moving from the cave entrance to the tarpaulin.

"Of course, Bender San. I will not be long. Our business will be brief."

Jack Bender shook Ishii's extended hand and in one motion pulled him towards him as he took the .45 out of his front packet and shot the man point blank between the eyes. The fire ants would be treated to a side order of brains along with the blood today. Jack dragged the man into the brush beside the cave and rolled him down a gully. No time to cover him up. It was late afternoon now. In little more than an hour the Almond Café, known as the "Almondo" in the broken English of the Japanese school girls, would be packed with humanity. A mosaic of men, woman, old and young. Every corner of the globe represented. All meeting here in this landmark for lovers that had been a favorite rendezvous for singles, cheaters, pedophiles, salary men and Office Ladies since World War II. Jack Bender would release his deadly cargo here amongst them all and finally his beloved Yumiko would be at peace.

Glad for the .45 now. Adam never did find out Jack had taken it from him. Guns difficult to acquire in Japan. Especially for gaijins. The .45, Navy issue, missing from the armory of the McClusky. Jack had absconded with it while Adam gave him an unauthorized tour of the ship during his duty day. Jack visiting him. Having dinner on his ship. He had asked to see the armory. A restricted area but Jack Bender had softened the resolve of his younger friend by reminding him that he had done twenty in the Navy.

"Adam, it's not like I'm a civilian. Just want to see what, if anything, has changed."

Jack had taken the gun while Adam was reading some A.A. literature in a corner of the armory. The incident was still under investigation but could never be traced to Adam. When and if they did, it would all be too late anyway, thought Jack.

Questions now though. A moment of clarity for Jack Bender. Perhaps. Shoko Asahara wanted him dead. Why? The answer coming in an instant. The death of Yumiko had made Jack unstable and thus unreliable. It made sense to Jack. He would have done the same himself. *What to do now?* These thoughts racing through the Disneyland roller coaster psyche of Jack Bender now as the truck rumbled up Route I towards Tokyo, Yes, Jack would go to the "Almondo," but he would make a slight detour first. Alas, Jack Bender could be a practical man as well. Asahara had failed. Jack would not. He fumbled for his dental floss as he accelerated down the highway.

Moments later a detachment of federal agents and marines descended on the now empty Ikego Cave 134. The bloodied body of a Japanese man was found nearby.

65

"I would like to leave the hospital. Please."

She looked so small. Delicate. How could something this petite and fragile hold so much grief? So much pain? The weight of the world, the first thoughts that came to Dr. Inoue. Harumi Inoue, staff cardiologist, on duty when Keiko Watanabe was brought in. So vulnerable yet something there. Unmistakable. Dr. Inoue had seen the look before. Only once but enough to permanently etch it in the deepest corner of her brain. Something that would come out only when invited by some dark and destitute mood. Working for the UN in Africa. Just out of medical school. It was the look of a young boy in Rwanda. Laurent, his name. She would always remember that look on his face. Brought in by one of the villagers. Both legs reduced to bloody stumps. Hacked off by the Hutu in another senseless disagreement turned to genocide. His mother and father butchered to death themselves. The boy, maybe twelve, if that. Just staring. Never cried. Didn't say a word. Just peered into some universe that he could only see. The price of admission, the horror he held deep inside.

Keiko Watanabe had that look now. She wanted to leave. The boy wanted to leave as well, Harumi remembered. He wanted to walk out. Not coming to terms with the loss of his legs. *Shock?* She envisioned him nearly every day now. It had been almost a year since she had left the horror of the Rwanda civil war, but she had brought Laurent with her. She saw him when she had occasion to visit that bad place in the abyss. Lying in the squalor, begging for loose change. Dead already, his soul gone.

The sight of Keiko bringing the doctor back.

"Keiko San, you must rest. You are still suffering the effects of your...ordeal."

"I will go now."

Keiko starting to remove the IV, the attendant gently yet firmly stopping her, with a look from the doctor.

The armed American guard outside the hospital room here in Yokosuka Naval Hospital peering in, turning away with a look from Keiko. Hard to hold her gaze. Penetrating. Something eerie about it.

"How did I get here?"

"You don't remember?"

Keiko not answering now. Needed to gather her thoughts. Regroup. Bide her time, as Adam would say. Unfinished business on her agenda. She didn't remember much, if anything, of the events of the previous day. The hotel, the room, all now just a blur. She knew that the Monster was gone, although she, mercifully, did not remember how. Enough for now. The staff at the American Naval Hospital here in Yokosuka had been cordial. Nice in fact.

Do I hate the Americans still? Had I ever? Perhaps it was my own self that I despised and hated. Loathed. Needed someone or something to focus my anger, pure rage, my heartache. Perhaps that had been it all along? Adam of course an American. In fact a member of the American military machine. The same rampaging, raping, military machine that he, The One, Shoko Asahara spoke of in such an all-consuming, mesmerizing, seductive way. Who was that person that had followed the Madman?

Dr. Harumi Inoue spoke.

"Keiko, may I call you Keiko?"

"Yes, of course, doctor."

"Harumi, please."

"As you wish."

"There is a visitor for you. An American..."

"Is it Adam?"

The flush in her cheeks now. Life pulsing through her.

"Ah, yes, I believe his name is Adam Welsh. He is in the American Navy."

"Please doctor…Harumi. No, I mean, I don't know…not ready, I mean."

The tear glinting in her eye. Like a beacon. Shining. A symbol. Hope perhaps. Rebirth. Harumi bent over closer. Her cheek almost touching Keiko. Looking into her eyes now. Clasping her hand.

What kind of hell did these hands banish just yesterday? These small fragile hands? They must have been transformed. A reanimation of sorts caused by a traumatic state that possibly only one person on this earth could remedy.

"Keiko San, I am a doctor of course, but I am also a human being as well as a woman. I see many patients in much sorrow and pain. I know sometimes that the medicines that we develop through modern science are sometimes not enough. You must see your Adam. It will be hard for you, but you must summon all your courage, every last bit that has carried your indomitable spirit this far. Take the last step. See your Adam."

Keiko Watanabe, in a moment of clarity, inexplicably and instantaneously realized that the evil that had lived within her was gone. She had felt this before but it was fleeting, perhaps because it wasn't built of anything of substance. She now knew with all her heart and soul that she indeed wanted to live. She had to live. She would live, and yes, she would love. Somehow. This was the ingredient that had been missing earlier. Love. The real variety. The tears came now. Unrelenting. A cleansing flood. Harumi held Keiko now. She stopped suddenly, body ceasing to convulse and looked up at the doctor with what Harumi Inoue would remember later and forever as the face of an angel.

"Yes, I will see Adam, doctor; my Adam. I will live. Thank you."

The doctor left the room with a smile.

Keiko lay in her bed staring at the ceiling, hoping that its white plaster would turn to snow and engulf her. Take her and Adam away to a different part of the universe. Someplace pure and white where nothing began and nothing ended and nothing had to be explained or regretted.

She felt the hand first. Trembling. Not as much as she had remembered though. Afraid to open her eyes at first. Lost in the whiteness. The snow drifts. No pain here. Nothing. Afraid to go back out. Something inside urging her to however. A survival instinct perhaps. Love more likely.

She opened her eyes.

Adam Welsh stared down at her. Into her very heart. Yes, there was a heart now. Born again. Beating. Tears forming. Adam's hand trembling a bit more. No words for what seemed like forever. Finally...

"How's my baby? Still beautiful as ever. More now. Are you sure you didn't go back to heaven for a while, baby? Don't talk. It's okay. Just hold my hand here for a while. Let me feel you. Your eyes. God, this hurts. A good hurt though."

She raised her hand and touched his lip. Still looking into his blue eyes. Still as blue as ever. Like the South China Sea on a bright day when you can see the gulls. Pure white against the azure sea. Like that now. The blue of Adam's eyes against the whites.

Her touch too much for him. Lips trying to move. Finally, "God baby, I'm so sorry."

The past flooding back in waves. The pain he had caused her. The desertion. All alone. So fragile. Yet, she had survived. Stronger now. Yet, still the delicate angel he remembered. He leaned down and buried his head in her breast. An avalanche of emotion now. Pouring down from him. A cleansing though. This was good. She stroked his hair. Said nothing. Just held his head to her breast. If they both died now it would be okay, she thought. No. No time for death now. Time to start living. The thought came and went in an instant. Still there though. She didn't miss it. She wouldn't forget it. In that moment she knew that the thought had been placed in her consciousness by something much more powerful than herself.

"Adam, I love you, and I forgive you."

The one sentence from the lips of this beautiful creature saving Adam Welsh. He would go on. They would go on. They would live now. Sleep came. The doctor passing by, stopped for a brief moment but then left to finish her rounds. No need to bother them now. Let the healing begin.

66

The tall figure moved across the room with a delicacy that hid the mass beneath his flowing velvet robe. As the shadow of Shoko Asahara slithered back and forth across the anteroom in the country estate of Ren Hideo, former respected university professor, current lost soul, one thought of the mythical hooded vestige of Death complete with sickle. The ornament here that was being waved through the air like a grotesque cheerleader from Hades was much more deadly.

"Ren San, you know I cut my father's balls off with this. Yes, one swoop. Balls, dick, everything. Gone. The look on his face before he bled to death, rapturous. Ah yes, such memories. The real beginning for me. For all of us. Yes, my friend. The beginning of the rebirth. Soon it will be complete. You are trembling my friend. Do I trouble you?"

Asahara had glided across the room. Now directly in Ren Hideo's face. His breath that of cold vomit. He had been pacing, seemingly levitating a few inches off the floor for what seemed like hours. Twirling and thrusting the Japanese banzai sword as he went. Hideo terrified. All alone here in the room. Himself and the Madman. The meeting had been held earlier. A council of sorts, Hideo not knowing all of the details. Not wanting to know them. Knowledge was death. The Arabs had been here. As had the Europeans. When word had come of the death of Haruki Okamoto at the Sanno Hotel, the meeting came to an abrupt end. All the visitors dispersing to the four winds it seemed. Plans changed. Atashi and Asahara himself meeting alone. Then Atashi leaving the room. Asahara would be departing himself of course. The Americans were on the scent. Plans had to be expedited. Changes made. Loose ends tied up.

"Did you know Okamoto San, Ren?"

The One calling him by his first name. Fear pulsating through his body now. He was dead. He knew beyond a doubt now. Strangely though, Ren Hideo did not feel so bad for himself. The loss of this house weighing far more deeply on him now.

"No, I did not, Omnipotent One."

"Please call me Shoko."

The familial, further confirmation of his demise.

"Yes, you two are very similar. Both sacrificing for the cause. The rebirth. The cleansing."

The sword held up now. Bristling in the light. The Van Gogh catching Ren Hideo's eye. A reminder before his impending death that he once was a man who possessed a soul. He had loved. He had been a good man. Once. A feeling of peace now.

The sword dropped to the floor. A smile from Asahara, a slight prick in the neck and then blackness.

"You will both be great martyrs as well."

The last thing Ren Hideo saw before the drug took effect and rendered him unconscious was the Van Gogh looking directly at him from the far end of the room. A look of commiseration. Possibly also of relief.

The two bodyguards and Atashi noticed the excitement in The One's eyes. A glow. Atashi knew what it was. He had seen it many times.

"Burn the house. Make the arrangements with the usual people."

A quick glance at Atashi as he entered the SUV.

"It will be done."

The SUV accelerating onto the gravel road that was once the play area for the small children of Ren Hideo in happier times. Hideo being administered to in the back of the SUV by the Cult doctors. The bedside manner of Joseph Mengele thought Atashi.

Poor bastard.

It would be important for him to be compliant in the next few hours. Ren Hideo's final service to the Aum approaching.

"I have made the changes you have directed Shoko."

Atashi resorting to the familial tone with Shoko Asahara. He did this only in times of crisis. No need or time for protocol.

"The French will be with us on this?"

Asahara, looking out the window of the SUV, not waiting for an answer.

"Yes, of course they will be. The minister has too much to lose. They will perform their duties. As they always have."

67

"Can't a man be granted even a tinge of human decency. For the love of Jesus, Mary and Joseph and all the saints. I can get the damn thing off myself. Please, go."

A bedpan in any hospital in the world can be an instrument of dehumanization notwithstanding its advertised reason for existence. This at least the opinion that Dan Bronsan had held throughout his life. This thought at least in this bizarre scene in his room at the Yokosuka Naval Hospital coming true to the nth degree. The sight of the minuscule, by contrast, bedpan protruding from the mammoth-like posterior of Dan Bronsan, two diminutive Japanese nurses grabbing at it desperately to no avail in a hopeless attempt to free it from its hairy captor was something that should have been left to some futuristic museum of the grotesque. Finally, for no apparent reason other than divine intervention, the pan released itself from the walrus-like cheeks of Dan Bronsan sending nurses falling backwards onto the bed and Dan spread eagled with his enormous ass raised to the sky like some Picasso rendering of Mt. Fuji.

"My God, Dad, is that you."

Kelley rolling into the room, the specter of her father lying sprawled on the floor a cause for alarm at first only to be followed by a convulsion of laughter. The nurses scampering to their feet immediately. Covering the massive bottom of Dan Bronsan who now actually wished that he had died in the hotel room a day earlier.

Getting to his feet now with the help of one of the nurses along with another, much larger figure. The arm shaking ever so slightly. Not as much as he remembered. Adam Welsh grabbing Dan around the shoulder and helping him up.

"Dan, I was in the neighborhood and thought I would drop in on you. If I had known you were having this much fun though..."

"God damn it man, have some respect. Jesus..."

Dan actually speechless. How much had Kelley seen? God he needed a drink now.

"Oh, Dad, don't be so embarrassed. It isn't like I haven't seen a naked man before."

"For the love of God, child...please."

"I'm sorry, I don't believe we have ever met. I'm Adam Welsh."

"Oh, of course, Adam. I would thank you for getting the room for me, but now I'm not so sure."

"Adam, please excuse my daughter here, I don't know where she gets the sarcastic streak."

"Oh come on, Daddy."

Turning back to Adam now. Flirtatious mode in full effect.

"Thank you so much for all your help. I do appreciate the friendship you have provided my father. Christ, you should be canonized."

"Now, girl, blasphemous language is not appropriate at this moment."

Kelley had been much less formal, much less Daddy's little girl since the ordeal at the Sanno. Thank God they had survived and only with minor injuries. Dan with a herniated disk as a result of his fall after the diversionary explosion and Kelley with some bruises and a sprained ankle. God, it could have been so much worse. Of course what Kelley would never know is the horror that had passed through her father's psyche as the white powder had been thrown on her face. Kelley not really having any idea of what it could be. Dan knowing of the demise of Rose, did not have that luxury. He knew clearly what it could have been and what he was sure it was, at the time at least. She was no worse for the wear though. At least on the outside. She had that Bronsan gene which adapted to change and also acted as a mask for any feelings one might have which might be construed as a sign of weakness. It would take a while before he or anyone else found out what damage was done within.

"I'm sorry that your visit has to be cut short."

"Cut short?" Kelley glaring at her father.

Dan glancing at Adam. A microsecond but enough time for Adam to realize that Kelley was not privy to the fact that she would be leaving Japan very soon. He winced.

Dan, for his part, looking away from his daughter but realizing it was no use. She must be confronted. Now, for her own good. For the good of all of them.

"Look, your mother has been on the phone all morning. She does have a point you know. You could have died for the love of God."

Dan almost in tears. Everything finally hitting him. The stress of the last few days. All that could have happened. Kelley forgetting her disappointment and hugging her father tighter than she could remember. They were alive.

68

Loss. The sense of complete and utter emptiness. The void that nothing could fill. Perhaps only hate. Maybe anger. When we lose someone or something that is in essence our entire world, we all deal with it in a different way. Sometimes the psyche, that phenomenal connection of checks and balances that enables the human being to go on despite pain of the most indescribable kind, kicks in and takes over the body and the mind. Mercifully. This is what had happened to Jack Bender. Twenty four hours removed from the bedside of his dear Yumiko. She had passed before he had arrived. He had ceased to exist as Jack Bender at that moment only hours ago. Now merely a receptacle of hate and retribution. This his fuel. This the new DNA make-up of one Jack Bender. Never meeting with Adam Welsh in the cafeteria as promised. Sliding out the stairwell of the hospital. Avoiding the all too obvious NIS tail that had been following him the last few days. A mission to be completed.

Jack Bender rumbling along in the U.S. Navy flatbed truck ostensibly on a routine waste dump. At least that is what was recorded on his sign-out sheet back at his office at the Toxic Waste Facility. The Lieutenant probably wouldn't even read it. Lieutenant Parker not really paying too much attention to things at the office. His wife about one month from dropping a future officer into the world. Eight months pregnant now. Yea, Jack thought to himself, what kind of world is that child coming into? Thoughts again of Yumiko. Never could have a child. Wondered if she couldn't or just wouldn't. The idea of bringing even a half-American into the world probably too much for her. Yea. The LT was a good man though. Trusted Jack like he would trust his old man. Even told him that one day. Jack grimacing, a bit of a twinge thinking of this. The LT's dream of a teaching post at Annapolis would surely never come to fruition once it was learned that a mole for a major terrorist network was operating right under his nose. Scapegoats would have to be created and the Lieutenant, unfortunately for him, was the perfect one.

Bloody hell, Jack screaming aloud now. They had tried to kill him. *Why? Of course, he was expendable now. His wife dead. A bit of a loose cannon perhaps. Fine. Plans would be changed. Retribution would be exacted. But first a visit.*

Jack Bender pulled the truck off Highway 1 entering the ramp exit for Roppongi. He would make one stop before the Almond Café - The Gas Panic bar and a meeting, albeit unannounced, with Shoko Asahara himself. Jack fumbled with his cell phone and dialed.

"Is he there? Let me speak to him. Now."

Voices in the background. Silence. Then, "Yes, Mr. Bender. Nice to hear from you. We were worried. So sorry to hear of your beloved wife. My condol..."

"Shut up, you piece of shit. You can find your errand boy's carcass in a gully near the cave. I'm sure you could care less though. Just answer me one question, "Why was it necessary to kill me?"

"Mr. Bender, Jack. May I call you Jack? Yes, again very unfortunate. I am sorry that you seem to be very distraught. Under the circumstances..."

"I have the sarin, asshole."

Silence. Some mumbling in the background. Sharp words. Orders. Then, "Where are you now? We must talk. You have no idea what you have there, Mr. Bender."

"Oh, we will talk. Gas Panic. One hour from now. Upstairs. Be there. Alone."

The large flat-bed truck did not blend in at all with the normal weekday traffic here in the Roppongi district of Tokyo. Of course this area was cosmopolitan, probably one of the most diverse areas in Tokyo and as such was known to be a bit eccentric. On a normal day or night, one could see anything from dancing Elvis impersonators to Japanese kids dressed like Middle Eastern terrorists. Therefore the sight of Jack Bender and his flatbed truck with tarpaulin covering the fifty-five gallon drum did not raise any eyebrows. Probably just another publicity stunt by one of the many nightclubs looking for the slightest edge. He stopped the truck in front of the Gas Panic bar. About 1700 or 5PM now.

The Aum soldier came out the front door on a dead run. Jack took the top of his head off with one round from the .45. Put it back under his coat and then pulled the tarpaulin off the fifty-five gallon drum. He stood staring at it for a moment, then raised the gun and pointed it directly at its center.

"Bender San. So nice of you to visit."

Asahara himself standing over the dead soldier. Leaning over now. Touching the brain matter. Very good shot my friend. Yes, but a bit messy. And of course now the police will be involved."

"A moot point now."

Jack's eyes glazed over. He would meet his beloved Yumiko soon. Pay off the promissory note. He fired one round into the drum. Nothing. He fired another, and the liquid began streaming out. Water. Brown water. Nothing more. Fifty-five gallons slurping out of the drum onto the flatbed and then onto the street. The sounds of laughter behind him. He turned to see the source. Asahara had raised his arm, pistol in hand. Fired. One round through the center of the tormented man's temple.

Jack Bender died sober.

The Japan Times would report that a mentally unstable American who worked at Yokosuka Naval Base had committed suicide after shooting an innocent bystander in front of the Gas Panic bar in the Roppongi District of Tokyo. It was rumored that the man, identified as Jack Bender, had recently lost his wife to cancer and was deeply distraught. The fact that Jack Bender had driven a U.S. Navy truck to the center of Roppongi with a fifty-five gallon drum marked Toxic Waste that contained nothing more than raw sewage water was never reported.

69

Hiroshi Aki thought the guy looked strange. Out of place. Hiroshi couldn't quite put his finger on why. Competent enough but definitely something amiss with this fellow. Keeping his eyes on him.

A visitor to the Tokyo Metropolitan Department of Water's website would note a new program which is described as - *An effort to establish an accurate grasp of customer needs while enhancing user understanding and appreciation of the water supply services provided in Tokyo. Under this program, department personnel and investigators from contracted companies visit customers to analyze individual water use and inspect water quality and leakage and otherwise assess the conditions surrounding water supply and usage.*

Over 11 million people each day used the water which was the subject of these investigations. This last bit of information could also be found in various Al Qaeda briefing memos.

"You really should stop talking so much you know. Let someone else into the conversation."

The blank look from Akeno Mori. Hiroshi Aki's attempt at levity would have been better used inside a morgue for the response it received.

Mori had said nothing since the trip to the Yamaguchi Reservoir had begun over twenty minutes ago. Hiroshi thankful that they would soon be arriving at their destination. The last inspection of the day. Hiroshi looking forward to leaving Mr. Personality and getting home to finally see his little girl, Honoka. He felt guilty at times because he had to work so much lately. Too many long hours away from the family. Not spending near enough time with his precious daughter. The work load had been much heavier these last few weeks. The terrorist activity culminating with the death of the American woman and the hostage situation at the hotel in Hiroo. The early morning meeting with Benjiro Zen, the head of security for the Tokyo water system.

"We need to keep a low profile about this, gentlemen. If people start believing that their drinking water could be poison, or worse; well gentlemen, we can all see the obvious consequences."

The new man had been there as well.

"Aki San meet Akeno Mori. Just transferred over from the Science and Technology division of Tokyo University. He will be assisting you with the sampling."

And that was it. As simple as that. The new man had not spoken since.

"So, are you single, married, kids?"

The distant look. Something there. Fear, anger, both?

"No."

Akeno Mori had enough ricin in the small compartment in his wallet that IRA soldier Rafferty Grogan had fashioned for him to kill at least one million people if it was put in the right place. The right place being the Yamaguchi Reservoir. Mori would do everything he could to place the ricin where Grogan and Cult scientists had instructed. He would do this since at this very moment, his wife, Kira, was being held in the basement of a country estate some 50 miles north of Tokyo. The final instructions delivered by Asahara's soldiers burned into his consciousness.

"You will inspect the Yamaguchi water supply. Nothing out of the ordinary. When you reach the bio-activated carbon adsorption treatment section you will..."

"I am not authorized to..."

"Do not interrupt, insolent scum. Shut up and listen. Time is of the essence. You will find a way to breach the security and place the ricin where it is shown on the schematic we gave you. If our instructions are not carried out to the letter, we will kill your wife. Of course it will not be a quick death. We will amuse ourselves immensely. Do you understand?"

Understand he did. Shortly thereafter, Akeno Mori had made sure that he was attached to one of the contractors that routinely sampled the water from the Tokyo Metropolitan system. He didn't have as much difficulty as he had originally thought he would. The Cult had evidently bought off a few security people. The chief of one of Tokyo's biggest police stations among others. Here he was now with this Aki character. Straight as an arrow. No way to plant the ricin where he had been instructed to do it unless he did away with the man.

"I have a daughter...oh yes, sorry I guess I've mentioned them about a million times. Very sorry. They grow on you though. Kids. It really is true. Once you have one, your only purpose in life is their well-being. God, I'm sorry. Please excuse me."

No response from the quiet one. True to form. Hadn't spoken all day. Why change now, thought Aki. He moved on.

"Well this is it. The last adsorption unit. You can take your samples right there."

The two men were at the edge of a platform which rose about thirty feet above the Yamaguchi Reservoir. Aki had actually pointed out the exact spot where Mori had been instructed to deposit the ricin. The packet set to dissolve upon entering the water. An easy task now. Simply drop it in. Aki putting his hand in his pocket. Feeling for the compartment that the deadly ricin now inhabited while it waited to be put to use. A smile came to his face as he turned towards Aki. His back to the edge of the platform. The water placid below. An idyllic day.

"Aki San, thank you so much for sharing your love for your daughter. I am so sorry that I have not been more responsive today. I have a family as well. A beautiful wife and daughter."

He seemed to be drifting off. Fumbling in his pockets. Moving backwards, towards the edge of the platform. Dangerously close to the edge, thought Aki.

"What to do now. A dilemma. Yes..."

The forced smile. Lips trembling a bit. Aki watching with great sorrow now. As if he knew what would happen next. Not knowing why. A feeling of impending doom. He tried to move. His legs couldn't or perhaps, wouldn't. In any case, something final would be happening shortly. Intuitively he knew this. He actually knew the man, perched now on the platform railing, much better than he had presumed earlier.

"My family, my family...."

Something coming out of an unseen pouch, beside his pocket. Bringing the packet to his mouth now. A look of anguish. Swallowing the contents. A slight grimace. Arms outstretched. Aki thought later that he looked Messianic at that moment. Christ on the cross. Collapsing backwards. Disappearing over the railing. Aki hearing the splash. Helpless. Rushing to the railing. Just in time to see the horribly bloated corpse of Akeno Mori sink to the bottom.

· · · · · · ·

Adam Welsh sitting in the waiting room, watching CNN over the Armed Forces Network. A picture of Jack. In his dress blues. Years ago. Happier times with Yumiko. She was actually smiling.

Where did they get that photo?

Adam too late to save his friend. Numerous calls to the office all unanswered. He never should have let him out of his sight at the hospital.

What the hell could I have done anyway?

He needed Keiko more than ever now. He rushed back to her room. The guards still there. They would always be there, he thought. Things had changed forever.

"You can't go in now, sir."

The marine private about twenty. Adam giving him the look that is reserved for marines and other sub-human life forms. He never did like jar-heads.

"Look, you don't need to be calling me, 'sir.'"

Jeez, why the hell did he bother. These clowns called the mailman sir for Christ sake.

"Okay...yea, no problem."

"Does she have visitors?"

"Yes, sir."

This last "sir" with a touch of distaste. Very obvious. The animosity mutual.

Deciding to just walk away now. An old lesson from Jack remembered. Needed to be with Keiko now. More than ever. Tell her about Jack. What he meant to him. Pressing business to attend to though. She would be okay here. Safe at least. The thought hit him like a shot of Jack Daniels the morning after. He needed to call Benny. Benny would know what to do. He would call Benny, and they would visit Dan. That was it. That's what he would do. Amazing the clarity one had when one was sober. Thoughts of Jack again. Tears welling up now. Strange, he didn't feel anything when he saw it on CNN. If he talked to Dan and Benny then maybe the emotions would all come out. His sobriety tenuous now though. Had to stay sober. For Keiko...hell, for himself. If not for himself, he would drink. Just the way it was. He called Benny.

"Yea, man I saw it on the news. I'm here at the Sanno bar now. Shit it feels empty here. Didn't know that Jack and you were that close. I never met the guy. I feel for you, Adam. This changes things though. Blasingame wants to see us. How's Keiko? Got to visit my little daughter soon. So much craziness. God, I'm glad you're with her. Don't fuck up again my brother. I will kick your ass. Yea, Almond Café. Sounds good. I'll be there in about an hour. And Adam...I love you buddy. Hang, baby. Just hang. The darkness before the light you know."

70

The Gas Panic was an alky's refuge. Dim light, strong drinks and no particular dress code. The homeless and hopeless all brought together by the common denominator of booze. alcohol and women. The fixers of all that is wrong with a tormented spirit, albeit temporary but after the initial relief, the warm blast, who cared? It was in this curious water hole for tormented souls that the American had sold his so many weeks ago.

"It is good to see you. You look well. A sake perhaps? Ah, yes. I am sorry. Your prefer the Budweiser. Good old American beer."

The irony not lost on Shoko Asahara as he sat across the table here on the top floor of the Gas Panic talking with this modern day Judas Iscariot. Celebrating all things American and yet selling out his country. God these people were confused, he thought.

"Cut the bullshit. Why did you have to kill Bender? He didn't even have anything. We had made the switch already. You knew that for Christ sake."

"For Siva's sake maybe, my friend. Certainly not for this Jesus Christ that you Americans parade around at your convenience. Particularly when some heathen, non-Christian people, not in lock-step with the political agenda of the reigning President must be obliterated from the face of the earth. All in the name of Jesus. Please do not speak anymore of this Jesus. You insult me. Bender San was...how do you say it? A loose cannon...Ah, I love the American idioms. He would have given us away, especially after he realized that he did not have any sarin at all, only fifty-five gallons of shit as you call it, I believe. Quite a nice touch. I must commend Okamoto San on that one. That was his idea. A beautiful twist. But, alas he is gone. Gone to a better place. Perhaps he and Bender are conversing now along with your Jesus Christ. I doubt it though. Bender will be burning in hell I believe. At least according to the dictates of your interesting yet paradoxical Christian faith."

The American glaring now. Muscles tensing. The vein along his temple pulsating like a horny toad ready for a fight. It wasn't supposed to be like this. Just a few isolated incidents to embarrass the Navy. The American Navy. The brass. The hypocritical assholes who had destroyed his old man. Ruined a brilliant thirty year career. It had gone too far now though. Much too far. No way of stopping it. Nothing he could think of now. Caught up in it like the proverbial "slippery slope."

"We need to end this now. Where is the sarin? I know it's not at Ikego. We agreed that it would be destroyed after the incident. The idea was to make the Navy look bad. Pin everything on Bender. The retired United States Navy guy. Destroy Bender and the Navy's reputation in the eyes of the Japanese. Base commander relieved. A scandal. Public outcry and all that. Eventually all the American military pulled out of Japan."

"Yes, of course, Commander...May I call you Commander?"

"You can call me god damn fucking Emperor Hirohito if you want. Just finish this. It ends now. Destroy the sarin."

A quizzical look from Asahara and then the laugh. The long guttural laugh. Atashi, sitting in the shadows behind them had heard this laugh many times. Usually a precursor to the horrible demise of the person or persons within earshot. Asahara had understood the allusion to Emperor Hirohito. A joke of course. Crude and tasteless if one understood anything about the Japanese culture, but he didn't really expect much from his guest along those lines. In any case, Steve Blasingame, Commander, United States Navy Intelligence Service was now Ashaara's most valuable mole so to speak. Recruited in much the same way as his Japanese cohorts. A bitter man. Brilliant career, yet unable to overcome the festering cancer within that was the destruction of his father's career. His father, the drunk. Destroyed by the alcohol yet Steve Blasingame would never accept that. When Aum had approached him, they had done it in such a subtle way.

"You do not want to avenge the destruction of your father?"

"Of course. But that's been done. Jesus, this has gone too far. You hear me? Get rid of the sarin. Now."

Blasingame to his feet now. Almost stepping towards Asahara. Thinking better of it. In any case, he would have been killed in an instant. A soldier with an AK-47 pointed directly at his temple just out of view. The military training in him sensed it. He turned to leave.

"The sarin has already been destroyed."

Asahara's words stopping the Navy man in his tracks.

"What are you saying? I thought..."

"We are not stupid, my friend."

"I'm not your friend."

"Yes, of course. We are not stupid in any case. We may be insane zealots following in the steps of Jim Jones and his cult, which is I believe how the Japan Times has referred to us in their latest editorial. The paper begins to bore me. Why is every once-reputable newspaper succumbing to the siren song of more yen and becoming a tabloid? Quite disconcerting. Well, no one reads any more. No matter."

Blasingame's patience wearing thin with this crazy.

"Please do not play games with me, I ..."

"Insolent bastard, The One never 'plays games' as you refer to it."

The table came crashing towards him, Asahara having kicked it with the force of a rugby player. Just missing Blasingame. Probably made of solid oak. Just as quickly as the rage started, he composed himself. Atashi, still out of Blasingame's view, had seen it before, but it still always managed to make him uneasy. He walked out from the shadows.

"Good Evening, Commander."

"You were here all the time?"

"Yes, please forgive the stealth measures. Necessary, unfortunately."

There is no more sarin, but this does not mean we are without a full house as you say in the poker world, I believe."

Blasingame momentarily disoriented. Watching Asahara, repulsed. The man was masturbating in full view of anyone who looked his way. Turning back to Atashi now.

"What the hell are you talking about? Look, I'm done. You've already killed at least three Americans."

"We have killed three Americans. I'm sorry to correct you, sir. But without your help we could never have brought this plan to fruition. We are indebted."

Blasingame slumped to a chair. His initial emotion of rage turning to remorse. Everything Atashi had said was true. He had sold out his country. He was responsible for the death of Bender and the woman at the train station as well as the marine at the Sanno, Sullivan. Of course he had no way of knowing it but he was also responsible, indirectly at least, for the death of Art Chambers.

"Yes, but we do not have a lot of time. We must move on. Would you please follow me, Commander? The One will not attend this experiment. He bids you adieu, as the French say. A very good segue if I may say so. Is 'segue' the correct word?"

"What in the name of God are you blathering about, man? I need to get back to my office. Any change in my schedule will arouse suspicion."

"Of course. This will not take long"

They walked to what appeared to be a storeroom door. Very dimly lit. The sound of the happy hour crowd could be heard below. The clink of glasses and animated conversation. Blasingame felt like he was a thousand miles away from them. He hardly drank. The curse of his father. Today might be a good time to imbibe heavily.

The stench was immediate. They had entered a small room. One light on the ceiling. Naked. Atashi turned it on. There in the middle of the room, a human being lying on a barren table, an animal-like gurgling sound emitting from deep within him.

"The subject was given ricin, a derivative of castor. The beauty of it is that castor is abundant throughout the world."

The sterile attitude that Atashi used around this man who was obviously undergoing terrible suffering inches away from him made Blasingame think of the Japanese medical unit that was exposed after World War II. The unit which was run by medical doctors conducted experiments on human beings. In some cases they actually dissected prisoners alive. Blasingame had read an article a few years back about one of the original members of the unit - an eighty-five year old man now living somewhere in Northern Japan was interviewed by the New York Times. What struck Blasingame was the man's ability almost fifty years later to look at the victims as objects rather than actual human beings. He said he had no problem with his conscience even to this day because these people were objects to him or Logs as he referred to them. Here now years later, Atashi displayed the same demeanor.

"The subject was given a dose of ricin thirty-six hours ago. As you can see, he is very close to expiration. Witness the shortness of breath, the choking and the dilation of the eyes. Ah yes, here it comes."

A loud other-worldly rumble from somewhere inside the man's chest. A red stain appeared through his white gown. Blood in the urine. A violent shuddering. Then, mercifully, silence.

"Yes, he is dead now I believe."

A quick look at the attending physician. A nod. Ren Hideo had died for the cause. Destruction before rebirth. The One would be proud.

"You sick bastards. What the fuck are you doing? What am I doing.? For the love of God, that is...was a human being."

"Please, Commander, remember your training. You are a military officer are you not? Compose yourself."

Blasingame's arm came down on Atashi's throat with the force of a sumo. Another ten seconds and the man's larynx would be broken. Out of the shadows, a blur and then a Japanese army boot, possibly size ten, struck his testicles. The pain agonizing. The grip withdrawn. Almost losing consciousness. Tears came to his eyes. Asahara standing over him. Next to him Minister Claude Lemieux.

"Deep breaths, Commander. Please bend over. You gave us no choice. I will decide if and when Atashi San moves on to the next world."

A soldier handed him a glass of beer. The one who had just practically obliterated his balls. He took it without looking up. Shaking in pain.

"We understand your wife is residing in Paris. Along with your child. A girl, I believe? Probably around thirteen now. Yes, a difficult age I am told. I had some growing pains during that period. Alas I was able to overcome them though."

The One looking off into the distance now.

Lemieux looking on nervously. Thoughts of his own brother's horrible demise flashing through his mind. Saying nothing. Watching Blasingame.

Asahara spoke.

"There has been a change in plans. A change as far as you are concerned. Of course we have never changed course. It was necessary to lead you in a direction which would enhance your cooperation so to speak. In any case, you will continue to help us. Your wife and daughter are currently comfortably ensconced in a location near Paris. When the time comes and providing you continue to cooperate in a manner that is acceptable to Aum, they will be released, and you will be given a considerable sum of money which you can use to settle anywhere in the world. Anywhere, of course, but the United States. I dare say that when your role in our victory is known, you will indeed be, how do you say, 'persona non grata'?"

A quick glance at Atashi to make sure the Latin phrase he had used was appropriate. The nod of approval from his mentor was enough to make him bounce up and down like a child. Surreal. Blasingame in the midst of all that he had just seen and heard could not help but think of the histrionics of Herman Munster from the TV show of his youth, awash with animated glee when given some type of approval from Grandpa or Lily.

Atashi sensing that matters needed to be brought to a close here. Danger of Asahara wandering a bit too far. He had seen it before. Needed his focus now.

"Gentleman, let us repair to a more comfortable meeting place. Please, follow me. The One will join us at his pleasure."

A bow to Asahara, a quick look to Lemieux as they were lead out of the room to what appeared to be a fake wall. An unseen button pushed and then brilliant light. The room resembling that of a large corporate venue. Possibly something that would be used by IBM or Sony. Scarlet chairs, about twelve of them, thought Blasingame as the pain finally began to subside in his groin.

A large screen at the head of the table which must have been at least thirty feet long. Made of mahogany he guessed. Two soldiers stood at either ends of the room. AK-47's at the ready. Blasingame marveled at how this much fire power could be here. Right in the center of Tokyo. A city known for its lack of gun violence. Of course the exception had occurred many times with the Yakusa, but since the public was not involved, people did not care. The death of Jack Bender by gun though had raised some voices in the media. Blasingame guessed that Aum did not really want him killed that way. Possibly strangulation or even this new ricin shit they were using. Asahara needed to be kept under control. Atashi was the real brains here.

Need to bide my time. Should have never kept Doris and Cheryl in Paris. The scumbag frog bastards could always be counted on to fuck the United States. Then again what was I doing? Sure, my father needed to be vindicated. But at what price? The former Aum soldier in the other room, recently expired. The heartless attitude of the Cult members present. No difference from Hitler years ago. What made human beings treat other human beings this way? Of course, then what of Hiroshima and Nagasaki? All in the name of God and Country. When did we stop being human?

Blasingame back to the present now. The gaggle of state-sponsored killers had taken their seats. Atashi walked to the screen.

"Gentleman, Minister Lemieux will now give an updated briefing. Certain events have taken place in the last few days that have forced us to be a bit more, shall we say, flexible. Minister Lemieux?"

Claude Lemieux. Minister of Cultural Affairs at the French Consulate in Tokyo. Well-respected, apolitical even by French Standards. Blasingame knew him well. At least his file. He had seen him at a few black-tie affairs at the American Embassy. Functions Blasingame was loathe to attend. The frog seemed like a pig in shit so to speak though.

I never did like the guy. Never liked the French either. Hated the fact that Doris insisted on living there after my posting expired as attaché in Paris. Cheryl loved it as well. Her friends were there. The usual excuses. Marriage not going very smoothly either in recent years. Many reasons why I didn't like the French. The French men a big reason. Doris in her forties now. Jesus why the hell did women decide to get horned out of their minds in middle age?

"Gentlemen, I believe you all know who I am. I hope you are feeling better, Commander."

A quick look at Blasingame then back to Atashi. Asahara wanking in the back. No help there.

"The sarin gas was essentially a decoy, a red herring as the Americans may refer to it. Ricin as you saw in the other room is a much more effective and easily handled substance. Lethal yet with none of the complications of the sarin. The ricin is taken from the castor plant. Actually a derivative of castor oil. It is water soluble which is extremely important as you will see and does not have to be made into a weapons grade form. As I said earlier, there has been a change in plan. Please."

"Mother of Jesus," Blasingame muttered as the detailed schematic of the Tokyo metropolitan water system went up on the wall.

The loud sigh behind him; Asahara's orgasm.

"The Tokyo metropolitan department of water supplies water for almost twelve million people. There are various purification plants that the water from the Tome River and other sources comes to before it is passed on to the public for their use. The ricin will be placed in one of these purification plants. In fact it is already 'staged' as I believe the military term is, Commander Blasingame?"

Blasingame beside himself. Fear and rage. Both fighting for supremacy now. Rage winning.

"Are you fucking out of your minds? Just from one purification plant you would kill thousands, possibly millions of innocent people."

"No one is innocent, my friend."

Asahara composed now. Uncanny. Strutting to the front of the room. At the dais now. Atashi bowing and moving to the side. The One back in control. At least for the moment.

"As we speak, Commander, forces from American and Japanese intelligence are on their way here. To be sure, I am surprised they have taken so long. They will arrest me as well as Atashi and some of my soldiers. The martyr, Ren Hideo, is now ash. His external shell put through the incinerator. I know you are concerned for him. He is now a great hero of the cause."

"Like he had a choice, you fuck-job," under his breath now.

"Excuse me…"

"Nothing. Clearing my throat. Bad air in here."

"I see. In any case the lawyers of Aum are well prepared, and I do not expect to spend too much time incarcerated. It is not about me or Atashi San, anyway. We will sacrifice for Siva as always."

A nod to Atashi.

"You will leave out the back, Commander A secret passage, you might say. Yourself and Minister Lemieux. It would cause too many questions if a senior American intelligence officer and a respected diplomat were found with such 'characters' as myself and Atashi San."

The pause for a laugh, none forthcoming.

"Yes. I will repair to the entrance, awaiting my arrest along with Atashi San. Minister Lemieux will brief you on your part of the plan. A very integral part, my dear Commander. Of course at first you may find it distasteful, but I'm sure you would find the rape and sodomizing of your wife and young daughter even more disturbing. Your daughter of course would go first, her mother watching. Distasteful, yes, but very necessary if we are to have your complete cooperation. Please understand. Nothing personal. Just business, I believe is the way your American Mafiosi would put it. Please, I must take my leave. The soldiers will escort you and Minister Lemieux to a location where you will be further briefed. I bid you adieu."

Lemieux looking down to avoid giving away his grimace. Asahara butchering the French language again. The man had the unique ability to be illiterate in multiple tongues.

• • •

The room awash with the smell of beer and death now two hours later at the Gas Panic. The American and the Frenchman now alone sitting on opposite sides of the mahogany table. Two folding chairs and a liter of green tea. The tea would go untouched. The silence too much for the American after the eerie tableau that he had witnessed just hours before.

"What the fuck is going on? What has happened here? How did we come to this, you and I? God help us."

"Yes, Commander. God or Siva. In any case we, you and I, do not have many options."

"You piece of shit. My wife and daughter are being held with the tacit permission of your spineless country. Of course with what you bastards did in Algiers, your alignment with torturous scum like the Aum does not surprise me."

"And you are without sin, my friend?"

The American started across the table but thought better of it.

"Please, Commander. Of course you are upset. I am upset."

The whole discussion taking on yet another aura of surrealism to Blasingame.

He looked at the Frenchman and for a brief moment, saw a human being.

"He killed my brother, you know."

Before he could explain further, the Aum soldier came in. It was time to depart.

Through a maze of trap doors, hidden walls and other ingenious devices of deception, the Commander and the Frenchman made their way out of the Gas Panic and into the street, a good half mile away from the building and out of sight of the arriving Japanese Special Defense Forces who had come to arrest Asahara. They never spoke. Both in their own self-made worlds of mental anguish and regret. Both trapped forever in the web that was Aum. No way out. Resigned to disgrace at best and indescribable horrors at worst.

The two guards motioned them into the Asahi Beer van. Doors shut behind them. They sped away. About an hour later, Blasingame found himself on the thirtieth floor of the Sony Corporate Office building in Yokohama. The Minister spoke first.

"You do not like me, I dare say, Commander?"

"Shit, what would ever give you that idea? I mean you're French, you're a traitor, partly responsible at least for the deaths of two Americans and countless other Japanese. Not to mention the fact that my wife and daughter are being imprisoned in your piece of shit excuse for a country and will be tortured and killed under the eyes of your government if I don't play ball in this game of genocide. No, I love you, Froggy."

Lemieux had developed the ability to ignore any insult. This gift, if it was that, usually reserved for those who had bartered away any sense of humanity or self-worth a long time ago. The minister now operating on purely animal instincts. He needed to survive, yet he could not intellectually say why or for what purpose.

"I told you he killed my brother. Of course I'm sure you knew that though, Commander. Your great intelligence apparatus. You are a competent man by all accounts. They abused him. Much the way the poor soul was killed back at the bar. Only they used sarin on my brother, not ricin. Frankly I don't know which is worse. Ricin easier to deliver I would think in any case. Asahara is insane. You realize that, I am sure?"

Blasingame seeing his nemesis in a different light now. Perhaps there was a man there after all. He would listen. Not give anything away. It could be a trap of course. A test of his loyalties. Too far into this demonic charade now. Only thing left was to save his wife and daughter.

"I'm listening. I need to get out of here. I've got a briefing, of all things. Don't want to be missed back at Hardy Barracks. Like it would matter now of course. Don't think I'll be the next CNO in any case."

No reaction from the Minister. The joke about reaching the most senior position for a military man in the United States Navy either lost on him or ignored.

"Why then?"

A curious look from Lemieux. No deciphering it. The sense there that the minister was a part of the whole bizarre scheme of things; the kidnapping of his wife and daughter, the Cult plans, everything. Something missing though. Lemieux not what one would call a true believer.

Blasingame of course with reasons. Tempered a bit since the events of the last few hours yet there nonetheless. The hideous demise of the former Cult member. A soldier reduced to a grotesque experiment. The status of Doris and Cheryl, his wife and daughter virtually imprisoned in Paris with the knowledge of the mass of ambiguity that sat across from him here in a secret briefing room high atop the Sony building. This lofty symbol of capitalism's incursion into Asia. The irony not lost on Blasingame.

The guy reminded him of John Cleese. The old Monty Python movies coming to mind. Cleese with a dark side. Tall, mustachioed. A large but appropriate nose. Distant now. *Was he in pain or holding back? Something or someone?*

"Commander, I am here, a part of this charade because I need to see the demise of Shoko Asahara. 'Pure and simple' I believe is the phrase used in America. Do you believe me when I express these sentiments?"

Of course Blasingame's belief was tied directly to whether he left this room alive. Lemieux knew this and sensed that Blasingame did as well. He prayed as much.

Blasingame, despite all the years of training in the nuances of the human condition, not ready for this. Off guard. Regaining composure now. The training kicking in. This could be a trick of course, he thought. A way for Lemieux to further solidify his standing with the Cult. For this to be true though, the minister would have to believe completely that Asahara would prevail. The man was a genius but with the flaws of the crazed as well.

"For the love of all that is human, do you fucking understand me?!"

The veins in the Frenchman's neck taking on the appearance of a Gila monster that Blasingame had seen in Sri Lanka years ago. Kids throwing rocks at something underneath a coffee warehouse. The building on stilts like most of the structures there due to the almost year round flooding. Blasingame a young junior officer on a tour to get away from his drunken shipmates. He could never stomach a drunk. Unable to come to terms with his father's alcoholism. The elder a victim of Navy politics he believed. Blasingame thinking a dog was hiding underneath the raised dwelling. When the seven-foot creature emerged, the young officer almost shit himself.

Lemieux's demeanor not far removed from the demon of days passed. Both displaying emotions based in fear and self-preservation. A rage at the injustice of life in general.

"Are we secure here?"

Blasingame knew the answer already but still scanned the room with the expert eye of one who had on occasion planted listening devices.

"Aum has a vetting process which is very effective although a bit unconventional, yet it is not as loyal a group as CNN would have us believe. We are secure. Here at least."

The minister able to move from unadulterated rage to an almost controlled serenity. Blasingame had seen this before. Only hours ago. Disconcerting.

"Are my wife and daughter in any danger?"

"They are fine. In fact as we speak, they are enjoying the comforts of first class aboard the regularly scheduled Paris to New York Air France flight, the premier airline in the world. Forgive my bias."

"Don't play with me, please, Minister Lemieux."

"There is no playing here, Commander. Asahara is being questioned at this very moment and thus is temporarily 'out of the loop' as your political pundits are apt to say."

Blasingame taking a moment to absorb this. Before it could fully sink in, the Frenchman handed him the cell phone.

"Please say hello to your wife, Commander. I will be happy when these wonderful products of communication's technology advance to the stage where they don't cost so damn much. Merde...I would appreciate it if you would make it a quick conversation. My embassy's budget is very tight these days."

A slight smile.

The phone feeling like a lifeline in his hand. *Please don't let this be a joke.* And then, "Hello?"

"Daddy is that you? Mom, Dad's on the phone. Wish you were here, Dad. This present is so rad! Love you, Daddy. Here's Mom."

"Cher..."

"Steve, what the hell is going on? Damn police van pulls up to the place this morning. All our stuff loaded up. No explanation. Just, "Sorry, madam, orders.' Is this some kind of fucking joke?"

Yes, there was no question it was Doris.

"Have to go, honey. I'll explain everything when you get to New York."

"You bet your..."

Click.

If it was a trick it was beyond diabolical. He believed the Frenchman. He had to.

"Thank you."

A moment to regain his composure and then, "Look, whether I believe you or not, what possible way out is there for us? I am finished. At the very least, my career is over. Worst case scenario which is realistic at this point is a long prison term and my family in disgrace."

The Frenchman nodded and then raised his head up. Looking directly into the American's eyes now.

"All is not as it appears, Commander."

71

Blackness all around. Claustrophobic. Like a velvet veil had been wrapped around her entire body. Translucent yet there nonetheless. Her own private cocoon. Something nearby though. Coming closer. A kind of light. No, a figure. Glowing. Trying to escape from the cocoon. The figure getting closer and closer. The scent of vanilla. Keiko had heard that sarin smelled of vanilla. Like the vanilla extract her mother had used to make white cake for her birthday. Hands on the cocoon now. Prying it open. A faint breathing. Labored. Now coughing. Coughing uncontrollably. The cocoon is ripped open. It is Rose. Blood streaming out of every pore. Her face, from a Picasso painting. Pure agony. Contorted with fear and pleading. "Why Keiko? Why me? Why me? I loved you."

Keiko's own screams woke her. The recurring nightmare. What to do now lying here in the hospital bed? Sterile yet peaceful. She had always had a love-hate relationship with hospitals. Her father had died in one. But they had a certain peace about them. One was safe. A bit different here though. The guard at her door only a few feet away. The blinds shut on the window which was always closed. They had left a few minutes ago. The security people. Members of American and Japanese intelligence. Congratulating her on her heroism. Interesting, a week ago she was one of the most sought after terrorists in Japan, probably the world. Now a hero. All was forgiven. She would never forgive herself though. Rose would always come to her. Pleading. Asking. *Why?*

She did not have an answer. Not now. Maybe never.

72

The Gaijin Boca was a throwback from another era. Literally meaning "foreign dead," it now was the resting place for scores of former warriors. Many of them the bright-eyed young Americans that had liberated the Japanese people and the world from the atrocities of the Japanese war machine. Tree lined, filled with spruce and oak and cherry. Here in the center of Yokohama this beautiful setting now filled with rows and rows of dead warriors. Most dying of old age or just bad living. Some lucky enough to have expired from a combination of both. The world here in 1992 a much different place then when these young warriors from Main Street USA saved Japan from itself. A world where the sons and grandsons of the militants of that war long ago had now taken root and begun a crusade of much more far reaching and lethal possibilities. The Age of Armageddon had replaced the world of, "The only thing to fear is fear itself."

The Tokyo Veterans of Foreign Wars Post 9450 gathered this day. A good turnout for one of their own, though, truth be told, not a very active member. Jack Bender had still been a Life Member who had paid his dues. Adam Welsh having a lot to do with the turn-out. Pretty much every man here coaxed into coming by Adam and Benny. After meeting at the Almond Café, Adam and Benny had decided on this memorial for Jack Bender. Benny here, Adam, Dan Bronsan. The latter had found the perfect excuse to get out of the hospital earlier than the doctors had wanted him to. Kelley here as well despite her father's objections. Benny had brought Joe Dickwell along. Dan not missing his daughter's obvious pleasure with Joe's unexpected appearance.

"A bit of an odd bird this Bender. He used to floss his teeth during lunch for the love of God."

"Yea, and you have the table manners of Martha 'Fucking' Stewart, Dan...Jeezus."

Adam and Dan about to get into again, Dan's back brace notwithstanding. Benny thinking maybe he should just let them go. Not here though. Not now.

"Gentlemen, or shipmates as you squid bastards would say, I believe; leave it to a civilized Air Force man to keep you knuckle-heads from going at it. Damn Adam, Dan here just had a helluva a couple days. And Dan, Adam here just lost a real good friend. Another one. Please. Kind of wish you were drinking, Petty Officer Welsh. At least you weren't so god damn ornery. Shit."

The bagpipe struck up almost on cue. Frank Waters, retired Army. Bagpiper extraordinaire. "Amazing Grace" lilting through the trees. The few birds that were there even stopped chirping. Attentive. A few Japanese guys that Jack had helped get sober standing to the side. Heads bowed. One or two in tears. Adam close to it now. He had fourteen days sober today. A miracle. Maybe this would actually be it.

Dan started first. A few in him before the service. Singing the first few bars. Holding the outstretched hand of his daughter.

"...to save a wretch like me..."

Yea, Adam had been saved, The wretch part applying as well. The pipes stopped mercifully. Joe Dickwell walking over to Kelley. The sun coming up in her eyes as she saw him.

"Hello, Kelley. You look great."

"You're not looking bad yourself. Been working out? Your butt looks even better than the first time I saw you."

"Kelley, Jesus, Mary and Joseph. Oh, what's the use. I need a drink. Would you gentlemen like to retire to the Sanno? All except for Adam of course."

"Actually I'd like to speak with Adam, yourself and Mr. Carter. I'm sorry it has to be under these circumstances. I have something to attend to right now, but in about an hour if you don't mind. Wherever is convenient for all of you of course. And Ms. Bronsan is invited as well."

"You bet your ass I'll be there."

Dan realizing that Kelley had had a few. Oh well. Under the circumstances, she deserved a drink, he supposed. Brave girl. He needed to tell her how proud he was. Her courage under unimaginable stress had helped save their lives. She and Keiko.

73

The plastic explosive had taken the door of the Gas Panic off as if it was made of cardboard. When the smoke cleared, the large figure in the crimson robe stood, hands stretched forward in a gesture of supplication. The bar below had been cleared as had all traffic within a mile radius. No mean feat on a Saturday night in Tokyo.

"Please come in, gentlemen. No need for guns or weapons of destruction here. I am a peaceful man, and, as you can see, I and my friend and lawyer, Atashi San, are the only ones present."

Shoko Asahara stood. An evil icon to most of the Japanese Special Defense troops who were here to ensure his arrest was done without any problems. American and Japanese authorities wanted Asahara alive. The warrant was for a complete search of the premises, and the arrest was on charges of suspicion of conspiracy to commit murder. Japanese law unlike its American counterpart assumed guilt before innocence. Asahara was handcuffed and led into the waiting van. Snipers placed on the rooftops surrounding the Gas Panic. Asahara needed to be alive. There were forces within his own circle who wanted a martyr. Perhaps The One himself.

HIROO POLICE STATION

"A very disturbing occurrence, gentleman. Of course I am sorry for the poor man's loss. No doubt a very deranged person."

The thought of Shoko Asahara referring to anyone as deranged was not lost on Joe Dickwell or any of the other participants taking part in the interrogation of this mass of flesh and psychosis.

"Is that why you killed Jack Bender, Mr. Asahara?"

"Do not answer that question, Asahara San."

Two Cult lawyers present here in the basement interrogation room of the Hiroo Police Station. Asahara had been brought in more for questioning than with any hopes of actually convicting him for the murder of Jack Bender. No witnesses. No weapon found. Dickwell knew that neither would ever turn up. Perhaps a few dead bodies. Nothing more though. Aum always tied up loose ends. Very careful. Sanitary. He watched as Dusty Rhodes tried to move questioning in another direction - The late Peanut and the subject of sarin.

"My client will not answer any questions that do not pertain to the matter he has been detained for."

"Ha!"

Asahara jumping up. Prancing. Quick on his feet for a large man, thought Dickwell.

One of the young lawyers ignoring it. He had seen it too many times before.

"Our client is tired. Are we finished here?"

Asahara dangerously close to morphing into "Demonic Whack-Job." His lawyers well aware of the potential for embarrassment. "Wouldn't be prudent" as former American President George Bush might have said.

"Can we hold him?"

Dusty Rhodes and the head of Japanese Intelligence along with Captain Osaka, Commander of the Tokyo Police huddled out of earshot.

The Tokyo Police Commander spoke first.

"Under Japanese law we can hold him for thirty days without charging him with any crime. You might say that we here in Japan consider the accused guilty until proven innocent. I believe that your American system lends itself more to protecting the rights of the criminal rather than the victim so this may be hard for you to understand. With all due respect."

He stared directly at Dusty. No love lost.

"Yes, Captain, of course your country is fairly new to concepts such as law and mercy. I don't believe you were burdened with concerns such as these during the Bataan Death March and other such escapades from your country's relatively recent past."

Dickwell barely concealing his approval. He loved Dusty. Red, white and blue to the core. Don't tread on me.

The Captain for his part, nonplussed.

The interrogation had been going on for at least three hours now. No progress. Going nowhere. Asahara moving from Madman to Buddha with ease. A smattering of childlike neuroses thrown in for good measure. Dickwell seeing the consistency throughout of the well-coached "talking points." The One staying on message. Atashi had coached him well before they were arrested and separated by the police. Bender had approached Asahara with a gun, and someone had shot him. Asahara of course did not know who. He had many who loved him after all. Would give their lives in an instant for The One. It could have been anyone, he explained. Many people worshipped Shoko Asahara. His death would not be tolerated. It could not be allowed.

74

Pounding. Shaking. *Why the fuck did I have to have that drink?* Always one more. Just one more. He blamed it on the city. This city. This Tokyo. This land of contradictions. Smile in your face, bow and then place the poker directly up the anal orifice. You wouldn't even know until later. Mesmerized by the smiles. The women making things more complicated. He needed to get home. Back to Long Island. Norma and normalcy. No more Asian trips. Time to retire.

Last night another night in a string of self-abuse that strung together like one of those carnival movies he had seen as a kid. The ones where the cards came flipping past so fast that it appeared the characters were actually moving. Almost puked thinking about it. All coming back in bits and pieces now. An innocent line of coke inevitably leading to another and then a drink and more drinks. With 8 PM becoming 10 PM, then midnight and then... The alarm rousing him at six. The big meeting. He had done it again. Incomprehensible demoralization. *Why?* Godamn, he had to stop, he thought. Almost out loud. Start all over.

Sam Wilson, investment banker for Lehman Brothers Japan, here at the Almond Café on a busy (it was always busy) Monday morning. Hung over. Sick. The need for a large coffee overwhelming. The momentary solace of the caffeine buzz. Yes, the coffee would do it. Pick him up. No more booze.

He looked around at the assembled array of Japanese businessman, foreign tourists and ladies of the night stopping in for a coffee before heading back to whatever hovel they resided in to begin the impossible yet necessary task of washing the sins of the evening away. The mind racing too god damn fast now. Needed it to stop. The coke and booze always took care of that of course. Able to figure things out. The problem was that life was still there when he woke up shaking.

He did not pay much attention to the kid at first. Music blaring from somewhere inside the ratty, Dead Kennedy stickered knapsack. Camel jockey, A-fucking-rab music thought Wilson. About to scream at the little ignorant punk. Turned to him. About to grab his arm. Thought better of it. The kid looked at him. He was not here. Not in the Café. He had already left. The body here but whatever passed for a soul already heading to some far off destination. Somewhere that Sam immediately knew he did not want to visit.

The boy an angelic visage. A disturbing peace. Odd.

"Turn that down. Please."

The last words Sam Wilson would speak didn't seem to be coming from his mouth. He was spellbound. Not knowing why. Something in the kid's face. *Serenity?*

"Allah be praised" was what Sam thought he heard. *Was that an Irish accent?* Sam's curiosity and building anxiety never getting a chance to achieve completeness. The boy staring directly into Sam as he pushed some unseen button within the bag. A circuit now complete. Five pounds of Semtex explosive melting Sam Wilson's face but not before he saw the kid smile.

• • • • •

Shamus Burlie, wearing a "Give Ireland Back to the Irish" tee shirt that his son and daughter had given him for his birthday, picked up the pay phone receiver and dialed the secure line. "The truth is rarely pure and never simple," he said before he hung up and walked away from the carnage that had once been a bustling café. The quote from *The Importance of Being Earnest* the signal to the Irish ambassador that the mission had been accomplished.

75

"Thank you all for your attendance. I'm sorry for my tardiness, but I had an earlier meeting that lasted longer than expected."

Joe deciding not to bring up the interrogation of Asahara. This briefing needed to be quick.

Joe Dickwell had reserved the Presidential Room at the Sanno. Not really Presidential. In fact no President had ever been in the room, let alone even stayed at the Sanno Hotel. The biggest celebrity, literally and figuratively, had been Akebono, the Yokozuna - Grand Champion of sumo. Half American, born in Guam and married to an American, he had stayed in the New Jersey Suite in point of fact with his wife and his two little daughters. Adam Welsh thought of the first time he had seen Akebono in this setting. The real person. Not the persona created by the sumo world. One morning Adam had been coming off another drunken bout and was on his way out of his room to get some drinks down at the bar. The hair of the dog that bit him. Akebono's door and his across the way had opened simultaneously to reveal the man-mountain and two sets of tiny eyes peering out from behind one of his tree-trunk legs. A quick smile from the cherubs before his little daughters disappeared behind the Sequoias. Adam had rode the elevator with the man. Liked him. Akebono had invited him and Keiko to be his guest that night at the Mongolian Barbecue. Adam worried that he himself would be devoured along with the Mongolian. Keiko had laughed.

One of the last times he remembered her as truly happy before the nightmare. Over now though.

Please let it be over, Jesus.

Here now in the Presidential Room, used by the VFW for their monthly meetings. Strict adherence to a no-booze policy which was irrelevant since most of the participants with the exception of the sainted Father Judd, who was one hundred and five if he was a day, had all gotten blasted before and would continue to do so after the day's business was finished. Adam remembered bringing a cup of coffee that reeked of Jack Daniels to one meeting. Never heard the end of it from Dan. Had to buy him four gins afterwards at the bar to finally get him to change the subject of how Adam had destroyed the sanctity of the venerable Veterans of Foreign Wars meeting. Oh well. Different now. Art had been there as well. The great conciliator, gone forever now.

Dickwell speaking.

"I'll get right to the point. Before I do however, please understand that everything I say stays in this room."

Adam laughing quietly. Dickwell caught it.

"Petty Officer Welsh? Something funny?"

"No sir, nothing. Just the "What you see here, what you say here, stays here. Here, here.' Jack used to say it at A.A. meetings. Anonymity and all that. Seems kind of ironic."

"Yes, I see. I'm sorry for your loss, again. He was a good man. Troubled. A good man nonetheless."

"Troubled, sir?"

"Petty Officer Welsh, I'm getting ahead of myself here. More will be revealed."

A slight wink. Trying to diffuse a possible inflammatory situation. Joe Dickwell had done his A.A. homework. Quoting the text of the Big Book, the Bible of Alcoholics Anonymous.

"Shoko Asahara, as you all may or may not know, is the head of an organization called the Aum Shinrikyo or Aum Cu ..."

Adam on his feet.

"Heard of him? The piece of shit killed Rose, might as well have killed Art along with her. He did as far as I'm concerned. Is he why we're here?"

"The meeting that Lieutenant Dickwell spoke of earlier was actually an ongoing interrogation of Shoko Asahara. He is in custody as we speak,"

Benny speaking now in a formal, military tone. Adam taking note. Benny Carter not missing anything. He had talked to Keiko of course. Knew the whole story. Not letting on to the others though. Especially Adam. Adam knew more than he was saying. Loyalty to Jack. He sensed the connection. Knew what Dickwell was up to. Break Adam, with his friends as the hammer. For his part, Adam keeping the eternal poker face. He wasn't very good at cards though. Benny knew it.

"Yes, Master Sergeant."

Dickwell staying on formal military terms with everyone. Couldn't afford to compromise the investigation. He liked all of them. Couldn't be one of them though. He had to remain what he was — Lieutenant Joe Dickwell, Naval Investigative Service. As if on cue, Kelley chimed in.

"Joe, or should I call you Lieutenant?"

Dickwell not taking the bait. He let Kelley continue.

"I see. Okay, Lieutenant. Anyone with half a brain knows that the bastard who almost killed my father and me is not a member of the Jehovah's Witnesses. He wanted to kill the Japanese girl..."

Adam couldn't control himself.

"Her name is Keiko. I believe she saved your life. It would be nice if you could remember her name."

"And, matey, I suggest you remember that my daughter would not have needed to had her life saved in the first place, which by the way was more due to the Jar Head incursion and her own quick thinking and a bit of blind luck I might add, than..."

"Why you ungrateful, fat bastard..."

"Petty Officer Welsh, stand down. Now!"

"Yes, sir."

Glaring at Dan. Stand by for heavy rolls.

Kelley seemingly unperturbed.

"I guess all I'm trying to say is that the girl Keiko is a big part of this. Am I right?"

"Again, Ms. Bronsan..."

Kelley wanted to castrate him on the spot and feed his balls to the squirrels. She smiled coyly instead. Progress.

"We seem to be getting a bit ahead of ourselves. Please be patient. All of you. Thank you. You have been asked here because Shoko Asahara is a central figure in an ongoing joint Japanese-American investigation into the Aum Cult and their possible role in the death of Rose Carney as well as various unsolved deaths of Japanese nationals. The common denominator, if you will, in all these deaths being traces of the chemical agent, sarin. Mr. Asahara was arrested by Japanese authorities approximately three hours ago. And now to continue with the briefing and to further explain why you are here, I would like to introduce the officer in charge of the investigation, Commander Steve Blasingame."

"Thank you, Lieutenant. Ladies and Gentleman. Some of you I have already had the pleasure of meeting. I am a military man utmost and foremost. As such I am also what was called in my time a 'straight-shooter.'"

"Yes, no bullshit, I believe."

"Yea! That's my daughter!" Dan unable to contain himself.

Benny laughing. Smiles all around. Blasingame caught off-guard but quickly regrouping.

"Yes, very well, Ms. Bronsan. No need for further clarification here."

A weak smile. Dickwell noticing Blasingame not in complete control like he remembered from their earlier meetings. Unknown to everyone but Dickwell and the Commander, the meeting had to be started an hour later than scheduled due to Blasingame's tardiness. Highly unusual thought Dickwell. A mental note filed.

"Please remember that this briefing is Top Secret and Compartmented. Do not even talk of the proceedings here among yourselves. Is that clear?"

"Yes, sir."

Adam Welsh smiling at the Commander. Tension here. No love lost. The alky and the alky's son.

"Navy Intelligence, indeed National Intelligence has known about the Aum Cult for years. Originally the organization was looked at more as a bully pulpit for the ranting of a crazy known as Shoko Asahara. An unstable zealot but harmful only to the hearts and minds of his weak...excuse me, vulnerable followers."

Adam unmoved. Staring intently at Blasingame. The commander continued.

"All of this changed with the tragic death of Rose Carney. I know that she was a dear friend to many of you here. My deepest condolences. Rose Carney, and I again remind you of the classification of this meeting, was murdered. We have laboratory forensic proof verified by Japanese Intelligence that Ms. Carney was killed with a lethal dose of the gas called sarin."

Adam shaking more noticeably now. Benny picking it up right away. Touching his friend's shoulder lightly. Reassuring.

"The reason you are all assembled here and are being given access to highly classified information is that frankly we don't have much time and you all were linked to Rose Carney in some way and thus can help us in the investigation. That is only part of the reason however. Since the death of Ms. Carney, NSA and various Japanese Intelligence and law enforcement agencies have noticed an increase in communications between Aum Cult operatives here and known terrorist groups in the Middle East as well as Europe. The death of Jack Bender gave us the excuse, if you will, to pick up Shoko Asahara for questioning."

"Why didn't we pick this scumbag up earlier?"

Benny Carter, visibly upset. The death of Rose Carney coming back to him now. The fact that Asahara had orchestrated it and almost killed his "daughter" Keiko. Killed one of his best friends in the world as well. Art Chamber's ghost no doubt present in the room now.

"If we had picked him up earlier, there was the possibility that Aum would have hit a soft target with the sarin they had. We did not know where the sarin was so..."

"Excuse me, Commander, you used the past tense there?"

The Navy Intelligence background in Adam Welsh still alive and well.

"Let me get right to the point. As it turns out, the Aum Cult does not have any sarin gas, at least not of the weaponized variety. The cave at Ikego where we believed Jack Bender had helped hide a large cache of it was searched. Nothing. Unknown to the media is the fact that Jack Bender transported a 55 gallon drum of what he believed to be weapons grade sarin to a safe house of Aum in Roppongi within the Gas Panic bar. We believed he intended to kill himself, Shoko Asahara and anyone within a ten mile radius of it with the cargo he thought he had. It turned out to be nothing but raw sewage."

"Jesus fucking Christ!"

Adam Welsh over the top now. Withdrawal from the booze and now the news that his best friend in the world, his surrogate father, had died for nothing. A barrel of shit.

"Petty Officer Welsh, please come with me..."

Before Dickwell could finish, the Commander's aide burst into the room. A few words spoken under his breath. Blasingame with the look of someone who had been told some very bad news indeed. Fighting for composure.

"Ladies and Gentleman, this meeting is adjourned."

76

Carnage.

NIS here to assist with the police due to the fact that the bombing victims could involve naval personnel. A possible connection to Aum, the first thought that came to Dusty Rhodes' mind as he arrived at what had only recently been a place of joy and happiness. A place where lovers met, old acquaintances reunited, business deals struck. Now these dreams and hopes lay scattered in the form of fingers, arms, bowels. Dusty trying to look away but couldn't. The attempt at professionalism a struggle. Finally winning. Nothing he saw in Nam could prepare him for the sight of the eyes of a once beautiful Japanese woman staring up at him from inside a face that was no longer attached to a scull. A mask now. Macabre in the extreme.

Dickwell threw up. Dusty ignored him. Time to get on with the task at hand. He had to. For his own sanity. For the sake of them all. Trying to speak over the din of the sirens and the sobs of the survivors.

Does one really "survive"? How does one go from the light banter of the young in love to the sight of ones future wife detached from her body. A bloody faceless mass? No. There are no real survivors of an atrocity such as this. How did the Israelis stay sane? Keep any semblance of civilization?

The task at hand.

"Sir, you say that you were half a block away or so, heading towards the Café when the explosion occurred?"

"My girlfriend! She is in there. Please, I need to see her."

"Yes, sir. Please just a few questions."

A quick glance at Dickwell. He had regained his composure. The puke helped. Dusty would join him soon. Needed to finish up here. At least a score dead. Many more maimed. Traces of C-4 or Semtex as it was commonly called had been found. The terrorist's calling card.

"Your name, sir, is Enimoto? Is that correct?"

"Yes, yes. I was coming here to meet my girlfriend. I am a university student. A loud explosion. So loud! Her name is Midori. Have you seen her? Midori Masai. Have you seen her?"

Dusty trying to keep the vision of the disembodied eyes from his consciousness. It could very well have been Midori.

"Enimoto San, please just a few questions and then you will be escorted to the information offices. Did you hear or see anything out of the ordinary before the explosion? Any person or persons that may have seemed suspicious?"

"No, nothing....wait, there was someone. This punk bumped into me as I was leaving the place for a moment to look for a rest room. I remember because I was looking back to see where Midori was. She was waiting for her drink. She always had to order the fancy drinks. You know, the ones that take forever to make?" Enimoto started to lose it. Regained control and, "He was in hurry. Had a knapsack with Dead Kennedy's stamped on it. Who the hell listens to them anymore? The eighties are over. Loud music coming from the knapsack though."

"What kind of music? Punk?"

"No, that was the weird thing. It was Arab music. Something that you might here at a Mosque."

· · · · ·

FRENCH CONSULATE, TOKYO

"Minister Lemieux, call for you, sir."

"Thank you. I will take it on the secure line."

Blasingame was on the other end.

"Are we secure?"

"As secure as the times allow."

The code phrase decided upon at the meeting inside the Sony building dispensed with to his satisfaction, Blasingame spoke.

"What in the name of Jesus H. Christ are you doing?"

"I'm sorry. What are you saying, Commander?"

"You know damn well what I'm saying. The Almond Café. It's dust as of this morning."

A pause.

"Yes, regrettable. Suffice it to say that some interests out of our control were responsible. I'm sure you know of whom I speak. They are, shall we say, concerned about the arrest of our former associate."

Blasingame's roar was cut off with, "Please meet me at the usual place. Twenty minutes."

Click.

The Frenchman held the phone to his ear even after it had disconnected. Finally returning it to its cradle as his hand began to shake violently.

The bombing at the Almond Café had been instigated by Peter O'Mara and the provisional wing of the I.R.A. The ambassador would say it was a necessary diversion of course. French intel had discovered the plan but too late to stop what Lemieux knew was the work of a feeble little man who simply resented being "left out of the loop."

77

"The death toll in the bombing of the Almond Café, a popular meeting place and landmark in the heart of the Roppongi district of Tokyo, Japan, has now reached 52 with the death of an unidentified young Japanese woman. In a surprising development, a fringe group connected to the Irish Republican Army not Al Qaeda as previously suspected, has taken responsibility for the morning bombing claiming retribution for the arrest of Aum Cult leader, Shoko Asahara who is himself a supporter of the Provisional Irish Republican Army. It must be noted that Ireland was an ally of Japan during the Second World War. Sinn Fein the political arm of the I.R.A. has denied involvement and has denounced the attack. This is Mary Otterbein, CNN reporting from Tokyo."

CNN reporting the latest on the Almond Café bombing. Old news to the Frenchman and the American seated at a corner booth in Paddy Foley's Irish pub here in Roppongi.

"You have spoken to your wife and daughter in New York?"

"Yes, yes. Thank God. I guess...possibly..."

The Frenchman ending the American's effort at a "Thank you" with a glance, a lowering of the eyes.

"Under Japanese law, Asahara can be held for thirty days without being charged."

"Seems okay to me. Keep the scum locked away, Course he'll probably enjoy it. Stroking away in blissful arrogance. What about the piece of leprechaun dung?"

The reference to O'Mara. Lemieux ignored the crude reference. He knew that the American was a clever man who used a redneck façade to hide a certain intelligence. In any case, the fact that the Almond Café bombing was just a red herring to distract the powers that be from the real Armageddon would be revealed in time. For now, the minister would use it to control Blasingame.

Paddy Foley's was an Irish pub in the true sense of the term. Guinness flowing from every corner of the room along with the occasional Jameson. The old-timers the only ones these days imbibing in the whiskey though. The younger crowd more health conscious, if that was possible within the confines of an Irish pub. Blasingame had read somewhere that the Irish and the Japanese had developed a bond during World War II that continued to this day. CNN had just mentioned it in fact. Various Irish-Japanese friendship days were celebrated all over Tokyo, usually at universities and right around St. Patrick's Day. He sipped his Diet Coke as Lemieux, Guinness in hand, continued his update on what had transpired since the meeting at the Sony Building.

"The incident this morning was directly related to Asahara's arrest. We now have a connection with certain elements in the Middle East who were not originally 'onboard' as you might say. This will make things complicated," Lemieux interjected.

"Please don't play with me. The Irish connection is real. No fake news from CNN this time. We have some pretty good intel as well. How long before Asahara realizes that my wife and daughter are no longer being held? I'm sure he can get that information even in jail."

A nervous pause by Lemieux.

"He knows already."

Blasingame barely able to contain himself.

"What, how..."

"Commander, they are safe. You have my word. Time is of the essence however..."

"Top of the morning. Sorry I'm late. Damn embassy business never stops. Not even on a Sunday when any self-respecting Irishman should be in the pub. I'm Peter O'Mara, I don't believe I've had the pleasure."

Peter O'Mara, Irish Ambassador to Japan. Pedophile and sometime tormentor of Adam Welsh took a seat and ordered a Jameson.

The fact that Blasingame did not kill the ambassador right then and there was a true testament to years of military training. How long he could tolerate this man who was responsible for the horrific scene just a few miles away was quite another story. Blasingame had seen O'Mara many times before at various embassy and DOD functions. The guy was always drunk but in a controlled sort of way. Got away with it due to his ancestry more than likely. An Irishman's reputation would be suspect if he didn't drink. Wary now. *Why was he here? What was the connection to Lemieux.* Questions. So many and so little time.

"Commander, I will get right to the point. The ambassador is an ally. He has been for a while."

"An ally!?"

The Ambassador gave the minister a a knowing look. Almost pixyish. He then turned to Blasingame. A leprechaun withholding the Pot of Gold possibly. He raised the Jameson to his lips and drained it. Grimaced. A glow appearing on his cherub-like cheeks. So much for sipping whiskey, thought Blasingame. Lemieux never took his gaze off Blasingame.

The ambassador spoke.

"Aye, to be sure, the nectar of the Gods. One of these days it will get me, but until that time I will float with the angels. Aye, where is Dylan Thomas when you need him. Why are all the great writers drunks and Irishman? Creativity my friend. Creativity and the sensitivity wrought from centuries of trials and tribulations. Christ the whole race would have died of pure boredom without the booze. You know Adam Welsh, do you not, Commander?"

The question meant to come into his unguarded flank. Test his reaction. O'Mara knew that Blasingame was familiar with Welsh. He also knew that he despised him. A test. O'Mara looked from Blasingame to Lemieux. The Frenchman seemingly reading his Irish associate's mind. Nodding in assent.

Looking back at Blasingame. The man was non-plussed. Well-trained. Poker face all the way.

"Of course I know Petty Officer Welsh. Washed out crypto type. A drunk."

He looked away a bit from O'Mara as he said this last. The ambassador smiling.

"Oh, no need to be embarrassed on my account, Commander. 'Drunk' is a highlight on one's resume as far as I'm concerned."

Lemieux laughing aloud. A nervous laugh. Blasingame finding this odd. A different side of the Frenchman. He continued to surprise.

"Yes, well, Commander, he is a good man nonetheless. A drunk is not a bad person necessarily. I believe your father was known to tipple a bit."

"Why you mick bastard..."

Blasingame coming across the table. Lemieux grabbed him midway. The ambassador never moved. He took another sip from his drink. Ordered another one. All the while looking directly at Blasingame.

"Never meant to offend, Commander. I knew your father. Good man. He was a young attaché, and I was just starting out in the mail room at our consulate in DC. Good man. You should be proud. Your Admiral Halsey had a few on occasion. Nothing to be ashamed off. Christ, Halsey even ran a ship aground. Different time though. Now, they relieve you for anything."

"Forget it. It's been a rough few days. Minister, why are we here"...and then looking directly at O'Mara, "and why in the name of all that is sane in this world were innocent lives obliterated at the..."

The Frenchman had shown no emotion up to this point. Letting the drama play out between the Irishman and the American. Analyzing before utilizing. He cut off the American before he could go any further. The bar was crowded but there could always be someone listening.

"Shoko Asahara is in the custody of the American and Japanese authorities. As we speak, he is being interrogated. We have a special detachment of Mossad entering the country in approximately one hour to add their, shall we say, 'unique' persuasion skills to the process."

Blasingame very familiar with Israel's intelligence agency. The very best. Of course if you are a tiny country surrounded by countries whose only goal in life is to remove you from the face of the earth, you make sure you have the very best Intel around. Blasingame mulling this as he peered over at the ambassador. The man seemed sober. If the booze was having any effect he hid it well. Very well. The new found information that the Frenchman was not only one of the "good guys" but obviously very highly placed just now beginning to sink into the Commander's consciousness.

The minister continued.

"The bottom line, Commander, is that Al Qaeda is now involved as well. This thing is world-wide. Aum had a very small amount of sarin. Asahara had his lieutenants thinking that they had much more. We believe now that Al Qaeda was the source of the sarin. A way for them to monitor the reaction of American and Japanese intelligence. They were able to find some holes. Holes we cannot talk about just yet. Suffice it to say that Jack Bender, a friend of Adam Welsh and Keiko Watanabe, was a part of the plan, knowingly or unknowingly.

"Petty Officer Welsh?"

The Frenchman noting Blasingame's surprise. It was clear that he did not know the connection between Asahara, Keiko Watanabe, Adam Welsh and Jack Bender. The music was loud here in the Pub. Starting to fill up now. Belly to belly at the bar. About two rows deep. A Gaelic quintet warming up over strains of U2 on the jukebox. Exactly why Lemieux had chosen this meeting place. No chance of eavesdropping either electronically or aurally.

"Ricin. You have heard of this, Commander?"

The ambassador staring at Blasingame with the look of a college professor addressing a freshman. Sober as the proverbial judge now.

"Yes. Of course. Made from castor I believe. We have a task force on it now. Some of our best biochemists looking into it."

"They need to look faster. Al Qaeda has it, and we know they will use it. Only not in the way we originally believed. We are talking an end of the world event, Commander. The bombing earlier carried out by forces within the IRA..." a quick look at O'Mara... "to make Al Qaeda think we are off their scent. The lives of scores a regrettable but fair tradeoff for the saving of perhaps millions."

The American lowered his head and gasped, "Dear God in heaven."

78

"You can make this a lot easier for yourself and your family. I believe you have a daughter, do you not, Mr. Asahara?"

Back in the interrogation room here in Hiroo jail. Joe Dickwell had gotten the little tidbit about Asahara's daughter from one of the Japanese guards. Strange how the Tokyo police commander had failed to bring it up.

"Her name is Mikasa. Pretty name."

Asahara began to shake. His back was to his audience. Hard to tell whether he was shaking with laughter or something else. The madness perhaps? Something gleaming. The guard lunged a split second before Asahara brought the shiv around and up towards the midsection of Joe Dickwell. A scream. The shiv had found its mark. The guard lay quivering on the floor. Asahara brought down by two other guards. The guard saving Dickwell's life. Bleeding on the floor. Asahara crying out like a wounded animal himself.

"Mikasa my cherry blossom. Why have you forsaken me. I will cleanse them. All of them, my daughter."

"Shut him the fuck up. How the hell did he get this in here. Get a medic in here now."

Dusty Rhodes beside himself with rage. Staring directly at the Japanese Police Commander.

"So this is your security?! Christ almighty, I've seen better security at a Philippine whorehouse!"

Nothing but a blank stare from the Japanese. The Madman muttering incoherently in the corner.

Dickwell turning.

"The guard saved my life. Jesus H. Christ. How the hell did he get the shiv, Dusty?"

"I believe the Inspector could answer that question. Couldn't you? Talk to me you piece of shit before I rip your fucking head off." Rhodes beside himself. The rage palpable. Joe had never seen this side. Dusty always in control although the cauldron was always simmering. Just below the surface. Mount Pinatubo had blown now though. No holding him back. Joe positioned himself between the black man and the Japanese and waited.

The Japanese moved towards the exit and Rhodes knocked him out with a roundhouse worthy of Jack Johnson. Dickwell staring in disbelief.

"Pick this piece of garbage up, and take him to the consulate for interrogation." The two Marines standing at the doorway picked the Japanese policeman up and took him away. The Japanese soldiers did nothing.

"I'll explain later, Joe. Suffice it to say that the scum is one of Asahara's soldiers. One of the reasons we haven't been able to pick him up for so long. Never could get anything on him. Tipped off at the last minute every time we got close. Unfortunately we had to let something like the shiv incident happen to get anything on the scumbag."

79

Keiko Watanabe walked through Harajuku on a beautiful summer's day. She loved this part of Tokyo. The fashion district, the young people and the outlandish outfits. This is where the Dancing Elvises could be found. A group of Japanese men all with outlandish pompadours, prancing through the streets. Passersby could not help but see the glow emitting from the young woman's face. A look not unlike that of one who had just been told that the initial diagnosis of terminal cancer was just a mistake. Charts misplaced. Very sorry. You will live now. Please enjoy. Once condemned now resurrected. Keiko did not merely look at the beauty around her, she devoured its entire essence. Keiko Watanabe was alive.

Given the circumstances surrounding Keiko Watanabe's life up to this point, it would seem ludicrous for the redeemed to now leave the idyllic setting of a glorious spring day in Tokyo, board the subway to Roppongi, leave the station and walk to the dark, whiskey-sated environs of Paddy Foley's Pub. This is what she did however. The price of her redemption. Not without consequences. Nothing in life for free.

The ambassador met her with open arms. She sat immediately without any acknowledgement. For this charade, done out of necessity, the old Keiko would take center stage. The snub not lost on Blasingame or the Frenchman.

"Yes, well, Ms. Watanabe..."

"Keiko, Keiko Watanabe."

She dismissed him.

Looking directly at Blasingame. No sign that the ambassador even existed as far as she was concerned.

"Commander."

"Please, Keiko, call me Steve."

Blasingame taking her hand somewhat uneasily. Regretting agreeing to the plan now. Too late in any case. The Frenchman standing and bowing. The music reverberating. The smell of stale alcohol and sated souls. Cheery, artificial conversation throughout fueled by the booze.

One night, eons ago she had found Adam here. Chatting up two woman right there at the bar. Their earlier date broken with deceit. He had to stay on the ship, he told her with fake remorse. She had come here that night hoping not to find him. Moving in behind him. Hysterical with rage and hurt. Flailing out at him. The crowd laughing at the spectacle of the small Japanese girl punching the American man almost twice her size.

A redemption of sorts now. Love returns. Keiko and Adam together again. Stronger. They were not really in love before, thought Keiko. A series of events and a kind of spiritual awakening had taken place for both of them.

Keiko Watanabe had one last thing to do before her rebirth was complete. The death of Asahara, his total destruction was imperative of course The ambassador a pawn. The history of Adam and the Irishman only recently completely explained to Keiko. Part of her new relationship with Adam. The complete unconditional honesty. The morning in the hospital when Adam had confessed the whole sordid past. Keiko knew that this was the end of Adam's cheating. He was hers forever now. She would never have to share him with John Barleycorn or any other woman. Adam's demons dying with the confession of the atrocities committed by the Irishman on his body and on his soul. A wreckage of the past. Just part of the tally that Adam had built up while drinking away his life. All in the past now. Business to be done. Plans to be made. Not much time.

"Are you with us, my dear? You seem distant."

Lemieux bringing her back. He sensed the tension between her and the ambassador. Knew it was there. That was enough. Needed to move things on. Blasingame looking on. The sooner this was finished, the better, *God save us all.*

80

"The guard will live , sir."

"His name please?"

"Oh yes, of course, sir. Makoto Mitori. He is 22. No family. His parents died in a car accident when he was young. He was going to make the police his career."

"I want him promoted immediately with honors. Arrange a note, some kind of statement from the Prime Minister. What about Asahara?"

"He is in the facility infirmary."

"Isolated I hope?"

"Yes, sir."

"And the police chief?"

"In custody being transported to Yokosuka Naval Base Brig for interrogation as per your orders, sir."

"Very well. Take me to Asahara. Now."

81

"Dad, I worry about Keiko. I had a dream about her last night. It was horrible."

The room here at Yokosuka Base Housing reminded Dan of more serene times. Times when he and Cathy, his first wife, actually his only wife were living the white-picket fence American Dream. Dan light years away from that now. Jeez how times had changed. The world was an evil place, thought Dan as he looked at the love of his life. His fragile angel. Dan wondered if it really was the vilest it have ever been. He remembered talking with Art about whether or not we were in the Last Days. Only a year ago now. Seemed like a million though. Eons ago. Art had said that we weren't. Not even close. Jesus, Man, half the population of the known world was wiped out by plague and war during the Dark Ages, Art had said. Yea, Dan thought, but they didn't have ricin back then.

"Kelley my dearest, you've been through a terrible time. We are safe here. Just like being back in the States." *Was that really safer?*

"I worry about her, Dad. In the dream she sees him and...."

Asahara, the scum, had had a lasting effect. Years of therapy ahead. Dan knew that Kelley covered up a lot. This was good though. Letting it all out. Good sign. Let her pour it all out. Sobbing now. Uncontrolled.

"Why does everyone have to die, Dad?"

Dan's first thought probably right on the money. Rose's death had not gone unnoticed. Profound effect. What else had his little girl hidden beneath the strong impenetrable façade that few could see but himself?

82

"What did you do to Adam? What the fuck did you do to my love? You destroyed him."

The Frenchman and Blasingame feigning surprise at Keiko's outburst towards the ambassador; although not really necessary as the boisterous crowd at Paddy Foley's were involved in their own drunken reverie. Keiko had never looked at the ambassador. Until now. The glare. Raising up. The knife coming out from under her Kate Spade knock-off. Too late. The blood spurting onto the table from the Irishman's jugular. Mixing with the Jameson. An odd combination. Blasingame would later wonder at his first thought. No wonder whiskey and tomato juice are never mixed. A distasteful concoction. The Irishman tried to stand. Never left his seat. Head crashing to the edge of the booth. Knocking over the shot glass. Dead. His bodyguards looking the other way. The Almond Café bombing the last straw for them as well.

The rape of Adam Welsh vindicated. And although Keiko would not know it, the lost souls at the Almond Café as well. All part of the plan from Lemieux and Blasingame. Once they discovered the connection between Adam, Keiko and the Irishman, it was easy to goad her into removing O'Mara. But at what price?

Blasingame leaking the information to Keiko that she had already suspected. It had been the Irishman all along. Meeting Adam years ago.

Striking up the false friendship that can be seen in every bar and pub throughout the world where men drink to ease the pain and then sell their souls for the company of strangers. Funny thing about bars. One can be mere inches from another and yet never really be conscious of that person. The booze, the fantastical atmosphere. Whatever. No one really saw Keiko Watanabe actually put the knife into the Irish ambassador's neck. Witnesses who included an underaged Japanese girl named Miho, a name which endeared her to American sailors as well as Bill Dwyer, journeying out from the confines of the Sanno Bar as he was wont to do only about once in a Blue Moon, said that the ambassador appeared to pass out. No knife was ever found although Colonel Dwyer was said to have lost a rather expensive combat knife from his collection that was kept at home. Nothing ever proven. The Frenchman and Blasingame displaying ignorance. Seeing nothing in the best tradition of Sgt Schultz from a show called Hogan's Heroes that Adam used to love to bring up in happier days with Art.

Two days later, the Sanno Hotel was severely damaged by what authorities later surmised to be a plastic explosive hidden in the kitchen area. Apparently planted by Peanut. He had killed one last time from beyond the grave. A Filipino girl of about twenty-two. She had just started working. Sending money to her province. Collateral damage.

83

Dan Bronsan had that feeling of foreboding again.

When was the last time? Years ago? Where? When?

Coming back now. The curtain parting. Early 1969, Christ Church Hospital, London. Low rent as far as hospitals went but with the Universal Healthcare system prevalent in the United Kingdom not really any difference among hospitals or physicians for that matter. Kind of a crap shoot, thought Dan. The doctor arriving at the waiting room of the Pediatric Intensive Care Unit. News about Kelley. The look on the Indian's face indicating the worst. M.S. Multiple Sclerosis. The doctor saying she wouldn't live past fifteen or sixteen. Sweet sixteen. Cathy with the stoic front. No outward feeling. Dan sure something had left his body.

The same feeling now. Here at Tokyo Metropolitan Water Treatment Plant No. 3, the impending doom returning. Behind the door. The sense that nothing good would be coming out from behind it. The knob turning ever so slightly. Almost imperceptible. Just a crack. Open nonetheless. Dan's thoughts turning to Benny Carter now. Outside the building. Standing watch. Cell phone in hand. Adam Welsh with Keiko far away. Better this way. Dan on his own. Somehow ever since the talk with Father Terry, so long ago, Dan Bronsan knew this would be the way he would end. The way to make amends. The way to salvation. The only way. Maybe this what Father Terry was trying to tell him. The good father unsure himself though.

Doubts. Dan needing to experience everything that had happened to him since. The miracle of his flesh and blood, Kelley, breaking the sixteen year barrier and now a woman of twenty-three. Healthier than most her age. She had beat the devil. In love now even.

Passing through the doorway now. Music. Seventies music. "Come on Eileen." Dexy's Midnight Runners blaring from somewhere inside the room... Louder and louder. Dan pausing as he felt for his cell phone with his other hand. Taking it out. The "No Service" text staring up at him. Mocking him. Taunting. Of course he should have known that the damn Swedish piece of crap wouldn't work in here. Early days for cell technology notwithstanding.

Dan sensing that God was punishing him for promoting the Svenson phones. Dan rationalizing with his standard "You get what you pay for" retort.

"Damn it all, anyway," muttering under his breath.

Then he saw it. The man in the lab coat. Dan started to speak, but the lab coat disappeared behind a partition.

Dan Bronsan here through an anonymous tip. One of his students at a seminar he had given on the Svenson cell phones that the Metropolitan Water Department was providing its employees had contacted him. Out of the blue. He had remembered Dan's boast that he knew various intel sources in the government. This basic Bronsan bullshit was in this case possible world saving bullshit. Dan had told Benny, and he had in turn passed it on to Dusty Rhodes and Blasingame. The decision was made to follow up the tip which stated that a colleague of the informer was acting very strangely and had talked about Aum and rebirth through destruction. Now, as Benny, Dusty and scores of Japanese Defense Forces and American marines surrounded the building, Dan's head telling him that this was complete insanity, yet he kept on moving further into what he now realized was a fully operating laboratory. The music louder now. The source a portable boom box sitting on some kind of a control panel at the far end of the room. Footsteps behind him now. Flashback to a horror not so long ago. The New Jersey Suite. The Monster. The feeling of impending doom. He turned. Hiroshi Aki, the father of Hanako who loved Barbie dolls stood before him.

"I was expecting you. Someone anyway. Interesting times that we live in, Mr. Bronsan."

"How do you know who I am? What are you doing here? Who the hell are you?"

The Japanese Water purification specialist stood at the control panel about three meters from the American. Various laboratory tools in front of him. This at least the perception of Dan Bronsan from his vantage point. All he could accurately make out were a few test tubes and what he had remembered from Chemistry 101 as a Bunsen burner. The burner on now, Dexy's Midnight Runners winding down their pleas to the long forgotten Eileen.

Aki holding up a test tube to the light. A liquid inside. Green in color. He addressed the American.

"You don't remember me? I was at your cell phone seminar a while back. I am the one who told you to come here. A tip I believe you call it. I have a daughter, Honaka is her name. As do you of course. I feel I know both of you, having followed you both in The Japan Times as well our own tabloids."

Aki turning the music down.

"Yes, the 80's. A truly unappreciated time in music, Mr. Bronsan."

"What the fuck is going on here?"

"As I was saying, I have a young daughter. I want her to grow up in a world that..."

Trailing off. Doing something with the test tube and the control panel.

"Do you think this planet of ours will be here in ten years?"

Dan Bronsan noting the man's trembling hands. Focusing on the test tube now. Yes, definitely a test tube of some sort. The color of the fluid menacing for reasons that Dan Bronsan could not explain. At least not at this moment.

"What are you doing there?"

No answer. Looking down. Some kind of knob. A control of some kind. The control panel of course. Aki turning the knob.

"Stop now!"

A smile. Placid. Aki looking directly at Bronsan now.

"The antidote. The salvation of the planet. The death of my beloved."

Aki began to cry. Turning to a whimper.

"My daughter will die. A martyr."

It all became clear to Dan.

"Aki San, Asahara is jailed. He is in solitary. He is unable to communicate with the outside world. All of his moles have been killed or captured. The nightmare is over."

"You can't be...you wouldn't lie to me, Mr. Bronsan?"

The look from Dan said it all. It was all true. Asahara was neutralized. His daughter safe. The threat of a Madman not carried out.

"I will ask you one more time. What are you doing?"

"Antidote. Yes. The antidote. Please, I must concentrate."

"Antidote for what? Please stop what you are doing and answer my..."

"The entire Tokyo Water Supply will be contaminated with ricin within hours. There is no time."

A button pushed. A low humming sound. Aki began pouring the contents of the tube into some unseen void. The button is pushed again. The humming sound stops. These actions taking place in a period of seconds.

"Now, Mr. Bronsan, please in the name of what goodness there is left in the world, take me to my daughter, my precious daughter and prove that you speak the truth."

Of course Dan Bronsan had spoken the truth. As had Hiroshi Aki. There were a few cases of nausea reported in the Meguro district of Tokyo. No deaths though. In any case, the fact that minute traces of ricin were found in the Tokyo water supply was never reported to the public at large. Enough for Hiroshi Aki and Dan Bronsan to know that thousands, perhaps millions of lives had been saved by Aki's quick action. The earlier incident with the poor lost soul, Akeno Mori at the Yamaguchi Reservoir had alerted Aki that terrible plans had been put in place. An initial test of some water samples near to where Mori had landed had indicated the presence of ricin. He had placed the antidote into the system after immediately closing the Yamaguchi Reservoir. As a result of this heroic feat, unknown to only a few high-placed intelligence operatives, Aki's beloved daughter, Honaka, along with Mori's daughter would be assured places at Tokyo University when the time came for Honoka to design her own Barbie doll.

. . . . .

The Japan Times covered the state funeral of the Irish Ambassador to Japan, the apparent victim of a brazen IRA assassination right in the heart of Roppongi.

A month later, Adam and Keiko, with Kelley as the maid of honor, were married in the Sanno Ball Room. A magnum of Perrier was placed in their suite by Dan Bronsan. The newly renovated New Jersey Suite. Keiko appreciating the irony in the choice of the room as well as the carbonated beverage which helped to ease the morning sickness that she had recently started to experience. The child that doctors said she would never have would be a girl baby named Rose.

The world would go on.

. . . . .

Unfortunately, due to what many in the West would consider very liberal sentencing guidelines, Shoko Asahara was not given the death penalty. Nor did he rot in prison. He spent less than three years in a high security mental hospital.

He was released in early 1995 after being deemed legally sane.

84

March 20ᵗʰ, 1995
Aum Cult Factory #1 Shibuya, Japan

"Do not puncture these until you are about to leave the train. Any earlier will mean death."

Ikua Hayashi, prominent senior doctor at the Ministry of Science and Technology as recently as one month ago, now sits in the dank warehouse in Shibuya that is Aum Cult Factory #1. The words from Shoko Asahara leave no visible impression on the thirty-eight-year-old father of three. He would carry out his mission and do it with the utmost precision.

"You have the umbrella and the masks?"

A nod from Hayashi. Expressionless.

"The car is in good working order?"

This question directed at Shigeo Yokoyama, former bank clerk, father of two, and getaway driver for Hayashi.

"It is working perfectly, Divine One. We will not disappoint. All glory to The One." The two men leave without further conversation. Everything understood. Their responsibilities clear. Failure neither an option or acceptable in any way. Repercussions would fall on their families. The dire consequences of failure clear.

They arrive at Shibuya Station now. Walk to the newspaper stand. A copy of the *Nihon Keizai Shimbun* purchased as planned. The lethal plastic bags placed inside the newspaper. The umbrella and the mask not unusual. Japan a very phobic country when it came to germs or weather. A chance of rain in the early morning forecast. A good sign. Asahara mentioned it at the briefing. Hayashi steals a quick look at his watch, 7:30. He enters the Roppongi bound train. Roppongi, symbol of all that the West had corrupted in Japan. The young women with their American boyfriends. The lust. The money. The disregard for all the old ways. This would change soon, thinks Hayashi as he stands with the newspaper in one hand and the umbrella in the other. The usual crowd on the train. Hayashi notices the little girl. About five. The same age as his Yumi. What was Yumi doing now?

Would this little girl be alive tonight? He blocks an image creeping into his consciousness of his Yumi now on the train, pleading for her daddy to come home.

Don't kill anyone, Daddy.

Hayashi takes the newspaper out and casually lets it drop to the floor just as the train enters Ebisu Station. He rapidly punctures the paper and the sarin bags. The doors open and he begins to leave the train.

"Mr. you dropped your paper, I can get it for you..."

The little girl. Inches away from the paper and the sarin. The little girl is now Yumi. Hayashi envisions her writhing on the floor of the train. Yellow liquid pouring out of her mouth. Her eyes dilated. Unable to breathe or to scream. Then motionless.

Hayashi kicks the newspaper out the doors just as they are closing. The paper and the sarin, now leaking, lands on the Ebisu Station platform.

"Don't bother the man, Yuko. I'm sorry, sir..."

Hayashi pushes past the woman. In an instant he is in the next car.

What have I done?! My family? What will become of my family. I failed!

The doors open at the Roppongi Station. Hayashi almost knocks over several people as he rushes out. Many would remember him later when they watched the carnage on the evening news. He dashes out of the station to the getaway car outside.

"In what appears to have been a coordinated act of chemical terrorism, five stations of the Tokyo Metro system were attacked simultaneously this morning. As of 8 PM tonight, eight people are dead and hundreds have been injured. Early, as yet unconfirmed police reports, indicate that at least three members of the religious zealot group called 'Aum Shinrikyo' whose leader, Shoko Asahara, pictured here, have been arrested in connection with these attacks. Asahara himself is still at large. Further updates as they come in. This is CNN reporter Bernard Shaw reporting from Tokyo."

"Shoko Asahara founded Aum Shinrikyo in 1987. The doctrines of Aum Shinrikyo are based on ancient yoga and primitive Buddhism and require worshipping the Hindu God Siva, believed to preside over both destruction and creation. The sect has tried to build its own 'kingdom' within its controlled compound facilities by establishing ministries and agencies under Asahara, its paramount leader. Among these, the sect 'Science and Technology Agency' consists of scientists who graduated from prestigious universities in Japan. It is divided into several teams specialized in chemistry, biology, physics and medicine. This organization provided the technical information required to synthesis the sarin."

JAPAN TIMES, 1995

EPILOGUE

SEPTEMBER 2001

"What did you think of the strip club last night, my brother? The clubs in Boston are much better than the ones in Florida, I believe."

The young Arab man changing the subject at hand. A trick to relieve the stress. Al Qaeda had taught the lessons well.

The polo-clad Reaper did not reply at first. It was almost as if he never heard the words of his young Saudi Arabian friend. Of course they had been friends since childhood. Carefree times, he thought for just a moment but then came back to the present. Important to stay in the present. Wasn't that part of the training that had led up to this moment? Occupied now with the newspaper.

"I am reading a very interesting story from the Japan Times. Yes, interesting. Did you know that years ago there was a group in Japan that fought the Infidel?"

Not waiting for an answer. Continuing now, "A story about the Cult leader Asahara. The One, they had called him. Very elaborate. They used chemical gases, sarin and ricin. The complexity. It amuses me."

"Yes, but... "

"All passengers departing..."

The flight boarding call cutting off the young man's reply. They must go now. Technology, so over rated, thought the polo-clad Reaper as he passed through security. The passport perused by the fresh faced attendant.

"And did you enjoy your stay in Boston, Mr. Atta?"

"Oh yes, very much. Thank you."

Then with a silent smile that the Logan Airport Screener would see for the rest of her days, Mohamed Atta boarded American Airlines Flight 11.

ACKNOWLEDGEMENTS

Roppongi is my second published novel, but it was actually started over twenty years ago. "Never give up," I believe is the operative phrase here. It was begun while I was stationed aboard ship in Yokosuka, Japan, in the 1990s. After the global insanity of the last two decades, I was driven back to a pre 9/11 world that existed before a seemingly daily dose of death and destruction became commonplace. The thriller is centered around the Aum Shinrikyo, an actual Japanese terrorist group active in the late 20th century. I witnessed first-hand their emergence in Tokyo while I was stationed in Japan. I simply added a few "What if's" and I was "off to the races" in a matter of speaking.

One important note: When I began this novel, I was drinking alcoholically. When I finished the final draft, I had been sober for a number of years. Thank God for rewrites.

Thank you from the bottom of my heart, Yuko Kishinami, Peggy Zibella, the late Gil Gaunce and Harry Brose, the officers and crew of the USS McCluskey (FFG-41), USS Curts (FFG-38) and the staff of the New Sanno Hotel for helping me create a work of fiction based on truth.

Once again, I am eternally grateful to The Meredith Brucker Writers Group: Meredith Brucker, Lynn Palmer, Ron Scibilia, Aly Kay, Cheryl Leland and the late John Leland. They listened to my weekly rewrites and gave me honest feedback, something that, in my opinion, is sadly missing from many writers groups today.

I would be remiss if I did not thank the person who nurtured *Roppongi* along during a UCLA Writer's Seminar that I attended, the uber talented critically acclaimed author, Susan Taylor Chehak.

I'm grateful to my late mother, Lucille, who told me I could do anything I put my mind to and to "stop thinking negatively;" no mean task for an alcoholic with self-esteem issues. I love and miss you, Mom. Everyday.

To my father, Walter Cox, a guy who tilted at windmills until one day the storm borne of a life of addiction engulfed him and carried him to the abyss. I found your unfinished novel behind the bar that summer day in August years ago. It was good, Dad, damn good.

To my brother Walter who is also my best friend. I love you man. I really do. Thanks for the constant positive energy even in the midst of many trials of the soul.

To my remaining siblings, Patrick and Maryellen, we made it and we came out pretty good, all things considered. To my beautiful nieces Tara and Ruth and Tara's wonderful spouse Eric along with Ruth's terrific dad, Rob and finally to Tara's little munchkins Easton and Graham, I love you all. To Bill Wilson and Doctor Bob Smith who met in Akron in 1935 and saved my life and the lives of millions of others, my eternal gratitude and the promise that I will always be there whenever another alcoholic asks for help. To my current and past life muses, some here, some gone, Bien Cox, Ron Scibilia, Steve Beilman, Jimmy Thomas, Gino and Jeanne Ardito, Art Chamberlain, and Mrs. Biggs, my 7th grade English teacher who taught me how to diagram a sentence and to always be a gentleman, God bless you all. Last, but certainly not least, to my wonderful creative team at Black Rose Writing: Reagan Rothe, David King, Justin Weeks, Christopher Miller and Minna Rothe; thank you!

Onward.
James Cox
May 30th, 2022
Phuket, Thailand

ABOUT THE AUTHOR

James Cox is an acclaimed author, playwright and actor. His solo show, *Love, Madness, and Somewhere in Between* was praised by critics and audiences alike at the 2019 Hollywood Fringe Festival while his debut novel, *Silver or Lead*, a psychological thriller, published in April 2022 is receiving rave reviews. *Roppongi* is his second novel.

James witnessed a terrorist attack in Tokyo, Japan, while serving in the U.S. Navy and brings real authenticity to this novel of love and redemption set against a background of global terrorism in 1990s Japan. James currently resides in Phuket, Thailand, where he is researching his next novel.

NOTE FROM THE AUTHOR

Word-of-mouth is crucial for any author to succeed. If you enjoyed *Roppongi*, please leave a review online—anywhere you are able. Even if it's just a sentence or two. It would make all the difference and would be very much appreciated.

Thanks!
James Cox

We hope you enjoyed reading this title from:

www.blackrosewriting.com

Subscribe to our mailing list – *The Rosevine* – and receive **FREE** books, daily deals, and stay current with news about upcoming releases and our hottest authors.
Scan the QR code below to sign up.

Already a subscriber? Please accept a sincere thank you for being a fan of Black Rose Writing authors.

View other Black Rose Writing titles at www.blackrosewriting.com/books and use promo code **PRINT** to receive a **20% discount** when purchasing.

www.ingramcontent.com/pod-product-compliance
Lightning Source LLC
Chambersburg PA
CBHW010514100726
47903CB00009B/2740